C000156815

Tangled Discoveries

Book 2 of The Malevolent Trilogy

By Carrie Dalby

Copyright ©2022 Carrie Dalby Cox

All rights reserved. No part of this publication may be reproduced, distributed, or transmitted in any form or by any means, including photocopying, recording, or other electronic or mechanical methods, without the prior written permission of the publisher, except in the case of brief quotations embodied in critical reviews and certain other noncommercial uses permitted by copyright law. For permission requests, write to the publisher.

Any references to historical events, real people, or real places are used fictitiously. Names, characters, and places are products of the author's imagination.

Book designed and published by Olive Kent Publishing
Mobile, Alabama

Cover art by Amanda Herman

www.carriedalby.com

For Megan Finnigan Grimes,

who loaned me her name for Sean Spunner's cousin,

and Charlie Cox

for inspiring Sean's smile—minus the chipped tooth

One

"Why are we here, Sean?" I asked my husband as we crossed the yard of a multi-level stucco house on the west side of Mobile.

"For a visit, Hattie." He lightly held my elbow, fingers caressing the sleeve of my blue dress as we climbed the steps to the deep veranda. Sean then entwined our fingers and opened the front door that was at least nine feet tall.

Stepping over the threshold with him, I looked about the cavernous space. "Do you know the owners?"

"Mr. Fearn next door was expecting us and left it unlocked." With his free hand, he made a sweeping gesture about the grand, but empty, hall. "Happy thirtieth, Hattie Spunner. This is for you—us. We can move in the first of May and be settled for your birthday on the eighth. Maybe even host a supper party if you'd like."

Unable to speak, I tapped my heeled shoe on the polished wood floor.

"It's a George B. Rogers design, the same architect who built many of my friends' houses—a one-of-a-kind showplace as well as a cozy home."

"Cozy? It has to be at least three thousand square feet!"

"It's over four, dearest." He locked his arms about my middle and leaned down for a kiss, causing a wave of brown hair to fall across his forehead. "We could fill it with children if you'd like. The yard would be perfect that, as well as for the dog. Now that Brandon is two, maybe becoming a big brother would mellow his mischievous streak. Helping care for Buster did that, too."

"I'm not sure I'll ever be able to keep track of more than one boy and his dog."

"I don't believe that for a minute." His chipped-tooth smile flashed amid his trim beard. "As an experienced teacher, you have more than enough skills to corral little ones."

"Students who are able to sit and listen to a lesson, yes. I never taught anyone younger than twelve, and you know it. Brandon is—"

"Intelligent, handsome, and an imp," Sean finished for me.

"Just like his father." I met his gaze before tracing the sensual curve of his lower lip. "I appreciate your generosity, but moving should be decided by both of us. You might be the breadwinner, but it's 1916, not the Dark Ages. I won't be hauled across town—"

Sean had the audacity to laugh. The twinkle in his amber eyes communicated that I had once again jumped to conclusions that did not match his intuitive mind.

"I'll not be offended, though you should know me better by now. Three years and three months you've witnessed my actions. And for three of those years come this June, we've shared our days and nights." He grasped my hips and gently pulled me against him. "The paperwork is drawn up, but not signed. I brought you here to get your approval and explain my reasoning. This villa might look exhaustingly large, but there's a reason we need the space."

Unwilling to concede to error, I adopted a sarcastic tone. "Besides me being a baby factory?"

There was a momentary loss of shine in his eyes, as though he recalled the halt to our actions that would result in babies. Out of fear of another pregnancy, I had denied him that pleasure for several months. Then the spark was back, and Sean spun me about as if we were at a masquerade.

"Though coupling would be an excellent way to spend an evening, I had other things in mind when seeking a new home." Taking both my hands, Sean smiled in his youthful way, though he was a mature thirty-six. "There's an additional bedroom, should we be blessed with more children, but my main concern was for a room devoted to your science and nature collections, suitable for hosting gatherings."

"Gatherings?" I slipped out of his grip.

"I know you've missed teaching since we were wed and thought you might enjoy hosting a science club. A weekly meeting for women and girls held after school hours would allow you the opportunity to teach those wanting to increase their knowledge but without worries over grading papers or bored students not wishing to be present for your stimulating lectures. An intimate group of eager minds for you to enlighten."

"I never dreamed such a scheme." Going to the nearest doorway, I peered around the corner, curious to the possibility until reality struck. "But what of Brandon on those afternoons?"

"There would be room enough for Althea to stay with us should we wish it. She's getting up in years, but I know she'd never admit to needing to slow down. I thought of offering to hire on a new cook for her to train and give Althea a nanny role with Brandon. What do you think?"

I felt a pang of guilt over Sean's excitement while I experienced nothing but resentment. Althea didn't have much more than a decade on Sean, but had played the role of mother to him since the day he arrived orphaned at his uncle's household when he was twelve and she was a kitchen helper. When he bought his own house a decade later, he hired Althea to cook and be head housekeeper, overseeing the maid and gardener. Even before marriage, I acknowledged the tie between them but turned a blind eye to Althea being the true mistress of the Spunner household through her practiced ways of managing Sean and the staff. No matter her kindness, having Althea as a live-in would be like sharing a roof with a mother-in-law.

"If you're really concerned about Althea's health, why would you want to place her over the care of a rambunctious boy?"

"Because it would be a joy to her and joy keeps people young. Not to mention it would get her out of the kitchen before the worst of the summer heat." His dimpled grin showed his love for the woman. "But I leave that to you, Hattie, both in accepting the house and choosing the best help for our home and son—no matter where we live."

"We both know if Althea accepts the opportunity to help with Brandon that *she* would be the one to choose her replacement in the kitchen."

I spoke out of bitterness, but Sean took it as more sarcasm.

"So she would, the old dear." He kissed my cheek. "Will you allow me to give you a full tour before you refuse my gift?"

Unable to stay upset with my husband despite his penchant for archaic male chauvinism, I nodded and accepted his arm.

"First, note the deep porch running the front and side of the house on this picturesque corner lot. It provides cooling shade while allowing the draperies to be left open for natural light and air circulation during the day—a blessing for Southern homes. There's nothing worse than being trapped in a parlor in August with no view of the greenery."

The impressive rooms on the main floor consisted of the massive living hall, formal parlor, dining room, breakfast room, silver room, kitchen, a half-bath, and a bonus sitting room in the front of the house. Sean then praised of the glorious leaded glass window in the stairwell. Upstairs, there was a large, screened in sleeping porch enclosed with lattice for privacy, as well as an extra room beyond for live-in help. The east bedroom shared a bath with that bonus bedroom, making it perfect for a guest.

The central room overlooked the front yard with a linking bathroom to another spacious bedroom above the parlor. The size of the rooms, dark paneling, natural light, and the lot itself were as inspiring as they were overwhelming.

"May I think a while about accepting the house?" I asked.

"Of course, dearest. The owner has promised not to entertain other offers until next week. But come see the carriage house. The apartment above the garage would be perfect for Althea."

***

Three afternoons later, Sean arrived home an hour earlier than typical. Caught unaware in the library, I couldn't wipe the tears from my face before he saw them.

"Dearest, there's no need to cry." His solid form embraced me, and I tucked under his chin, resting my cheek on his navy suit. "You've been melancholy for weeks, and I thought thinking of a new house would help you improve. If it's been too stressful, forget it was an option."

His loving attention caused more tears to fall. I knew I did him a disservice by hiding my sorrows. But now, after my emotional wounds had festered and scabbed, Sean's arms felt delicious around me. Strengthened by his regular time at the gym, his firm embrace was my solace.

He kissed the crown of my brunette hair. "Hattie, will you finally allow me entrance to your pain? I want nothing more than to comfort you."

I raised my chin and caught his lips with passion I hadn't explored since the previous year. Relishing his eagerness, a pang of disappointment caught my middle as he leaned back to look down from his half-foot advantage.

"I've missed your taste and ardor, Hattie. Welcome back." His grin matched the lightening I felt in my heart.

"I'm sorry, but I couldn't feign desire while I struggled to breathe these past months."

He escorted me to the leather sofa across the room and settled me on his lap.

"Now tell me what's plagued you." Sean pulled the pins from my bound hair and stroked through the locks to loosen them. "We're alone, aren't we?"

"The maid is gone for the day and Althea has Brandon and Buster out for a walk." I kissed Sean's neck. "What has you home early?"

"I won my case in court and didn't fancy returning to the office when my mind was occupied with you. Will you share with me?"

Nodding, I exhaled. "I'm not sure if you noticed, but Brandon has been nursing less since autumn and was down to just twice a day come Christmas."

"You bet I noticed. I've missed seeing those beauties." He bit his lip and eyed my chest.

From a young age, I'd been endowed with ample measurements that all the binding in the world couldn't minimize. Height, dainty ankles, and a button nose I had not, only an hourglass shape on my compact frame that Sean wanted to hold from the first night we met.

"By Valentine's Day," I continued, "he only wanted post-supper snuggles and milk. I felt the emptiness in my arms and fear in my mind."

"Fear?"

"Nursing mammals are less likely to become pregnant. As Brandon weaned himself, I felt more vulnerable. I'm not sure I'm ready to have another child." I mustered a tiny smile of embarrassment. "I'm sorry for withholding my affections, Sean. I hope you haven't suffered too much."

"Apparently not as much as you, though I may have taken matters into my own hands a few times." He took my mouth with a deep kiss. "But I've missed your touch."

"I've missed our moments as well, though I was too busy mourning the loss of my baby to explain anything."

"The loss—"

"That little imp spurned me, Sean Francis Spunner."

"What? When?"

"After his birthday supper he played the worst April Fool's Day joke on me because it was true. I washed and dressed him for bed, telling him stories as I always do. When I settled in the rocking chair in his bedroom and opened the buttons on my dress he said NO. He ran to you for a kiss and you carried him to bed, telling him what a big boy he was, and he laid down with Buster without so much as a smile at me. He's refused my lap after supper the last three weeks, going instead to you and his dog."

"Oh, Hattie." Sean kissed my forehead. "You should have told me."

"Fortunately, there wasn't much for my body to get used to as he'd only been nursing a minute each night, but I felt the swelling the first few evenings and the disappointment has been constant."

"Are you in pain?"

"There's been nothing physical for over a week."

His eyes widened. "Nothing?"

I shook my head before dropping against his shoulder.

"The boy is a fool for refusing your bounteous bosom, but we must see it for what it is. As the Psalmist said, 'To everything there is a season, and a time to every purpose under the heaven.'"

"Don't get religious on me, Saint Francis. It's nothing more than nature. All children go through stages as they grow, but I didn't expect it to affect me as much as pregnancy did—both physically and emotionally."

"To me it *is* a religious experience. I see no better way to express my feelings than to shout the glories of your luscious curves being my sanctuary once more." Sean went to his knees beside me. Bowing his head, he gifted a kiss to the peak of my blouse before looking up with his disarming smile.

"I'm not ready for another baby," I whispered.

"There are ways of prevention," he countered.

"I won't have you purchasing sheathes as though trying to avoid whorehouse diseases." I folded my arms. "Besides, I know your feelings on marriage and procreation. I wouldn't ask for anything you would object to."

He left a gentle kiss on my lips. "Speak to the midwife."

"She's as Catholic as you and the Pope!"

"But she knows things—preventative measures that even she approves of."

"And how do you know *that*, you cad? She must be a dozen years younger than you!"

Laughing, Sean pulled me onto his lap. "From conversations at the gym. I've sparred with Henry since before they were married and know for a fact Darla wanted to wait before having children. They were married in April, and she didn't have a baby until October the following year."

Eyes wide, I stared at my husband.

"Doing the math, dearest?" He smirked. "And before you say anything about her putting her husband off that long, I can tell you no newlywed would have strutted around like Henry Adams did without being regularly *well* fulfilled by his bride."

"Have the men noticed you're no longer strutting?"

"Your powerful loving has given me stores of swagger to call upon." Sean undid the top three buttons on my blouse. "Telephone Darla Adams tomorrow to set up a consultation. For now, there's plenty we can do to satisfy each other while keeping my virile seed from your womb."

"You arrogant—"

His questing kiss silenced me. "You love me as much as I love you."

I wrapped my arms about his neck. "So help me, I do, even though it's against my better judgement for personal freedom and rights for women."

"My sexy suffragette. There will never be equality, especially in my house. You're my superior, Hattie. I'm a weak puddle of natural man at your feet." He went to his knees at the side of the couch and clasped his hands in prayer. "Will you bestow a token of affection to your humble servant or grant me permission to shower you with my—"

"Sean!"

"Don't *you* have a naughty mind? I wasn't trying to be vulgar." His hands went to my hips and he rested his head in my lap. "Though if you wish to walk that line of debauchery we so thoroughly explored our first year together, I'm more than happy to indulge."

Heart racing with his hot breath near my core, I shifted enticingly. "I'd like that very much. I've missed our experimentations."

With a primal growl, he opened the rest of my blouse. He kissed along the edge of the brassiere, his short beard tickling my breasts. "Hattie, never withhold from me again, I beg you."

"I'll tell you all and share my love as long as I'm able."

Our hands were on his trouser fasteners when the patter of booted feet struck the hall.

"Sean Francis, are you home?" Althea called as Brandon scampered into the library.

"Yes, and I've got the lad!" Sean replied as he buttoned his suit jacket to hide the bulge below his waist.

Brandon ran for his father, who scooped him into his arms as I closed my shirt. Then Althea stopped in the doorway. The straw hat she always wore when out of the house still perched atop her tight curls as she looked from my disheveled appearance to Sean's joy.

"Welcome home, Sean Francis. I'll start on supper now since you've got Brandon Patrick. He was a good boy all the way around Washington Square and back."

She left without further word, though I caught a glimpse of amusement in her dark eyes as she turned away.

Hoping to take control of the situation, I reached my arms to my son. Brandon eagerly transferred, warming my heart. I kissed the wave of brown hair that matched Sean's.

"What shall we do now that Daddy's home?"

"Play piano!" Brandon lunged for his father. "Daddy plays colorful music."

Sean set him on the floor and caught me about the waist. "Will you join us?"

"I'll be there in a few minutes."

"I look forward to your arrival *and* tonight, dearest." He kissed the shell of my ear and whispered, "I'm going to taste every inch of you."

Watching him strut out of the room, I found myself smiling as I went for my corner of the library. All my science books were in a narrow section of bookcase and my boxes of samples stacked on the bottom shelf, where they had to be pulled out to be enjoyed. Sean had offered more space when we married, but he was so settled in the house after years of living alone I didn't want to disturb his extensive library. He had, of course, thousands of books of his own I was welcomed to, but I thought they were best kept as he'd arranged them—even the science ones.

The image of the spacious rooms of the house Sean wished to buy came to mind. I knew which room I'd choose for a science area—the one in the front center of the first floor, flooded with natural light. Ideas on how to arrange the furniture around the built-in bookcases while leaving room for display cabinets for my fossil collection filled my thoughts. Maybe a telescope at the window seat, though that would be better suited for the second floor. I had been comfortable in Sean's house, but it was *his*. I wanted to create a home that was *ours*. With a final look around the library, I inhaled the aroma of Sean's pipe tobacco he liked to smoke after supper and followed the boisterous sound of Brandon belting out an Easter hymn while Sean accompanied him on the piano.

Brandon stood on the piano bench beside Sean. A little hand on his father's shoulder steadied him as his near-perfect pitch and diction sang the glories of the risen Lord. Sean claimed he wasn't gifted with music, but to my untrained ear, he was flawless in his accompaniment. A jack of all trades he was with his keen mind. Though over a thousand miles from my Boston roots, I knew home was wherever those two were. When Brandon's wavering voice sang out the final word and Sean's hands lifted from the keys, I clapped.

"That was lovely." I kissed Brandon and then my husband. "I accept your generous gift, Sean. Sign the papers for the house."

Two

"**I wish I could keep one**, Winnie, but my parents are still mad I skipped school yesterday," Christina said as she held a squirming mass of brown fur to her face.

"These are already spoken for," I said from my perch on a wrought iron bench under a sprawling oak in my family's yard on the afternoon of May sixth. A blanket was spread at my feet on which my friend lay with the newest litter of puppies from my mother's German longhaired pointer.

When she sat up, Christina flipped the brassy blonde hair that fell over her shoulder so the giant bow that held it secure lay on the nape of her neck. She went to a different church and was graduating high school in a month—a year ahead of me in classes—but she was my closest friend.

I shifted my legs to nudge one of the puppies back onto the blanket with the toe of my boot. "Did your parents find out you met Luke?"

"Fortunately not. I told them I had a hankering for ice cream and didn't want to wait until after school." She gathered all four puppies into her arms and looked up at me. "I wonder if Luke likes dogs. I'll have to ask him."

"What did you do when you met with him?"

"I helped him dust the organ pipes. We were way up in the church balcony. Not even the elder knew I'd arrived because Luke hurried me in a side door. When the dusting was done, we kissed. A lot." Her pale cheeks blushed rose beneath her brown eyes. "You'll never know joy, Ethelwynne Graves, until you kiss a man."

Irritated with her using my full name, I straightened my black skirt and squared my shoulders. "I've been kissed."

"A school yard peck on the cheek doesn't count. Besides, that would be a boy, not a man." Christina had made our nearly two-year age difference feel even more pronounced since she fell in love.

"Winnie!" My mother called from the kitchen steps. "Get those pups back to the stable. They've been out long enough, and you need to prepare for supper."

"Yes, Mama!" Looking to Christina, I nodded to the blanket. "Do you want to bundle them into that or carry two?"

Scowling, Christina scooped up the nearest puppies. "Don't listen to that meanie. I won't let her put you in a sack like a barbarian raiding a village."

"It doesn't hurt them." I displaced the other two and tossed the blanket over my shoulder before grabbing the loose puppies.

Christina followed my lead to the stable that used to hold the horse and buggy. It now acted as a kennel and parking area for my father's automobile. Our corner lot across from Washington Square was the length of the block, allowing plenty of lawn space for my mother to raise healthy dogs. I had run the acre as a girl, and my eleven-year-old brother still did, but in recent years I was more often sedentary with reading and piano playing—and dog-watching when forced.

In the stable, I set the puppies in the stall near the straw piled in the corner.

"How can you not gush over these dear little creatures?" Christina asked when I draped the blanket over the half-wall.

"Year after year, they all look alike. Besides, they'll be gone in a few more weeks."

"You're the coldest girl in town, Winnie. No wonder you've never had a beau."

"I made the mistake of becoming attached to a litter when I was seven. I cried for days when the puppies were all sold." I leaned against the stall from the outside. "My parents felt sorry and offered me first choice out of the next litter, but I declined. Since then, I've favored none of them with one exception."

Christina plopped into the hay and corralled all the pups onto her dress. "When was that?"

"Last year. Mr. Spunner asked Mama to choose the best one from the winter brood for his son's first birthday, and I was tasked with training him."

She giggled. "Mr. Spunner sure is handsome. I bet you liked doing a favor for him."

"It's not like that. He's nearly as old as Mama, and my parents are his son's godparents."

"The old family friend, rescuing the young damsel in distress through the love of a dog. But not even that could melt the girl's heart."

"He's been coming to supper once a month since I can remember. I probably puked all over him as a baby. He'd never look upon me as anything but a girl."

"So you've thought it out!" Christina laughed.

"There's nothing to think through. He's married now and—"

"*Now*. But he wasn't *before*."

I exhaled in frustration, hoping my face wasn't as red as it felt. "I might have thought myself in love with him when I was younger, but I no longer daydream about him. I'm no homewrecker."

"Nor am I. Luke might be twenty-five, but he's never been married."

The hopelessly soft look on Christina's face worried me that my previously tough friend would make a fool of herself over her infatuation with the new organist at her church. I was reserved and quiet, happy to spend my lunchtime reading alone, but Christina had defended me against bullies my first week at the high school, and we'd been inseparable ever since. I could tell Mama didn't approve of

Christina by her mannerisms when she was around, but she never came forward with anything to discourage our friendship.

"I need to go in now," I reminded Christina.

"But what of the puppies? I think their mother abandoned them."

"Not by half. She's been watching you all this time. As soon as you step out of the stall, she'll come to them."

We had to wait by the doorway for Velvet to rejoin her family before Christina would leave.

"Have fun with your supper party," she said when I walked her to the front gate.

"It isn't a party. It's a standing engagement the first Saturday of the month."

"Your romantic supper with Mr. Spunner." Christina fluttered her eyelashes.

Ignoring her parting remark, I made a point to pass under the satsuma trees and touch one of the colorful bottles hanging from the branches. Our tiny grove of trees was planted by my namesake, Great Aunt Ethel Allen, who passed away when I was too young to remember. Well, half my namesake. The Wynne in Ethelwynne was for Winifred Ramsay, one of Aunt Ethel's nieces. It was because of Winifred the bottles from the previous century hung in the grove. From what I could weasel out of my father, Mr. Spunner hung the bottles for Winifred in 1897, just weeks before she passed away from yellow fever at the age of fifteen. Sean Spunner and Winifred Ramsay had been sweet on each other. Each month he came for supper, Sean carried a little ball of twine and a pocketknife in his suit and checked the trees, keeping the bottles in good condition through the years.

Once, when I was six, he set me on his shoulders to cut down a blue bottle with fraying string, in order to rehang it. That was the day I knew I loved him, for he trusted me with his sharp penknife while my mother still cut my food and my father never let me lift a finger to help him at his store. I held Mr. Spunner's blade in my trembling hand while I perched on his shoulders. It was a rare, chilly August evening, and he pretended my shaking was from the cold rather than nerves.

"Ethelwynne," he'd said, for he never called me Winnie like everyone else, "don't forget to breathe. In through your nose, out through your lips. When you've got hold of the old twine, line up the knife and cut through on an exhale. It's sharp and will give you no trouble if you control it."

I did as he instructed.

"There!" Mr. Spunner had exclaimed. "I knew you were capable."

But he missed his usual supper the next month, and when he came in October, he brought a girl with him he said he was going to marry. I see her face in my dreams sometimes—her blue-violet eyes the prettiest color I'd ever seen. She looked like a princess with black hair and a fine silk gown. I wanted to hate her, but she was kind and beautiful. Eliza Melling didn't give my baby brother any attention, but she asked to draw me—told me I had bewitching dark eyes behind my spectacles and an old soul. Mama didn't appreciate that. She stayed tight and quiet, like she does around Christina, but Papa was enchanted. He set me on the piano bench, and Miss Eliza loosened my braids and arranged my hair about my shoulders. Quick as a wink, she presented the sketch to Mama. My mother smiled politely, but it was Papa who kept the picture on his desk.

After supper, when Mr. Spunner and his lady left, Mama stormed about and said that Sean had no right to marry a chit like that—that she would do him wrong. Papa told her she was jealous and needed to forget the past because Sean deserved happiness. Mama didn't talk to Papa for two days.

That winter, Miss Eliza died. Once, I came home from school and saw Mama hugging Mr. Spunner on the settee in the parlor while he sobbed. To this day, he's the only man I've ever seen cry. I didn't want him to be embarrassed, so I waited on the stairs. When Mama walked him to the door half an hour later, I jumped for his arms.

He laughed and kissed my cheek. "You're a ray of sun, Ethelwynne."

Mr. Spunner is the only one to compare me to sun. My hair and eyes are brown, not golden locks with sky blue eyes, but I felt warm and glowing when I was with him.

I loved those monthly suppers with Mr. Spunner, not to mention his other visits, for he bestowed kindness and brought books from his personal collection for me to borrow from the time I was seven.

All was well for years, and I approached adolescence with daydreams of him waiting for me to come of age. I imagined he'd take me to one of those masquerades he told stories about, and I'd be a glittering lady like the others he had danced with.

Then he brought Hattie Fernsby to supper when I was thirteen. She wasn't as glamorous as Miss Eliza—for she was a school teacher, not an heiress—but she was spritely, kind, and bold. Once again, Mama didn't approve of Mr. Spunner's choice because this one preferred science over religion and was too outspoken. Of course, Mama never said that to Mr. Spunner or his guest, but to Papa after they left. There was another fight, and it was Papa who spurned Mama for her ridiculousness.

Knowing Mr. Spunner was lost to me forever, I studied Hattie when she accompanied him to our house—which was to every monthly supper since then, except the few they'd missed when on their honeymoon and again when Brandon was born. I wanted to be as daring and kind so I too could be the type of confident woman capable of anything, like Hattie Spunner.

Mama was stubborn and tense much of the time since then, though her and Papa were mostly at peace. Papa said she thought too much about the past, and she nagged me about brooding because she saw herself in me. But what did it mean when all my parents' disputes were over another man?

I washed and dressed in my Easter frock. Mama couldn't complain as I'd worn it two weeks ago to church for the holiday.

Now it was another Sunday dress, and I was encouraged to wear those when company came. After brushing my hair until it shone, I braided it into a thick plait that hung down the middle of my back. I was old enough to wear my hair up, but I didn't want to do it for the first time on a night the Spunners came and never thought of changing my style for school because I didn't wish to be teased about it. Maybe over the summer I'd make the change—if I couldn't get my hair cut short like I really wanted. I doubted the boys at church would make a big deal about it. They'd been ignoring me for years, though Nathan Paterson typically smiled when we accidentally made eye contact.

Downstairs, my mother—red in the face though it wasn't unbearably hot—hurried around the dining table, fidgeting with silverware and the vase of fresh flowers from the yard. Her pointy chin and sharp nose gave her a regal quality, but I was glad to have inherited my father's softer features, even if it came with his need for eyeglasses.

"You cleaned under your nails when you came inside?"

"Yes, Mama." I clasped my hands in front of the white eyelet dress and waited to be dismissed.

"You may play the piano if you'd like."

I headed for the parlor because if I was at the piano when Mr. Spunner arrived, he was likely to begin singing. He had a lovely baritone. Mama sang too when he asked her. She was her prettiest when singing—especially for him. I knew that she loved him, but I was going on seventeen and beginning to understand all the different types of love there were in the world.

Andrew sulked in the corner chair. He was a miniature version of our father, which meant he was a masculine form of me— though I hoped my ears didn't stick out as much.

I played "Sympathy" on the upright grand when the Spunners arrived. As hoped, Mr. Spunner sang his way across the parlor.

"Come join me, Merri!" he called for my mother as his wife and son entered the room with Papa.

Mama arrived with a girlish bounce in her step, nodding to Hattie and Brandon before joining Mr. Spunner beside the piano. Without being asked, I started the song again. When her clear soprano rang through the room with Mr. Spunner's deeper tone for the chorus, my skin tingled with the combination.

Breaking free from Hattie, little Brandon ran for his father. Sean held him while he finished the tune. At the close of the song, Papa and Hattie clapped.

Brandon wiggled out of Mr. Spunner's grasp and ran to Andrew. "Can we play firetruck, Drew?"

"Not now, boys," Mama said. "Wait until after supper."

My brother gave a relieved grin patted Brandon on the head. "In a while."

Brandon came to me next, pulling himself onto the piano bench until he stood beside me. He kissed my cheek and smiled. "Winnie plays purple. Do you sing?"

"I usually leave the singing to others, Brandon."

Mr. Spunner came behind us, resting his hand on each of our shoulders. "I haven't heard you sing in years, Ethelwynne. Why is that?"

"Mama sings better than I do, so I keep with accompaniment for guests."

"Your voice is just as sweet, Winnie," Papa said from his seat beside Hattie.

"Will you sing for me tonight, Ethelwynne?" It was a line from my old fantasies. His voice, warm hand on my shoulder, and his very presence caused my face to heat.

If I waited until after supper, I'd worry myself sick. "I will right now, Mr. Spunner."

"No more 'Mr. Spunner.'" He lovingly squeezed my shoulder. "You're a young woman, and it makes me feel terribly old to hear you address me like that. Call me Sean as your parents do."

I didn't look back at him when he lifted Brandon into his arms, but I felt the loss of his touch and saw the pinched look on Mama's face.

Without further thought of my audience, I started on "All Creatures of Our God and King." I might have chosen the hymn over a popular song because I knew Sean was devout in his Catholic faith, no matter that his wife was not. Was it an unconscious way of showing him I was a more godly choice? I shoved the doubt that crept across my mind as I sang of the glories of creation.

Sean joined me on the final verse. I nearly stopped singing when his rich voice bloomed behind me. Then his hand was on my shoulder with a reassuring touch. No matter what I had talked myself into believing, I felt myself smitten once more.

Upon completion, Sean took my hand and brought me before the others to curtsy as though I were at a recital.

"That was marvelous, Ethelwynne." He gave a dazzling smile. "Your voice is lovely. Don't hide it from us."

"Thank you." I bowed my head to hide the blush on my hot face. "Please excuse me a moment."

I made myself walk calmly from the room.

On the stairs, my mother's voice carried from the parlor. "It's getting dark, Sean. Allow me to go to the grove with you before we eat."

Upstairs, I washed my face in the bathroom, then went through my room to the sleeping porch beyond. I caught glimpses of Sean's beige suit and Mama's blue dress through the satsuma trees as they walked, but their voices never hid.

"She's too young to call you by your Christian name."

He laughed. "She's going on seventeen, Merri. The same age I was when we met, and we called each other by our first names."

"I'm only two years your senior. You have two decades on her, Sean. It isn't proper."

"She may not be wearing her hair up, but she's a young woman. Parents are always the last to see how much their children have grown."

"It's not that." Her voice had lowered, but they'd finished their inspection of the bottles and were halfway to the kitchen steps below me.

"Then what?" He crossed his arms and looked at Mama in a challenging way.

"It's the way you speak to her as an equal. She's always looked upon you with a rapturous gaze. I don't want you leading her astray."

"Is that what you think of me, Merritt Hall Graves? That I would seduce your daughter!"

"Not on purpose, but—"

"I speak to her as an equal because she's intelligent. I've tried to encourage her natural talents and abilities from the beginning."

"Can't you see how that might feed fantasies of love to a girl, even if it's not there on the man's side?"

"I do love her, as I love all your family. I've felt like an uncle or godfather to Ethelwynne and Drew all these years and see them more often than your own brother does."

Hearing him speak of his love and then renounce it as an uncle set a knife in my already aching chest.

"But she might not understand it as such," Mama said.

Sean gripped her arm and leaned close. "She's no simpleton, Merri. Give her credit where it's due."

"But she's been watching you. I know she has. You might not mean to, but your charm still draws people and a girl like Winnie who grew up with her head in books can't help but be swept away. Don't you remember what you did to Winifred and me that summer?" Her voice grew hard with jealousy. "And then you've paraded your train of lovers before me all these years. I saw the way my daughter looked at you when you brought them here, and it broke my heart."

He gave a sardonic laugh but kept hold of her arm. I found myself leaning toward the screened wall to better hear as he dropped his voice.

"A *train* was it, Merri? You might have called me a cad and still think of me as one, but I've only loved two women since your cousin died. *Two* in as many decades. Don't you dare cheapen my feelings for those I've lost or for my wife."

"Sean, I—"

"Are you ready to admit you're a sore loser, Merritt? How often have *you* wanted another taste of what we explored after my Winnie died?" His left hand rose to her cheek and the gold of his wedding band winked in the setting sun as he caressed her face. "You could have had me any of those days we lived together. You know it and regret it, but don't project your unfulfilled desires for me onto your daughter."

"You pompous bastard!"

Mama knocked his hand away, and I gasped. It could have been my imagination, but Sean appeared to cock his head toward the balcony.

"A pompous bastard I might be, but I'm not the scoundrel you think I am."

He stalked out of sight through the kitchen porch while Mama ran for the stable.

Three

Sean returned from his inspection

without Merritt and sat resolutely beside me while the boys tinkered at the piano. Brandon played his fingers across the piano keys trying to mimic Ethelwynne's earlier song, Andrew looking on with a glazed expression.

"Is everything okay?" I asked.

"None of the twine needed replacing, Hattie."

Bartholomew stood and looked to the door. "Did Merritt stop in the kitchen?"

"She was behind me the last I saw," Sean replied.

Our host left the room to search for his wife. I took Sean's hand into mine, caressing his knuckles. He dipped his head and kissed me as Ethelwynne walked in.

Sean stood. "Drew, would you please show Brandon how much the puppies have grown since last month? It's still light enough outside."

"Yes, sir."

Andrew took Brandon by the hand and left. Then Sean waved Ethelwynne over.

"Mama ran to the stable," she stated as she approached.

"I thought you were on the balcony." He gave a sad smile and opened his arms to her. Hesitantly, Ethelwynne stepped close enough for Sean to embrace. "I need to talk to you about what you heard. I'm sure some things were distressing and others confusing."

She nodded and moved back a few feet.

"Your mother and I have had a strange relationship from the beginning, but she's one of my closest friends. She orders me around and we argue like family, but we've shared much and comforted each other through several heartaches. We used to talk about everything without shame, but that's changed in recent years. She's laid a wall for propriety's sake, but I tend to ram my head against it in attempt to go back to how we were. I'm beginning to see that might not be possible."

"Mama has always worried about your choices," Ethelwynne said.

"She knows the errors of my ways and is overly protective of my heart since she was with me the first time it broke. But no matter what happens with Merri, I want to be here for you, Ethelwynne." He took her chin and gently raised it so she would look him in the eye. "Do you fear me?"

She shook her head, large brown eyes threatening to fill with tears behind her wire-rimmed glasses.

"You mother is stubborn and growing as uptight as an aging Victorian schoolmarm—no offense Hattie." His subtle humor cause both Ethelwynne and me to smile. "Come to us if you ever have questions your mother refuses to answer. Hattie and I are happy to help. We love you, Ethelwynne."

"I—I love y'all too." Her voice trembled with the words.

He put an arm around her shoulder and kissed her cheek. "I'm glad to hear that."

Merritt walked in while Sean still had an arm about Ethelwynne and scowled. "Supper is ready. Bart is having the boys wash. Winnie, go do the same."

I stood as Ethelwynne left the room. "Thank you for hosting us, Merritt."

She gave me her tight-lipped smile and turned on Sean. "How dare you get close to her after what I told you?"

"Ethelwynne understands how I feel, and that Hattie and I are here for her."

Merritt huffed and stalked out of the room.

I turned squarely to him. "Sean, what was said between the two of you?"

He took my hand and kissed me. "We'll talk later, dearest."

We gathered in the dining room, Bartholomew and Merritt at the head and foot of the table, with Ethelwynne and Andrew on one side and my family across from the children. As typical, we kept Brandon between us, and Sean was set closest to Merritt. In hopes of smoothing the ruffled air, I started talking after the blessing on the food.

"It's extra pleasant to be here. Everything was moved to the new house from the old this week, but there are still crates in all the rooms. Althea is finishing with the silver closet while we're here."

"How is the old bird doing with the change?" Bartholomew asked.

Sean laughed. "She's pleased as punch as I've given her the apartment in the carriage house. No more cross-town jaunts before dawn to get to us. We'll be hiring on a new kitchen girl, and Althea is going to take on a nanny role with Brandon while overseeing the rest of the help."

"Switching to a live-in is a big deal." Bartholomew passed the shrimp platter to me.

"Althea is more of a live-out, as she isn't under the roof," Sean said. "There's room for a domestic off the back stairs, but Hattie and I prefer our privacy at night."

Bartholomew chuckled but Merritt turned fuchsia.

"If you insist on being vulgar in front of mixed company and children, I'll have to ask you to excuse yourself from *my* dining table, Sean Francis Spunner."

"My apologies, Merritt." Sean's eyes twinkled under the chandelier, and I knew he held back several retorts. Hopefully they wouldn't erupt later.

Brandon started drumming his fork against the edge of the china and nodding his head to the beat. I moved to grab his hand, but Bartholomew touched my elbow.

"Let him. He's being gentle and won't hurt anything." Bartholomew took a bite of green beans and smiled. "He sure is musical. I've never seen it in one so young."

"He gets it from Sean," I stated. "I have no musical abilities."

"But Hattie," my husband said, "music is the math and science of the art world. Brandon has your mind for patterns and order."

Brandon took the pause in the conversation to increase the tempo and sing a few lines of "Sympathy."

"You know," Sean said, "I think he was trying to work out that tune on the piano earlier. I bet if he had more time, he would have figured it out."

Merritt scoffed. "Don't be ridiculous. He's only two."

"Children are more capable than we give them credit for." He glared at her with narrowed eyes until she lowered her gaze.

Brandon finished his tune with a smile big enough to light the room. Bartholomew clapped and everyone joined—except Merritt.

"That was wonderful, Brandon, but it's time to eat now." I shifted his plate closer to the edge of the table to encourage him.

Once everyone was back to eating, I allowed myself a minute of respite before doing my best at polite conversation.

"There's going to be an addition to our routine at the new house," I said. "Sean had the wonderful idea of me hosting a science club. I plan to open the house to women and young ladies seeking to discuss topics of scientific interest one afternoon a week. I would love for you, Merritt and Winnie, to be my first members."

"I hardly have time or interest for something like that," Merritt said in a dismissive tone.

"But Winnie would love to." Bartholomew spoke for his daughter.

Sean looked to Ethelwynne with a hopeful gaze. "Would you?"

I saw her hesitation and the refusal to look at her mother. Ethelwynne respected her parents, but there was a wall between her and Merritt. Her father, though, she was willing to appease.

She met Bartholomew's eyes and smiled, then turned to Sean—careful not to look at her mother beside him. "I'd be happy to be part of the club." Then she focused on me. "Thank you, Hattie."

We made it through supper without further issues. Brandon fell asleep during dessert, giving us a valid excuse to leave early.

"He's tuckered out form the excitement of moving," I explained as Sean stood with our son in his arms. "Thank you for having us. Could we do the honor of hosting next month?"

"Yes," Bartholomew was quick to say. "That will give Merri an opportunity to see the house. I told her about it after I stopped by on my way home from work Thursday. It's fantastic."

"Ethelwynne will get the next tour when she comes for the first club meeting," Sean said as we passed through the hallway.

I turned to catch her eye. "I look forward to seeing you, Winnie. Four o'clock on the fifteenth, but come early if you'd like. Invite your friends too."

We all said goodbye on the front porch. When Sean and I were halfway down the walk, the door slammed behind us.

"I don't understand why Merri gets upset with me," Sean muttered.

"It's because she loves you," I replied as I opened the passenger door for him. "How have you owned a piece of her heart all this time?"

Sean laughed as he slid into the automobile. In his arms, Brandon stirred but stayed asleep. "You don't want to know."

"I wouldn't ask if I didn't, and you told me before supper we'd talk later." I sat behind the wheel and started the engine, but turned to look at him.

"Get us home, Hattie."

"Not until you tell me."

Sean kissed Brandon's forehead and whispered. "You have a stubborn mother."

It was my turn to laugh.

He grinned at me, raising his eyebrows. "Start driving and I'll tell you."

"Fair enough." I put the automobile into gear and looped the long way around Washington Square.

"I gave Merritt her first orgasm," Sean stated matter-of-factly when we were on the far side of the park.

My foot mashed the brake, and I turned to him with my mouth open. He had to put a hand on the dashboard to keep steady from the sudden stop.

"God in heaven, Hattie, you could have hurt Brandon!"

"Why on earth didn't you tell me that when we were safely parked?" I stared at him in the shadowed space.

"I didn't think you'd react like that."

"Not be shocked that my husband and the woman we've shared monthly dinners with for over three years had an intimate relationship? I'm open-minded, Sean, but I was under the impression all your previous loves were deceased."

"*Loves*, yes. Winnie and Eliza both rest in peace, but–"

"But *lovers* are a different thing. Leave it to a lawyer to leave himself an out. I see how it is." I shook my head in disgust and released my foot from the break. "And don't start in on your tales of the tenderloin district during Mardi Gras."

"I would never, especially with Brandon here."

I scoffed and slowed as we came back around to the Graves's house. "You and Merritt! Really, Sean, how could you keep that from me?"

"It wasn't much of anything. She was curious about sex, and I was more than eager to experiment. She had found a naughty book of her uncle's after he died. You know the one with all the color illustrations of positions we've tried out?"

"Yes, though you failed to share how you acquired it." I turned west on Government Street.

"Merri gave it to me thinking I'd burn it for her, but I admitted I had every intention of keeping it. We talked about things, which mostly consisted of me shocking her as she was so naïve. What we did together happened after Winnie died. We were both upset and needing to feel alive. We were mostly clothed and took turns lying on top of each other, rubbing and grinding like a couple animals staying warm until she yelled for me to stop."

"Why did she do that?"

"I went too far by trying to lick her tits."

I couldn't help laughing. "I can't imagine any of that. She seems such a prude."

He chuckled. "But I got her wound up and set her off."

"You scoundrel. And then yourself?"

"No, unfortunately. Bart stormed in and found us. I thought he was going to kill me."

"And he still welcomes you into his home?"

"Technically it's Merri's house, but he saw I was a young fool and felt sorry for me. Bart didn't hold it against either of us."

"That was good of him."

"I even lived there with Merri for a week afterward until her aunt came back from the hospital." Sean sighed. "I was there the week before too, sharing a bed with Winnie most of the time."

"And you told me hers was an innocent love."

"It was, but I went off like a blast of dynamite when I tried to pleasure Winnie. I spent inside my pants like the schoolboy I was. Merri just laughed when she understood what had happened."

"Serves you right, you scoundrel." I drove in silence the last block until I pulled into the driveway. "Can you truly reach climax while clothed—both people?"

"I'd be happy to show you if you question my abilities, Hattie."

I parked the automobile inside the carriage-house-turned-garage and gazed at my husband with a smile. "I expect a demonstration after you get Brandon in bed."

***

Monday evening, we awaited the Davenports to join us for an intimate supper party. As it was my birthday, I opted to invite the couple that introduced me to Sean rather than the priest we hosted regularly or Sean's best friend, Dr. John Woodslow. With the Davenports, there would be Louisa for Brandon to play with. Fortunately, Melissa encouraged her husband Freddy to leave his two oldest daughters with their mother and stepfather for the evening so we wouldn't be too overrun with children.

Sean and I wore a previous season's masquerade apparel—a purple gown with a tiered skirt for me and a tuxedo trimmed in coordinating violet for him. We stood on the veranda as the Davenports walked from their automobile to the front steps. Melissa led the way in a tasteful green evening gown with her copper-red hair done up in a fancy twist that drew attention to her height. Louisa skipped at her side in what was probably her Easter dress, and Freddy in his tails carried their youngest in a travel basket.

"Happy birthday, Miss Hattie!" the almost three-year-old exclaimed as she handed me a bouquet of yellow gladiolas.

"Thank you, Louisa. They're lovely. Do come in, all of you." I accepted a hug from Melissa and guided her through the looming front door.

"It's positively massive." Melissa looked impressed though her own home was equally as large. "You must be overwhelmed with it."

"Yes, but Sean is so proud."

"Isa!" Brandon waited at the foot of the stairs with Buster. "Come see my room!"

Holding hands, the two climbed the stairs—the dog following them.

"Set Junior down wherever you wish, Freddy." I pointed to the right. "We'll keep the doors to the parlor open and the dining room is directly across. Sean will follow the children, won't you?"

"As soon as I get your flowers in water, dearest."

Freddy brought the basket into parlor, carefully setting his sleeping four-month-old's travel bed onto the floor. I had purposely kept the light dim in the room for that very purpose. Freddy straightened his sleeves and came to me with an outstretched arm.

"Happy birthday, Hattie." He kissed my offered hand and grinned in his friendly way. "I'm glad you're on the proper side of Government Street now."

"It will be easier to stop in for a visit while on my walks, if you don't mind," Melissa added.

"Of course not."

"All are welcome," Sean said as he returned from the kitchen and went for the stairs. "Hattie should be more than pleased with a plethora of friends in the neighborhood. Come see the upstairs, Davenport."

"Come whenever you wish, Melissa, but especially on Monday afternoons. Starting next week, I'm hosting a science chat for women and young ladies at four o'clock. I hope you can join me from time to time. Bring the children. Althea has already agreed to watch over a few extras that mothers might have with them. I don't wish to exclude anyone because they don't have a nanny."

"No class distinction?" Melissa mocked with her brassy Long Island accent. "What will the neighbors say?"

"To hell with what they think. There will be no age or class regulations here. Any woman or girl old enough to sit quietly is welcome, as well as babies who might need their mothers for nourishment. This is my science room—front and center of the house. The total of mine and Sean's science libraries are in here, as well as my fossil collection and other things I've collected over the years."

I opened the folding glass doors to the room between the main door and the dining room and motioned Melissa inside. Brandon's room was directly above and the soft rocking motion of his wooden horse could be heard through the high ceiling.

"Sean ordered two display cases and a microscope that should arrive by Friday. The room will be snug for up to a dozen ladies, but if more eventually join, we can open these doors and use the living hall for seating space. What do you think?"

"I think you've planned it wonderfully, Hattie. I'm excited for you. Who else is coming?"

"Just Winnie Graves, so far, but she's supposed to invite a few friends from school. Her mother, Merritt, down right refused."

"Sean's friend who raises dogs?"

I nodded. "I was hoping she'd come. A talk on animal breeding would be informative."

"Maybe she'll change her mind," Melissa offered.

"She's as stubborn as they come." I sighed. "But Sean adores her."

"No more dwelling on that now. It's your birthday, and you only have one thirtieth. I would love a personal tour of your home."

"I'm glad you're here, Melissa." I hugged her. "Both tonight and in general. You're the only one who understands what it's like to go from career and independence to being in Southern society's holding pen. I never expected to turn over every duty from making the bed I sleep in with my husband to child care to another when I'm not even employed. Yet there's already been another domestic hired, and I still haven't figured out how to manage the original ones."

"I don't envy you that. We only have a part time cook who also helps with the larger housekeeping chores, plus the man who cuts the grass once a week. Freddy insists on working the rest of the yard ourselves. I do enjoy it, but I admit it's handy to be able to pass it off as a joke to those who don't understand by saying an accountant loves to save a few dollars."

I laughed. "Sean is humble about many things but egotistical about others. I can never be sure when he'll take offense to something I try to refuse—from this house to a new teapot. But enough of our men. Let me show you around while they're busy with the children. Sean brags the dining room is the same size as the Mellings' though I've never set a foot in their mansion. Our table seats ten, but he wants to buy a larger one."

"Men always want things bigger," Melissa joked as she walked around the table. "Sean and Alex are old friends, but Lucy's social circle is extremely small."

Freddy's oldest two daughters were from his marriage to Lucy, so Melissa was well-acquainted with the Mellings—a couple I've always wanted to get to know, as Sean was once engaged to Alex's sister. "I've met Lucy a few times at masquerades, but we didn't talk much."

"She's very private. The space is about the same. I've had enough meals there to know."

"And how is it to dine with your husband's ex-wife?" I asked as we finished walking the downstairs.

"I'm used to her moods now, so it isn't too painful."

We stopped in the shadowed parlor to see that Junior was still sleeping before climbing the stairs. I bypassed the sleeping porch and the extra room beyond with a quick remark before showing Melissa into the guest bedroom. The children were playing in Brandon's room, and Sean and Freddy were wrapped in a conversation, so we hurried to the master suite. Melissa took in the bookcases lining the walls between the windows, doors, and fireplace.

"I've never seen so many bookshelves in a bedroom before."

"Sean claims we need the maid just to keep them dusted." I motioned to the writing desk in the nearest corner, the set of wing-backed chairs before the hearth, and the chaise by the window overlooking the front yard. "It's his library as well as our bedroom. He gave up his private space for me to have the science room."

"I always knew he was a romantic." Melissa's broad smile widened as the men entered. She immediately took Sean's hand. "Well done, Sean. Isn't it lovely, Freddy?"

"It gives the room warmth without the fuss of artwork and certainly breaks tradition," Sean's boxing friend remarked.

"Your home is lovely, Sean," Melissa said. "Please excuse me while I check Junior before supper."

Freddy took his wife's arm and they left the master suite. Sean turned to me with a devilish smile. "Was it just me, or was that a bit arousing to have another couple in our boudoir?"

"That's all you." I wrapped my arms about his shoulders with a sensuous caress across his tuxedo. "You alone satisfy me, though I know your stamina could easily see to more."

"I didn't mean it like that, though I love your debauched way of thinking." Hands at my hips, Sean kissed his way down and nuzzled into my décolletage. "Your delectableness would be legendary, though I'm not sure I'd want to share these with anyone except our babies."

"And you're mine. I crave your magnificence to fulfill my own needs."

"Then my magnificence you shall have, Hattie." The spark in his eyes told me I was in for a lavish night after our guests left.

Four

"You were right, Winnie," Christina told me over our boxed lunches in the school yard Wednesday. "When my parents heard Mrs. Spunner was hosting a club, and Mrs. Davenport would be there, they said there could be no better way for me to spend an afternoon. They hope spending time with esteemed ladies will improve my manners."

I chewed a mouthful of sandwich before speaking. "And my mother cringes at the thought of me spending extra time with Hattie."

"I didn't tell them it was a science group. I left it broad—a women's club—and they assumed it was a charity-type function."

A whistle came from one of the boys' classroom windows in Barton Academy. Christina flipped her ponytail over her shoulder and rolled her brown eyes. I continued on, knowing no one would whistle at "four eyes."

"Who else should I invite?" I asked.

"For fun or girls who want to learn more science?"

"Serious girls. I don't want to disrupt Miss Hattie's club. She's in earnest about it and has always been nice to me."

"Then Jessica and Faith. They answer the most questions in science."

They were both girls from Christina's year that I wasn't familiar with other than names and faces. "Would you take me to them when we finish eating so I can invite them?"

She nodded. "Let's eat faster so we have more time."

The silence allowed me to reflect on how grateful I was for Christina. I never would have been brave enough to approach older students to invite them to the science club alone.

"Don't let them intimidate you—Faith especially. She's intense."

I felt their disdain as soon as we approached the two sitting on a corner bench. They both wore gigantic bows—the brunette the biggest black bow I'd ever seen at the base of her skull, and the fair girl a huge white floppy one on top of her head. It was a fashion I never was comfortable with, but they wore it well.

"What do *you* want?" the strawberry blonde asked as she narrowed her eyes at Christina.

"My friend has an invitation I'm sure you two would be interested in, Faith."

The dark-haired one snorted. "That's doubtful."

Christina nudged me forward when I froze before the seniors.

"My name is Winnie Graves. Mrs. Hattie Spunner is starting a science club for women of all ages to gather weekly. The first meeting is next Monday at four o'clock. They just moved into the house near the end of the Government Street trolley line at the corner of Houston. Christina thought of you both when I asked her for recommendations on students who would be interested."

"Hattie Fernsby Spunner!" Jessica jumped from the bench. "Miss Fernsby was my favorite teacher. I was disappointed when she stopped teaching to marry. Lawyers are so droll, and she was a shining star. She's the reason I plan on studying medicine in college."

"Then you'll come?" I asked.

"I wouldn't miss it," Jessica replied. "Right, Faith?"

She nodded, keeping a skeptical eye on Christina.

"Faith's sister was in Miss Fernsby's last class that year when one of the girls asked about Charles Darwin," Jessica explained. "She didn't shy away like other teachers might."

"Charles who?" Christina asked.

Faith huffed with disgust. "You're a simpleton, Christina Wilmer."

Jessica ignored both of them. "There was rumor that Mr. Gentry fired Miss Fernsby over that, but she was still teaching after Christmas break. That's also when she showed up with her engagement ring. Maybe the lawyer did something to help her out."

"How do you know the Spunners?" Faith asked me.

"Mr. Spunner is an old friend of my parents." The bell rang while they stared at me. "I need to get to class. Goodbye."

As I walked away, Faith kept talking. "What does her family do?"

"Her father owns a mercantile just beyond the trolley line, and her mother raises the most glorious dogs. Pointers of some sort. If you want, I'll go with you Monday and take you in the store for a cola before we go to the club. It's a respectable shop."

Hurrying toward the door so I could escape the conversation, I tried not to remember the snide looks Jessica and Faith dealt me when I first approached. I didn't wish to know if Christina was rebuked or my father not good enough for them. If they decided against me, that was fine. I invited them to support Hattie.

***

Monday after school, I rushed out the front gates to catch a streetcar. Not wanting to stop at home and be pestered by Mama, I rode straight to the Spunners' place.

I had visited their old house many times and recognized the cook in the yard with Brandon and his dog as I walked up. Letting myself in the gate, I called out. "Good afternoon, Miss Althea and Brandon."

"Afternoon, Miss Winnie."

"Winnie!" Brandon ran for me, and I hugged him.

Buster ran in circles around us and then sat, smiling in the way dogs do.

"Hey, Buster. Are you being a good dog?" I scratched behind his ears.

"He keeps Brandon Patrick safe as well as I can," Althea said.

"I know I'm early, but—"

"Go on in." Althea motioned to the house. "Miss Hattie is expecting you."

I went for the steps, and Buster tried to follow me. I gave him the hand signal to sit, then stay. Pausing on the veranda, I made sure the dog waited in the yard before walking through the towering front door into the vestibule. The interior door was open so I stepped inside.

"Hattie?" The hall was more of a room of its own with the stairs and several rooms radiating from this central hub. The dark wainscoting added a warm richness to the space, and all the windows from the exterior rooms flooded it with light. I called louder. "Hattie?"

To the left, a door swung into the dining room and Hattie came through.

"I hope I'm not too early."

"Not at all. I was just checking the status of the refreshments. You're always welcome, Winnie." She smiled and looked to the clock on the mantel. "Would you like a tour? You'll be the first to see something in the master bedroom. I found it this morning in the back room with a bunch of things that came out of Sean's attic from his bachelor days. I'm sure he tucked it away because he thought it too scandalous for a bride to look upon, but the painting is a true masterpiece and the woman captivating. I thought it would be fun to hang over the fireplace."

We climbed the stairs and went down a private hall to the master suite. My gaze followed the bookcases around the room until it fell upon the painting above the hearth. Spellbound, I went toward the face from my dreams. Her back was bare and she clutched a purple sheet to her voluptuous chest as she looked over her shoulder with a devilish smile at all who looked upon her beauty. Reaching for a tendril of her raven hair, I smiled at the portrait she had created for her fiancé—an intimate gift for a lover.

"It's no wonder Sean acquired it," Hattie said. "Have you ever seen such a beautiful young woman?"

"Yes," I said without thinking as I fingered the texture of the lock of hair against her spine. "I had no idea she painted as well as she sketched. I only met her once, but I was as enchanted by her as Papa was when Sean brought her to supper."

"Who—"

I touched the scratched signature that was little more than an E and M in the bottom corner and turned to Hattie with a smile of remembrance. "It's a self-portrait of Eliza Melling."

Hattie blanched and reached for a finial on the footboard of the massive tester bed. Registering her shock and how my words must have wounded her, I was quick to her side.

"You were right in seeing the beauty and skill, Hattie."

She sank onto the corner of the bed. "Eliza—I had no idea! Sean told me I favored her, but I look *nothing* like that."

"Dark hair and blue eyes, though hers were more periwinkle, like hydrangeas. I thought she was a princess, but you have that same spirit about you—bold and intelligent."

She looked to the painting once again. "Sean will remember and—I have to take it down."

"He looks upon you with the same adoration he looked upon Eliza with. And it hasn't changed, Hattie. Every time you come to supper, Sean's gaze communicates he wants to do nothing but hold you."

"You can see all that?"

I nodded and blushed. "I've always watched him closely. The love in his eyes when he looks at you is breathtaking. As much as you think he's proud of this house, he's even prouder of you and your son—and it boils Mama to see it. She and Papa got into as big of a fight the first night he brought you over as they did over Eliza's visit."

Hattie laughed and the spark in her eye that made all the difference in her beauty returned tenfold. "Don't even get me started on your mother."

"She's jealous of you, Hattie."

The doorbell chimed.

She took my hand. "That must be the first guests."

***

I hurried downstairs, Ethelwynne right behind me. Melissa wearing a simple day dress and a broad smile, stood on the front porch holding Junior. I ushered her in and gave her a quick hug.

"Winnie," I said as I turned to her, "come meet my dearest friend in Mobile, Melissa Davenport."

"Hello, Mrs. Davenport. My father often speaks of your husband after the boxing tournaments. He loves to attend them."

She laughed. "And Freddy loves to win. Please call me Melissa."

"Yes," I said as I took Melissa's bag from her, "I want everyone on a first name basis at club meetings. No societal formalities. Did Louisa settle in with Brandon?"

"Settle? No. They're running about the lawn like a heard of zebras on the Serengeti. Althea might rethink her willingness to watch extra children after today."

We laughed and migrated further into the house.

"Come into the club room. The display cases are up since you were here, Melissa, and Winnie hasn't seen the space yet."

My room was set with a semicircle of assorted armchairs, a built-in window seat, and sofa surrounded by bookcases—those around the window seat and freestanding ones. The available wall space was hung with shadow boxes displaying my insect collection. One table in the corner held a microscope and notebook. The coffee table in the center of the seating arrangement was hinged with a glass top, displaying dozens of rocks and fossils in neat rows.

"You're like a girl with a new toy," Melissa remarked as she took an armchair in the middle of the grouping. "Sean knows how to spoil you."

Gazing out the window as Brandon and Louisa kicked a ball, I smiled. "He knew exactly what I wanted without me having to explain myself."

Ethelwynne self-consciously adjusted her wire-rimmed glasses.

Melissa looked at my young guest. "I understand you've known Sean your whole life, Winnie."

"Yes." Ethelwynne turned to Melissa. "He's like an uncle to me."

"He's as charismatic as any man I know—and probably the most intelligent. Sean is larger than life in some ways, but don't let that fool you. His flaws are there, as Hattie can attest. No man is perfect. Don't place him as your measuring stick for possible beaus."

She bowed her head. "How did you know to warn me?"

Melissa laughed, her kind brown eyes warm and intuitive. "I've been where you are, Winnie. We all have because we're human."

Hoping to change the topic, I offered refreshments. "Would either of you like something to eat or drink?"

"I'll wait until my friend arrives, thank you," Ethelwynne said.

"Iced-tea would be lovely, Hattie." Melissa shifted the baby in her arms then smoothed his tuft of auburn hair as she smiled.

"How old is he?" Ethelwynne asked.

"Nearly five months," Melissa's voice carried while I poured her drink. "He was born on Christmas Eve."

"And your daughter outside?"

"Louisa will be three next month, and I turned thirty-four a few weeks ago. I had a later start in marriage than most—even later than Hattie's. I introduced Hattie to Sean. Well, I tried to introduce them at my Christmas party in 1912, but they were drawn together before I had the privilege. Sean still claims it was me. I knew they would be a perfect match."

"You're telling that old story again?" I asked as I delivered the glass. "Winnie's known about me from the beginning."

The doorbell rang and I went around the corner from the club room to answer it. Three young women were on the front porch, one of whom I knew.

"Hello, Mrs. Spunner. Winnie invited us to come over. I'm Christina, and this is Faith and Jessica."

"Jessica! Why I'd know you anywhere. I'm so glad you came. How are you?"

"Very well, Miss—Mrs. Spunner."

"No formalities while you're here, girls. We're all equals. Call me Hattie. Set your things on the bench by the stairs, then come say hello to Winnie and Melissa. After introductions, help yourselves to food and drinks in the dining room and get comfortable. I'm so glad you all came."

Melissa and the students were introduced, and Ethelwynne followed Christina, Jessica, and Faith into the dining room. They weren't shy about helping themselves at the massive table under the chandelier. Ethelwynne used the silver tongs to place a cookie on her crystal plate.

"I took Jessica and Faith by your father's store before we came," Christina told Ethelwynne. "Mr. Graves was glad to see me, wasn't he, girls? He even gave us each a peppermint stick and told us he hoped we enjoyed the meeting."

"Yes," Jessica said, "and he told us to stop in every week if we could."

Faith looked Ethelwynne up and down twice. "Mr. Graves is very distinguished looking for a shopkeeper."

Christina rolled her eyes and stalked to the club room.

"You do your family credit, Winnie," Faith stated in a superior way. "Don't bring yourself down by being friendly with the likes of Christina Wilmer. She's nothing but trouble."

Jessica nodded in agreement, and they returned to the other room with their refreshments. Wanting to follow them to see how Ethelwynne handled that information, I instead had to answer the doorbell. Sean's best friend's wife stood on the veranda along with a younger blonde.

I plastered on a fake smile. "Grace Anne Woodslow, I didn't expect you."

"Oh, I'm not staying," the doctor's wife said. "When John told me of your plans to embark on a science club, I knew it would cut into my schedule too much, but I thought Marie would enjoy it. I brought her this first time to introduce her and make sure there were girls her age before leaving."

"There are several high school students." I looked to Marie Marley with her Catholic school uniform and smiled. "You're welcome to join us, Marie. Why don't you both come in and say hello?"

Grace Anne's eyes roamed the club room in her calculating way. "Hello, Mrs. Davenport. It's lovely to see you. And such a pretty grouping of students too. Yes, you'll do fine, won't you, Marie?"

"Yes, Grace Anne. Thank you for having me, Mrs. Spunner."

"Think nothing of it, Marie. And call me Hattie."

"Marie has permission to walk to my house afterward. Father is picking her up there." Grace Anne looked to the dining room and parlor. "It's a lovely home design—almost as large as John's and mine. It will be handy having you and Sean close. I'd love to host you for suppers, and maybe you will finally come over for tea."

"I'm sure I could at some point. Thank you."

I saw Grace Anne out and returned with a genuine smile of relief. "Do you ladies know Marie?"

Everyone shook their heads but Faith spoke out. "*Private school girl.*"

Christina snickered.

"First and foremost, my club is for *all* women, no matter their education, religion, or social class. We will treat each other with respect and use a first-name basis. If you don't agree to these basic rules of civility, you may finish your refreshments and see yourself out."

"I went to private until high school," Jessica said. "I wanted to get to know a larger cross-section of humanity before going to college. My mother still thinks it's scandalous to attend with non-Catholics, but there's so much to see outside a world run by priests and nuns."

I smiled at hearing words I would have said myself, but before I could speak, the doorbell rang again.

"Darla, how wonderful!" I brought in the midwife several years my junior with dark hair twisted into a bun. "Would you like something to eat before you sit?"

"No, thank you. I can never eat directly after a delivery, but a drink would be lovely."

Darla exchanged greetings with Melissa before she kissed the baby on his forehead.

"Ethelwynne, could you show Marie the food while I collect a drink for Darla?"

I left the room with the girls and quickly poured a glass.

"Delivery?" Jessica asked Darla. "Do you speak of babies?"

"Yes," Darla replied with a relaxed grin as she sat near Jessica. "I'm a midwife. I work with Dr. Hughes now, but I trained under my mother on Dauphin Island since I was fourteen."

"I just found out Marie is fifteen," I said as I handed the tea to Darla. "And Winnie is sixteen. How about you ladies?"

"We're all in our final year. I'm eighteen, Faith is seventeen," Jessica answered.

"Eighteen," Christina said, "and I can't wait until I graduate."

"And your plans after graduation?" I looked from Christina to Jessica and then Faith.

"True love!" Christina declared.

Jessica rolled her eyes.

"I plan to be a secretary or teacher," Faith stated. "There will be more need for female workers if our country gets involved with the war."

Not to be outdone, Jessica stood as though answering a question in class. "I'm going to Mount Saint Agnes College in Baltimore and plan to transfer to Johns Hopkins University if I can get accepted into their medical program."

"They've accepted women from the beginning," Darla said. "I wish you well. I'm sorry, but I didn't get your name."

I instructed everyone to introduce themselves by name and age—the adults included their profession—current or past. Besides my former years teaching, and Darla's midwifery, Melissa was a travel writer until her youngest was born, having written both magazine columns and two essay collections. All of us were mothers and could drive automobiles, too.

"I'm happy to speak of my travels and the nature and wildlife I've explored on five continents," Melissa told us.

Faith gasped. "Have you seen savage natives?"

"Nothing is more savage than a charging hippopotamus, but I'm acquainted with various tribal customs from around the globe."

Jessica turned pink with excitement. "Fascinating!"

"It's been a few years since I've been abroad. My last trip out of the country on assignment was to Jamaica, but I've traveled this region extensively since marriage."

"As a midwife," Darla said, "my field of expertise is the female body, especially as it relates to reproduction. In working with Dr. Hughes the past five years, I've also gained extra on-the-job medical training equivalent to a nurse."

"More like a doctor." Melissa adjusted her son in her arms as he opened his eyes. "Darla Adams is a true gem to have on your side."

"As you can see," I said, "our club members thus far have many skills and much knowledge to share. Even as students, you are each unique. You'll have gleamed different facts over the years, your personal interests have led you to special studies away from the classroom, and your daily life has molded you into extraordinary individuals capable of teaching others. I propose we use these two hours each week as an environment of discovery."

Jessica, Faith, and Marie began clapping, but Christina yawned as though bored.

"We have a lovely group right now, but more are always welcome to join us. We don't have to stick with a special schedule for topics, but getting an idea of what everyone is most eager to hear about will be helpful." I picked up the notebook and pen from the corner table. "For a beginning list of topics, what are some areas of interest? No need to raise hands, just try not to talk over each other."

"Sex!" Christina blurted.

Faith crossed her arms, and Marie turned red.

"Sex is a very important aspect of life. Without it, species— including humans—would become extinct." I looked at the students. "We each have different interests and beliefs, and we're not created to learn at the same speed. If there is ever a conversation that you are not ready to explore, you may go to the parlor or veranda and someone will collect you when we move to a different subject. And if you're simply not in the mood to talk or need a quiet place away from home to think about things, come eat and settle somewhere quiet about the house rather than join the group. There's no reason to feel shame or fear while you're here. Is that understood?"

"Yes, Miss—Hattie," Faith said. "I'd love to discuss Darwin's theory of evolution. My sister was in your class when it was brought it up the year you taught at the girls' high school. I was jealous to miss it."

"I only gave the basics of his early career, Faith, but here is the perfect opportunity to dive into his fascinating work. I'd be happy to guide a discussion on that as well as point anyone who is interested to the right books for more information."

Faith looked pleased for the first time, then Jessica jumped in.

"Medical things are my interest, especially psychology. I'd love to dive into Freud and other schools of thought. I aim to put a stop to this nonsense label of 'hysteria' men are so quick to slap on females. One of my aunts was put in an asylum when I was ten but I never believed half of what the doctors said about her."

"There's much to be learned, ladies." I looked about the room. "I have hope in the future with bright minds like all of yours seeking truth."

Five

The new cook, Pearl, and her friend—both approved by Althea—were busy clearing the serving pieces from the dining table in preparation for supper. I stood in my science room and reflected on the past two hours with pleasure.

"The girls have things under control, Miss Hattie. I'm going to bathe Brandon now," Althea informed me.

"Thank you." I turned with a smile and reached for Brandon. "Did you have fun with Louisa?"

"Isa is orange and bright!" He kissed me before following Althea up the stairs along with Buster.

I reset the seating into more natural conversation groupings. When I had the final chair in place, Sean pulled me against his solid chest. He smelled fresh from the shower as he always did after time at the gym. I leaned against his firm body with a sigh.

"How did it go, dearest?" He kissed my neck.

"Wonderful." I turned in his arms to look up at him. "There was a bit of animosity between a few of the younger girls, but I think we've straightened it out. I have nothing but high hopes for the club after today's strong beginning."

His dimpled grin shone as he trailed his thumb over my jaw. "I haven't seen you glow like this for a while. It's wonderful, Hattie."

"It's all thanks to you and your idea for the club. I love you, Sean."

Our lips met with a passion that would never be sated. My hands fingered through his hair, skimming over the softness of his beard on their way to the tie at his throat. "Supper isn't until seven o'clock, and Brandon is getting his bath."

"I love the way you think." Sean kissed me again and locked his gaze with mine. "Are you clear?"

I nodded.

"Lock our bedroom door, and I'll enter through the bath after seeing Brandon. This is going to be good!" He bit his lip and rushed for the stairs.

I clicked off the lights in my room, just as excited as Sean over fully sharing ourselves once more. My monthly had finished the day before and—according to Darla's methods of tracking the reproductive cycle—I had about a week of uninhibited time with Sean before the window of fertility opened. Then it would be almost a week of seeking other means of pleasure before we could share the ultimate until the next monthly struck. Scientific knowledge equaled power over fears and the means to take control in life.

Pulse thrumming with thoughts of my husband, I shut and locked the hall door to our oasis. From the bathroom that sat between our room and Brandon's bedroom, laughter rolled. Sean could always break Althea's seriousness, a skill our son inherited.

Heart light with joy, I turned toward the bed. The corner of my eyesight caught the painting I had hung. Remembering Ethelwynne's revelation as to who it was, I paled. In all the excitement of the afternoon, I'd forgotten about it. Sean expected an intimate moment with me but his previous fiancée smiled down on our bed.

"Keep my boy a bit longer. I'll see you both at the supper table."

Sean's voice carried into the room before the click of the bathroom door followed him. I studied his face as it raised to the center space on the opposite wall. A smile quirked at the corner of his mouth, and his eyes dimmed with a level of loss, but not quite sadness.

"I'm sorry, Sean. I found it in the back room with the other things from your attic, and I was struck by the beauty and quality of the work." I took a breath and his eyebrows rose, wrinkling his forehead. "I didn't know who it was. Winnie arrived early, and I gave her a tour. She was captivated with it and told me the name of the subject and painter. I meant to take it down, but there wasn't time before the guests arrived. I'll remove it now, and you can relax before supper."

"I didn't come here to relax." Want colored his voice with a deep, golden tone as he dropped his suit jacket on the floor before moving toward the bed that separated us. He pulled off his tie and stepped out of his shoes.

My body reacted to his seductive air with a flood of need to my center. But I could only stare at the intensity in his usually playful eyes.

"I came here to share a passionate hour with you." He tossed his cufflinks onto the bedside table and opened his shirt. "Has something changed in the last three minutes? Do you not want me anymore, Hattie?"

"Not want—no. I thought you wouldn't want *me*."

"I'll never lose my passion for you. You're my wife, my lover, the mother of my son." His shirt went to the floor, and then his hands were at his waistband. "Shall I do this alone?"

Hungry for the feel of him, I removed my shoes, hiked up my skirt, and crawled across the bed. When I reached the other side, my hands traveled his torso as I stood.

"The vision of you coming to me has me ready for anything, Hattie. Feel if you don't believe me."

I laughed and kissed his pectoral muscles. "I know how potently masculine you are."

"Then why are we not both naked?"

"Because the curtains are still open." I passed him and closed the pair of drapes fronting the house. "Please get the far side."

Sean closed the north facing curtains. "No one can see the bed from the street."

"But we don't always keep to the bed, do we?" I countered.

Sean's laughter filled the room as he pulled me to him before the mantel. "And I love that. Every day is a surprise with you, Hattie."

I glanced up at the painting. "I'm not a young seductress."

"Your intelligence and beauty surpasses all because it goes to your heart and soul." He took me around the waist and turned us so he stood behind me, both facing the portrait of Eliza Melling. "She blinded me with her wit and allure, but Eliza is my past. You are my present and future. And it's so much brighter than I ever dreamt possible."

Sean set to work on the buttons and had my blouse half off a few seconds later. Devouring my collarbone with his lips, he scattered all semblance of control I might have had over myself. I opened his trousers, and he yanked my shirt free. A few seconds later, I was shimming out of my skirt and he his underdrawers. Sean took a moment to trace my shapewear with his fingers before they too were divested. The deliciousness of our skin meeting our full length had me trembling as he enfolded me in his embrace.

"Oh, dearest love." His kisses rained across everything as we migrated toward the bed. "The taste of you is all I need in this life."

Sean lay across the width of the bed and beckoned me to follow him to the middle. I knelt beside him, smiling down on the glorious view he afforded me as he stretched and flexed.

"It's been six months, Sean. It might be a tight fit."

"I'm hoping for that, for both of our pleasure, but *you* are in control."

I glanced to the painting.

"Hattie, if you must think of that picture, let it be to show her who has power over me now. Prove that you dominate me, that you rule my life. There's no room for her image in my heart because you possess me thoroughly." He removed the pins from my hair and dark waves tumbled about my shoulders. "But Eliza was debauched. She probably would have wanted to watch to be sure you fulfilled all my needs. Let's give her a good show and then we'll have an encore or two after supper."

Laughing, I leaned over his body. He uttered blasphemous words mingled with explicit phrases as took him in my mouth. I kept on until he couldn't speak, relishing the power I wielded. The absolute mind, body, and soul connection between us as we gazed into each other's eyes—like two atoms on a collision course—brought complete security, reckless abandon, and the freeing power of the universe into one all-encompassing rush of bliss as he entered me. We both gasped.

"If this feels half as good to you as it does to me," he whispered, "then I'll know I've done my part well."

"It feels incredible, Sean. Better than our first time together."

"That's it," Sean coaxed as he assisted my rhythm. "Write the evolution of your climax on butterfly wings and take flight."

Allusions to Charles Darwin from the lips of my devout Catholic husband always heightened my passion. Coupled with his kneading hands and well-placed kisses, I soon orbited the galaxy amid the birth and death of suns as moons rose and set beyond a blinding horizon.

His gentle rocking beneath me slowed as he trailed a finger down the side of my face. "You're so beautiful."

"Make me fly again, Sean."

He never bragged when he took command, but there was a glint in his eyes that shouted of his domination. There was no room to be upset with myself for shirking control with a capable lover at the helm. With a gentle roll, we exchanged positions and he immediately resumed his sensual assault with a brisk rhythm. I don't remember the exact words he shouted with his pinnacle because I was dizzy with my own, but our bodies were in a sweat tangled mass on the bed afterward.

Sean's fingers combed through my hair, brushing it back from my face. "I'm going to return straight home every day this week. We'll exercise each other in this room—no gym needed."

"Won't you miss your friends?"

He kissed my breast. "I've been staying on the rowing machine and punching bags this past year. Davenport is the only man I'd call a friend there, maybe Henry Adams, but he's a lot younger. I've got more than a decade on all the others and have no interest in climbing through the ropes for a boxing match. I need to keep my face flawless for my wife."

I laughed and snuggled under his jaw. "You're too handsome to wish black eyes or a broken nose upon."

"I could set a rowing machine in that back room or hang a punching bag on the porch."

"Or both." I caressed his torso. "You're a topnotch physical specimen, Sean Spunner. Da Vinci could have used you as a model."

He motioned to the painting of Eliza. "She used me as one for sketches—capturing my youth and virility with her practiced eye. I wish I could show one to you, but I'm sure her mother destroyed them after the accident. Alex never mentioned anything about them, and he would have ribbed me if there were survivors."

"What will the help say with the noise we made and seeing this painting in here?"

"I doubt the kitchen girls heard anything."

"You sounded a bit like Tarzan with your release."

Laughing, he pulled me closer, nestling a leg between my thighs. "I offer my Jane a heap more than Tarzan did. That was monumental, Hattie. And you don't need to worry about Althea. She's spoken to me before about it."

My instinct was to bolt upright, but Sean held me to his hot body.

"Once, not long after our wedding, she told me, and I quote, 'I sure am happy you found a lady with enough fire to satisfy you, Sean Francis. Boys like you need a lot, and it's been a long while since you've strutted around like the cock of the walk after a good crow.'"

Looking to his face, I saw the joy and love and returned his smile. "You deserve every bit of pride over what you just accomplished, Sean."

***

The next four days were overflowing with putting the final touches on the house, making sure I spent ample time with Brandon during the day, and satisfying myself with Sean in the evenings and before he left for work. I was grateful I didn't have to spend my mornings scrubbing grits out of the breakfast room rug. If that made me a society snob, then maybe I'd judged the ladies in my new social group too harshly. Sleeping sated and deep every night, I readied each morning with energy I hadn't experienced in years. Sean couldn't keep his hands off me, Brandan enjoyed our daily adventures, and Althea kept a knowing smile on her face.

Saturday morning, Sean stayed at the grand piano with Brandon for two hours, teaching him three new songs to sing. When our lunch was served, I settled across the table from Brandon and smiled as Sean kissed our son's forehead.

"You'll sing for Uncle Patrick and Aunt Cecelia tonight, won't you?" Sean asked as he lifted Brandon into his seat.

"Yes, Daddy. I like to see the colors."

"The colors?" Sean took the head of the table and looked to Brandon while my mind reeled with the information.

"All colors! I like your colors best, Daddy."

"And what are those?"

"Blues and greens when you play piano. Gold when you sing."

My hand went to my mouth to cover a gasp as everything clicked into place.

"What is it, Hattie?" Sean asked with concern.

"Synesthesia!" I reached across the wide table to take Brandon's little hand. "You're blessed to see the colors, Brandon. I've often felt Daddy's voice as golden too."

"My colors are good?"

"Yes, Brandon, very good."

He clapped his hands in an odd beat. "I clap red and gold!" His pace increased. "Red and purple!"

Pearl carried in the tray with our vegetables, chicken, and rice.

Althea followed with the pitcher of iced-tea. "Do you wish me to sit with your boy, Sean Francis?"

"Not today, Althea, but thank you." He smiled at her. "We'll put him down for his nap too. Enjoy a few hours to yourself." Sean blessed the food and then dished a small amount of everything onto Brandon's plate, quickly cut his chicken, and then held each dish for me to serve myself. "What does this all mean?"

"He has synesthesia," I whispered. "More specifically, it's chromesthesia. I've read about it in scientific journals. Synesthesia is a specialized way some brains function in which one sense that's experienced leads to a reaction or reflex in another sense. Those with chromesthesia involuntarily see colors for different tones. Their vision is stimulated by their hearing, making things like music a rainbow-creating experience."

Sean glanced from Brandon to the bowl of rice he was dishing from. "Do I laugh in gold like when I sing?"

He nodded vigorously.

"And Mommy?" Sean added chicken and greens to his plate.

"Mommy is pink like azaleas."

"Those are pretty flowers, aren't they?"

"So is Mommy."

"Yes, she is. What about this?" Sean tinged his fork against the china.

"Silver!"

"Silverware?"

"Silver. Gray with pink." Brandon went back to eating his chicken.

"Don't draw too much attention to the colors," I whispered to Sean. "He's not a parlor trick, and I don't want him to begin to despise it."

"A parlor trick?" Sean sounded aghast. "Hattie, this is brand new to me. I'm trying to understand my son, not parade him in front of guests."

We silently ate for a few minutes. Buster's tail brushed my ankle, and Brandon's hand disappeared under the table with a piece of chicken.

"Are you full, Brandon?"

"Yes, Mommy."

"Go ask Miss Pearl to help you wash up."

He was down in a flash and running for the kitchen.

Sean leaned closer. "Hattie, what of his intelligence? Is this a sign of trouble?"

"All the studies so far point to it being a sign of *increased* intelligence."

"I knew he was above average! Merri can eat humble pie when—"

"You said no parlor tricks."

"He's always loved singing for an audience. That won't change."

"If it isn't made a fuss over."

I stopped as Brandon ran through. He climbed onto the piano bench. After a moment of listening to his simple notes, I took Sean's hand.

"Allow him to make music and sing when he wants, but don't push. I think he's enjoyed it so well because for him, it's painting. He sees it and the abstract music becomes physical in his mind's eye. He's too young to understand that no one else around him sees it. If he learns we don't see the colors, he might lose interest. I have vague memories of seeing colors when I was little, but I suppressed them after telling my brothers and they teased me about it."

"But that's my boy! He's gifted and possibly a musical prodigy."

His countenance burned bright with pride. How could I protect our son while allowing Sean a bit of bravado to share?

"Don't encourage him more than you already have. And not a word about synesthesia to anyone. He's too young to be made into a novelty."

"But our boy—"

I kissed his lips and leaned my forehead against his. "Our son is as amazing as his father. I've never met a smarter person, Sean. You memorize passages of scripture, poetry, plays, and more. Not only that, you can recall them at a moment's notice and recite with such enthusiasm. It's breathtaking to watch."

"But I didn't try, it just happened. And no one remarks on it."

I took his face in my hands, my thumb tracing his lower lip. "You must have hundreds of pages memorized that you've been adding to your whole life without conscious effort. All because no one drew attention to it. Your gift is part of you—something numerous people love and enjoy—but it's not a novelty. It's in your soul, Sean. Allow Brandon that same experience of self-acceptance. Don't make him superior in his mind or before others. Let him be himself and shine that way."

"But people might not have thought me special."

"Ask your uncle when he comes to supper tonight if he thought you blessed with intelligence when you were a boy. Find out if he didn't see your talent and discover ways to encourage you without drawing attention."

"He rode me hard with schooling. Urged me through courses so I graduated early and—"

"Because he knew what you were capable of, Sean. Ask your uncle, then I'll serve *you* humble pie."

Six

Sunday after church, I sat in the yard with a puppy and a pocket stuffed with dried turkey bits. Tasked with training one from the litter with the same hunting signals my grandfather had taught my mother's dog when she was a girl, I worked hard to earn my five dollars for the feat. Whenever a litter was more than two, Mama hired me or Andrew to work one of them.

After five failed attempts at getting the dog to lie down with only the visual signal, the back screen door opened.

"Winnie, telephone!" Mama called.

I tucked my charge under my arm and went for the house.

"Not in here," Mama said from the porch. "You know the trainees aren't allowed inside."

"I'll hold her."

She shook her head. "And you know better than to leave her alone in the yard."

"Then what am I supposed to do when I'm called to the telephone?" I knew my tone wasn't polite, but it was absolutely infuriating to be treated as a naughty child for what would amount to a minute of time on the telephone.

Mama folded her arms across her slight frame. "Return the dog to its rightful place in the stable before coming inside."

Seeking comfort, I cradled the puppy to my chest. "Then could you please take a message for me? I'd rather not make the person wait all that time."

She nodded curtly, and I stalked across the yard.

"Velvet," I said when I approached the dogs' stall, "your owner is the most uptight woman in the world. Here's your fourth puppy. I fear she'll be more than five dollars' worth of trouble."

I set the little one beside Velvet and stroked the mother's silky ears.

In the far corner of the stable, my father stood from behind a pyramid of stacked barrels. "Winnie, I don't like to hear you bad mouth your mother."

"I'm sorry, Papa." I closed the stall door, cut down to two-feet in height so Velvet could come and go but the puppies couldn't. "What are you doing in here this afternoon?"

"You want the truth or what I told your mother?" He wiped his forehead with his handkerchief against the heat.

"The truth, please."

"You're old enough for it, Winnie. I trust you won't hold it against me."

"Never, Papa." I took his hand and kissed his cheek like I'd done as a girl.

"You know your mother never liked alcohol, even before the state prohibited it."

I nodded, thinking of the times Sean would come to dinner with a bottle to share with Papa and how he'd try to coax Mama to take a shot for "old time's sake."

"I was never one for daily drinking, but I like a nip of something every now and again. I've got a contact that stops in the store and sells me a bit to fill my flask." The sunlight streaming through a crack in the side of the barn caught his spectacles in a glare and shower of dust particles as he looked to me. "I keep the flask back here when it's been filled and get a shot when I feel like it."

"But it's the Sabbath, Papa."

"I'm glad you've listened to your mother about such things, but I'm sure my soul will survive the wickedness." He smiled at me. "Truth be told, I've only got a drop or two left and it's my second fill for the month. I've been running out here a lot since supper with the Spunners."

"Why does she keep inviting them over if she hates them?"

The whiskey on his breath blew like fire when he laughed. "She doesn't hate them—it's the opposite. Merritt loves Sean—she always has—but she's jealous of Hattie."

"But she married you."

"She did, and I know she loves me. I love her more today than I did nineteen years ago. But her love for Sean is different. He's always been one to charm the ladies, and Merri fell for him while he was romancing her cousin. Sean has been this enigma, within reach but forbidden fruit all this time."

"She thinks I'm in love with him too. I heard her tell him."

"Are you?" Papa put a hand on my shoulder and kept eye contact.

"Sometimes I think I am, but it's like loving the hero in a novel. I know the man isn't for me, but it's nice to think about. And I really like Hattie. I'm glad he married someone so smart and kind. I'm happy for them."

"So am I, Winnie." He patted my shoulder. "Sean has been through a lot in his life—more scrapes and sorrows than me, and I've got six years on him. I'm glad you're going to Hattie's club. She's still a bit of a fish out of water here. I hope this will help her find more friends because Merri has been treating her terribly."

"She's not been kind to me either."

"Winnie, she loves you. Her mother was hard on her, and she knows she needed that firm hand and high expectations to make the best of herself. She's sees so much of herself in you, and she's doing the best she knows how to raise you right."

"I'm not bad, Papa, but she makes me feel inferior with how she talks to me like I'm Drew's age. I'm a few years away from the age she was when you married, but I've experienced nothing and never gone further than Grandma and Grandpa's house in Grand Bay."

"What is it you'd like to do?"

"I'm not sure of anything beyond the opportunity to make my own choices."

"Will you do me a favor, Winnie?"

I nodded.

"As soon as you decide what you'd like, will you tell me so I can do everything in my power to help you accomplish it?"

"Yes, Papa. And thank you."

I went for the house, my father followed, but slowed in the yard to light a cigarette.

"It masks the smell of the whiskey." He winked. "I'll be behind you in a minute."

Glad to have my father's support, I passed under the satsuma trees with one hand raised to set the glass bottles swaying. I entered the kitchen smiling.

Mama turned from the counter where she was organizing her recipe box to look me over. "Did the pup give you trouble?"

"No, Mama. I stopped to talk to Papa. Who was on the telephone?"

She smoothed a hand over the gray streaks at her hairline. "Christina. She said she had an urgent matter to discuss with you about her history homework. Isn't she a grade above you?"

"Yes, but we have the same history course. She had to retake it."

"Go ahead and call her back."

Papa came in from the porch with the last words and kissed Mama.

"Christina gets hopelessly lost with history dates," I said. "I'd rather go to her house so I can show in the textbook what she needs to focus on."

Mama frowned. "If she spent more time on her studies rather than her appearance, it would be better. You don't need to put yourself out of your way to help a girl like that."

"She's my friend, Mama. I like to help her."

"What has she ever done for you?"

"Merri, there's no need for that tone." Papa took her arm and turned her to face him. "We're to help our neighbors no matter what they do for us."

"Christina helped me first," I blurted. They both looked at me, and I almost lost the courage to share my secret shame. "A group of girls found me sitting alone on the first day of high school. They pestered me about my glasses. Christina happened by and shoved them away. She gave them a talking to with enough venom that no one else has bothered me since. I just wish we'd gone to the same grammar school because I've been teased my whole life."

"Winnie, my girl." Papa embraced me. "I'm sorry you inherited my poor vision. I had no idea you had such trouble at school. Your reports were always good and you never complained."

"There wasn't anything you could have done to protect me at recess or lunch."

"I could have taught you to fight to defend yourself. For a start, if a boy bothers you and won't back off, kick him in the groin."

"Bart, my daughter will not participate in violence!"

"She will if it saves her from a worse fate. But that's not the point. Right now, you need to meet Christina." He nudged me toward the hall. "Be home in time for supper."

"Thank you, Papa."

I could feel my mother's eyes burning into my back as I left the kitchen, but I didn't turn around. I took my straw hat from the hall tree and exited the front door.

On the other side of the park, I met Christina.

"There you are!" She hooked her arm through mine and nodded the way I'd been going. "Meeting you here saves a bit of time."

"I'm happy to help you with your history—"

"That was a bunch of rubbish to be sure your mother told you I called. We're meeting Luke!"

"What?" I kept beside her as she quickened her pace.

"We need to go to the church. After he's done with his organ duties, we'll take a walk or something. It will be our first time in public, but I want you with me in case someone who knows me sees us and tells my parents."

"And what if someone sees me and tells my parents I was out on the town on a Sunday afternoon when I was supposed to be tutoring you?"

She laughed. "Your family doesn't mix with as many downtown people as my folks do."

At the edge of the neighborhood, we turned north on Broad Street. Before disappearing into the Methodist church building, I glanced at my family's spiritual home—First Baptist Church of Mobile diagonally across Government Street. My church was as looming and pretentious as the Catholic cathedral with its Greek rival portico standing nine feet above the main road. By comparison, the Methodist congregation's building had a tall façade with no place to wait out the rain that frequented the city. It had undergone enlargement and improvements over the past several years, and now the stucco entry boasted ornamentations that made it look distinguished, though still flat.

Christina held the massive door open for me. As we slipped into the coolness of the church, I was immediately assaulted with the deep rumblings from a pipe organ as we neared the chapel doors.

"Isn't he glorious?" Christina whispered. "He stirs my soul just listening to him so no one need claim I'm smitten with him only for his looks."

Her eyes closed, and she swayed in the doorway.

I took hold of her arm. "Where are we to meet him?"

"Around the side of the building, but I wanted you to hear him first."

"I've heard him. Let's go."

We escaped through the main door and double backed to the Broad Street side so we were in the shade.

"You really are chicken, Winnie. I don't know why I'm friends with you."

"Then I'll go home. Maybe we'll say hello to each other at school tomorrow."

I took a step, and Christina yanked my braid. "You don't have to be such a hothead."

Down the sidewalk, a tri-colored mutt barreled toward us. Its matted fur reeked of garbage. Jumping at me, the dog dirtied my blue dress as its heavy paws pressed in my thigh. I pushed the mutt away and Christina gave a startled cry.

"What's this?" An amused voice asked.

"Luke, help! That dog came out of nowhere at Winnie."

I turned toward Christina and found myself looking at the lightest blue eyes I'd ever seen on a man. Luke's countenance was angular with a jaw that gave his face a triangular look beneath his brown hair. Above his left brow was a port wine birthmark smaller than a penny and shaped like a dove in flight.

"The infamous Winnie Graves?"

I pushed the mongrel back once more.

"Yes," Christina said. "Now help her, Luke."

"I can handle dogs," I said with a superior attitude though this one was nothing like my mother's sleek pointers. It pawed at me once more and stuck its nose at my hip.

Luke laughed. "Do you have a meaty bone in your pocket, Winnie?"

The treats! I shoved the dog as hard as I dared then thrust my right hand into my pocket, scraping up all the turkey which I then flung on the sidewalk. The mutt immediately snuffled them into his mouth and ran off.

"Winnie, that was disgusting!"

I held my soiled hands before me. "Where can I wash?"

"There's a spigot around the back of the church." Luke touched Christina's shoulder and smiled. "Wait here a moment. I'll bring your friend around."

Her adoring brown eyes met his light gaze. "I want to come too."

"There's always mud back there. I don't want you to soil your pretty shoes. The infamous Winnie has practical boots on. We'll just be a minute."

Luke took my arm with a firm grip and marched me to the rear of the church building. There he looked back to wave at Christina before leading me through the jumble of construction supplies. My heart rate increased as the reality of being with a strange man in a private location flooded my senses. I wished my father had told me more about fighting before I left the house, but knowing where to strike a man helped me stay somewhat calm.

"It's over here." He released my arm and trailed his hand down my back, keeping a light touch low on my spine.

My stomach churned as we went deeper into the shadows. How could Christina be blinded by such a schemer? I saw the faucet and stepped to the side as Luke turned on the water. While I leaned over, my hands scrubbing each other under the water spout, Luke touched the side of my waist and leaned over me to wet his handkerchief in the flow. His palm spread and flexed around my hip.

"Christina told me you were young, but you're a woman in all the right places."

I straightened so fast, I knocked him off balance and he set his shiny loafer in the fresh mud.

"You little—" He laughed. "You need a firm hand, but keep your pluck."

I walked as fast as I could back to the sidewalk.

"Christina, whatever do you see in him?"

She looked beyond me. "What? Where's Luke?"

"Right here." He came up behind me and patted my shoulder as he passed. "I had the exact mishap I warned you about. I'm afraid I ruined my best handkerchief in the process."

She looked to his shoes and shook her head. "Winnie will think you're a clumsy fool, but we'll give her time to see how wonderful you are. Where are we going?"

"Not too far. I have to be home by four." I purposely moved my time up to protect myself from Christina's penchant for shirking rules.

"Then let's get going," Luke said. "How about a stroll to Bienville Square?"

"That sounds lovely, doesn't it, Winnie?"

I lifted a shoulder in a half shrug.

"You're still put out over that dog business. It serves you right for walking around with food in your pocket." She took Luke's arm when he offered, but I ignored the one he extended to me and went to the far side of Christina as we headed for the corner.

"I was training a puppy when you telephoned. I'd forgotten there were treats left."

"Winnie's mother raises the prettiest puppies," she told Luke. "Do you like dogs?"

"Not as much as Winnie does, feeding strays like that."

Christina laughed when we paused at the corner to wait for it to be safe to cross Government. Luke's profile boasted half a dozen tiny lines that radiated from the corner of his eye, and the lines about his mouth were deeper than they should be on a man of twenty-five who worked indoors.

"I'll tell you now, Luke. I want one of the puppies from Winnie's mother once I'm married. She tends to only do two litters a year, but maybe there would be some next Valentine's Day. My dog wouldn't need the extra training with hunting hand signals—that costs more and takes longer. I just want a cuddly puppy to play with."

"They don't stay little," I reminded her. "You've seen how big Velvet is."

"But she's still pretty, nothing like that mongrel who attacked you."

We were quiet as we crossed the main road. Once we were heading east on the north sidewalk, Christina moved to a new topic.

"That's where Winnie attends church." She pointed to First Baptist.

Luke leaned around Christina to look at me. "How's the organ?"

"We only have a piano. The congregation is saving up for something spectacular, so it's taking a while to fund it since the construction on the new building finished."

"A stately church like that without pipes is a disgrace."

"The building is impressive, but I prefer ours don't you?" Christina asked Luke.

"Ours? Oh, United Methodist? I just work there. Didn't you know, Christina?"

"But you must be a believer."

"There's a God and all that, but I take the position of organist where they'll have me. I play their drivel to pay the bills, then I cut loose with Ragtime at the clubs at night. I've played everywhere from New Orleans to Memphis to—"

"I thought this was your first job since graduating college and moving from Atlanta." Christina shook her head. "But I can never keep places and dates straight. That's why I have trouble with history."

Luke looked sideways at Christina. She was too distracted to notice how thoroughly he had stuck his foot in his mouth, but he didn't fool me. The problem was how I would get my friend to see the truth before the man fooled her to an extent she might never be able to recover from.

***

"I've been invited for tea Saturday afternoon," I told my mother as soon as I arrived home Monday evening from Hattie's meeting.

"Tea?" She looked up from setting the dining table. "Who does tea parties these days with war going on?"

"Apparently Mrs. Woodslow does."

"Why would a surgeon's wife—Hattie. This is her doing, isn't it?"

"I'm not even sure if she's attending. Marie Marley invited me. She attends the club meetings, and Mrs. Woodslow is her oldest sister. I walked with her to the Woodslows' house afterward. Marie's father picks her up there so she doesn't have to travel far after the club dismisses."

"Do you know her from school?"

"I met her at the first meeting. Her brother-in-law is close friends with Sean."

"I know he is. And I bet the girl goes to a Catholic school. I don't see how you fit in with her."

"Marie is nice, Mama. And they aren't old money. Her father made a fortune in the lumber business two decades ago, but he started with nothing, like Papa."

"What's this?" My father asked as soon as he was in the door. He took Mama in a hug and kissed her square on the mouth.

"Mama is upset I've made a new friend who invited me to a tea. She can't stand Christina, and apparently my new friend isn't up to her standards either."

"Don't put words in my mouth, Ethelwynne Graves."

"Then please stop being petty about everything in my life." I went for the stairs.

"Don't walk away from me, young lady!"

I turned to my mother. "I don't want to listen to more complaints over the Spunners or my friends."

"When the Spunners are taking over your life and—"

Papa laughed and slung an arm around Mama's thin waist. "Merri, Sean and Hattie aren't taking over Winnie's life. She goes to Hattie's meeting once a week. How is that hurting anything?"

"Besides being around more Catholics than ever—"

"You sound as bigoted as Aunt Ethel. Don't you remember how you hated her speaking badly of Catholics?"

Her face flamed red, a familiar sight in recent weeks. "That was before I'd seen for myself what a bad example they can be."

"Bad example?" Papa shook his head. "You seem to have forgotten your own choices. Who was it who welcomed Sean to live with her when she was nineteen?"

"How dare you speak of such things in front of our daughter?"

"She's old enough to know the truth, and you're beyond the age to deal with your feelings, Merri. Are you truly so disappointed with being married to me rather than Sean?"

"No, Bart. Of course I love you more." Tears filled her brown eyes, and I inched toward the hall to escape. "Sean was Winifred's, but I cherished the connection to him that their relationship created between us."

Papa took her in his arms. "You've been closer to Sean than you have been to your own family back in Grand Bay since you moved here, but you don't need to be a prisoner to your emotions over him."

She nodded.

"And Winnie is smart enough to choose her own friends. If she's to go to a tea, she'll need a new dress for the occasion."

"I'll see to it, Bart." She looked up at him. "And I'm sorry if I ever caused you to doubt my feelings for you."

As they kissed, I went to my room to hide from their dizzying display of emotions and tainted words about the past.

Seven

Early Saturday morning, I lay awake.
Physically comfortable with Sean tucked behind me, I hated to move
even when I heard Buster's nails on the bathroom tile. I stole from
the bed as gently as possible but Sean still groaned over me leaving.

"I'll just be a minute," I whispered.

Brandon was finishing up with the toilet. Then he clapped his
hands under the water faucet as I held him to the sink to wash his
hands.

"We need a step stool. But for now, let's put Buster outside
and get in bed with Daddy."

Using the back stairs on the screened-in porch, we easily let
the dog into the yard before hurrying back up. Brandon climbed the
side of the bed and snuggled against Sean.

"We need to buy a step stool," I said as I settled my head on
the pillow, facing my boys. "Brandon will be more self-sufficient in
the bathroom with one."

"I'll take him downtown while you're at Grace Anne's. We'll
drop you off for the tea, and then go to the furniture store to look at
stools. Maybe a stop for I-C-E C-R-E-A-M. as well."

"All that while I'm stuck with a gaggle of society women? It's
not fair."

He caught my eye over the top of Brandon's head. "Don't be
so judgmental, Hattie. You might meet someone who would be a
perfect fit for your science club."

"I highly doubt that. I'm not like them, and they don't like me." As though feeling my self-defeat, Brandon shifted toward me as a message of love, eyes falling closed.

"You get on great with Melissa and Darla." Sean lowered his voice.

"Exactly. *They* are career women who weren't raised in this elite society, nor are their husbands lawyers or doctors."

"So all lawyers' wives are snobs?" His amber eyes were bright beneath the lifting dark brows.

"Don't even tease me."

"Alex's wife isn't stuffy. And she's a writer—earning an income higher than her husband from what I've heard."

"Melissa has already told me that Lucy Melling doesn't go out much."

"I wish you got on with Grace Anne better. She likes you, and John would love for you to educate her a bit."

"She's pleasant and an excellent hostess, I'll give her those two compliments. But the good surgeon's wife has no grasp on world events or basic scientific principles. I have absolutely nothing in common with her."

Shifting as though to climb over Brandon, Sean stilled—body supported by one arm—as he observed our boy snuggled fully against my thin nightgown. The rush of motherly emotions I'd been bereft of for weeks flooded back. For a moment, I yearned for another baby to experience that closeness with.

"It appears he's dreaming of the good ol' days, when he was in the land of milk and honey. He's blessed to have your nurturing, Hattie." Sean bit his lip and slowly lowered on his side so he could watch Brandon sleep. "I love you both so much it hurts to think I had to wait as long as I did for my family."

"I hope we were worth it," I whispered.

Finger trailing my cheek, his words were just as soft. "I'd go through the years of loneliness again for a moment with you. As Lord Byron said in 'Stanzas for Music,'

'There be none of Beauty's daughters

With a magic like thee;

And like music on the waters

Is thy sweet voice to me:

When, as if its sound were causing

The charmed ocean's pausing,

The waves lie still and gleaming,

And the lull'd winds seem dreaming:

And the midnight moon is weaving

Her bright chain o'er the deep;

Whose breast is gently heaving,

As an infant's asleep:

So the spirit bows before thee,

To listen and adore thee;

With a full but soft emotion,

Like the swell of Summer's ocean.'"

Maybe I was as hopeless as a society wife reading romances, but I didn't need the fantasy of the books when I had Sean before me. I captured his caressing hand and brought it to my lips, kissing each finger as I held his gaze with my own. I meant to study Sean's face—the dark hair across his chin, the curve of his lips, and the lines radiating from the corner of his eyes when he smiled. But the warmth of Brandon's little body against mine and my husband's secure hand resting on my hip surrounded me with comfort that urged me to close my eyes to soak in the rare moment of quiet togetherness.

I woke an hour later to an empty bed. Water running in the next room accompanied Brandon's giggles.

"Go get some clothes, young man," Sean said a moment before he stepped into our room wearing only his underdrawers.

"Good morning, once again, Hattie. I loved watching you sleep even if there was a bit of jealousy over Brandon's prime real estate."

Brandon ran into the room with shorts in one hand and a sailor top in the other.

"Climb on the bed," Sean told our son. "I'll help you dress."

I escaped to the closest, pulling out a blue calf-length skirt with a coordinating blouse that buttoned down the front beneath a modest V-neck and a broad collar. Setting my bust in a brassiere, I topped my matching underwear with a princess slip to smooth my lines before donning the new ensemble. I stepped out of the closet barefoot and Sean nuzzled into my neck before he grabbed a pair of trousers off one of his shelves.

"You're too pretty to keep inside all morning. Let's go for a walk after breakfast. Go get your shoes and socks, Brandon."

After we ate, Brandon leashed his dog and the three of us headed north on Houston Street before cutting east, toward the Davenports. We visited with them in their yard a few minutes before resuming our walk. On the return trip home, Sean held my hand and allowed Brandon and Buster to lead the way on the quiet side streets. He paused to greet each neighbor we passed.

"It's everything I dreamed it would be," Sean said as he held the gate open for me when we reached the yard a few steps behind Brandon.

"What's that?"

"Being happily settled in marriage to a woman I adore and having friends to compare parenting with." His lips brushed mine as he leaned close on the back step.

"I'd stay with you all day if I could." I pressed against him in a seductive embrace.

"No you don't!" He took my arm and marched me through the back porch. "You're going to the tea party, and I'm dropping you off there myself to see that you do. Althea!"

She appeared in the living hall as we arrived there. "Yes, Sean Francis?"

"Brandon is in the yard with Buster. Could you watch them until our luncheon is served?"

"I'd be happy to."

I tried not to dwell on all that Althea had witnessed—both with me and before I entered Sean's life. I was sure he had brought Eliza to his house, but was he more discreet as they weren't married? Or was Althea and her devotion to him means to forgo propriety where his lovers were concerned? I knew it wasn't worth pursuing, but I found myself thinking of Sean's past since the move—especially after I unknowingly hung the portrait of Eliza Melling in our bedroom.

Her haunting smile welcomed me as Sean led us into our space. Neither of us had spoken of it since that first day, but we looked at it. A lot. I think it brought a bit of youthful exuberance to him. I crossed the room to close the door to the bathroom while opening the buttons on my top. On the way back, I shut the drapes and laid my clothes over the chair by the mantel. My shoes and skirt were removed, and Sean deftly lifted the slip over my head.

"This is a pretty set." He fingered the lace trim on my underclothes and kissed the swell of my upper breast. "Gives your tits a good lift too. Are they from Mademoiselle Bisset's shop?"

I nodded as his hands followed my full hips down to my thighs where he played with the garters holding up my stockings.

"Would you leave these on?"

"All right, but I'm in control otherwise."

"And what do you have in mind, dearest? We can't take too much time."

Even with all we had done together and our open conversations, I blushed.

Sean saw my hesitation and embraced me. "It must be positively scrumptious, Hattie. Whisper in my ear what you want to do with me."

***

Sean pulled the automobile into the Woodslows' semicircular drive and called out to Ethelwynne, who was almost to the front steps. "Hello, Ethelwynne! Would you make sure Hattie goes inside?"

"Of course." She waved to Brandon in my lap, and he returned the gesture.

Sean leaned across the seat to kiss me, and I set Brandon on the bench seat beside his father.

"I'm glad I don't have to walk in alone," I told Ethelwynne on the front porch.

"So am I. I've never been to a tea party before."

"You'll do fine, Winnie. It's not much different than a club meeting except the sandwiches tend to be drier, as well as the conversations."

We were both laughing when Mrs. Woodslow opened the door, causing a wave of floral scent to escape.

"Welcome, Hattie and Winnie. I'm so glad you're both here." Grace Anne's dark blonde hair was pulled into a chignon, but a few frizzy curls escaped, and they swayed as she turned toward the parlor. "Marie, your friend is here!"

We shifted further into the long hall between the doorways to the front parlor and dining rooms.

Marie came in from the parlor on the left, taking Ethelwynne's hand. "Winnie, thank you for coming."

"Before you two run off," the hostess said, "let's get in a quick introduction to those already here."

We followed Grace Anne into the frilly white and pink room that Marie had just vacated. "Everyone, this is the wife of my husband's dearest friend, whom I've been waiting ages to get to one of my teas. I fear she's too clever for me, but maybe someone could help entertain Hattie Spunner."

The stares I received from the up-turned noses of the ladies sitting on the dainty furniture made me straighten my posture.

"And this is my sister's friend, Winnie Graves." Grace Anne motioned to the younger guest. "Winnie and Hattie, meet Kate Stuart, Mary Margaret Easton, and my middle sister, Sadie Beauchamp."

After smiling and nodded her head, Ethelwynne whispered to Marie, "Should we stay?"

"It's frightfully boring. We have permission to sit in the sun room so we can talk freely, but I promised Grace Anne we wouldn't serve ourselves until after they do."

As Marie and Ethelwynne made their escape, I looked between Grace Anne and her equally blonde sister sitting near the doorway before stepping further into the room that looked more fitting for a Victorian house than a modern home.

"Thank you for having me, Grace Anne," I said as I passed her.

I sized up the two brunettes on the tufted sofa. I'd seen both and been briefly introduced to them when I attended Mass and at masquerades, but I'd never had an extended conversation with either. Knowing Mary Margaret was a mother of an ungodly amount of children, I chose to sit in the chair closest childless Kate.

The divorced woman was at least as tall as Sean and she held herself well—so well, I wouldn't be surprised to learn she wore an archaic corset. The gold watch on a chain about her neck shifted on her white blouse when she leaned toward me.

"Welcome, Mrs. Spunner. It will be a pleasure to get to know you better this afternoon."

"Thank you, Ms. Stuart. It seems I've been slow to meet people in my years in Mobile."

"It's not for lack of excursions. You were a teacher at Barton Academy's high school for girls your first months here, were you not?"

"Yes, from the fall I arrived almost four years back until that summer I married."

"Sean Spunner." The gleam in Kate's dark eyes was difficult to read. "He was a rascal in his youth—both he and Grace Anne's John. I feared they would never grow up, but fortunately for you two they did, though they still seem capable of mischief come Mardi Gras season."

I smiled. Unsure if she laid a trap for me or not, I kept silent.

"Sean loves parading you about, but you don't attend the cathedral often."

"I promised him I would go at least monthly."

"Why not more?"

"I prefer science to religion. Sean respects my choice."

"Surely a woman would rather attend Mass for the morning than worry about her husband sitting alone—or worse—with *other* parties. Oh, not that there is anything to worry about with Sean these days. But what of you sitting alone those hours?"

I matched her bold stare with one of my own. "I read, Ms. Stuart. I receive a dozen different science and medical journals and relish quiet Sunday mornings as a time to catch up with my subscriptions."

She shifted, angling her shoulders in a way that communicated dismissal as Grace Anne welcomed three more ladies into the room.

We were soon brought across the hall to the dining room to fix our plates. I wanted to peek in at Ethelwynne and Marie in the next room, but Mary Margaret stopped by my side.

"Tell me, Mrs. Spunner, why have you not joined us before?"

"I nursed my son and didn't like to leave him for extended periods of times."

There was a gasp from one of the new arrivals and the murmur of more voices before Mary Margaret spoke again. "You know, Mrs. Spunner, there are formulas these days. A child is no reason to inconvenience yourself from social engagements."

"My son is no inconvenience. I made him my priority his first two years. It's been proven in the natural world that a strong mother-child bond from the beginning helps nurture the growth of the baby's brain. This solid foundation of love and nourishment between mother and child has given Brandon a firm foundation for the rest of his life."

"And all that coddling doesn't upset your husband?"

"Why would it? I never treated my husband as a child, therefore he was never replaced."

"But it might make him jealous," Kate said.

"There is a huge difference in the type of love I give Brandon verses what I give Sean. If you're sharing the same type of love to all your family members, you might wish to reevaluate your choices."

Mary Margaret gave a snorted chortle of distaste. "Whatever we do, men go where they want for *their* coddling."

"I don't know about *your* men, ladies, but my husband is perfectly satisfied with our sexual liaisons." I grinned at the shocked expressions staring back at me. "Why just before our noon dinner today, my husband led me to our room and watched me undress."

"Hattie," Grace Anne said with a quiver in her voice, "I'm not sure this is the appropri—"

"Obviously your friends want to know or they wouldn't have brought forth the subject. Maybe education about healthy marriage relations would be of assistance because it sounds like some of the gentlemen in your social circle still cling to the whoring habit from their youth. If they're going to use the lack of response from their wives as the excuse, at least take away that option by engaging your sexual nature with your husband more often. Don't feign alarm, ladies. You've all been married, and most of you are mothers, so you've completed the deed at least *once* in your lives. If you found the act distasteful, I'd say you're doing it wrong, or your husband is."

"Really, Hattie!" Grace Anne exclaimed. "I'll have to ask you to cease with this."

"I want to hear what she has to say," Kate said.

"Yes," Mary Margaret agreed. "If she can keep a man like Mr. Spunner satisfied, there would be hope for me—and every other lady in attendance."

"It isn't about me *keeping* him—it's about enjoying the act for myself and for how it bonds us. It boils down to science and nature.

I'm open to discussing all things about that at my science club on Monday afternoons, if anyone is interested. It's an open salon style for all young ladies and women from four to six o'clock."

"But you'll speak to us now, won't you?" Mary Margaret asked.

"As long as Mrs. Woodslow agrees."

Grace Anne sighed. "Let's bring our plates to the parlor so we can all sit comfortably."

Eight

Marie and I sat in the space beyond the dining room. It felt like a greenhouse with its massive windows and tropical plants. A wall with a fireplace divided us from the food. There were open doors on either side of the hearth, so it wasn't exactly private, but the ladies didn't seem to notice us with Hattie on center stage. Marie's ivory complexion was the color of a beet, and I was afraid I looked much the same.

Worry over Hattie spilling too much private information—thereby damaging her own and Sean's reputations—gave way to the thought that if anyone would cheer her on it would be her husband. Despite his gentleman status, Sean was a braggart and enjoyed shocking people.

The rustle of skirts and click of heeled shoes on the hardwood floor migrated back to the parlor.

"We'll have to relocate to keep listening," Marie whispered.

After the sounds of the last lady leaving quieted, Marie crouched and went for the door to the right of the fireplace, then pushed through a swinging door on the next wall to the right, waving at me to follow. I found myself in a butler's pantry with a scowling maid and cook. Undaunted, Marie went out a door to the left, which put us at the far end of the entry hall, beyond the staircase.

"Stay here a moment," she whispered. "I need to make sure John's curtains are closed."

She snuck through the folding glass doors across the hall. It was the same style of doors that separated the Spunners' downstairs rooms, but Hattie always kept open. A moment later, Marie motioned me in.

The room was dark. Rich wainscoting, built-in leaded glass bookcases, and a window seat on the opposite side of the room filled the lower third of the walls to the bottoms of the tall windows, and a broad molding reached from the tops of the windows to the twelve-foot ceiling. To the left, another pair of folding glass doors led to the parlor, but they were closed and curtained with emerald brocade drapes for privacy. Skirting the desk before the gigantic Greek-detailed brick fireplace, Marie pointed to the two arm chairs between the desk and curtains and took the furthest for herself.

From our new seats in the cool darkness of the doctor's study, we heard everything.

"Do you really speak of things like sex with young ladies in the club?" someone asked.

"None are too young to learn how their bodies work, though I've told them that if there is ever anything they don't wish to hear, they can respectfully sit in another room."

"Have any of them left?"

"Not yet," Hattie replied. "But I think you mistake my point. We don't discuss sex every week, but we let talk go where it will—Charles Darwin, fossils, climate. But isn't it better to have informed young women rather than unsuspecting innocents that are easily taken advantage of? We need to empower young women so they can take charge of their bodies rather than allow men to manipulate them. Where our mothers may have failed, we don't need to."

There were murmurs, but I couldn't tell if they were in agreement or hostile.

"And you and Mr. Spunner are happy?"

"Blessedly happy, as he says. Earlier today, for instance, he wanted me to wear a certain article of clothing while we shared our bodies. Did I want to? Not preferably, but I wanted to experience the coupling in a location we had never attempted."

Gasps.

"Where else is there than the master bed?" someone asked.

Hattie laughed. "There are no regulations, ladies. Two bodies can join anywhere there is space for them. I agreed to wear his chosen items if he allowed me to be in control."

"Goodness!" A lady shrieked.

A set of footsteps clicked down the hall.

"Can we do that?" a timid voice asked.

"Why ever not? Demand a new location or position. Don't just lay on your bed in defeat—climb on top and claim your mate from time to time."

Marie giggled but my stomach churned. I didn't like to hear that from Hattie because it made me think of her and Sean in all sorts of ways.

"Is that what you did today?" a bold voice asked. "Did you take charge of your lawyer from the top?"

"Yes and no." I could hear the smile in her voice, and it gave me shivers. "Sex is fluid, in more ways than one. Don't keep it stagnant in one position the whole time. Most of the animals who hold still are those that feign death during the act, which isn't the way for humans. Allow the build—both yours and his—to inspire movement. It will feel better for both of you."

Nausea threatened to overtake me. I covered my ears to block what Hattie next shared.

Marie looked gleeful with the secret, but then noticed my distress. Still smiling, she took my arm and whispered. "You must be hungry. We'll go back to the other room."

When we were a foot from the door to the hall, it opened. I nearly screamed, and the blond man looked equally startled. He wore a white shirt and tie with suit trousers, but no jacket.

Marie put a finger to her lips. "John, you're home early."

We moved back a few steps to allow her brother-in-law entrance into his room. He smiled at us and gently closed the door behind him.

"What's going on in here?" he whispered.

He knew we were up to no good—and trespassing in his private space—but he wasn't angry, only curious. I liked him at once. I adjusted the new white lawn dress and prayed I didn't look like I was trying too hard with my prissy braid and bow almost as large as the one Marie wore.

"We were listening to the tea ladies," Marie whispered,

"Why would you want to do a boring thing like that?"

"Hattie was speaking about sex."

"Hattie is here?" He maneuvered around us and leaned toward the curtains.

Marie followed him. "I think you missed the good parts."

"Shh." He waved at her to quiet.

They both hovered inches from the door. I shifted uncomfortably by the other exit.

"Is that Kate Stuart?" Dr. Woodslow whispered.

Marie nodded.

"And Hattie—" He interrupted himself with his own chuckles. Marie punched his arm, and he took her hand and brought her to me. "Now please introduce me to your fellow intruder."

"John, this is my new friend, Winnie Graves. Winnie, this is the best brother-in-law in the world, Dr. John Woodslow."

His blue eyes widened. "Winnie Graves? *The* Winnie Graves? Daughter of Merritt Graves?"

"Hush!" Marie hissed.

I nodded, and he pumped my hand in the heartiest handshake I'd ever received.

"It's a pleasure to meet you. I've heard so much about your family since, well, before you were born."

The doctor looked me up and down as though weighing me against some visual he had in his mind. I blushed and pushed up my glasses, thinking he might know all Sean's secrets as they related to my mother.

"I look more like my father than my mother," I offered.

"Then your father must be real pretty." He winked.

Marie giggled. "Come on, I need to be sure our guest eats."

"Lead the way," Dr. Woodslow said. "I did five surgeries this morning and never got a dinner break."

The three of us crept into the hall and then through the pantry. Since we had the man of the house with us, we were smiled at as we walked through the prep area on our way to the dining room.

We were piling our plates when someone caught sight of us from the parlor.

"Dr. Woodslow!"

He rolled his eyes before turning for the doorway. "Kate, how are you?" He met the tall brunette in the hallway, holding his plate in his left hand as he leaned over her extended glove to kiss the back of her covered hand.

"Fine, as always, Doctor. Have you been hiding from us?"

"I was trapped in the surgery all morning, and our youngest guests were kind enough to share their food and keep me company while I eat." He looked back at us, raising his brows before turning back to the lady and then taking a step closer to the parlor. "Hello, ladies. Gracie. I hope all is well for everyone."

There was a polite murmur.

"I don't wish to intrude on your party, so I'll return to Marie and Winnie." He retreated, stopping long enough to pour a glass of ice tea before retreating to the conservatory.

Marie and I finished gathering our refreshments and joined him. Dr. Woodslow had loosened his tie and sat with an ankle on his opposite knee, balancing his plate on his folded leg. He was as easygoing as Sean, but had more distinguished good looks as opposed to Sean's boyishness. I knew from hearing Sean speak of his friend that they were within a year in age, but the doctor looked several years older, though his sandy blond hair hid the hint of gray at first inspection. He was old enough to be Marie's father, but she adored him like a cherished brother.

We ate in companionable silence several minutes, all apparently straining to hear what might be said in the parlor. Nothing but a constant hum of voices and a few high bits of laughter reached us the next quarter of an hour.

As the doctor stood, Hattie stopped in the far doorway.

Dr. Woodslow immediately set his dishes on the side table and went to her. "Hattie." He kissed her cheek and pulled her into our hideout. "I'm glad you made it. I'm sure it's meant the world to Gracie."

She laughed. "I'm not sure about that, but we'll see what happens."

"Did you cause trouble?"

"It's my middle name, John. Didn't you know?"

"Trouble does seem to fit you, and you look lovely. What else do I need to say to encourage you to invite us over for supper sometime?"

"I'll discuss it with Sean and have him ring you to compare schedules."

"Thank you, Hattie."

She turned to me. "Are you doing okay, Winnie?"

I nodded. "Everything is great."

Marie giggled, and I shot her a warning look.

"Well, I better get back," Hattie said with a smile. "I don't want to give those ladies too long of an opportunity to speak about me."

After she left, Dr. Woodslow looked to Marie. "She really got them riled up in there, didn't she?"

"You don't know the half of it!"

"If Mr. Spunner arrives before the others leave," I said, "be a friend and don't allow him inside. Tell Hattie he's here, and keep him company until she goes out."

"God in Heaven, help that woman," Dr. Woodslow said with a laugh. "If you don't tell me the details, Marie, I'll be forced to believe her talk was more fitting to a men's locker room than a ladies' tea."

"I would shudder to think men would speak of anything more intimate than what she confided. Keep that in mind if my sister does anything…unexpected in the future. Just don't let on that you know the source of it."

Hattie had been correct in proclaiming the sandwiches would be dry. I had to refill my glass of tea before finishing my plate. Within the next half hour, a few ladies left. Not wishing to see an awkward exchange between the Spunners and any of the guests, I looked to Marie.

"I should be going. Thank you for inviting me. And you, Dr. Woodslow, for not being angry we were in your room."

He laughed. "Shenanigans are nothing new to me. I'm pleased to have met you, Winnie."

Crossing to the parlor, I found five ladies—including Hattie—still with Grace Anne.

"You have a lovely home, Mrs. Woodslow, and I enjoyed my time with Marie."

"I'm glad you joined us to keep her company."

As soon as I stepped onto the porch, Sean's automobile pulled into the driveway.

"Get Hattie," I whispered to Marie before descending the steps.

"Ethelwynne, would you like a ride home?" Sean called to me.

"No, thank you. It's a nice afternoon."

"Spunner!" Dr. Woodslow called from the porch as he took Hattie's arm. "Allow me to return your wife to you."

I forced a smile and waved before making my escape.

Nine

I stood in the living hall, overlooking the mass of guests at the refreshment table and wondered if I needed to rework my science gathering into a sexual freedom club. Not only was Grace Anne Woodslow at my meeting, but three ladies from her tea party: Sadie Beauchamp (her sister, who was married to one of Darla's cousins,), snide Kate Stuart, and Mary Margaret Easton. Darla and Melissa were both there, as well as the five high school girls.

As the ladies began to settle, Grace Anne shooed Marie toward the parlor as though to keep her baby sister away from the bulk of the dialog. Marie and Ethelwynne took dining chairs placed just outside the open club room, which I was pleased to see. As much as I proclaimed educational freedom, I knew how innocent those two were. The other high schoolers were nearly graduated, and I felt no concern over them hearing anything these women might discuss.

"Did any of you take action with your husband based on Hattie's stirring words at Grace Anne's tea?" Kate asked without fear of anyone asking her likewise because she was divorced—the only female in Mobile society to survive such a scandal.

When the Davenports had stopped by yesterday afternoon, I'd told Melissa of my tea party experience. She discreetly whispered the basics to Darla. Both looked at the new guests expectantly.

After a minute of awkwardness, Mary Margaret cleared her throat. "I did and my husband accused me of getting into his whiskey because, according to him, only a drunk or a whore would initiate anything out of the ordinary. I wanted to counter that the whore might need to be drunk to put up with his attitude."

"You poor dear." Grace Anne put her arm around her friend. "Don't let that discourage you. Edmund has been disgruntled for years. It might take time to reach him."

"Is he worth reaching?" Melissa asked. When several ladies gave her a harsh stare, she straightened. "It's all well and good to strengthen your relationship with your husband, but remember that no matter what we do on our side, there has to be movement and growth on *his* side for things to work."

"Easy for you to proclaim with amiable Frederick Davenport as a mate," Kate said. "When a man has gone rotten, there's nothing we can do to stop it. But Edmund, Mary Margaret, has been improving himself. Don't give up hope."

Wishing to change the topic to something more pleasant, I opened my mouth, but Sadie Beauchamp spoke first.

"My Saturday night was a smashing success! Richard loved everything I did and asked if I'd taken a correspondence course on seduction."

"Newly-wedded bliss," Grace Anne remarked with a smile for her middle sister.

"She was married last autumn!" Mary Margaret complained. "The rosy-tint of my newlywed days expired after the first week."

"Edmund isn't the easiest person to get along with," Melissa said with compassion. "You do as well as you can with him, everyone sees that."

"He was so charming and attentive when we courted. And his brother is a darling with his wife." She was near tears.

"But Maxwell doesn't have a problem with the bottle." Melissa was well versed with the Easton family dramatics as her stepdaughters were half-Easton.

"And Alabama prohibition means nothing in Mobile. It isn't easy for anyone." Kate's words had a tone of finality to them that closed further conversation about Edmund or Mary Margaret's woes.

"Hattie," Grace Anne said, "what do we do about babies if we increase our intimate time with our husband?"

"That," I replied, "I'll refer to Darla. She's the one who advised me."

"I think I might already be beyond that," Sadie said.

"Oh, Sadie!" Grace Anne jumped to her sister's side. "Have you told Mother?"

"No, and don't you dare. I need to see the doctor first to be sure."

When the sisterly chatter settled down, all eyes turned to Darla. She described the monthly cycle, to which all present—including the youngest—listened intently.

"So you can have sex without worry right before and right after the flow?" Grace Anne asked.

"For most women, yes. And I recommend using a calendar to mark your days. Don't rely on memory with something as important as family planning." Darla looked at all those assembled. "Not every woman has an exact pattern to her ovulation, but for the majority, this method works. Listen to your bodies and remember when you're fertile is when your body craves the connection the most, which Hattie is keen to remind us helps insure the survival of the species. Some women can feel ovulation—that's a good marker for counting the after days—but no matter when the egg is released, there are only a few days each month when it's possible for a woman to become pregnant. As much as men like to believe otherwise, their seed is not immortal."

A tinkling of laughter from the adults.

"But the only fool-proof method to prevent pregnancy," I paused to make sure Christina was still listening, "is to *not* allow consummation. You're in control of your own body. Don't let a man—husband or not—to take advantage of you if you're not willing."

More questions from the married women came to the midwife. While Darla answered them, Ethelwynne and Marie took their plates to the dining room, then relocated to the parlor with their refilled dishes. I checked on them ten minutes later, and the girls were happily discussing an L.M. Montgomery novel.

Jessica and Faith had to leave at half past five, and Christina and Mary Margaret slipped out along with them. Seeing that the other students had left, Marie looked in on her sisters, whom she had arrived with.

Sadie conversed with Darla about early pregnancy signs, and Grace Anne tried to gleam information from Melissa about her marriage while she nursed Junior, but she was tight-lipped with everyone except me and Darla. Marie returned to the parlor with Ethelwynne and the two sat at the grand piano, playing a duet.

Kate joined me in the hall. "Why did you start this science salon, Hattie?"

I knew that Kate was one of the biggest gossips in town, but that she carefully selected what news to spread and which secrets to keep for future power, so I chose my words carefully.

"I didn't dare admit that I missed teaching, but Sean could tell. He chose this house especially because it would suit entertaining and encouraged me to begin a science club as an outlet for intelligent conversation and to share all the science journals I subscribe to. It was his idea to invite some students, to give me that feeling of contributing to younger minds." I nodded toward the parlor. "Winnie's parents are old friends of his. She brought a few girls from the high school."

"I never realized how intelligent Sean is," Kate admitted. "He tended to hang around the wild ones in his youth, and that grin of his makes him look like a silly school boy."

I laughed. "His smile keeps him approachable, but he's the most intelligent man I've ever met. He is more widely read than anyone I know, and with a memory as long as an anaconda that he pulls from to recite poetry, scriptures, the Constitution, and even Charles Darwin."

"And now you're glowing like a newlywed." Her brown eyes narrowed. "Three years, is it?"

"Yes, this June."

"Never forget how much you have, Hattie. So many of us have nothing that matters." For a moment, Kate's eyes looked wounded and her words were so quietly spoken, I knew she would refute them if I ever told anyone. Kate returned to the club room and pretended to look through the microscope, but never adjusted the dials.

Following the sound of Ethelwynne playing and singing "At the End of a Beautiful Day," I stopped in the middle of the parlor to watch her.

A minute later, Brandon ran in the front door. "Winnie sings pretty colors!"

His dirty knees were on the piano bench, and he gazed up at Ethelwynne as she finished the tune. "Teach me, Winnie!"

Darla and Melissa managed to wrangle themselves away from the older Marley sisters on the pretense of getting their children home. A minute after they left, Kate, Grace Anne, Sadie, and Marie were in the hall, ready to leave as soon as Ethelwynne finished her song the second time. We all clapped for her—Brandon the loudest.

"Walk with us back to Grace Anne's, Winnie," Marie said. "My father will give you a ride home from there."

Brandon held Ethelwynne's hand and jumped all the way to the door, causing her to nearly drop her school books. "Stay and sing!"

"I can't, Brandon. But I'll be here Saturday for supper. Five days. I'll sing with you then." She looked to me and smiled. "Thank you, Hattie. I had a great afternoon. I'll see you Saturday. It was nice to seeing you again, Kate."

"And you, Winnie."

I stepped onto the veranda with Kate, Brandon following us.

"She is a charming girl. How does Sean know her family?"

"He lived near them for years. They live across from Washington Square."

"They aren't Catholic or from here, are they?"

"No. Winnie's mother was raised in Grand Bay and her father in McIntosh. They're Baptist."

"*Country* Baptists." Kate pursed her lips. "But they're raising that girl right. She's accomplished with music. I didn't hear her speak much, but she carries herself well."

Althea came around the veranda from the back of the house. "Sorry, Miss Hattie. The rascal heard the music and took off. I knew he was safe inside, and I couldn't leave the other children alone."

"The only trouble is the dirt that might have fallen around the piano."

"Come on, Brandon Patrick." Althea offered her hand. "It's bath time."

Left alone on the porch with Kate Stuart, I motioned to the rocking chairs. "Would you like to sit?"

She checked the watch she wore on a gold chain. "My driver is infuriatingly punctual. I told him five minutes before six o'clock, so it will be several more minutes before he arrives."

We took the matching rockers outside the south facing parlor windows.

"The girl," Kate said. "Winnie. Tell me that's not her given name."

"Ethelwynne Graves."

"That's most unfortunate."

A black, fully enclosed automobile pulled to a stop in front of the house. I stood with Kate. Before we reached the steps, Sean exited the front door.

"Hattie," he paused a brief fraction of a second before snaking an arm around my hips and kissing me. "I didn't mean to intrude on your final guest. May I assist you to your vehicle, Ms. Stuart?"

Kate's gaze traveled every inch of Sean in his well-fitted gray suit, a naughty smile curving on the corner of her lips. "I wouldn't dream of taking you away from your wife."

"That's good of you. There's nowhere I'd rather be than with Hattie."

"She's certainly a rare treat. Enjoy *all* of her, Mr. Spunner."

We watched her walk the curving path to the front gate. Sean waited until she was in the back of the automobile and the driver had closed her door before speaking.

"Was it just me or did Kate Stuart undress me with her eyes and make more than one innuendo? And what is the city's gossip queen doing at your science club?"

"I may have gotten a tad carried away in conversation at Grace Anne's tea last Saturday, but four new ladies attended today."

"That's wonderful, Hattie. What did you say to invite them?"

"I encouraged them to be bold, demand more, compromise when needed, and even initiate sexual moments."

"Hattie, darling." Sean kissed me and laughed. "You are the most brazen creature in town."

"Today, Kate asked how things went for everyone. Edmund brushed his wife off, complaining she must be drunk."

"He's been a lost cause since Eliza. The jerk didn't know what he had before him."

"Your Eliza was with that over-grown blowhard?"

"Just once, at his bachelor party no less."

"And you knew?"

"It was months before we began courting. I was in the house when it happened—across the hall at a poker game with a bunch of other Mystics of Dardenne members while they were going at it. I've told you two things before that you need to keep in mind. I was a scoundrel in my youth, and she bewitched me."

"Always an out with a lawyer," I teased.

Behind me, the hustle and clatter of the dining table being cleared for supper continued. Sean must have thought our tantalizing discussion was too fresh for the young help to witness and led me to the stairs, where I continued the conversation.

"Several ladies wanted to know how I kept such a fine specimen as you completely satisfied. I may have shared our most recent example to illustrate compromise, control, and changing positions."

He froze in the hall before our bedroom door. "Our most…Saturday…oh, Hattie!"

"I didn't tell them about the stockings, but they know I was on your lap and then climaxed on top of the desk. I'm sorry if I went too far."

Three things were prevalent when Sean escorted me into the room and shut the door with a bang.

Our drapes were already closed.

The door to the bathroom was shut.

And Sean was shaking with laughter—not anger.

"Those poor ladies must have been shocked out of their minds to hear that. John has wanted you to spend more time with Grace Anne to encourage her toward intellectual improvement, but he might consider sexual enhancement a better bonus. You can be sure I'll weasel it out of him when we take supper at the club Wednesday." He dropped my dress on the floor before devouring my cleavage. "And all those hens can think of your boldness as they seek their own man to fill them on a desk."

I held him as I lay back on the bed, relishing the way he fit against me. The coupling was quick but thorough. We were breathless and had new love marks when we climaxed. Lying in his arms afterward, I trailed my fingers across his firm middle as I smiled over the successful afternoon.

"You look pleased," Sean said.

"Every aspect of life with you is fulfilling. Brandon heard a new song today he liked. He proclaimed Winnie sang in pretty colors and listened to it twice before she had to leave."

"Win—oh, dear God!" He sat up, bringing me with him. "Ethelwynne was at the tea when you spoke about us, and here this afternoon! Merritt will kill me if she finds out what you've been speaking of around her daughter."

"Give me some credit, Sean. At the Woodslows' house, Winnie and Marie were in the space beyond the dining room and we were in the parlor. They never attempted to join our conversations. And today, after Darla spoke about monthly cycles and family planning, the youngest girls were in the parlor the last half of the time."

"Monthlies and family planning! Hattie, how many students are attending now?"

"The same five, all three weeks so far. Marie Marley is the youngest, but Grace Anne is fully aware of the range of topics we cover. The others are ready to graduate. One is even going to Baltimore for college."

"And you've potentially armed these young women with the means of engaging themselves sexually while avoiding pregnancy."

"It's not like that. These girls have their heads on straight—well, all but one. And that one, in my opinion, will benefit from hearing things that might help her make a somewhat less stupid choice from the one she's already set on."

Sean took my face in his hands, gazing intently into my eyes. "Hattie, you must take care with your discussions. Someone might accuse you of contributing to the delinquency of a minor if any of these girls were to act upon something they learned here."

"You're mad at me."

"No, dearest, I'm the farthest thing from angry. I love your passion to see this new generation be given the knowledge you never had." His lips on mine were soft, creating a tingle that traveled from my mouth to my core. "As your husband, I will always support you in your ambitions, but as a lawyer, I will advise you to use caution from time to time."

I climbed onto his lap, straddling him. "And is my legal counselor ready for an exploratory interview?"

He laughed and wrapped his arms around me. We melted together once more, fused in our mutual love and pleasure. Afterward, Sean covered me with kisses before we dressed for supper. I paused before the mantel as I buttoned my blouse.

"I noticed something at the Woodslows' during tea."

"What's that?" Sean asked as he finished securing his necktie.

I pointed to Eliza's signature in the corner of her painting. "Grace Anne's portrait in their parlor is a Melling."

Sean grinned. "Yes, one of the few Eliza-painted debutante portraits in existence."

"I always thought you gazed at it because you found Grace Anne attractive, but you look at it to feel closer to Eliza, don't you?"

"No, not closer, but in admiration of her talent. She was blessed with the gift of artistic expression, like our son is with music." He kissed me. "I promise to nurture Brandon and allow him to grow the way he wants with music—unlike the confining guideposts the Mellings set for Eliza. Fortunately, she wasn't dull enough to follow the rules."

We collected Brandon from Althea on our way downstairs. The supper table was laid beautifully for us with the china Aunt Cecilia gifted us for our wedding. Sean settled Brandon in his chair and escorted me to my seat. I tapped the call button in the floor under the table to signal we were ready for the food.

When Brandon finished eating, Sean excused him to wash his hands and then play at the piano. We ate in silence until Brandon began plucking out a few random notes. A minute later, Brandon's pace picked up and a single-note tune evolved from his tapping.

Sean's eyes widened. "Is that 'At the End of a Beautiful Day?'"

"That's what Winnie was playing this afternoon."

"She played it twice?"

I nodded, catching the wonder he felt.

"God blessed our boy, Hattie." He wiped his mouth with the linen napkin before hurrying across the broad hall to the piano.

By the time I joined them, Sean accompanied Brandon singing "The Lord is My Shepherd." I took the corner of the sofa, tucked my leg under my dress, and rested my head on the backrest, dreamily watching my husband and son shine with their musical talents.

Ten

During lunch on the first Friday in June, I sat with Christina in the schoolyard. I pretended to study for a literature test the next hour though I couldn't concentrate on the definitions. It was better than listening to Christina drone on about Luke.

"Why are you even bothering with literature? It's your best class."

"History is my best, but how do you think I do well if I don't put in effort?"

"Because you're naturally smart." Christina twirled the tip of her ponytail. "Listen. I want you to go with me to see Luke in concert tomorrow night so I don't have to go with my parents. There's a choir performing in the church at eight, and he's the accompanist."

"I can't," I said with honest relief. "We have our monthly supper with the Spunners tomorrow evening."

"What about to the dress rehearsal? I bet we could sneak in and watch."

"Two of the puppies are supposed to be picked up tomorrow and one is my trainee. I have to be on-hand to speak with the new owners about the progress and teach them the signals." It was a partial lie. I used the signals my mother taught me, and she knew them better than I did.

Christina pursed her lips. "How many will be left?"

"The last one is picked up next week. The first one should be gone by the time I get home from school."

"That's sad. No wonder you're so cold about them."

"I told you they were all spoken for."

"Well, maybe the next litter. Luke did tell me he adores dogs."

"Of course he does," I mumbled. I spoke the next sentence louder. "Has he met your parents or mentioned wedding plans?"

"No, but he's seen me with my parents at church. I'm sure they believe me in love with someone in the congregation because I've never wanted to go to church, and now I jump at the chance to go to any meeting that needs music. My mother has mentioned the quality of the hymns have improved since we got a younger organist. The previous man was so feeble he could barely press the pedals his final month."

"But that doesn't mean she would approve of Luke as a match for you."

"That won't matter if we elope to Mississippi for a weekend."

The bell rang, and I happily gathered my supplies to escape Christina's ridiculousness. I sailed through the test in my literature class, and the rest of school passed quickly.

All was quiet when I arrived home. Seeing no one on the main floor, I hurried to the barn. Only Velvet and three of the puppies were there. I returned to the house, brushing my hand against two glass bottles in the satsuma trees on my way.

"Mama?" I hollered once I was back inside.

I climbed the stairs, a sense of unease growing. Even if she went to a ladies aid meeting or visited friends, my mother had never failed to be home when I returned from school.

She sat on the edge of her bed, staring into her open wardrobe. "Mama, are you okay?"

"Winnie." She wiped the back of her hand across her shiny cheek. "You're home early."

"It's nearly half past three. I see the first pup is gone."

"His new owners were pleased. He followed Mr. Inge's hand signals right off."

"Then why do you look sad?"

"I don't know what to wear to Sean's house. I haven't had a new dress since Christmas because I skipped an Easter frock when I had that cold and didn't attend services."

"Anything will do, Mama. Sean and Hattie don't judge people be their clothing styles."

"That's no reason for me to appear any less fashionable than one of their society friends when I'm invited over. We're just as respectable as any of those people you've been to club meetings and tea parties with."

"Of course we are, Mama."

"Do you know where those ladies shop? Certainly not department stores or patterns from a general store."

"There's a Parisian shop I've heard mentioned. Bisset's. It's on or near Dauphin Street."

"Would you go with me in the morning, Winnie? I want a new dress to wear to supper tomorrow night." She moved before the mirror above her dresser and peered at the fine lines on her forehead. "I'm willing to put everything from today's sale in for it."

"You don't have to impress the Spunners."

"Ethelwynne, sometimes a woman has to prove to herself that she can still turn heads. It might involve showing a man what he missed out on or reminding another what he's lucky enough to have, but it's done for the benefit of the woman—even if that result hinges on the reaction of the men involved." Her brown eyes bore into mine with a fierce determination. "I haven't felt pretty for a long time."

"Mama, you're petite and pretty—two things many women want most in the world."

"I haven't had a proper gown in years. While I'm brave enough to put it on, I'm nervous to walk through the doors of a strange shop. Will you go with me at ten o'clock tomorrow morning?"

I nodded, bewildered at the level of vulnerability she allowed me to see.

"Thank you, Winnie, but please don't say a word about it to your father."

That night, I woke twice from dreams about Christina and Luke. I was grateful I'd been spared the curse of love thus far. I wasn't ready to make a fool of myself like Christina. No man would ever be worth throwing away my self-respect.

After breakfast, Mama sent Andrew off with Papa to work. She spent an hour in the bedroom readying for our shopping trip, and emerged in a navy A-line, calf-length skirt with front pockets that were all the rage, paired with a crisp white blouse that never went out of style. Her thick, brown hair was piled on top her head in a loose bun, soft and full.

"You look nice, Mama." I wanted to say it was certainly good enough to wear to the Spunners' house, but knew better than to voice my opinion when it was contrary to hers.

She looked over my own plain blouse, gray skirt, glasses, and braids—shaking her head. "You look like a schoolgirl."

"I *am* a schoolgirl, Mama."

"Not for much longer, Winnie." She sighed. "I fear I've done you a disservice, trying to raise you in the city as my mother did me in the country. Our situations are too different, yet here you are, going on seventeen and still wearing braids. Sean was right. I need to allow you to grow up."

We walked to Government and took the streetcar down to Royal and looped back to the north side of the road, exiting near the shopping district. Asking directions from a policeman, we found the proper block. Mama paused to stare at the sparkling evening gowns in the store window.

As soon as we were in the shop, a buxom brunette dressed in all black approached us. "New faces! Such pretty new faces. Welcome, ladies. I'm Mademoiselle Bisset and I will personally outfit you for any occasion. Come. Tell me what is needed."

"Hello, Mademoiselle Bisset. I'm Mrs. Graves. I have a supper party to attend tonight. I'm afraid I waited to the last minute to find a dress."

"It is wonderful to meet you, Mrs. Graves. It is rare to find a lady of your dainty frame with such elegant lines. Do you happen to be connected to Bartholomew Graves at Allen's General Store?"

Surprise lit her face. "Yes, that's my husband."

Mademoiselle Bisset laughed and patted Mama's hand. "That dear man! I shall fuss at him for not sending you to me before now. He has been most kind in taking my overstock to sell at his store. With the war going on, my friends in France send what they can when they can, but sometimes the shipments are too much for me to handle. Not wanting to place the merchandise in any of the city stores and have too much competition, I contacted his store because several of my customers living west of town have spoken of the high quality goods and exemplary service there. I don't give him the evening gowns, of course, but the simpler dresses and basic foundation pieces."

I thought of the silk nightgown Papa had given Mama for her last birthday and smiled at knowing where he'd acquired such a piece.

"How very clever of you," Mama said. "I don't usually have the need for an evening gown, but it's a bit of a special occasion. We're going to Mr. Spunner's new house, and I want to look my best."

"Sean and Hattie Spunner are some of my favorite people! He brought her to me to outfit for her first Mardi Gras masquerade. When a man accompanies a woman here, I take him aside and question him for *his* likes. I find out what colors he likes best and what part of the body he focuses on so when he looks at her in one of my gowns, she will see the excitement in his eyes and feel even more beautiful. How long have you been friends with the Spunners?"

"Almost twenty years. They're friends with our children, too. Sean and Hattie are both fond of Winnie."

"I see the keen mind of your father in your eyes, Miss Graves. Your mother's elegance and your father's intelligence is an excellent combination." Mademoiselle Bisset turned back to my mother. "I have just the gown for you. You might think it bold, but you have the perfect figure for the fashion. It only flatters a woman who is small on top, if you understand."

Mama blushed. "Yes, of course."

"I think that it might need to be taken in a bit in the waist and length, but my seamstress is in today, and as it is for the Spunners' supper, I would allow it to be placed on the top of the work pile and delivered to you this afternoon should you like the dress."

"That's very generous of you, Mademoiselle Bisset."

"Caroline," she called to a shop girl behind the counter. "Bring the newest silk House of Worth to us in the first dressing room."

Mama's eyes widened. "House of Worth? I could nev—"

"Mrs. Graves," Mademoiselle Bisset said in a calm, low voice as she took my mother's arm. "I always treat my business associates well. Your husband qualifies because of his sales in my behalf. I am sure I will be able to outfit both you and your daughter for less than you believe possible."

Before they reached the curtained room, Mademoiselle Bisset turned to me. "Sit there, Miss Graves, and I will see to you once your mother is happily settled with a gown."

I sat on the chintz chair without explaining that I wasn't to receive a new dress. When the assistant carried an orange and silver gown with very little on the top to Mademoiselle Bisset, my mouth hung open. I clasped my hands in my lap and strained to hear the conversation going on behind the curtain.

"No upper shapewear can be worn with this as the dress is cut too low, but you are not in need of lifting or tucking. My dear, you are positively the daintiest thing I have ever seen! The men will be in awe when you enter the room. Mr. Graves will have to fight them back."

Mama laughed, then gasped. "Oh, no. I couldn't!"

"But you must. This was made for a woman like you and there are not many in Mobile that compare."

"I feel naked."

"But beautiful, no?"

"Yes, but it's so much skin!"

"Pale skin that has never seen the light of day, capturing the shine of the metallic beadwork on the trim. For a woman of your slight form, this gown excites—not because of exposed mountains of flesh, but because the drastically low cut reveals all without being flashy. I would suggest a choker style necklace or nothing at all. Go on and show your daughter how lovely you are."

Mademoiselle Bisset opened the damask curtain, and I stared at the stranger who stepped out. A fairy princess couldn't have been lovelier. The silver, gauzy lacework of the short sleeves was repeated on an underdress that was exposed on the bottom third of the front by the cutaway of the creamy orange silk fabric of the gown. The broad, deep square neckline showcased nearly ten square inches of chest from neck to décolletage and shoulder to shoulder.

"Well, what do you think, Miss Graves?" Mademoiselle Bisset asked.

"Everything you said was true. Mama is flawless."

"Is it what I was looking for?" My mother turned, showcasing a deep V-cut on the back of the bodice and a short train of the orange silk.

I nodded.

Mademoiselle Bisset smiled at my agreement. "Caroline, fetch our seamstress from the back to see how much she needs to nip this in at the waist and hem. Now for your daughter."

"Yes, please find her something that she could wear to day parties as well as evening socials. Church, too, would be a plus."

Mama must be out of her mind! She sewed most of my clothes and never bought me more than one dress in the spring, and she'd already purchased the white lawn for Mrs. Woodslow's tea and my traditional Easter dress.

"Stand before me, Miss Graves." Mademoiselle Bisset circled me like a hawk. "You're between your mother and father in stature, a fine figure for a young woman. Are you near eighteen?"

"I'll be seventeen in August."

She stared at my face. "Spectacles must always be worn?"

"Yes, ma'am."

"But as your father, you have kind, intelligent eyes. Do you like blue?"

"Very much."

She turned to the shop girl. "Fetch the tiered blue dress with the puff sleeves."

Despite my worry over Mama's gown, a thrill went up my arms upon seeing the party dress. It was the prettiest sky blue tone, and the three tiers on the bottom portion weren't too ruffled to be considered childish. The scooped neck line was modest, but mature, and the short, puffed sleeves were trimmed with the same ruffle as the dress tiers.

"It's darling," Mama said.

Mademoiselle Bisset smiled. "I told you I will dress you both for any occasion, Mrs. Graves. Walk around the shop while your daughter tries on the dress to make sure you are comfortable. Now in you go, Miss Graves. Caroline will assist you."

I found myself closed in the curtained space with a stranger. I stared at her, my face heating at the thought of disrobing in front of her.

"It's policy, Miss, but I'll turn around so long as you don't need assistance with your buttons."

I turned my back to her as well, opening my blouse and then stepping out of my skirt. I hung them on an empty hook and faced the worker in my underwear and full slip. "I'm ready."

She lifted the dress she held. "Raise your arms as I pull it down. This one isn't as tricky as some, so you'll be able to secure the fasteners in back without assistance."

Having ladies' maids that laced you into corsets and buttoned your dresses seemed so last century, but I supposed there were still a few families around town who used them.

Once the dress hung on my shoulders properly and the pearl buttons on the nap of the neck were fastened, the worker tied my sash and nodded.

"Thank you."

She opened the curtains and I stepped out.

"It's as lovely as I thought. Do you approve?" Mademoiselle Bisset looked to my mother.

"Yes, but the hair and shoe—"

"New stockings and shoes," she agreed. "I have just the thing. Caroline, the white ankle-strap shoes, please, and shite stockings."

I gave the assistant my shoe size and turned back to my mother.

"You must wear your hair up now, Winnie."

"I'd rather have it cut, Mama—that 'round the face style with finger curls."

"But that's practically like a boy!"

"Mrs. Graves," the shopkeeper said in her kindest voice, "I have to agree with your daughter. A feminine cut like a Castle Bob would be glorious on her, framing her face and working well with her glasses too. And though it is not my specialty, I would venture that seeing you and knowing your husband, she would have enough body and natural wave in her hair that might eliminate the need for rolling to achieve the desired outcome."

I smiled in relief, Mama catching me with the relaxed grin.

"You'd really like that?"

"More than anything!"

Mama's hands nervously traced the pleats at the front waist of her gown. "I've always cut Winnie's hair. I wouldn't even know where to go."

"Say no more, Mrs. Graves. I shall telephone my friend right now and see if she can work her in this afternoon."

"I have an appointment I need to—"

"I could go by myself, Mama."

"I bet she could even sell her hair, getting far more for it than the haircut would cost," Mademoiselle Bisset said.

My mother looked from me to the proprietress and back. I think it was the pleading in my eyes that pushed her over the edge, but it might have been the thought of not having to pay for the cut. "We'll take both outfits and an appointment at the hairdresser's if you can claim one for Winnie within the next two hours."

"I knew Mr. Graves had to be married to a sensible woman." Mademoiselle Bisset clapped her hands and motioned to the assistant. "Help Miss Graves back into her clothes, then her mother."

Mama stepped closer to her before I was out of earshot. "I'm not certain I have enough with me to cover the total."

"I shall charge the rest to Mr. Graves without trouble."

"He doesn't know I'm here today."

She laughed. "My dear, isn't that typical? I send the bill to the husband's office the Monday after the event. The man is so pleased with how his wife looked, he happily pays every penny. I expect Mr. Graves to be so happy, he will send you back within a week to purchase more."

We both changed and Mama surprisingly settled the bill with her own cash—a testament to both Mademoiselle Bisset's generous discount and the high price Mama was able to collect for the puppies of her prize-winning dog. My haircut appointment was set for the next hour, so we stopped at a restaurant for a quick luncheon before walking to the hairstylist.

"I'm going to set the dress boxes in your bedroom when they arrive. I'd like to ready in there so your father doesn't see me."

"All right, Mama."

"Cutting off your hair scares me. I hope you like it as well as you think you will." She handed me two dollars. "Keep that in case she doesn't want to buy it. And remember tipping is customary. I hope to see you home before two."

I kissed her cheek. "Thank you, Mama."

The hairdresser was more than pleased with my hair. Because of the length and condition, I walked out with nearly twenty dollars in my pocket and more self-confidence than I'd ever felt in my life.

I crossed Government Street at Broad as I typically did, my shortened locks swinging freely above my shoulders. As I passed the eastern edge of the United Methodist, the strains of choral music drifted out. I thought of Christina's plans that day and hurried through a cloud of cigarette smoke wafting from the construction area at the rear of the building.

"Winnie, is that you?"

The voice made my skin crawl. I didn't stop, but footsteps pursued me.

"Wait a minute, girl. I'm talking to you!" Luke grabbed my arm, yanking me to a stop but I refused to turn to him.

"Let go!"

Still holding my sleeve, Luke weaseled himself in front of me. His putrid breath leaked from his grinning mouth. I yanked my arm from his grip.

"That's some haircut you got—makes you look older than Christina—but I knew it was you by those glasses. Stop and talk to me a minute, will ya?" He raised his brow, wrinkling his dove-shaped birthmark.

"No, thank you."

"Why are you acting like I'm a stranger? I've brought you around town." He took my arm again.

"And I had a horrible time. Now let me go."

I tried to pull free so I could run, but he held tighter.

An automobile coming up the road crossed to our curb, pulling to a stop.

"Winnie!" Mr. Finnigan—Sean's uncle—called from the driver's seat. Beside him, his wife looked on with wide eyes. "Are you having trouble with this man?"

"I ain't trouble," Luke said as he released my arm.

"Then go back to wherever it is you came from."

Luke took a slow drag from his cigarette as he sized up the gray-haired couple in the Cadillac. Maybe he noticed their fine clothes or Mr. Finnigan's no-nonsense attitude. Whatever it was, he sauntered back to the church.

"Are you headed home, Winnie?"

"Yes, Mr. Finnigan."

"Get in and we'll see you there. I don't want your parents or my nephew upset at us for leaving you out here when that man is hunting you."

Mrs. Finnigan straightened her gloves. "I almost didn't recognize you with your new hairstyle, but I saw that man bothering a young woman and made Patrick pull over. Climb in the backseat, Winnie."

I did as directed, and we soon drove down Palmetto Street. Mr. Finnigan parked in front of his house two blocks before mine and turned to look at me.

"That man isn't a friend of yours is he, Winnie Graves?"

"Not at all." I raised my hand to fidget with my braid, but it wasn't there.

"But you know him."

"One of my friends from school fancies him. I meet him two weeks ago when I walked with her. I ignored him when he called out to me, but he grabbed my arm."

"I'm glad you see through him, but you need to be more careful. The world is a dangerous place these days. Things are changing when a young lady can't be alone without a man making a pass at her. Your parents—"

"Please don't tell them, Mr. Finnigan. I was with Mama all morning on errands. She left me at the hairdresser because she needed to get back in time to meet the new owners of one of the puppies."

"Those darling puppies!" Mrs. Finnigan sighed. "Our Pudding is such a dear. Your mother has that magic touch with them."

"Your father should show you a thing or two about defending yourself."

"He's told me to kick the man in the groin if he doesn't listen to me."

Mrs. Finnigan gasped, but he laughed.

"Bart could teach you more than that. He busted up Sean a time or two in the old days," he said as the automobile pulled back into the road. "Sean Francis always managed to find trouble whenever he took his head out of the books."

"But he turned out fine because of your rearing, Patrick," Mrs. Finnigan said.

"I did my best for the lad." He stopped before my front gate. "Listen to your parents and stay safe, Winnie."

"I'll be more careful, Mr. Finnigan. Thank you both for your assistance."

I waved as they pulled away, grateful they came along when they did but hoping they wouldn't speak to anyone about the altercation.

Eleven

"Are these too much for tonight?" Sean held out his arms, flashing the nickel-sized gold cufflinks engraved with his initials he'd gotten last Christmas from Uncle Patrick.

"They'll keep people's attention off your passion marks."

He rushed to the mirror and tilted his head up, searching for the remnants of our lovemaking.

I swatted his rear. "There's nothing showing—this time."

Sean laughed and took me in his arms from behind. "Never change, Hattie. I love you and this dress of yours is quaint."

"You aren't bored with it?" I touched my hand to my covered chest—one of my modest evening dresses I'd chosen specifically to detract from my breasts when Brandon was a newborn.

He kissed my ear. "Not at all. It's matronly, just the thing for the Graves family."

I'd worn the gray dress quarterly the last two years for our supper gatherings as a show of respect to Merritt's more conservative lifestyle. When I wore anything showcasing a bit of cleavage, she spent more time frowning at my chest than speaking to anyone.

Brandon ran in. "Mommy, Daddy, I'm ready!"

"You look sharp, young man." Sean scooped him up. "Mommy needs a touch of jewelry before we go downstairs. What shall we give her from the treasure box?"

Sean held Brandon over the jewelry organizer on my dressing table, and he dug his little fingers through the shiny items.

"Pearls!" Brandon brought forth a pearl earring.

"Great choice." Sean found the matching one and handed it to Brandon before collecting a short strand.

Standing before me, Brandon held the earrings in his open palm. "Gifts for Mommy!"

"Thank you, Brandon." I kissed his cheek when I took the first one, fastening it on my lobe, then again for the second.

Sean set him on the bed. "And now the necklace, Brandon. You must always kiss a lady's neck when you place a necklace on her."

He giggled as he watched us, and then Sean carried him downstairs. I stopped in Brandon's room. As expected, Althea had turned down the bed and was placing his nightshirt out.

"Thank you for getting him ready, Althea."

"It's my job and I love it, Miss Hattie. Would you like me to stay in the kitchen to oversee things during your party?"

"If you'd like to."

Sean and Brandon sat at the piano singing "Love Is Mine" and the table was laid perfectly. Since it was our first meal with the Graves family in the new house, I'd opted for place cards, but maybe it was time to break the seating arrangements Merritt had settled on at her house.

Through the open windows, a light breeze rustled the sheer curtain panels. The rumble of an automobile pulled into the driveway. I moved toward the vestibule to welcome our visitors. Standing by the open door, I was the first to see Ethelwynne's new haircut.

"Winnie, it suits you well—the dress and more especially the haircut." I hugged her as Andrew slipped past us into the house and then I brought Ethelwynne into the parlor. "Just look at her, Sean! She's absolutely adorable and more mature at the same time."

"Ethelwynne, why I hardly believe it." He took her hands. "I can't call it a transformation, but it's most definitely a magnification of everything that was there before. I heartily approve and hope your parents do as well."

She laughed, but before she could reply, her parents entered the hall. Bartholomew paused to close the door behind them, leaving Merritt shimmering in an orange gown trimmed with metallic beads. I recognized Mademoiselle Bisset's touch at once and stood aghast at the amount of exposed skin on the Baptist woman. I looked twice—sure her nipples would be on display with obnoxiously low décolletage, but nothing unseemly showed. The natural lay of her nearly-flat bosom cast only the hint of a shadowed valley on her chest, but she was somehow the most feminine image I had ever seen with the expanse of moonlight skin beneath her unadorned neck.

I fingered the pearls lovingly hung around my throat and looked to Sean. He had dropped Ethelwynne's hand and stared opened-mouth at Merritt garbed in his favorite color.

"You're as beautiful as one of Keats's fatal women he wrote odes about."

Fortunately, Bartholomew joined Merritt, an air of superiority about him in his Sunday best as he put his arm around her tapered waist.

"Buster," Brandon said to his dog dozing beside the sofa, "Miss Merri's here!"

No matter how long it was between her visits, Buster always remembered Merritt. The dog charged toward the hall. Sean caught him by the collar to prevent him jumping on her fine gown but Merritt went to her knees.

"Allow him to come to me," she said.

"Easy, Buster," Sean said as he dropped to his own knee beside the dog, eyes not leaving Merritt.

Being well-trained, Buster calmly crossed the final inches. Then his front paws were on the lap of the exquisite gown, his neck stretching so he could lick Merritt's face. Her smile was so pure and youthful I saw of glimpse of Ethelwynne in it.

Seeing the adults on the floor, Brandon went right between Sean and Merritt. "Do you like our new house, Miss Merri?"

She smiled at Brandon before glancing around the space. Then her eyes were back on Sean. "It's lovely."

Sean rose and offered his hand to help her stand. "Allow me to give you the grand tour. Bart and Ethelwynne have already seen the house so I'll give you a private one."

"Don't forget Andrew," I said in my sweetest tone. "Boys love exploring new locations."

"Of course," Sean said as he took Merritt's bare elbow. "Come on Drew. Brandon, don't you want to show him your room? We'll begin upstairs."

The two boys ran ahead with Buster while Sean took his time escorting Merritt up the stairs. As soon as they were above, I turned on Bartholomew, poking him in the chest though he was a decade my senior and a foot taller.

"You might want to keep an eye on her. Anyone who can do an about-face on something like modesty is capable of shirking *anything*."

Bartholomew flashed me an annoyed look but ascended the stairs. Thinking of the future, I dashed to the dining room and rearranged the place cards so my name was beside Sean at the head of the table and Bartholomew at the opposite end with Merritt.

Joining Ethelwynne in the parlor when I was done, she offered a grim smile.

"Mama wanted a new dress to help her feel pretty, but I think she went overboard."

I nodded as the telephone rang.

Miss Althea stepped into the rear alcove off the main living hall to answer the box at the same time the adults made their way downstairs. Sean led the procession and Bartholomew followed, holding his wife's hand.

"Sorry to interrupt, but the there's a telephone call for you, Sean Francis."

"I'm in the middle of a tour, Althea. Please take a message."

"It's your uncle, and it sounds urgent."

Ethelwynne's head snapped up.

"Excuse me a moment," Sean said to our guests.

As Sean went to the telephone, I stepped forward. "Allow me to show you my club room. It's more put together than the last time you were here, Bart, and Merri may see where Winnie spends her Monday afternoons. Have either of you ever used a microscope? Winnie, would you like to show them how to focus the slides?"

Putting Ethelwynne in charge of her parents allowed her to showcase what she'd learned as well as freed me to mill around the doorway so I could keep an eye on Sean. He looked agitated with a hand white-knuckled around the earpiece. As soon as he hung up, I met him in the hall.

He distractedly kissed my temple, a hand on the small of my back. "I need Ethelwynne," he whispered.

My brow furrowed. "She's showing her parents how to use the microscope."

"Send her to me as soon as possible." He nudged me toward my room.

"Will you look at that!" Bartholomew said as he peered through the scope. "Merri, you have to see this blade of grass."

One of his hands went to her hip as she bent over the table and the other showed her where to focus the dial. Both of them busy, I waved Ethelwynne over and pointed to Sean pacing the parlor. The girl actually lowered her head as though she were about to be punished. I crossed to the stairs and hollered up for Brandon and Andrew and ushered them into the science room.

When Merritt finished her turn with the microscope and had seen her fill of the fossil collection, I intercepted her exit.

"I was wondering if you would be willing to speak to the club sometime about dog breeding."

"Dog breeding?" She leaned away from me as if I'd asked her to recite in public, naked.

"Animal breeding is a science of its own though you might not recognize it as such. Choosing the right mate, deciding which pup to keep for the next generation of breeding, the timing, and so many other things cover topics such as genetics and biology, not to mention how it ties into women's issues like pregnancy."

"And those are topics of interest for your club members?"

"Yes, we have a midwife, a girl about to graduate who plans on going into medical school, and—"

"I really don't see how Winnie finds any of that interesting, but more importantly, that those are appropriate subject matters for a girl her age."

The soft rumble of the table top gong on the buffet in the dining room gave its vibrating wave. Before I could step into the hall, Merritt did. She glanced at the dining room before turning to the parlor.

"What do you think you're doing to my daughter, Sean Spunner?"

He had gripped Ethelwynne's wrist and she looked to be struggling to get away from him, but they both froze. Bartholomew rushed onto the scene.

Sean's hands went up in a show of being unarmed. "I'm merely teaching her how to escape if someone grabs her. I taught her how to outmaneuver someone stronger—something every girl should know. Could we please demonstrate before Bart attacks me?"

"But supper is ready," I interjected in hopes of switching their focus.

"It will only take a moment. All right, Bart?" Sean asked.

The man nodded and Sean took hold of Ethelwynne's wrist.

Ethelwynne grabbed her entrapped hand and yanked herself free.

Leverage against a stronger force—we could work self-defense into the science club!

"Well I'll be!" Bartholomew exclaimed. "Did you let her do that?"

"No, I didn't. You hold her and see how she does it."

Ethelwynne had to perform again for her father's benefit. Grinning Sean was about to add more to the display, but I interrupted.

"If we want a fresh supper, we need to get to the table," I politely reminded him.

Sean affectionately patted Ethelwynne's hand. "Just remember what I taught you and you'll be a step ahead."

Then he slapped Bartholomew on the back and hurried to Merritt's side, offering his arm. "Allow me, Merri. Did I tell you how beautiful that dress is on you?"

"In more ways than one, though please keep your hands off my daughter from now on."

Upon noticing my name on the place card by his seat, Sean frowned. "It looks like one of the new kitchen girls mixed up the cards. Do sit, Merri."

Merritt sat in the chair he pulled out for her and gave me a smug look that let me know she understood I was the one who put my name beside Sean's. Everyone else naturally migrated to their typical seating arrangements. Annoyed I'd bothered with the place cards—for all they did was empower Merritt in knowing she'd struck me a blow—I didn't enjoy my favorite meal of blackened shrimp.

My only consolation was Brandon beside me. I helped him often, thereby keeping my eyes off the shameless flirting happening on the opposite end of the table. It was so blatant, Ethelwynne was a permanent shade of pink, and Bartholomew nearly choked twice. Merritt was often the initiator, but Sean dished it right back with a side of Keats quotes. If we sat closer, his shins would have been bruised from kicking.

"I think we had better go," Bartholomew said when he finished his last bite of pie. "We had a long day with Drew coming to work with me and the ladies out on the town and puppies being sold."

"I'm not tired yet, Bart." Merritt angled her shoulders in a coquettish way that sent Sean's eyes straight down her décolletage.

"Well I am." Bartholomew pushed back from the table.

"Please, give us two more minutes. Brandon and I practiced a song we wish to sing for you." Sean stood and collected Brandon without a glance in my direction. "It will only be a few minutes more, Bart. Those still eating may listen from here, otherwise join us in the parlor."

Sean settled at the piano, Brandon standing beside him. With a nod and an opening note, Brandon sang the first verse of "Let Me Call You Sweetheart" in his angelic voice while Sean accompanied him. By the time they got to the chorus they sang as a duet. Everyone but Andrew—who helped himself to another slice of pie—made their way to the parlor.

Sean sang the second verse alone. Brandon joined the first line of the chorus, but then Merritt was there, singing in her high soprano of being in love while her hand rested on Sean's shoulder.

As soon as the song was over, Bartholomew had Merritt's elbow. "That was terrific, Brandon. Thank you for having us, Sean and Hattie. Allow us to host next month."

"Of course, Bart. We wouldn't miss it," Sean said.

"There's one more thing," I said as I stood. "All of the adults, please join me in the science room. Winnie, would you and Andrew mind entertaining Brandon on the piano for a few minutes?"

Ethelwynne nodded and approached the piano. I took Sean's arm and we crossed the hall behind Bartholomew and Merritt. Closing the doors, I glared at Merritt. Her husband loosened his tie and shifted away.

"How dare you come into my home like a society wench, wearing a gown that happens to be Sean's favorite color, and showing more skin than even your underclothes reveal?" My words were as straight as my deadly gaze. "You have no right to play innocent when your tits were nearly bared at my supper table when you previously turned your nose up at *me* for showing an inch of cleavage in your house."

Merritt was speechless, but Sean caressed my arm in a soothing manner. "Hattie, it's Merritt, not a society strumpet. There's no need to be jealous."

"This is beyond jealous! This is a wife who has endured a blatant attempt at the seduction of her husband by the previously mousiest, most pious prune in the city, in front of the woman's husband and children. Not to mention you drowned her with flirtations in return. No, this isn't jealousy. This is *fury*!"

"Forgive me, Hattie," Sean said, "but I didn't see things like that."

Merritt had the audacity to laugh. Bartholomew tried to shush her, but I turned on them both.

"I don't believe Merritt was ever a defenseless little sprite." I went toe to toe with her. "Sean gave you your first orgasm, but it wasn't enough, was it?"

"Now just a minute, Hattie." Bartholomew went to his wife's side and her doe eyes filled with tears as her cheeks heated.

Sean got between us.

"Hattie, I know you feel wronged, but please don't be cruel. Merri had lost her uncle and her aunt was hospitalized from the shock. I helped as best I could, but after Winifred passed, Merri and I were frantic with the loss. In our grief-stricken haze, we explored each other to feel alive." Sean looked to Merritt. "I don't think you've forgiven me for that encounter, but I'm not sure if it was because what we did or what we *didn't* do. We got on swell, even after you married Bart, but you turned cold when I attached myself to Eliza. After Eliza died, you went back to your old ways with me, but you've been a bitch to Hattie from the beginning. As much as it would pain me, I'll cut my ties to you before I subject my wife to your attitude any longer. What do you want, Merritt, friendship with me and my family or isolated misery?"

A few tears spilled over. "That's hardly a choice, Sean."

"How do you think I've felt the times I brought those I loved to meet one of my dearest friends, and she treated them with contempt?" His hand touched her cheek. "Eliza saw through you immediately and had a good laugh. She knew you were jealous and found it adorable an old married lady still pined after me."

"That conniving trollop wasn't good enough for you! I knew she'd break your heart the moment I laid eyes on her shallow smile and devious eyes. I couldn't fake politeness to save my life with that horror. Dying before you were married was probably the most humane thing she'd done in her spoiled life."

"That might be true, but what's your excuse with Hattie? There's not a devious bone in her body." He curiously did not defend his first fiancée.

Merritt glanced at me dismissively. "She's no innocent."

"And neither am I, as you well know."

"But you deserve a lady who would be only yours—one who loves your church as much as you do."

"Merri, I love Hattie's mind. It's her passion about science that first drew my attention to her. Before I saw her dear face or ample curves, I heard her voice an opinion about women scientists at a Christmas party that electrified me. As much as I loved Winnie, when I think of what life would have been like with her, I realize she didn't challenge me mentally. She was a girl to love and cherish, a face and body to adore. I would have happily watched her play the piano and sing every night, but there would have been no stimulating conversations between us. I didn't understand it then, but I need that."

"She worshiped you, Sean. We both did."

"I know, and I reveled in it. I felt like a king with his own harem of innocents to train." He flashed his devilish grin. "I often thought Winnie's body with your mind would have been the perfect girl. Looking back, that was my way of telling myself I wouldn't have had long-term happiness with Winnie. Part of me knew it then but it still hurt to let her go."

"When you were connected to her, I was attached to you as well. I knew through marriage to my cousin was the only way I'd have claim to you, but I wanted that thread, no matter how thin. I could have shared you with her, as we had those weeks."

"You knew I needed your banter, your fire."

"But I couldn't compete in the physical ways."

Sean laughed and took her hands. "Merritt, you have everything a man needs, as I'm sure your husband will attest."

"You're beautiful, Merri." Bartholomew put an arm around her waist and kissed her cheek. "But it's hidden when anger gets in the way."

"I found your slight form beguiling," Sean continued. "When I went to the district for the first time during Mardi Gras the next year, it wasn't Winnie's outline I looked for—it was yours. Some of the fellows laughed, saying I was too inexperienced to choose a bawd properly. But I knew from our brief explorations that a slim figure was capable of much softness. Not to mention the thrill of feeling powerful against your wispy frame."

"You loved me?" Merritt whispered.

"I still do, Merri." He raised her hand to his heart. "I keep a piece of you in here but I knew from the beginning that you and Bart were right for each other. I was just a moment of your life as you grew from girl to woman, but I selfishly took that night when we were in sorrow. Do you forgive me?"

She flung her arms around him. "I wanted it too, but I would have been ill if we had done more. Bart deserves my devotion though I've been haunted by the piece of you I believed I lost when Winnie died."

Sean kissed her forehead. "You still have it, Merri, as does your family. Will you allow my family the same by finally accepting my wife and son with open arms?"

"Yes." She hugged him, face wet with tears. "And I'm sorry for my behavior."

He held her at arm's length and shifted her towards me. "Now humble yourself, Merritt, and apologize to Hattie."

Her lips tightened and her cheeks colored further. "I'm sorry for being jealous of you, Hattie. I couldn't stand to see Sean with anyone superior to Winifred. You're his perfect match, but seeing you together broke my heart. Bart's been telling me I was jealous for years, but I haven't wanted to admit it. I wish you both well—I always have—though I could never celebrate your marriage. It felt unsympathetic to my cousin, though I know relationships with the living should carry more precedence than ghosts from the past."

I allowed her to hug me, and offered a stiff smile to her and Bartholomew before we exited the room. They collected Ethelwynne and Andrew, and I turned Brandon's nighttime care over to Althea. After our guests were gone, I met Sean in the hall.

"Are you all right, dearest?"

"I'm still a bit furious I stood by in my matronly dress, chosen specifically to respect Merritt's conservative values, while you ignored the change I made to the seating arrangements. And she knew! She *knew* the place cards were right and lorded over me with that superior smile and shift of her skinny shoulders. She watched you chose *her* over me."

"Hattie, I didn't realize. I know that doesn't sound like much, but it comes from my heart. You, my one and only wife, are the keeper of my desires and the key to my soul. You deserve my utmost respect and attention and I failed you in that regard." He moved toward me hesitantly, waiting for my reaction. When I didn't recoil, he fingered my cheek, remorse in his eyes. "I promise I'll never let you down like this again."

"But in other ways?"

He shrugged and gave his adorable chipped-tooth smile. "I'm sure I'll leave my dirty socks in the wrong spot or forget to do something you've asked of me."

"Like moving those boxes from the back room into the attic?" I laughed and rested in his arms a moment. With a sultry gaze, I looked up at him. "Did you enjoy your view of the daintiest tits in town?"

"It was a novelty." A hand trailed to the swell of my bosom, then both of his hands cupped me. "Your curvaceous body is all I crave, Hattie. You're all I need. All I want. Will you welcome me once more?"

I kissed him and led him upstairs. Upon entering the guest room, I closed the door and went for his buttons. We claimed the guest bed for the first time.

Afterward, when we lay together, I spoke my thoughts aloud. "This is the first time we've been in a bed other than our own since our honeymoon."

Sean nipped my earlobe. "Have we really been at home for nearly three years?"

I nodded. "Two houses now, but always our bed."

"Other locations create a thrill, don't they?"

"Yes, but they don't need be as far away as Boston."

"We'll have to introduce Brandon to your family at some point, but it sounds like we're in need of a private getaway."

"I'd enjoy that."

We checked on slumbering Brandon on the way to our bed, where we snuggled skin to skin.

"Sean, what was that telephone call from you uncle about?"

"Winnie, the poor dear, got herself into a bit of a bind this afternoon. Fortunately, Uncle Patrick was on his way out of the neighborhood when it happened. Aunt Cecelia had him pull over to intervene."

"That sounds serious."

Sean rubbed my back with his warm hand. "It could have been, and right there on the sidewalk at Government and Broad in the middle of the day. I'll be paying a visit to the Methodist church tomorrow to let the church elders know what type of man they hired as an organist."

"Do you think it's right to get involved? Winnie looked scared when she heard your uncle was on the telephone."

"She's worried about her parents finding out and banning her from leaving the house, but that's why I needed to do something about it. Ethelwynne is completely innocent in all this. It isn't right for a young lady to be traumatized by a predator." He was silent a moment, then hugged me tighter. "I knew a man—a friend I might have called him at one point—that wouldn't think twice about grabbing a girl to force her to talk to him, or worse. He took advantage of plenty of women over the years in one way or another, but I never stood up to him. I always looked the other way because it wasn't my girl or the woman in question was a whore. I rationalized everything. In the end, it was Alex who stood up to him, though it was too late. His last victim died."

"Do what you think best, Sean."

"Ethelwynne needs to be kept safe—and all the other young ladies in Mobile." He stroked my loose hair.

"They couldn't ask for a better protector."

Twelve

At the breakfast table Sunday morning, Mama said she was staying home from church. It was the first time I remembered her missing when no one was sick. Papa told me and Andrew to walk ourselves to chapel service, though we didn't have to go for Sunday School.

Since our parents were closed up in their room after eating, I changed from the plain Sunday set I'd put on that morning into the new blue dress. I'd been careful at supper the night before and hung it on the sleeping porch all night to air. Except for a few wrinkles on the ruffles that were hardly noticeable, it was as good as new. And my hair—as Mademoiselle Bisset expected—looked carefully coiffed with minimal brushing. I polished my glasses and called for Andrew to meet me on the front walk.

"Mama's gonna be sore when she sees you in that dress," he said as we exited the gate.

"She especially asked for a dress I could wear to parties or church. It will be laundered tomorrow anyway, so it's not creating extra work."

"Mama's been weird lately, especially with that awful dress she wore last night. I bet she'd never wear *that* one to church." Andrew retrieved a stick from the ground as we walked the edge of Washington Square and proceeded to whack it against every tree we passed. "But she's always been moody."

But she hadn't. I remembered my joyful mother—the one before Eliza Melling came. In the months after Eliza's death, happy Mama returned when the light in Sean's eyes did as well. All was good for years. That changed when Hattie arrived.

"Don't you remember your first years of school, how Mama would sing while she worked around the house and we were allowed to play with the puppies rather than only train them?"

Andrew shrugged. "That was ages ago."

"Mama needs to find that happiness again."

As we climbed the steps to the portico, I felt the stares. Sure enough, a group of women waited for me at the top to gush about my hair—all complementary. They were hoping to tell my mother and were disappointed she wasn't there. They were further let down when I gave them no explanation for her absence.

After the hot walk in the June morning, the welcome coolness of the chapel's soaring ceiling enveloped me like a summertime dip in the creek near my grandparents' house.

When we exited an hour later, I allowed Andrew to join with a group of boys his age on the side of the church. Two young men my age I'd known in the congregation since childhood lounged against the side of the church, each with the sole of a foot propped on the stone behind them.

"You look swell, Winnie. All grown up," Nathan Paterson said.

"Thank you."

"Yeah," Teddy said, "you're the prettiest girl here."

I smiled and looked to my brother, hoping he was ready to go. Andrew was in the middle of a modified baseball game that the mothers would put a quick stop to when they saw their boys taking part of on the Sabbath.

Nathan pushed off from the wall and shuffled closer to where I stood on the edge of the bottom step. His blue-gray eyes sparkled in the sun, bright compared to the brown eyes of everyone in my family. I hadn't been this close to him since grammar school, and my heart raced a little.

He gave me a shy smile as he ran his ink-stained hand through his blond hair. "Are you stepping out with any guys yet?"

Unsure if I heard his whispered question correctly, I twisted my fingers together. "N—no. I don't know if my parents would approve before I graduate."

"Are you going on the Sunday School picnic next Saturday?"

"Yes."

Nathan angled away from Teddy. "Would it be all right if I look for you there, Winnie?"

My smile couldn't be stopped that time. "That's sounds fine, Nathan."

I went to the edge of the ball game. "Come on, Drew! We need to leave after the next hit."

A chorus of boys groaned. "But he's our best player!"

"Your game won't last much longer," I countered. "The mothers are almost out of gossip."

Nathan laughed. In our younger years, I had always been the tallest in class but now he was slightly taller. "Would it be okay to acknowledge you if I see you at school?"

Knowing it would be rare because Barton Academy kept the male and female students separated, I nodded. He caught my gaze and I turned away, trying not to look at the strong line of his jaw, but the energy that passed between us created a surge of anticipation that reached my toes.

Andrew hurried over from the game but didn't stop as he headed for Government Street. "Let's go!" he called back to me.

I turned to Nathan. "Goodbye."

"I hope to see you soon, Winnie."

Andrew was already at the corner of Broad Street, waiting in a throng of church goers to cross Government to the south side. Knowing Nathan and Teddy watched, I moved as quickly as I could without running, weaving between families to make it to the corner before the group crossed. I caught the tail of the migration.

"Wait up, Drew!" I hollered.

He paused on the edge of the sidewalk halfway down the Methodist church. A second later, my pulse lurched at the sight of Sean Spunner coming out the church's front door. He looked like a tycoon in a hand-tailored three-piece charcoal suit he probably wore for important court cases. There was a grim set to his jaw as he placed a derby atop his head and turned the opposite direction. I rushed to Andrew and took his hand.

"I ain't a baby!" He jerked away.

I poked his back. "Just walk fast."

"I was until you stopped me. I want to get home. I'm hungry."

"Then you choose the route."

Giving him control allowed my thoughts to carry me away. The only thing I noticed was our pace didn't change, and it cooled a bit when we turned into the neighborhood. My mind was a collage of Nathan. Something had switched on inside me when he told me I looked nice. I recalled a sampling of exchanges I had with him from the time I was three: a church picnic scuffle over the last cookie, the way he yanked my braids when I was eight, and the time he carried my books home for me when I was eleven were the highlights.

Andrew stopped at the next corner to look both ways, and I nearly ran into him.

"Hello, Mr. Spunner!" Andrew called out.

My gaze snapped to the right. Sean walked toward us from Government Street.

He lifted his hat and bowed. "Hello, Drew and Ethelwynne. Where are you two headed alone?"

"Back home from church," Andrew said. "What are you doing on our side of town?"

"I had some business to see to after Mass, so I parked my automobile at my uncle's house and left Brandon with Aunt Cecilia while I made a visit." He put a hand on each of our shoulders. "Come back with me and say hello. I can drop you at home when I leave."

"I gotta get home and eat dinner, Mr. Spunner."

"I happen to know there's a coconut crème pie and cookies at the Finnigans' house, you know, in case you change your mind."

"Dinner can wait!"

Sean motioned Andrew ahead, took my elbow, and dropped his voice. "I went by the Methodist church to get a look at that man. You were right about him, Ethelwynne. He's at least as old as me. I spoke to one of the church elders who was involved with his hiring. They didn't telephone any of his references or the church he supposedly played at in Atlanta because of the cost involved in long-distance calls. I told them I would telephone in their behalf, at my own expense."

"Did they ask why you were concerned?"

"I told them he was lying about his age to young women and making inappropriate advances toward them." He gently squeezed my arm. "I didn't mention your name."

"Thank you."

Andrew ran into the Finnigans' yard, but Sean and I paused at the front walk.

"I can't let him get away with his treatment toward you."

"And Christina. He's stringing her along with dreams of marriage."

"I'll do everything possible to clear him out before he accomplishes anything that can't be undone."

My heart plummeted at what the words implied as I followed Sean into the house.

"We have company, Aunt Cecelia! I found a hungry boy on the street and brought along his sister, too."

Mrs. Finnigan was elegant in a pink and gray ensemble as she rose from her chair in the parlor.

"Winnie, you look spectacular," Mrs. Finnigan said. "Turn around so I can see that dress. That's not one your mother made."

I laughed and spun, which made the ruffles of the dress pouf out. "It's from Mademoiselle Bisset's shop."

"She always knows how to match the perfect dress to the woman as well as the host if she's attending a party."

Sean cleared his throat, color rising to his cheeks. "Shall I take our guests into the kitchen for their treats?"

"Please do. The cook isn't here right now. Brandon, do you want more to eat?"

"Cookies!" Brandon jumped off the piano bench where he'd been plucking out notes.

Sean laughed. "No boy ever refuses cookies. Show Drew where to go, Brandon."

"Thank you for having us, Mrs. Finnigan," I said. "I'm sorry if it's an intrusion."

"Our home is always open to Sean and anyone he wishes. And I'm glad to see you looking well after your frightful ordeal."

I followed Sean down the hall, where he paused before the swinging door.

"Did Mademoiselle Bisset know why your mother wanted a new gown?"

"She told her we were going to a supper party at your house."

He shook his head. "Hattie was right—I don't know how to handle Merri. Let's hope I do better with the organist problem."

***

Monday morning, Christina waited for me on the steps of First Baptist to walk the final five blocks to school together.

She hurried to my side and leaned close. "I had the most glorious afternoon yesterday. Luke met me out behind a vacant house with a little picnic and some moonshine. I only took one sip. Maybe two, but he wouldn't let me drink more because it wouldn't have worn off by the time I had to go home."

"How was the moonshine?"

"Awful! I wouldn't have wanted more even if he offered. But his attentions were amazing."

"Attentions?" I played dumb hoping she would drop the subject.

"Winnie, you're such a child. I don't know why I bother talking to you." Christina huffed the next few steps before continuing. "His touches and kisses. We would have done more, but some kids in a neighboring yard came out and made a ruckus. I was worried they'd peer through the bushes and see us."

"What's there to see with two people kissing?"

"You're a simpleton, Winnie Graves. I thought you would have learned something from the discussions at the science club." She pulled me to the side and looked around at the others pedestrians. "My clothing wasn't properly on. Luke had my blouse open to—"

"He's a foul, old man and you need to stop seeing him!"

"Listen to you having a fit like a jealous girl!"

"When he took me to the faucet for me to wash my hands, he touched me. Then he saw me on the sidewalk Saturday and grabbed my arm to force me to talk to him, but I got away."

Christina rolled her eyes. "You don't even know how to talk to an adult man, do you?"

"I get along fine with adults and you know it."

"Your precious Spunners don't count. I mean *unmarried* men."

"Why would unmarried men want to talk to school girls?" I paused to drive my point home. "The only reasons I can think of are scandalous."

"Everything isn't as sensational as a novel, Winnie."

"If *you* don't open your eyes, you're going to have your heart broken—or worse."

I started walking. Christina's hard-soled heels followed a few paces behind. As I crossed Cedar Street, I smiled at seeing who waited along the schoolyard fence.

"Hey there, Winnie." Nathan's shirt sleeves were rolled up and he held a stack of books under one arm. "Could I walk you to your first class?"

"How about to the hall?" I asked, not wanting to get in trouble with the faculty.

He nodded. "Allow me to take your books. What's your homeroom?"

I passed him my books but kept hold of my lunch. "Mathematics."

Christina slowed as she approached us. "Don't waste your time with that little girl, Nathan Paterson. She's a simpleton when it comes to men."

A few people around us laughed and my face heated. Nathan ignored everyone as we walked into the building. "I'm glad to see you this morning, Winnie."

We paused by my hall. "It was good to see you too, Nathan."

"Mr. Paterson, boys are *not* allowed in the girls' corridor!" Miss Stimson said from the doorway to her French classroom. "Give Miss Graves her books and be on your way, or I'll be forced to call Mr. Gentry's attention to your actions."

Not wishing trouble with the principal, I whispered my thanks to Nathan.

His fingers brushed mine as he released the books. "Goodbye, Winnie."

At lunch, I didn't know what to do since Christina was mad at me. Deciding to keep with our typical spot—a prime shady patch of grass—I rationalized she could avoid me if she wanted because I'd done nothing wrong and shouldn't have to hide.

I settled with my sandwich, thermos of tea, and a copy of *Wuthering Heights*. A few minutes later, there was a whistle from one of the upper windows. When it happened again the nearby students giggled.

"Winnie," a girl called out as she pointed up. "I think someone is trying to get your attention."

Nathan perched sideways in an open third floor window. He waved and one of his classmates came up behind him. After an exchanged word, Nathan pointed to me. The students in the schoolyard giggled, and I hid behind my book.

By the time I arrived in my last class, several girls had asked me about my relationship with Nathan Paterson.

"I know him from church," I replied each time, not knowing what else to say because I wasn't sure where our conversations were leading.

After school, Nathan waited for me where he had that morning. "Do you always carry so many books?"

"Usually."

Other students filed past as we stood together. "May I carry your books home for you? Or maybe just as far as the park if you don't want your mother seeing me."

Pleased he'd remembered where I lived, I found myself smiling. "I go to a science club on Mondays. I ride the streetcar west to the loop."

"Do you have to ride, or could I walk you to give us time to talk?"

"It doesn't start until four."

"Then hand over your books." He took the stack with a smile and hefted them on top of his. "I live halfway to the loop, on Ann Street. If you don't mind, I'll drop my books there."

"That's fine."

"You seem practical, but then carry all these books around. Why not utilize a knapsack or something?"

"Do I need one with you around?" I realized too late that my remark could be considered coy.

Nathan's mouth curved into a smile, and for the first time in my life I had the urge to kiss a boy. "You're a sly one, Winnie Graves."

I looked away. "I don't mean to be."

"That's what makes you fun."

I reflected on that for several moments. "Why did you finally talk to me yesterday after all this time? Was it my dress or haircut?"

"Both. You've been shy in recent years and dressed plain. I figured with the new style you might be ready to be more social, but you still didn't respond to my whistle at lunch."

"I never assume attention is directed at me."

"Why not? You're intelligent and pretty." His chin lowered as though embarrassed. "School finishing next week was another factor that spurred me to talk to you. I want to make the most of these final days."

I blushed at his compliments. "What are you doing over summer?"

"Apprenticing with my uncle. He works for The Daily Register."

"A reporter?"

"An editor these days, but he'll be able to get me in all the departments. I think he even plans to make me sell newspapers for a bit. He told my father I need to know every aspect of the business."

"You want to write?"

"I don't tell many people, but poetry is what I enjoy best. I know it's a tough go with that, so I'll need a job that will allow me to write and see life until I can make a name for myself."

"I love poetry."

We spoke the rest of the way to Ann Street about favorite poems. Half a dozen houses up the road, we stopped by a picket fence.

"This is it. Would you like to come in and get something to eat?"

"I'd rather wait here, but thank you. Hattie has a good spread of refreshments each week, but get something for yourself if you'd like."

He nodded and dashed through the gate before I could take my books from him. I found myself gazing about the picturesque street, thankful for the shade of a crepe myrtle tree budding with pink blossoms. A few boys ran up the road, slowing to look at me.

"Ain't you Drew's sister?" one asked. "He's got the best arm out of any of the boys at school."

I nodded. "Do you have him playing pitcher?"

"Naw, we need a guy that can throw to the bases to get the runners out," another said.

"He's been working on his fastball. Try him out on pitcher sometime and see for yourself."

The boys continued up the street at the same time the front screen slammed shut. Nathan ran down the steps, a messenger style bag slung crosswise over his shoulder and a piece of banana bread in his left hand.

"I hope those kids didn't bother you."

"Not at all. We talked about Drew and baseball."

"You like the game?"

I shrugged, not wanting to seem weird for enjoying it. "I went to most of the exhibition games at Monroe Park with Drew and our father last year. Did you leave my books inside?"

Nathan patted the leather bag. "I'm using more brain than muscle this time. It frees my hands."

"So you can eat."

"Yes, but I'd like to hold your hand."

"Not today, Nathan."

"But soon?"

I nodded, pleased he didn't take it the wrong way. Our conversation about literature returned.

"So where are we going exactly?" he asked when we passed the Woodslows' home.

"To the Spunners' house, at the corner of Houston, where I'll eat and listen to the others talk about science, medical, and travel topics. It's a mixed group of adults and students. I'm not so much interested in the science aspect as the life and travel topics that come up, but the Spunners are good family friends, so I support Hattie's vision."

He whistled as we crossed Houston Street. "That's a swanky abode."

"Sean Spunner is a highly respected lawyer."

Nathan nodded. "He's frequently mentioned in the newspaper. My uncle thinks he'll be a judge within a few years."

"Good or bad things in the paper?" I asked when we stopped outside the pedestrian gate.

"Usually complimentary, with a lot of high profile cases. It's often noted about the random things he recites that play in with the trial, both humor and serious in nature."

I laughed. "That sounds like Sean."

Nathan narrowed his brow. "You call him by his first name?"

"Old family friend, as I mentioned. He's like an uncle to me." Amazingly, the words didn't sting.

"Well, enjoy your club meeting. Use my satchel as long as you'd like." Nathan pulled the messenger bag over his head and held it for me to accept. I ducked under the strap and he settled it across my shoulder. "Could I wait for you before school tomorrow?"

"I'd like that."

"I'll see you in the morning, Winnie."

Thirteen

Tired of waiting alone—for the newness of the club had worn off, and there were no early arrivals—I stepped onto the veranda to see what caused Buster to bark. Ethelwynne was outside the gate with a young man. He removed the bag he wore and slipped it over her head before leaning close as he held the gate open. When his gaze lifted enough that he caught sight of me on the front steps, he raised a hand in greeting. I waved back and smiled.

"Good afternoon, Winnie," I called when she was halfway across the yard.

"Hello, Hattie." Buster jumped around her, but she didn't stop until she reached the bottom step. She sat and allowed the dog to climb into her lap to be scratched and rubbed.

Looking to the road, I watched Ethelwynne's escort retreat. "And who is the friend who walked you here today?"

"Nathan Paterson. He walked with me all the way from school. He spoke to me for the first time in years after church yesterday."

"I bet he likes your haircut. And Sean told me you wore your new dress again."

She nodded and rubbed behind Buster's ears. "But Nathan says he's always liked me."

"I'm sure he has. He has an air of honesty about him."

"You like him, just from seeing him across the way?"

"I do. If he walks you next week, invite him in for refreshments before he goes home."

"Thank you, Hattie. I think he'd enjoy that." Ethelwynne nudged Buster away and stood. "I'll go wash."

Darla and Melissa arrived in the Adams's automobile. Brandon's greeting to Horatio and Louisa could be heard inside, and I welcomed the women soon after. Ethelwynne joined them in the dining room as they dished up their food.

"Winnie, your hairstyle is utterly charming!" Melissa exclaimed. "I've often thought of cutting my hair, but I love when Freddy brushes it every night. It makes the pain of handling it the rest of the day worth it."

"It gives you a certain glow," Darla remarked.

"That might be more from the attentions of a young man," I said before answering the doorbell. "Come on in, Jessica and Faith."

"Is Winnie here?" Faith asked. "We saw her leave school with a boy!"

"She's in the dining room."

"Winnie," Jessica said as she crossed the hall, "what's the story about you and Nathan Paterson? It's all anyone could talk about after lunch."

"He may be a junior, but he's one of the handsomest boys in school," Faith said.

"He must be intelligent if he likes Winnie," Melissa remarked.

Faith took a plate and started dishing up. "He writes good articles for the school newspaper. Have you kissed him yet?"

"I didn't even allow him to hold my hand."

"Playing hard to get is risky," Jessica said over a glass of tea.

"I'm not *playing* anything. I just don't want to get carried away."

"Pacing is an excellent idea." I smiled at Ethelwynne. "Don't feel like you have to meet certain expectations. Only allow what you're comfortable with."

The girls prattled on as I welcomed the Marley sisters—Grace Anne, Sadie, and Marie.

"Kate couldn't make it this week," Grace Anne said.

"Does anyone know if Christina is coming today?" I asked the girls as Marie joined them.

"I saw her going in United Methodist when the streetcar passed on my way home," Faith replied.

"We'll give her a few more minutes before we begin things officially." For Christina's sake, I hoped she arrived soon. After all Sean told me about that man and how he acted toward Ethelwynne, I didn't want to imagine what he was capable of in private with a young woman who was in love with him.

Ten minutes later, we were all settled in the club room with refreshments and still no Christina. Ethelwynne looked nervous, which I disliked, especially after seeing her joy when she arrived. Melissa shared stories and photographs from her travels through central and southern Africa—flora, fauna, climate, and the natives. Everyone was mesmerized with the information Melissa provided. I had heard many of the stories before, but they were equally fascinating the second time.

Six o'clock came quicker than any of us wanted. Jessica and Faith rushed home, then Darla and Melissa. Althea brought Brandon through on the way to the bath, but the Marley sisters and Ethelwynne were still in the living hall when Sean came in the back door.

"Hello, ladies."

I could tell by the slight waver in his voice he wasn't expecting anyone to still be here, and from the blush on his cheeks I could see he remembered that Grace Anne and Sadie knew about our intimate times together.

"Hello, Sean." Grace Anne smiled.

He took her hand and gave his best friend's wife a peck on the cheek. "You look exceptionally pretty today, Gracie, and your sisters. How is married life, Sadie?"

"Very well, thanks in part to these club meetings." She giggled. "I'm glad to know you're not the wallflower you were several years back."

"Hattie knows how to keep life stimulating." He put an arm about my waist and winked at them. "And I hear John is satisfied with his life at present as well, Gracie."

The sisters laughed, but I nudged Sean and motioned toward the girls in the club room. He winked at Grace Anne once more, and then went to Ethelwynne and Marie.

"And how are you two doing?"

"Fine, thank you, Mr. Spunner." Marie blushed more than Sean, and I wondered if her sisters had shared anything with her.

"I'm good, but I need to get home." Ethelwynne looked to Marie. "Are we leaving soon?"

She nodded and then encouraged her sisters to say goodbye.

We saw them onto the veranda and waved them off.

"Winnie walks with them to Grace Anne's house, then Marie's father drops her off on their way home," I explained to Sean.

"I'm glad to hear that. I don't want her out alone in the evenings." Sean guided me inside. "Does she arrive with girls from school?"

"A boy walked her today."

He raised his brows. "The full two miles from Barton Academy?"

I nodded.

"Who? I'll beat him into the ground if he mistreats our girl. I might need to give him a warning message first."

"He appeared honest and respectful, even if he couldn't keep his eyes off Winnie." Sean growled low in his throat and I laughed. "God help me if we ever have a daughter. You're barbaric when you get in protection mode."

"Can you blame me, especially after that man chased her?" Sean's countenance darkened.

"Christina didn't come today. One of the girls said she saw her going into the church. Were you able to make those telephone calls?"

"Yes, and it's as I feared. No one named Luke ever worked at the Baptist church he said he interned at in Atlanta, but a man matching his description, right down to the birthmark over his eye, played the organ at the neighboring Methodist church and was run off after three months because he got a sixteen-year-old in the congregation pregnant."

I gripped Sean's biceps. "Did you offer assistance in capturing him?"

"I told the preacher if the parents wanted to press charges to get with me within the next forty-eight hours, and I would work with the local police to detain him. I couldn't promise longer than that because he's liable to flee when he knows we're onto him. I did collect information on where he was before he went to Atlanta—Memphis—and the name of the congregation he supposedly played at there. I fear his trail could crisscross the Southeast for a decade or two with his despicable acts. I did speak with the minister and church elder at United Methodist this afternoon. They're supposed to talk to Christina's family this evening."

"It's going to destroy Winnie's relationship with her."

"Christina will thank her one day."

I gave a dry laugh. "You don't know girls."

After supper, piano time, and putting Brandon to bed, Sean worked at his desk, prepping files for the next day. I was across the room, curled on the chaise in an attempt to disperse the pain in my abdomen from my monthly cycle. The book about bird migration across the Americas sat untouched on my knees.

Sean glanced over and lifted the pipe from his mouth. "I'll be at least another fifteen minutes, Hattie. Will you survive that long?"

"I survived twenty-six years without you. I'm sure I can handle that many minutes without your full attention."

His smile warmed me long after he returned to work. I was able to ignore my cramps and read for half an hour. Sean clicked off his desk lamp and crossed to me, waiting for my nod signaling I was done with my page before he turned off my reading light. Once he was in bed, I laid my head on his bare shoulder and his arm went about me.

"Your club meeting was good?"

"Yes, though two less ladies than last week."

"Who else besides Christina?"

"Kate."

He gave a soft laugh. "I bet that was a nice break. She made numerous ladies miserable and ruined the reputations of too many to name. You escaped that by arriving in Mobile after *Snitch* magazine was put in the grave. I can assure you, you're exactly the type of woman she would have targeted."

"I don't have the required pedigree."

"You'd like to think that, but you married *me*. Freddy's first wife was from Pennsylvania, a frail, quiet, and completely respectable young woman, yet Kate was rude about her, therefore no one befriended her before she died of consumption."

"We all evolve. Kate might still be a snide gossip, but she's carrying a load of shame and wounds."

"That makes her even more dangerous. Guard what you tell that woman, Hattie."

"I do." I tucked against his warmth.

"You never told me the name of the boy who walked Winnie over. Someone needs to watch out for her, especially if her parents don't know."

"Nathan Paterson."

"Paterson..." I could almost feel him mentally flipping through the files in his head. "Benjamin Paterson, editor at The Daily Register. Unmarried. No claimed children. Baptist. Doesn't drink alcohol or participate in Mardi Gras festivities other than as an observer. He'll go to print with any scandal you raise during Carnival—like the Mystics of Dardenne masquerade of '04. No one questioned how *he* had a firsthand account of the police raid, but he laid it out as though there. The sneaky bastard was probably right under our nose and we were too smashed to notice. But Paterson has a brother who's an inspector at the state docks. *He* is married and has a couple children. Nathan must belong to him."

"Winnie told me she knew him from church."

"Even a sober young man gets unholy ideas about pretty girls."

"None of that now. Rest that amazing brain of yours. You need sleep to function at your best tomorrow."

"Yes, dearest."

I smiled in the dark, loving the feeling of secureness I had in his arms, but I didn't sleep for almost an hour.

A nightmare about Brandon being lost at Monroe Park woke me before dawn with a gasping cry.

"Shh. Shh, Hattie." Sean stroked my arm.

I tried to wiggle free. "I need to check Brandon."

"I will." Sean's footsteps padded across the tile in the bathroom. The light from the other bedroom spilled through the open bathroom door when switched on. "Brandon!"

Fear raced up my spine and I bolted out of bed.

I hurried through the bathroom and blinked against the brightness in Brandon's empty space. "Where is he?"

Panic twisted Sean's face. "I don't know!"

"Where's Buster?"

"Buster!" Sean shouted as he ran for the hall.

There was a soft bark in reply, but I couldn't tell where it came from.

Sean ran down the stairs and I to the guest room, throwing on lights and racing through the space all the way to the back room beyond while my arms trembled and my heart pounded.

"Hattie! Hattie, I've found him!"

I held the banister to keep from stumbling head-first in my rush. Sean was on the piano bench beside a groggy Brandon, Buster lying beneath the instrument. I fell to my knees, pulling Brandon to my chest as tears erupted.

"He was sleeping against the keys, his head on his arm for cushion," Sean explained.

"Never come downstairs alone at night," I scolded.

"Buster was with me. Don't be sad, Mommy. I made you a song."

I clung to him, tears dripping down my face.

Sean came around behind me and loosened my hold before tugging me upright. "Allow him to share his song. It's important to him," he whispered.

"Listen, Mommy! It's pink and purple for you."

Brandon played several notes with his index finger, then repeated the tune before adding his sweet voice.

"I love my mommy, the prettiest mommy.

    She shines like the sun and is lots of fun.

    She lets me play, each and every day.

    I jump in puddles, but she prefers cuddles.

    She cannot sing, but wears Daddy's ring.

    We love her so, much more than she knows.

    My mommy, the prettiest mommy in the world!"

Sean clapped. "That was amazing! I need to write that down—his first composition!"

As he went in search for paper, I lifted Brandon into my arms.

"You like it, Mommy?"

"I love it, and I love you, Brandon Patrick Spunner. I'm blessed to be your mother." I kissed his cheek. I wanted Brandon to be brave enough to move about the house at night, I simply didn't want him to do so at his tender age. Brandon needed to keep his sense of adventure and passion for his creativeness, though. I wouldn't be responsible for crushing that. "Just promise to only come downstairs in the dark with Mommy, Daddy, or Buster. And only to the piano if it's with Buster. He's a good piano dog."

Brandon giggled as Sean returned with one of my tablets from the science room. "Help me with those lyrics, Brandon. 'I love my mommy, the prettiest mommy.' And then what?"

He went to his father, reciting his song as Sean wrote the words. I sank to the sofa. Once Sean had the lyrics down, he dug in for more.

"Now the song, Brandon. Did you know every key you press on the piano equals a dot on a page, signifying a note? Your song for Mommy is made up of dots. I'd like to write them down. Do you want to play it again so I can write down your notes?"

"Yes!"

Brandon ran for the piano. He played and sang his song, warming my heart once more.

"That's wonderful, Brandon. I'll bring special music paper when I come home from work. Your song will make a rainbow of color on the page once we write it down properly."

Brandon clapped, causing Sean's grin to double.

"Music composers need lots of sleep. How about I tuck you back in bed?"

"Buster can tuck me in. Goodnight, Daddy."

Like a brown shadow, Buster crawled out from beneath the piano and trotted to Brandon's side. I watched the duo until they disappeared.

Sean took my hand. "Hattie, our boy is a genius! Not only does he recall what he composed, he can pick up the song from any point without pause."

"It was a short tune." I freed myself.

"Don't make light, dearest. Brandon—"

"I'm not making light of Brandon. We've already established his brilliance. I have nothing but love and respect for his natural abilities. It's his father treating him like a lab animal that I scorn."

"You can't expect me to *not* test a few points with him along the way."

"I expected you to keep with what we agreed—no extra attention, no bragging to extended family or friends, and no pushing him about music or chromesthesia."

"I can't ignore something like his first composition—this is a milestone that needs to be recorded. Think of what the world would be if Charles Darwin didn't record his early finds in his journals. The stepping stones are needed and records of them are of utmost importance."

Anger flared at being called out for the errors in my hasty judgement. If Sean wasn't so smug, I wouldn't jump to the defensive about everything, but I couldn't speak the words—only stare.

Sean embraced me, filling my soul with love. "You were scared and the switch of emotions after being freshly awakened was disorienting. Your fear needed an outlet. You switched it to anger and channeled it at me because my perfection is too much for you."

I freed my right arm from his hug and pinched his rear. "Don't be an ass, Sean. Bring me back to bed and allow me a few more hours of sleep. I'll try to forget this conversation in the morning."

Fourteen

Tuesday morning, Nathan waited for me at the corner of Government and Broad. I removed the satchel from my shoulder. Nathan placed the strap over his head and added his own things to the pouch. He didn't ask about holding my hand, but his ink-stained pinky—compliments of being left-handed—brushed my fingers several times over the next few blocks.

Approaching the school, I saw Christina outside the fence glaring at everyone who passed. She met my eyes as Nathan and I crossed the road.

"There you are, you scheming bitch!"

Nathan flinched.

Eyes wide with shock, I felt the heat rush to my face with the attention from the crowd.

"And don't stand there like the picture of innocence. You know exactly what you did!" Christina shoved me.

I slipped off the curb but stayed upright. Nathan belatedly took my elbow.

"Don't be fooled by her new haircut and friends. Ethelwynne Graves is nothing but a lying fink!" She grabbed me by the hair and marched down the side street.

"Now wait just a minute!" Nathan hollered. "I never thought I'd have reason to hit a girl, but you better get your hands off her, or else!"

"Or else what?" She paused and stared him down. "I thought so."

Christina started pulling me again, but I jerked out of her grasp—losing a sizeable chunk of hair in the process. I moved back toward the corner, keeping my empty hands up in defense.

"I don't know what you think I did, but I didn't lie or—"

"So you're going to claim to know nothing of your precious Mr. Spunner showing up at my church to tell the elders about Luke?"

"Sean's uncle happened by the sidewalk on Saturday when Luke had me by the arm. Mr. Finnigan had to tell him to let me go because he didn't listen to me when I told him to. But I didn't tell Sean. Mr. Finnigan was so upset over it, *he* did."

Christina gave a snorting laugh. "Luke wouldn't do anything with a baby like you when he—oh, you're a simpleton! But because of you and your high and mighty friends, he's lost his position. He's going to have to rely on his piano playing in the clubs, which destroys any hope of my parents ever liking him."

"He's never going to go through with anything between the two of you, and besides which, even Sean says he's lied about his age. He's estimated Luke to be at least in his mid-thirties."

"What does age matter when we're in love? And he promised to marry me. I made sure of it."

"He's not to be trusted!"

"You're the one not to be trusted, Ethelwynne. I'll never forgive you for making Luke out to be a monster."

I stepped to the side to avoid her when she went for the nearest gate. Christina pushed her way through the crowd as the school bell rang.

Nathan was immediately at my side. "You handled that splendidly, Winnie. Are you all right?"

I nodded, rubbing my scalp. "I need to get to homeroom."

Throughout the day, I fielded questions about Christina and Nathan from classmates. Seeing Nathan waiting for me by the school gate that afternoon renewed my soul. He took the satchel, added his books to it, and we set off. He saw me all the way to the east side of Washington Square. From that far corner, he watched until I was through my gate, where I turned to wave.

Wednesday morning—and every morning the rest of the week—Nathan waited for me a few blocks closer until I found him Friday morning in front of the park. The smile on his dear face fortified me.

On the way home that afternoon, Nathan and I discussed "The Chambered Nautilus" by Oliver Wendell Holmes.

"It's too preachy to be a great poem," Nathan declared after we had gone back and forth about it for several minutes.

"So good poems can't have a message?"

"Of course they can, but the beauty of the words needs to mask it on the first read. The message should unravel like the layers of an onion—little by little."

"But onions are one of the most potent foods. You cut into one and you *know* it's an onion. That would be the same if you read a poem once and know what the message is."

Nathan laughed and grabbed my hand, tenderly squeezing it. "I suppose you're right about my metaphor. Besides, people these days don't take the time to savor a poem. It's a sad state of affairs. But you, Winnie Graves, have a keen mind and aren't afraid to show it. I admire that in you."

As we came into my neighborhood, the sounds of Government Street faded and the cooling relief of shaded sidewalks increased. Nathan moved closer and lowered his voice.

"You'll look for me at the picnic tomorrow, won't you?"

"Yes."

He nodded, his pinky reaching to mine for a quick touch. "You won't mind if people see us together, will you?"

"No, why should I?"

"Then you'll allow me to walk you all the way to your gate today?"

"Oh." In my mind, Mama was only at home, but people from church would talk if they saw me spend the whole picnic with Nathan. I paused in the middle of the sidewalk and looked into his blue eyes, knowing there was nothing my mother could say against his good character. "Walk me to the gate, Nathan. And meet me there Monday morning if you'd like."

We soon found ourselves before the front gate on Chatham Street. He passed me the satchel.

"Tomorrow can't come soon enough, Winnie."

For the first time all week, my mother saw me enter the front door. She was coming out of the kitchen, using her apron as a fan. Velvet was at her feet, back to being anywhere she wanted to go because she was puppy-less.

"Winnie, where did you get that bag?"

"A friend noticed the pile of books I carry around and is letting me borrow it."

Mama fingered the soft leather. "I don't like you borrowing something that expensive. If you needed a bag, you should have told your father. He can pick up something tomorrow if he doesn't have anything suitable at the store."

I held the satchel against me defensively. It felt like a hug from Nathan when I wore it.

"I don't think Papa needs to rush to buy me one when I have use of this."

"Winnie, it needs to be returned. We can't have people thinking we can't provide for you properly."

"You and Papa don't need to spend more money on me this month—not after the dresses and everything. School ends next week.

Allow me to use it a few more days, and I'll find a bag over the summer for the autumn term."

"I suppose that will be all right." Mama was always one to see the bottom line. "I'm finishing the cookies I promised for the picnic. Your father will drive you and Drew to Monroe Park after breakfast so you don't have to handle the boxes on the streetcars."

"Thank you, Mama."

I hurried for the stairs and then flung myself on my bed. After a minute, I went to my desk, unloading my books onto my work station. A folded piece of paper fell to the floor. Thinking it one of Nathan's he forgot to retrieve, I almost tucked it back into the bag. Curiosity got the best of me. I unfolded the page and caught my breath.

For My Brown-eyed Lady

Throughout life

I searched for color

Bold splashes

Bright hues

Then you smiled

Lips like the pink within a shell

Chestnut hair

Eyes as rich as soil

From which life springs

For nourishment

Of body and mind

My soul needs to see you

For my skin cannot touch

Your tanned complexion

Smooth, soft, and scented with beauty

Infused with intellect

I wish to trace those shell-pink lips

Run my fingers through your bewitching hair

Drown in the depths of your eyes

I didn't believe it was possible to feel more from words than I did at that moment. I read it again, then hastily removed my shoes and stockings before retreating to the hammock on the sleeping porch. I reread Nathan's poem until I had it memorized, smiling so much my face ached.

I needed to share my news with someone. Christina is who I would have normally told, but that was now impossible. Marie never had a beau and I didn't want to look like a braggart though I had more questions than pride. I never dreamed a boy would write me a poem—and did he leave it for me on purpose or did it fall from his own stash? How should I react in either circumstance?

Hattie!

There was just enough time to telephone her before I had to set the supper table. I tucked the poem into my pocket and ran downstairs. Velvet was on the settee in the parlor, but I heard my mother in the kitchen. I snuck into Papa's study and closed the door.

After I asked the operator for the Spunners' house, my palms grew damp with perspiration.

"Spunners' residence."

"Miss Althea? It's Winnie. Is Hattie available?"

"Sure thing, Miss Winnie."

I fidgeted with the cord to the earpiece as I waited.

"Winnie, is everything all right?"

"Hattie, I simply have to talk to you before I burst!"

"Did something happen with Christina?"

"Well, yes it did, but there's more."

"I'm listening."

"Oh, I couldn't possibly over the telephone. Could you ring in a little while and ask about coming to pick me up for a visit this evening? Please, Hattie, there's no one else I can talk to about this. Sean said I could speak with either of you about anything, remember?"

"Yes, of course."

"Thank you!" I hung the receiver, wiped my sweaty hands on the back of my black skirt, and went for the kitchen to collect the dishes for the table.

"It's about time, Winnie," Mama said as soon as I pushed through the swinging door.

"I got to reading and time slipped away." I gathered four dinner and four bread plates before going across the hall.

When the glasses I got on my next trip clinked together, Mama sighed. "Do be careful, Ethelwynne."

"I'm sorry, Mama."

But I was so distracted with thoughts of Nathan, I dropped half the silverware a minute later.

"What is wrong with you today?" she asked as I placed the fallen forks in the sink for washing.

"I guess I'm excited about the picnic tomorrow. It'll be difficult to sit around all evening while I wait."

My father came in the backdoor just then. "Difficult sitting around for what?" he asked.

"The Sunday School picnic tomorrow."

"Apparently Winnie is all aflutter about it," Mama said as she reached for Papa.

He smiled at her and they embraced like a pair of young lovers. I hurried out with the fresh silverware to finish the place settings.

I jumped when the telephone rang. Papa came out of the kitchen for it, and I did my best not to look like I was listening from the dining room.

"Hello, Hattie. Yes, we're all well."

A pause.

"That little rascal? I bet Winnie would enjoy that. She was just complaining about having nothing to do tonight. Yes, eight o'clock is fine. Goodbye."

Papa found me in the dining room.

"It's your lucky day. It appears little Brandon was asking for you. Hattie telephoned to see if you'd come over for a bit after supper and play the piano for him. I told her you'd love to. And if you don't, make sure you keep your complaints to yourself the next time you're bored."

Fifteen

Ethelwynne waited on her front

porch when I pulled the automobile alongside the curb. She ran down the dark walkway and opened the door with a huge smile.

"Thank you, Hattie! I just had to talk to someone."

"I'm afraid what I told your father was partly true," I said as I drove. "When Brandon heard me tell Sean you were coming, he was ecstatic about your visit. He wants to show off his piano playing. Sean has been working with him this week."

She laughed. "That's fine. I adore Brandon."

"You sound happy. Did you have a good week, even with Christina trouble?"

"It was wonderful, all because of Nathan."

The affection in her voice was alarming, but I didn't wish to upset her by being harsh or negative. First love was treacherous ground. Most of my memories involved heartache where men were concerned, but maybe Ethelwynne would cope better when Nathan eventually let her down.

"Did he walk with you more?"

"Every day, before *and* after school. In the mornings, he kept meeting me closer and closer to my house, and finally this afternoon I allowed him to walk me to the gate—not caring if Mama saw him. We'll be meeting at the Sunday School picnic tomorrow. I'm sure Mama will hear about me sharing my time with him, but Nathan has been so sweet this week, there's nothing bad she could say about him. I haven't even let him hold my hand yet."

I was sure Merritt would think of plenty of negative things to say about any male who attempted courtship with her daughter, but I held my tongue.

When I parked the automobile, Ethelwynne touched my arm.

"Nathan wrote a poem about me." She pulled a folded piece of paper from her skirt pocket. "He loaned me his messenger bag for my books, which he carries when we're together. He adds his own things to it, then takes them out when we part. I'm not sure if he's giving it to me or if it's something he wrote in private and accidentally left behind. Would you read it and tell me what you think?"

"Of course, Winnie."

I followed her up the front steps, noticing how her shortened locks accented the womanly shape her body had developed in recent months. It had been coming on for a while, but her youthful braids had camouflaged her maturing form. Ethelwynne was already curvier than her mother—her father's solid genes more prevalent though there was nothing masculine about the girl.

"Winnie, Winnie, Winnie!" Brandon grabbed her hand as soon as we were in the door. "Make colors with me!"

Buster barked as Brandon pulled her into the parlor, but Sean intervened.

"Just a moment. I'd like to greet our guest." Sean paused before Ethelwynne, studying her face. "Something has changed, Ethelwynne."

The shine in her eyes practically glowed when she smiled.

"Please say it isn't so!" He brought her into a tight hug. "Who did you fall in love with?"

"His name is—"

"No, don't tell me. You're here to talk with Hattie and play with Brandon."

"It's piano time!" Brandon tugged her again.

"May I be your audience?" Sean asked them.

"Yes, Daddy. You can clap."

I escaped into my science room and left the door open so I could hear the music. Sitting in my armchair under a side table lamp, I unfolded the poem. My mouth fell open as I read the tender words. Twice. There was no mistaking the scribe's longings.

The sound of Ethelwynne playing "All Creatures of Our God and King" while she sang with Brandon filled the house.

I peeked around the corner, grateful the piano bench faced the other way. Waving to get Sean's attention, I then put a finger to my lips and motioned him over. I returned to my chair and read the poem for the third time.

When the duet finished the hymn, Sean clapped heartily. "Now see if he wants to learn some of the notes to play, Ethelwynne. Or sing something else together. I'll be back in a few minutes."

Sean walked into my room with a huge grin. "I love watching him when he's with another pianist. I pick up on more of his body language than I do when I'm busy accompanying him. He's an incredible boy, Hattie."

I nodded, lips pressed together.

"Dearest, what is it?"

He pulled the nearest chair closer, sat so our knees were almost touching, and reached for the paper I held. As he read, his eyebrows went up, then furrowed. His mouth gaped, eyes widened.

"Where is this little Romeo so I can beat him black and blue?" Sean's voice rose with each word.

"Shh. They haven't even held hands, but there's a bit of a dilemma." I took the poem back and explained about the paper being in the bag they both used and Ethelwynne not knowing if it was purposely left for her.

"You bet your perky tits he left it on purpose!" Sean pointed at the poem, lips in a snarl. "There's only one reason a guy writes a poem like that and it's to soften the girl so he can make his move."

"They're attending a Sunday School picnic tomorrow, not having a clandestine meeting."

"She's in love! Girls in love lose all reason just as boys in love think of only *one thing*. I did telephone Benjamin Paterson the other day to check on this nephew of his. He gave Nathan a glowing report and even said he's interning with him this summer." Sean flicked the paper. "But that poem negates everything. It says right there in black and white that he wants to touch her. She practically floated in here with the mere thought of this treacherous boy. I don't know how Merri and Bart could have missed the signs so clearly on her face. We need to focus on the problem with Ethelwynne since they aren't."

"There's no problem—and she came to me, not you."

"But *you* came to me for the expert opinion on young men." He swaggered out of the room.

I left the poem on the side table and followed Sean to the sofa in the parlor. We sat snug beside each other, his arm around my shoulders, as we watched the antics at the piano.

Brandon stood beside Ethelwynne on the bench—leaning against her as he sang—and Buster's head rested on her knee.

They finished their tune and turned when they heard me clapping along with Sean.

"I play my Mommy song!"

Brandon nudged Ethelwynne until she stood, and she came around to the loveseat, Buster lying at her feet. Brandon rifled through the sheet music, found the hand-written page Sean created several days ago, then centered the pages on the music rest and himself on the piano bench. He played the opening notes and his pure voice sang out the melody. Ethelwynne looked to us in surprise, and Sean grinned in response. At the end, the three of us gave

Brandon a standing ovation. He ran directly to me. I lifted him for a hug and he snuggled to my breast.

"I love you, Mommy."

I kissed the top of his head. "And I love you, Brandon. You had fun with Ethelwynne, but now it's time for bed. Say goodnight, and Daddy will bring you upstairs."

"Goodnight, Winnie." He dashed to her for a hug. "Thank you for coming to play."

"I had fun, Brandon."

When they went upstairs, I motioned Ethelwynne to the sofa.

"Did he really write that song by himself?" she asked as she sat beside me.

"Sean only transcribed it for him. He's using it as a way to teach Brandon how to read music since he was beginning to play by ear, but we could expect nothing but brilliance from Sean's son."

"Brandon is adorable." In an instance, Ethelwynne switched from open to guarded as she looked to her hands. "What do you think of the poem?"

"It's—"

"You showed it to Sean, didn't you? I want to know what he thinks as well."

I laughed. "I'm not so sure you will, but he's certain the poem was given to you. No mistake in it being left behind."

"All the feelings I developed for Nathan this week came alive when I read his words. It's like he validated my heart. I truly feel at peace with him, Hattie. Even when Christina was yelling at me in front of the school Tuesday morning, I felt stronger knowing he was standing behind me."

"What happened with Christina? Why didn't she come to the club Monday?"

After she told me of Christina's accusation and behavior, I squeezed her hand. "I'm sorry you got pulled into this, Winnie. Sean wanted to be sure you're protected from this man, but he promises he never mentioned you by name."

She shrugged. "Sean isn't the guilty one. And it's only because Christina knows of our friendship that she linked me to his involvement. Even if we aren't speaking, I worry about her."

"Any good friend would." I took her hand. "But don't feel guilty. None of this is your doing. Keep enjoying your time with Nathan and try not to allow Christina's drama to infringe on your happiness."

"I really like him, Hattie. He's become my dearest friend this week."

Warning flags waved in my mind. "But what of Marie Marley? You've gotten close with her in recent weeks. Don't allow a relation with a boy to replace female companionship."

"Marie is fun, but we don't see each other much besides at the club meeting since we go to different schools. We plan on spending time together during the summer. We're just a few blocks away so it should be easy. And Nathan will be working, so he wouldn't interrupt that."

"Make it a point to carve out friendships. Don't put your life on hold because you're feeling sentimental about a handsome face."

Ethelwynne gave a joyous smile. "He *is* handsome."

"I'm glad you think so, Ethelwynne." Sean strutted in and winked.

She smiled at Sean—no hint of her previous schoolgirl infatuation on her countenance. "I was speaking of Nathan."

"You and I need to have a talk about your Nathan. Do you mind if I smoke?" She shook her head and he went for his supplies on the mantel. "Now, Ethelwynne, young men who give poems to sweethearts are after one thing."

"Did you ever write a poem for a girl?" she countered.

"Just once, for Winifred Ramsay after she died. I left it on her grave, but I've recited more than my share of poems to woo a pretty face. Believe me when I say the purpose is the same as one who pens his own words."

"Which is what—beyond expressing emotions?" A defensive sharpness shaped her words.

Sean smirked around his pipe from his overbearing stance before the mantel. "He does it to soften the girl so she's willing to accept him when he makes a play at her."

"And how did that work last Saturday when you were quoting Keats to my mother at the supper table?"

He choked on an inhale and sputtered a few coughs before looking upon Ethelwynne's confident stature beside me. Sean knew she had won that round, but his debate fists were up.

"What your mother and I say is different. We're old friends and married so—"

"I'd say that would make it ten times *worse* than two unattached people. How do you think all that poetry and flirting makes your spouses feel?"

"Blazing hell, Ethelwynne, this conversation isn't about me, it's about that boy who wants to get a feel under your skirt!"

"Sean, I'll not have you talk like that to Winnie," I said with sharpness.

"But it's true." He puffed on his pipe. "She needs to be prepared for what this boy or anyone after him will try. I don't think I need to tiptoe around meanings when Nathan is penning her poems that spell out his desires."

"That still doesn't excuse your behavior in doing the same thing you accuse him of doing," Ethelwynne said with the confidence of a wronged soul. "Don't point the finger at Nathan who hasn't even held my hand when you act like an arrogant peacock strutting his wares around my mother!"

Merritt had completely disappointed her, and Sean was right there for the fall. A second later, Ethelwynne crumbled over the arm of the sofa, sobbing.

Sean immediately set his pipe on the holder and went to his knees before Ethelwynne. As soon as his hand touched her back, she collapsed on his shoulder, wetting his shirt with her tears. He pulled her onto his lap and rocked her like a child, smoothing her hair.

"Cry, my dear little Winnie. Cry out the hurt. I'm sorry for adding to your pain. You're completely right about me. Your mother and I—we might have hurt each other at different points in the past, but now we're hurting everyone around us. Forgive me, Winnie. Please forgive me."

His own tears fell as he continued to rock her. In over three years of knowing Sean, I had never heard him refer to Ethelwynne by her nickname. It was a profound moment in more ways than one. Not knowing what to do or say, I stayed on the sofa, inches away from the tender scene. As her sobs slowed, Ethelwynne gathered her words.

"I haven't been able to talk to Mama for years, and Papa has been too distracted over her this past month to burden him with anything." She sniffed. "Days ago, my best friend publicly denounced me as a liar. I've had nothing this week except Nathan. I'd be alone without him."

"You always have us, Winnie." Sean fished a handkerchief from his pocket and wiped her face. "Hattie and I are here for you and the Lord is a prayer away. He knows your pains, including what a pain in the ass I am."

She hiccupped a laugh, and I smiled over them.

"I'm honored you feel safe here. Hattie and I want nothing but the best for you, and that means we're willing to discuss difficult subjects. Am I thinking the worst of Nathan Paterson? Probably, but that doesn't negate the potential dangers and heartaches involved with relationships. Thanks in part to Hattie's club, you understand the basics, but those all fly out the window when emotions are involved."

They stared at each other a moment, wet eyes glistening.

"Here." He helped Ethelwynne stand and motioned to the sofa. "Before anyone gets the wrong idea, you sit with Hattie, and I'll go back to smoking and pacing the room like a father giving a lecture."

I hugged her when she settled beside me, then she took my closest hand and held it as we watched Sean prep his pipe once more.

"Winnie, you're a beautiful young lady, both in form and personality. The natural instincts of men aren't always proper. There are plenty who bridle their passions and show young ladies the respect they deserve, but even the best intentioned souls are tempted beyond reason when alone with someone they're attracted to."

"Like you and Mama."

"Exactly like that. I respected her, but we rationalized everything to fit our physical needs. You can see the depth of emotional havoc that moment in time had on her." Sean stopped before Ethelwynne, pain-filled golden eyes gazing upon her. "I'll do everything in my power to see that you aren't wounded like your mother and other countless girls who get caught up with a well-meaning beau. I'll arm you with knowledge and pray when the times come—and they'll come in spades—that you'll choose wisely. Now, we've had you here long enough, but I must say one more thing before Hattie drives you home. Promise me you won't run off with Nathan tomorrow. Stay with the picnic group and stay in the open. Will you do that for me?"

"I promise."

Sean pulled Ethelwynne to her feet and kissed her cheek. "Now go wash your face so your parents don't think we sent you into hysterics—even if I did."

She laughed and hugged him. "Thank you."

After she was gone, I stood before Sean with a bemused smile.

He lowered his pipe. "Did I manage to dig out of the hole I expertly trapped myself in?"

I nodded.

Sean's brows lifted in an effort to exude innocence. "And you've forgiven me for everything?"

"You know I have."

Sixteen

On the way to Monroe Park, I sat in the backseat with the boxed cookies. In the front, Papa lectured Andrew about spending his money wisely. I had been put in charge of the streetcar fare for our return trip, but Papa had given us each enough coins to be able to ride the carousel and roller coaster, as well as buy ice cream, play a few arcade games, and even attend a baseball game or concert at the grand stand if we wished. It was the most money my brother had ever carried on his person at one time.

When we pulled to a stop in the parking lot on the southeast side of downtown, my father looked back at me. "Enjoy yourself today, Winnie."

"I will, Papa."

"And you," he told Andrew, "won't be going to any baseball games for a month if you cause trouble."

"Yes, sir." Andrew scrambled out the door.

"You get at least one of those boxes, Drew. Don't leave you sister with the lot."

My brother opened the backdoor. I handed him one of the boxes and lifted the second as I climbed out.

"Winnie." Papa waited until I looked him in the eyes, kind behind his glasses. "I'm serious about you enjoying yourself. I know things have been stressful for you. I hope to show your mother a good time when I take her downtown for dinner and shopping so we'll all be in a better mood come supper tonight."

I smiled. "I hope so too."

All thoughts of my parents fled as I followed Andrew's lead down the path toward Mobile Bay. A banner proclaiming FIRST BAPTIST ANNUAL SUNDAY SCHOOL PICNIC was raised above our designated area. A dozen chaperones and twice as many students were already assembled.

My brother was soon surrounded.

"Drew's here. Let's play ball!"

He shoved the box at me, pulled his mitt from his pocket, and ran with the boys for the nearest expanse of grass.

"Winnie, let me help you," the preacher's wife said as she took the top box. "Are these your mother's famous shortbread cookies?"

"Yes, ma'am."

"The desserts go over here." She saw me look back at the boys after I set my box beside hers. "Don't worry about Andrew. My husband promised to play ball with them."

No one close to my age was there yet. Besides which, there were only two other girls within three years of me in the congregation, and I didn't want to sit around and look like I was waiting for Nathan.

"I'm going to walk the Yacht Club Pier before it gets too hot, if that's all right."

"Sure, Winnie. If any of your classmates come, I'll tell them where you are."

The stretch of the dock under the glaring sun was overwhelming, but I started down the wooden planks, enjoying the sound of the seagulls and the gentle lapping of the blue-gray bay against the pilings. As I got further from shore, the shouts of children playing dimmed into nothing.

Alone in my thoughts, I focused on Nathan's poem. I mulled over the words, feeling them anew like the sun on my skin—my bare forearms as well as my face and neck. Mama didn't like me getting sun because it bronzed my skin so easily. She always told me boys preferred pale skin that easily showed a blush, but Nathan had written of my "tanned complexion" as though it were a good thing.

When I was halfway to the two-story Yacht Club building at the end of the pier, running footsteps vibrated the planks. I turned to the stampede. Nathan, Teddy, and another boy came to a stop a few feet away.

Nathan inched closer. "Hey, Winnie. How are you?"

"Good, thank you." I smiled.

"Do you mind if we walk with you?"

"Not at all." I returned to my leisurely stroll, and Nathan fell into step with me.

The other two skirted around us and ran ahead to get a better look at a jumping fish. Not wanting to waste our small window of privacy, I looked to Nathan's blue eyes.

"Thank you for the poem."

"I had hoped you'd find it, but I didn't want to ask in case you hadn't." His smile was the most perfect of all. "I meant every word, Winnie."

A glance ahead showed his friends leaning over the railing to better see the fish. I took his right hand with my left, linking our fingers together. We didn't speak as we walked past his friends, but Teddy took note and nudged the other in the ribs.

"Come on," Teddy said. "Let's go join the baseball game and leave the lovebirds."

Nathan looked back to see that they turned for the park, and then caught my gaze with a smile that set my heart pounding. His hand tightened around mine. "It's delightful to be here with you. With school ending in a few days, I'll miss our daily walks and conversations."

"I will too. I'd like to keep seeing you, Nathan."

We reached the clubhouse and stood a moment in the shade of the porch that wrapped the building. Afraid my hand was turning sweaty, I released our connection and went to the railing. Elbows on top of the wood, I extended my hands over the bay. The breeze cooled my palms and my hair tossed about my face.

"Do you ever go fishing?" I asked.

Nathan leaned on the railing too. "I haven't in years. The last few times I went, I brought a book and stuck the end of my pole in the ground. I read until something pulled my line, which wasn't often. Apparently fish prefer bait that gives chase."

I turned to him, admiring the definition of his jaw, square chin, and perfectly straight nose—poetry in form. "And what type of bait do you bite at?"

His hand rose to my cheek, fingers creating all sorts of electricity as he brushed the tousled hair behind my ear. "The sincere type."

My mouth went dry. I fought the instinct to lick my lips because his gaze was fixated on that location. He wanted to kiss me and I wanted him to. The thought of what I had promised Sean flittered through my head—not going anywhere private with Nathan. But Nathan and I weren't hiding. We were before a row of windows on display to anyone inside the Yacht Club. Our chaperones knew where we were and could see us as tiny forms at the end of the pier.

His fingers trailed to my neck and he shifted closer, eyes still on my mouth.

"Yes," I whispered in response to his unasked question as I angled in for the contact.

Soft and warm. The sweet kiss created a line of communication directly to my middle. The second of contact wasn't enough for either of us. Nathan leaned toward me as soon as he'd stopped, his hand going around my neck to increase the firmness of our connection.

Everything was a blur when we separated. Nathan laughed and slipped off my eyeglasses that had fogged over. He wiped them with his handkerchief and then placed them back on my nose.

"Better?" he asked.

I nodded, took his hand, and started our journey back to the park.

"I have to return your bag on the last day of school. My mother noticed it yesterday afternoon, but I talked her into allowing me use of it until school closes."

"Did you tell her it was mine?"

Feeling as though I failed a test, I shook my head. "I said it was a friend's."

"I hope you consider me more than a friend. I'm fond of you—I have been for a long time. Will you be my girl, Winnie?"

"I'd like nothing better." I leaned my shoulder briefly against his.

He stopped and took hold of both my hands. "I'll treat your heart with the utmost respect."

Gooseflesh to erupt on my arms. I wanted to cling to him and feel more of the thrill his connection created, but he went back to holding one hand so we could continue our walk.

"I'm prepared to face my mother when I return home. One of the chaperones is bound to telephone her with news I spent all my time with you."

"You'll spend all day with me?" Nathan asked, sounding hopeful.

"I planned on it. I need to check in with my brother every once in a while, but I think Drew will be busy playing and watching baseball."

"He's great at ball."

"He dreams of going into the major league."

"Drew is the best I've ever seen at this age. I'd say his odds are good for going into the majors." He paused when we reached the end of the pier. "Would you like to ride the roller coaster?"

"Yes."

"I was hoping you wouldn't think it too babyish. I love the front row—how about you?"

I smiled. "I do like the front best."

When we reached the looming wooden structure that was at least five stories high and crisscrossed beneath with skinny support beams, I paid my own way from the coin purse in my skirt pocket. The line for the coaster wasn't long, allowing us to climb the stairs without pause.

"We'd like to wait for the front, please," Nathan told the operator before we could be herded into the holding area.

The guy smirked and eyed our held hands. "Sure ya don't want the back?"

"I'm certain," he replied with a straight face.

I didn't understand what the man inferred until we were seated and the machinery started up the first hill. The *clackity-clack* of the gears was almost deafening as we were shakily pulled up the track, but it faded to nothing when Nathan's right arm went around my shoulders. Everyone behind us could see his face come to mine at the top of the rise when he kissed my cheek.

We plunged down the first hill and around a corner, which pressed me into Nathan's side. Up, down, and around we rode, but my mind became more focused on the physical closeness of our bodies rather than the thrill of the speed and dips. I think I cried out a few times, the wind ripping the excitement from me as soon as it was expressed.

As the ride came to a jerking halt back where we began, Nathan helped me stand. I was glad he assisted me because my knees were weak and I was dizzy. The other riders passed us. As we got down the exit stairs, the roller coaster started clacking on the tracks above.

Nathan stopped and looked around. I followed his gaze, seeing we were caught within the shadows of the wooden structure like a spider's web.

"May I kiss you, Winnie?"

I nodded and his left hand—the side always stained with ink—trailed my neck, under my hair as his right hand went around my waist. We moved closer until our fronts were nearly touching. Then we both closed our eyes when contact was made. His hand on my neck caressed down to my shoulders and the lower one spread his fingers at the small of my back as his lips continued their quest. My arms were around his middle, hands splayed while hoping I was kissing properly. After the long, nibbling connection, he gave me a series of three quick kisses before slowly stepping away. The roar of the roller coaster had stopped and the sound of dozens of feet tramping down the stairs headed our way.

Nathan linked his hand in mine and led me toward the carousel—trusting his lead as the steam on my glasses slowly cleared. I allowed him to pay my fare, and Nathan made up a poem about galloping through a magical forest while we rode side-saddle, facing each other.

After the carousel, we checked in with the picnic group. The boys were already clamoring for food, so I helped the women arrange the luncheon, and Nathan assisted the preacher in lining up the boys to march them to the nearest spigot to wash.

"You sure are spending a lot of time with Nathan this morning," one lady remarked while the preacher's wife kept an eye on us.

"We've been in the same Sunday School class forever and figured with it being a picnic for that, it would be fun to pass the time together."

"You've hardly spoken to each other the past few years in class," the lady who taught us when we were fourteen chimed in.

"And how often have you seen boys and girls during these sensitive years being overly friendly with one another?"

"Really, Winnie Graves! I've never heard you be disrespectful before."

"I didn't mean to be. I've been attending a women's science club and am used to hearing opinions expressed and thoughts shared from all sides."

"Science club?" the preacher's wife asked.

"I suppose the members are suffragettes," the Sunday School teacher remarked.

"I believe many of them are," I said. "Several of the women drive their husbands' automobiles, and one of the other students is going to college to pursue a medical profession."

"And Merritt allows her daughter to attend this progressive group?" someone said behind me, chilling my blood.

I had said too much.

When the boys returned from washing up, I found Drew and stayed by him in the scraggly line.

"Do you want to eat together?" I asked.

He snorted. "It's bad enough having you hang around like I'm too little to dish my own food. Next thing I know, you'll want to tie a bib around my neck."

"Fine." I gave him a shove, causing his friends to chuckle.

I went to the front of the line where the other girls were—all younger than me. After filling a plate and getting a cup of lemonade, I found a shady bench on the edge of the area to claim. Nathan joined me a few minutes later. I warned him of the watchful eyes.

"I made it ten times worse by mentioning the science club when I was accused of being disrespectful. I was merely asserting my opinion."

"Is that Monday meeting part of your transformation this past month?"

"I think it is. We talk about everything, much like you and I do."

We chatted while we ate the sandwiches and chilled salads.

Fifteen minutes later, Nathan noticed the boys run for the desserts and stood. "Allow me to gather some sweets before they disappear."

With cookies and fresh lemonade, we spent a pleasant quarter-hour on our bench. Then Nathan was recruited for the relay races. I cheered him and Andrew on.

The relays were followed by a mass exodus to the baseball park for a minor league game. Nathan and I joined the others and spent three glorious hours side-by-side. We talked as much as we observed the teams on the field.

After the game, I caught my brother on the shoulder before he could disappear with his friends.

"We need to head home, Drew. If you have any money left, you can play a few games in the arcade while we wait for the streetcar."

"I only have enough money left for one game."

"That's your own fault for buying so many treats." I nudged him toward the exit gate. "But since you've been good, I'll give you a penny."

"Thanks, Winnie. The guys are right about you being better than most, even if you are getting lovey-dovey with Nathan." He ran into the crowd.

Blushing, I looked to Nathan.

He took my elbow on the congested footpath. "Is it all right if I ride the streetcar with you?"

"Of course, though I couldn't stop you from taking public transportation."

He laughed and trailed his fingers between mine. We waited in the arcade while Andrew played a few games, then the three of us sat together on the trolley for the ride north. We transferred downtown, taking the Government Street line west. Rather than cross the busy road, we rode it around the loop, passing Nathan's street, then the Woodslows' house, and finally the Spunners' before we were along the south side neighborhoods.

When we got off the streetcar, Andrew took the lead.

"I had a lot of fun today," I told Nathan.

"So did I. We'll have to try for weekly expeditions like this over the summer—a whole day of exploring together."

"I'd like that." We stopped before the gate—Andrew already going into the house. "Thank you for a wonderful day."

He held the gate open and kissed my cheek when I walked through. "I'll see you at church tomorrow, Winnie."

"I've already sent your brother upstairs to bathe," Papa said when I came into view of the parlor. He was in his chair in the corner with the newspaper in hand. I perched on the edge of the settee. "You look happy. Did you have a good time?"

"Yes, thank you, Papa. Would you like the leftover money back?"

"No, you keep it." He pulled his glasses down the bridge of his nose and looked at me over the rim. "I do believe you're glowing, Ethelwynne."

I couldn't stop the huge smile that bloomed on my face. "I spent the day with a boy. He even walked me and Drew home."

"My little girl has a beau?"

I nodded.

"When do I get to meet him?"

"You already know him, Papa. It's Nathan Paterson."

"The towheaded rascal?" He laughed when I nodded again. "You two used to fight like cats and dogs when you were little. You'd start a row over everything from cookies to parts in the Christmas pageant. When you were about five, the director made you both sheep and you spent the scene trying to out *baa* one another. Y'all did such a fine job of it, the audience couldn't hear the shepherds speaking their lines."

It was my turn to laugh. "I'd forgotten about that."

"He seems a good lad and is from a nice family, but it's my duty to give him a talking to about treating my daughter well."

"Nathan has been respectful and kind."

"And I'll make sure he stays that way." He pushed his glasses up his nose and winked at me, though I knew he was serious to a certain degree.

I turned for the hall and came face to face with Mama. Her hands were on her hips and she scowled like a scarecrow.

"How dare you make a fool of me today, Ethelwynne? I got a telephone call to tell me you were inseparable from Nathan Paterson and the few minutes you weren't with him, you managed to insult your old Sunday School teacher." A hand went to her heart. "How do you think it made me feel to receive a call like that from the preacher's wife?"

"I didn't mean to insult anyone. I asked an honest question." I glanced at Papa, who got to his feet.

"And she complained about you attending women's clubs with progressives—and blamed that on you spending all your time with a boy—including eating with him in an isolated location."

"Isolated? We were in full view of the chaperones in a public park. Papa, you know how those women twist things. My day was nothing like this sounds."

"Don't bring your father into this. I'm the one who received the telephone call. It was all I could do to hear such negative things about my daughter. Why have you not told me about Nathan before?"

"Merri, she and Nathan have been going to church together almost as long as they've been alive. They're at that age when boys and girls start to get back together after the rift that comes with growing pains."

"Must you always take sides with other people?"

"There are no sides because there's nothing to argue," Papa said. "Those old biddies at church will make a mountain out of a molehill to create a bit of gossip."

"Don't talk about my friends like that!"

"What do you think they would have said about *you* if they'd seen you last Saturday?"

Her lower lip trembled.

"Let's not spoil our good day, Merri." His voice softened. "We had a nice time downtown, the children had fun at their picnic, and supper smells great."

"Fine, but Winnie isn't going to church tomorrow."

"Why ever not?" I cried.

"You can't keep her from church as a punishment," Papa said. "If you think she's done wrong, she needs church more than ever."

I appreciated his sentiment, but I didn't think my behavior warranted any punishment.

"I'll not give her the chance to be around that boy until he properly introduces himself to us, and I hear about today from more sources."

"Introduce himself? Merri, we've known the lad since he was in short pants. And as for sources, you heard our daughter's side. That's enough for me."

She shook her head. "Ethelwynne stays home tomorrow, and you'll stay with her to make sure she doesn't leave while I attend church with Drew."

"You've got a lot of nerve, Merritt Hall Graves."

"One of us has to. Supper is in ten minutes." She stalked back to the kitchen.

Seventeen

Sunday, I attended late Mass with Sean. The problem with going to the cathedral with Sean was leaving afterward. He loved to stand on the portico and speak to everyone he knew—which was practically all who exited. When Brandon was a baby, Sean would hold him in his arms, but now he set him on his shoulders so he had a bird's eye view of the Mobilians in their Sunday best.

After Sean exchanged words with Edmund Easton, Edmund turned on me with his roving eyes. "Hattie, your club seems to have flustered my impressionable wife."

"I doubt that. Mary Margaret is clever. I'm sure if you took the time to hear her out, you'd be in agreement with her ideas."

Mary Margaret was pink as she herded her children away.

"Loosen up, Eddie." Sean slapped Edmund's shoulder and dropped his voice. "I know you aren't priggish, just try practicing some of that freedom in your own bedroom. There's a wealth of pleasure to be had within marriage. A wife is more than a means to produce offspring."

Edmund looked like he was ready to strike Sean with a right hook when Alexander Melling came up behind him.

"Hello, Brother!" Alexander took Edmund in a hug.

"Get off me, Melling." Edmund easily freed himself from the smaller man and straightened his suit before stalking away from his brother-in-law.

"Thanks for that," Sean said to Alexander.

"It's the least I could do since you helped ease the judge's annoyance with me at our last trial." He turned to me, blue eyes merry. "Hattie, I've wanted to congratulate you on your excellent marksmanship. Never have I seen such a fine display of passion marks on a fellow until Sean walked into court the other week. And the teeth marks on the ear—exquisite!"

"Sean told me you two had fun in court, but I'm sure it was nothing to what he and I enjoyed before he left the house."

Both men laughed.

"Obviously not." Alexander looked around the thinning crowd.

Brandon bopped him on the head. "Where's Asher?"

Alexander gazed up at Brandon when he spoke his son's name. "You've got a good arm like your daddy. Asher stayed home with his mother today."

Sean put a hand on his friend's shoulder. "It appears we both have wives whose church attendance is fleeting. Stop in with your family for a visit sometime. The boys could play while we chat. Let Lucy know Hattie doesn't bite unless she's married to you."

Alexander laughed. "I'll see if I can talk her into that one Sunday afternoon."

"Then I can show you the house. There's something I especially want to share with you."

"That sounds fine. I'll see you both later."

Once Alexander hurried down the steps, I turned to Sean. "Don't tell me you're referring to the painting of his sister."

"All right, I won't tell you." Sean grinned.

***

At a quarter 'til four Monday afternoon, Althea was inside preparing a tray for the children as I kicked a ball with Brandon in the yard. I found it amazing he looked so unsteady while playing because he was all coordination when focused on music.

A few minutes later, I heard Ethelwynne's laughter. She crossed Houston Street, holding hands with Nathan Paterson.

"Winnie!" Brandon ran for the gate.

"Hi, Brandon."

Nathan reached past Ethelwynne to open the latch.

Brandon stopped before the young man, staring up at him. "Who are you?"

"Nathan. Nathan Paterson. Who are you?"

"Brandon Patrick Spunner. I like to hold Winnie's hand too. Are you friends?"

His grin was pure and bright, showing me in an instant what Ethelwynne saw in him—beyond his stirring poetry. "Yes, we're special friends."

"Come meet Hattie." Ethelwynne took the lead. "Hattie, this is Nathan Paterson. Nathan, Hattie Spunner."

I extended my hand, forcing him to drop his hold on Ethelwynne. "It's nice to meet you. And please, call me Hattie, not Mrs. Spunner."

"It's good to meet you, Miss Hattie." He smiled and reclaimed Ethelwynne's hand.

"Please go inside and get some refreshments. I'll be in as soon as Althea returns."

After they walked up the front steps, I realized I had sent them inside unchaperoned. As soon as Althea came around the far side of the veranda with the children's refreshment tray, I hurried inside.

Nathan and Ethelwynne stood by the dining table, both glowing with the essence of young love.

Over the next few minutes, Jessica and Faith arrived, as well as Grace Anne and Marie.

"Sadie couldn't make it today," Grace Anne explained. "She's helping our mother host a Bridge party."

Then Melissa and Darla arrived, accompanying the sound of boisterous children in the yard. Kate Stuart was last. Everyone was eager to speak with Nathan. He handled the attention with little stammering.

Slowly, the ladies migrated into the club room with their plates and cups. The students stayed in the living hall, clustered around Nathan. Without being told, he made his excuse.

"It was great to see you all and meet Marie, but I should go before I overstay my welcome."

Jessica, Faith, and Marie said their goodbyes, and then Ethelwynne walked with him to club room doorway where I lingered.

"Thank you for inviting me, Miss Hattie." He leaned into the club room. "And it was nice to meet so many distinguished ladies."

"Stop by anytime, Nathan," I said.

Ethelwynne went to the entry with him. "I'll see you in the morning."

As soon as the door shut, Marie was jumping beside Ethelwynne. "He's the prettiest boy I've ever seen!"

"He's smart too, even if his ears are a little odd," Faith remarked.

"Who looks at ears when a boy has a face like that? And he's a good writer," Jessica added.

"He's interning with his uncle at The Daily Register this summer," Ethelwynne said as she came into the club room.

"Benjamin Paterson is his uncle?" Kate asked. "He's the brightest reporter and editor we've had in this city for decades."

The room continued to buzz with chatter about Nathan. A few minutes later, when the talk had run its course, the doorbell rang. My mouth nearly dropped open when I found Merritt standing outside in a smart new dress suit.

"Hello, Merritt. Are you here for the science club?"

"Only out of necessity." Her words were as clipped as the mincing steps of her heeled shoes.

"Would you like some refreshments before you join us?"

"No, thank you. I'm sure Winnie didn't mention it, but she behaved poorly at her Sunday School picnic and several of the ladies seemed to think her participation here was to blame. I plan to supervise the meetings she attends from now on."

"Mama, there's no need." Ethelwynne stood from her seat beside Marie. "I told you I didn't mean to be impertinent, and if I was, Hattie's club isn't at fault."

"I'll be the judge." Merritt's sharp gaze moved across those assembled.

I went through quick introductions between Merritt and all the others. Despite her being the smallest woman in the room, she managed to convey a dominate aura that several shrank from. But not Kate or Melissa. Kate looked ready to strike, and Melissa was nonchalant.

Merritt sat rigidly in a single chair, and Ethelwynne returned to her previous seat by Marie, arms crossed.

"What are we discussing today, Hattie?" Jessica asked.

"I thought pollination and plant reproduction would be timely, but if any of you have other ideas, now is the time to voice them."

Junior in Melissa's lap began to fuss. She opened her blouse in preparation to nurse him—making Merritt turn scarlet.

"Pollination sounds interesting, but how about psychology?" Jessica said. "That's what I'm leaning toward for my studies in college."

"To better understand your aunt?" I asked.

Jessica nodded. "They labeled her with hysteria eight years ago, and her husband had her committed."

"Do you know what her symptoms were?" Darla asked. "I've read in many medical journals lately that several of the old labels placed on women are being shown to have real medical conditions behind them, rather than the emotional instability previously assigned to all females."

"Some," Jessica said hesitantly, "but I don't know everything."

"Share with us what you're comfortable with and we'll discuss from there." I smiled reassuringly. "Her age, living arrangements, and so forth are a good place to begin."

"She'd been married for about twenty years. Four children— my cousins were between six and seventeen when it happened. A solid family life, but my uncle said she went off the rails."

"So she was around forty?" Darla mused aloud. "That's the average for women to start going through the change."

"What change?" Marie asked.

"Just as young women mature from girlhood into childbearing years with the start of your monthly cycles," Darla explained, "after a few decades, women transition out of it."

"Yes," I said. "After a certain age—and it's different for everyone—the stress of pregnancy would be too much strain on a woman so the body takes away that option. This change in a woman's life is another testament that nature knows what's best."

"Nature, as planned by God," Darla added.

I nodded in acknowledgement of my friend's polite way of calling out my perceived heresy before continuing. "There are often upsets during this transitional time, similar to emotional swings that happen in our younger years with that body change."

"We know all about those," Jessica said with an eye roll as she adjusted the giant bow on her ponytail.

"With women transitioning from fertility to infertility, there is often an urge to try once more for motherhood. For married women, this sometimes means looking to a younger, more virile man because we are often married to a man older than us."

Melissa laughed. "Not me. I have three months on Freddy."

I looked around the room. "Procreation is a natural instinct, and there's no shame in that. But there's *no excuse* for women of enlightened society to cave to these base desires."

"My aunt did that," Jessica whispered. "Her husband caught her with his best friend. They locked her up for it, claiming hysteria and listing adultery as one of the symptoms."

"That's not madness, that's poor decisions," Darla stated.

Kate shifted in her chair. "But I'm sure the man involved walked away with nothing against him."

"Do all women go through this promiscuity phase?" Grace Anne asked, pretending to look bored.

"Not all, but often there will be a phase of trying to attract attention to prove she's still desirable, even if she doesn't plan on acting on it." Merritt visibly flinched at Darla's words. "But that's just as dangerous. Playing with the affections of men and seeking to get them to lust after you is as sinful as the act itself. Are we not taught in The Holy Bible that to commit something in our mind is the same as doing it?"

Merritt jumped to her feet. "Winnie, you needn't hear any more of this filth."

"Mama, she was speaking of the Bible."

"The topic is completely unacceptable. We're leaving, Ethelwynne."

"Papa gave me permission to attend the meetings, and I'd like to stay with my friends."

"Then your father will collect you!" Merritt slammed out the front door, crossed the lawn, and headed up the sidewalk toward Bartholomew's store.

"And that," Kate said in a sarcastic tone, "is an example of a lady going through *the change*."

Ethelwynne ran to the bathroom.

There was an awkward trickle of laughter before I turned back to my guests. "Please, ladies, don't mention anything of this to Winnie unless she brings it up. She's gone through a lot with her mother in recent weeks."

"Is Merritt"—Kate paused for dramatic effect—"sniffing around *your* virile husband?"

"I refuse to continue this topic as it relates to people within our group."

"But what happens to women after that second change?" Grace Anne asked. "Will we no longer want sexual relations if we can't get pregnant?"

I could have hugged her for switching back to the topic in a safe way. Perhaps I'd judged her too harshly, but seeing discomfort in a group was part of her skillset as an excellent hostess.

"Each woman is different," Darla explained. "Overall, the average is a decline in sexual desires, but some find it more freeing as they aren't hampered with the thought of possible pregnancy. There are some herbal remedies that have been passed down through the generations that can ease symptoms—both physical and emotional."

"It can also depend on the type of relationship you're in," Melissa said as she burped Junior. "In my travels, I've seen couples of all ages in dozens of different cultures. Some are just as affectionate in old age as newlyweds."

Ethelwynne returned with a freshly scrubbed face. I met her in the hall, opened my arms to her, and led her to the parlor sofa.

"Mama told me before she bought that dress that sometimes women have to prove to the men in her life that they are lucky to have her so she knows her worth."

"Self-worth isn't based on what others think of us. Your mother was raised wrong in believing that, and she's doing you a disservice by perpetuating the myth." I took her hands. "We're born worthy, Winnie. No one can take that from us but ourselves through self-pity and neglect. Don't think you need a man in your life to tell you you're pretty—know in your soul that you're strong, beautiful, and brave."

Her arms were around my neck, nearly strangling me as she cried.

Over her shaking shoulder, I watched Melissa pace the living hall, swaying Junior. When the doorbell rang, she answered it.

"I'm sorry to disturb the club meeting," Bartholomew said from the vestibule, "but I'm here for my daughter, Winnie."

"Come in, Mr. Graves. We're all fond of Winnie. I'm Melissa Davenport."

"Mrs. Davenport, it's a pleasure." He shook her hand. "I enjoy watching your husband at the seasonal boxing tournaments. His form is as good as the professionals."

"I'll pass along your kind words. Winnie is in the parlor, having a tough go of things at the moment."

Bartholomew stepped inside, heartache etched on his face.

He laid a hand on his daughter's back. "Winnie, I'm sorry, but I need to bring you home now. You can come back next week—but not your mother. I'm putting my foot down about that. You'll need time away from her during the summer."

She raised her head and looked up at him with her wet face. "Thank you, Papa."

He tucked her glasses into his shirt pocket and passed her a handkerchief. "Hattie, I'm sorry for Merri's disturbance. I hope the ladies don't think poorly of Winnie because her mother caused a scene."

"It's forgivable, Bart. And as Melissa said, they're all fond of Winnie. But Merritt might need a little help. Darla Adams is here. She's an experienced midwife and knows much of women's issues. A consultation with her would be beneficial to Merritt. Darla knows of herbs and other remedies to help balance a woman's system when her body is going through the change."

"Do you think that's what's plaguing her?"

"She's overly concerned about Winnie, but those varying body symptoms and emotions don't help. Darla is knowledgeable and a great listener. Would you like to meet her before you go?"

Bartholomew nodded, and I collected Darla from the other room.

"Darla Adams, this is Bartholomew Graves. Bart, meet Darla, Mobile's best midwife."

"Miss Darla, it's good to meet you. I was wondering if you think you might be able to be of assistance with my wife, Merritt. I believe you met her this past hour."

"Yes, and she appeared flushed. Has she complained of overbearing heat, beyond the climate?"

His eyes widened behind his glasses. "How did you know?"

She smiled, a spark of humor in her blue eyes. "It's a story as old as time, Mr. Graves. I'd be happy to have a consultation with her."

I brought Ethelwynne into the hall to give them a moment to discuss details. "Don't forget your bag."

"Never." She collected the satchel and hugged it to her chest.

"Was part of your mother's issue with your behavior at the picnic because you were with Nathan?"

Ethelwynne nodded. "But he was a gentleman. Be sure to tell Sean we never snuck away. He kissed me for the first time on the Yacht Club Pier, before the whole world."

"How was it?"

Her tear-stained face broke into a bright smile. "Magical, but my glasses fogged over."

I laughed with her and smoothed her hair behind her ears. "Hold to the good, Winnie."

Before Bartholomew could escort Ethelwynne to the door, the bell rang. I stepped ahead of them to open it and came face to face with my previous boss—Mr. Gentry, the principal of Barton Academy. He had just as much disdain on his face as ever.

"This is quite a surprise, Mr. Gentry."

"Unfortunately not for me, Mrs. Spunner. You may have changed your name, but you seem to still be up to your old practices."

Brandon and his friends ran by, laughing and playing across the lawn while Althea watched from the corner of the veranda.

"I'm sorry, but I'm in the middle of hosting a gathering. Perhaps you could return at a more convenient time." I motioned to

Bartholomew and Ethelwynne. "Please excuse us, but a few of my guests are on their way out."

His cold eyes assessed them. "Are you removing your daughter from this profane club, Mr. Graves?"

Bartholomew stopped short and stared. "Excuse me?"

"A concerned citizen recently brought Mrs. Spunner's group to my attention as several of the students from the girls' school have been in attendance. I aim to put a stop to Mrs. Spunner's vulgar teaching habits in regards to evolution and sexuality."

Merritt came up the front steps, head high. "Those are exactly my concerns, Mr. Gentry."

Ethelwynne's mouth gaped and she leaned away. "Mama, did you—"

"It was not Mrs. Graves who came to me, but I applaud her stance. I'm here to directly assess which Barton Academy students are involved so I may properly inform the girls' parents."

"I refuse to allow you entrance into my home, Mr. Gentry." I stepped toward him, arms crossed.

The coward looked to Ethelwynne behind me. "Miss Graves, will you please inform me which of your classmates are inside?"

"She will not." Bartholomew nudged his away around his daughter and stood at my elbow.

Behind Mr. Gentry, Merritt reddened. "Bart, he's the principal. Winnie must—"

"Mr. Gentry has no authority here, and I won't allow my daughter to be a pawn in some power struggle. Winnie, go to your mother. I want both of you in the automobile immediately."

When the Graves ladies walked away, Bartholomew stepped in front of me. He had a good two inches on Mr. Gentry and several more in the way of muscles. I laid my hand on Bartholomew's arm.

"I appreciate your willingness to step in on my behalf, Bart, but I can handle things." When he turned to me, I continued. "Get Merritt and Winnie home. I'll be fine."

I nodded to him before he went down the steps. Then I narrowed my eyes at the instigator.

"You're trespassing, Mr. Gentry. I demand you leave my property at once. If you wish to speak to me, telephone for an appointment. Maybe I'll grant you one."

Someone came to the door behind me.

"Thank you, Hattie, for another stimulating meeting. One never knows what will happen at these gatherings," Kate said as she passed me. "Ah, Mr. Gentry."

The knowing look the two schemers shared immediately soured me. Then Kate's automobile arrived—early.

"Good afternoon, Ms. Stuart. It seems I'm on my way out as well. May I see you to your driver?"

I watched them stop outside the gate and exchange words. Mr. Gentry left first, but Kate smiled at me before climbing into the back of her automobile. I had ignored Sean's warning about her, thinking I was above her reach. Obviously I wasn't.

Eighteen

Mama and I were silent on the way home.

Papa spoke once we parked. "What time is Drew expected?"

"Six-thirty," Mama replied. "Supper will be late."

"Do you want help in the kitchen?" he asked.

"I want to be left alone."

I took that as an excuse to go to my room. I didn't attempt to study or even read for pleasure—it would have been a wasted effort.

On the sleeping porch, I stretched out on one of the hammocks and reviewed the events of the afternoon. The walk to the Spunners' house with Nathan was more enjoyable than last week as we were holding hands. I loved introducing Nathan to the group. Seeing the admiring eyes made my feelings for him stronger. Then Mama arrived and shattered my day. But now my friends all knew that even with a handsome beau, my life wasn't idealistic. Hattie's arms around me had been comforting. She smiled more than she scowled and understood I was a person with real emotions. Why couldn't Hattie have been my mother?

Then my thoughts drifted over all I had heard at the science meetings so far. Beyond learning more about my own body, I loved hearing about Melissa Davenport's travels. I knew I could never run off to another continent, but there was one location that always seemed beyond reach though it lay a short distance away. Remembering Papa had told me weeks ago to inform him when I chose an adventure, I decided to tackle the subject that evening.

By the time I wandered downstairs, the supper table was already set. I went to the parlor and rubbed Velvet's silky ears.

My father lowered the newspaper and offered a smile. "Did you get your studying done?"

I shook my head. "But I don't have any tests tomorrow."

"And Drew?"

"I heard him in the bath when I came down."

Papa nodded.

"Do you remember when we spoke of me getting out and experiencing new things? You told me to let you know when I discovered what I wanted to do."

"Yes, Winnie."

"I want to visit Dauphin Island and see the Gulf of Mexico, not just the bay or Mississippi Sound. I want to climb the shell mounds, walk in the sand, and see the goats in the trees."

"Goats in the trees?"

"The goats sleep in the oak trees to keep away from alligators."

Papa laughed. "That does sound like something. Where did you hear about all the wonders of the island?"

"Hattie, Melissa, and Darla. The meetings aren't all what Mr. Gentry said, Papa. Melissa Davenport talks about her travels a lot at the meetings. She's been all over the world except Australia and Antarctica. Darla grew up on the island, and they have friends there—including one who is a captain. Sean has hired him a few times to bring Hattie there for exploring."

"And do you think the Spunners would like to travel with you when you go?"

"They might. I'm not sure they've been since Brandon was born. But wouldn't you want to go, Papa?"

"Yes, but if we're hiring a boat, I think we should bring as many people as possible. Maybe that new friend of yours, Marie Marley."

I sat forward. "And Nathan?"

He took off his glasses and rubbed the bridge of his nose. "Let me find out about this captain, and we'll go from there with planning. Fair enough?"

I nodded because my smile was too big to speak around.

As though waiting for Andrew to come downstairs, Mama announced supper just as his noisy feet touched the hall floor.

Papa escorted Mama to the table, pulling out her chair and effortlessly pushing her in.

After the blessing on the food, Papa started the platter of baked chicken around the table and Mama the green beans from her end. Andrew was intuitive enough to know there was a problem, so he stayed silent, brown eyes watchful. I tapped his foot beneath the table and smiled at him. One corner of his mouth lifted and his eyebrows rose.

"How was your final Monday of the school year, Drew?" Papa asked.

"Good, though playing at Jacob's house was even better this afternoon. We can't wait for Friday afternoon and summer break."

"What are your plans?"

Andrew shrugged. "Play ball, fish, swim. Whatever you and Mama allow me to do."

"You'll need to help keep up the yard," she said. "And work in the store from time to time."

"Yes, Mama."

Velvet padded into the dining room and lay by Mama's chair. The dog didn't whine, but Mama slipped her a bit of chicken and rubbed the back of the dog's head. I wished my mother would spoil me every once in a while.

***

I made it through the next few days avoiding Mr. Gentry at school and Mama at home. She finally opened a conversation at the breakfast table in the kitchen Thursday morning.

"What do you expect will happen with Nathan Paterson after tomorrow afternoon?"

I stared at her over my plate of eggs and toast. Papa and Andrew both looked between us.

"I've seen him meet you at the gate every morning this week and bring you home the last two afternoons." Her eyes narrowed. "And yes, that included seeing him kiss you."

Andrew made a retching noise and our father covered his mouth with his napkin.

"Just on the cheek, Mama."

"And how many boys have you allowed to do that?"

"What exactly do you think of me?" My voice rose with each word.

"Winnie," Papa said with a warning tone. "Speak to your mother with respect."

"Can't she do the same for me?" I sounded more hurt than angry. "Nathan is my first and only beau. I don't like being spoken of as though I've been hiding something."

"Then why are you sneaking around with him? Why does he stop at the gate and not come to the door?"

"We're not sneaking anywhere. He holds my hand down Government Street for the whole town to see." I maintained her brown-eyed stare with my own. "And if you want to know why I haven't invited him to the door, you don't need to look further than the mirror."

"Ethelwynne Graves!" Papa snapped.

Mama left her chair so fast, her coffee cup spilt on the white tablecloth.

"Darla Adams is coming to speak with her today. We must be patient," Papa admonished before climbing the stairs to follow her.

I pushed the remainder of my food around my plate while Andrew finished his breakfast.

"I'm glad I'm not you!" He took his lunch pail and went for the back door.

Alone, I scrapped my uneaten food into Velvet's bowl on the back porch and washed mine and Andrew's dishes. Not knowing what my parents would do, I removed the soiled tablecloth, but reset their places. I was well acquainted with doing laundry—something Mama made me help with every break from school—so I brought the linen to the porch and started it soaking in the washing sink while Velvet ate my leftovers.

I gathered my lunch and the satchel before exiting the front door. Nathan waited for me at the gate. Without word, he transferred the bag to his shoulder, loaded his things into it, took my lunch with one hand and held my other as he kissed my cheek.

"What's wrong, Winnie?"

I leaned against him a moment, not caring if anyone saw us. His hands were too full to offer a hug, but the closeness brought enough healing to lift my mood.

"Nothing's the matter now." I squeezed his hand and stepped toward the road.

We crossed to the park and skirted the edge with what I thought of as our tranquil pace—neither of us in a hurry to get where we were going.

I looked to his profile and smiled when he turned to me. "Could we go for an ice cream or cola after school?"

"We'll do both."

"I have a quarter with me I can put towards it."

"There's nothing I'd rather do than treat my girl. I even know which soda fountain does the best floats in town. Meet me at the back gate after school."

The monotonous day was broken at lunch when I came into the hall early to escape the midday heat and ran into Christina.

Her dark eyes were filled with tears and her lips trembled.

"Are you all right, Christina?" I reflexively reached a hand to her arm.

"I'm fine!" She jerked away.

I tried to forget her the last few hours of school, but the despair on her face haunted me. Christina was different from the girl who had yelled at me before school the previous week. In case miracles were possible, I prayed Luke—if he was still in her life—was treating her well.

When the final bell rang, I hurried out of class.

"Winnie!" Jessica called to me from the doorway of the science classroom. "Are you coming back to the club next Monday?"

"Yes, my father said I could."

Jessica narrowed her eyes. "And your mother is okay with that?"

"She's been overruled."

"Good. I want to be sure to see you before I leave for Baltimore in a few months, but Faith won't be back. Mr. Gentry paid a visit at her family's house last night and shared all sorts of sensational things about Hattie and the club."

"Oh, no! Did he get hold of your family too?"

"He caught my father while my mother was gone. Fortunately, my father thinks it best for me to learn the ways of the world before I head to college."

"Fathers are superior when it comes to trusting us, aren't they? If I don't see you tomorrow, I'll see you at Hattie's on Monday."

Half the crowd was gone by the time I reached the back of the school property. Nathan leaned against the fence, a notebook in his right hand on top of his books as he scrawled with his left. I studied the way the sun brightened his hair to gold above his white shirt. The wave of it that covered his eye when his head was bent over the page begged to be brushed back and his firm lips kissed.

I ran to him, stopping just short of colliding. His bright eyes locked on me with wonder as I leaned in and kissed him fully on the mouth.

"Winnie, it's against school rules."

"What is Mr. Gentry going to do, expel us the day before summer?"

The weight of my actions, the casual dismissal of rules, and the excitement of the contact kept us in suspension several seconds. Then we both laughed and he kissed me.

"There! That'll show them." He took the satchel, loaded his books, and then his fingers were locked in mine.

When we were on the next block, I bumped my shoulder against his. "What were you writing?"

"I'm working on a new poem." Nathan smiled, making my insides feel fuzzy. "A copy might make it into the satchel tomorrow."

"In the morning, I hope. I have to return it after school."

"I'll place it directly into your hand if needed."

For the first time, our pace was swift. We wove between the crowds when we reached the business district, Nathan offering his apologies. At the drug store, he paused to allow a lady to exit before motioning me inside. We settled on two padded brass stools at the end of the counter and Nathan immediately removed his notebook from the bag and the pen from his shirt pocket, moving the instrument smoothly across the lined paper.

The soda clerk threw a small towel over his shoulder and approached us. I recognized him in an instant. Sean had brought me to this drug store a decade ago and told me he had accompanied my mother and her cousin there just before the yellow fever outbreak.

"What can I get you kids?"

Nathan looked up from his notebook. "Hello, Mason."

"Paterson. I should have known it was you with all that scribbling going on." The man looked to me a moment and back to Nathan. "Be careful you don't lose your girl because you're ignoring her to write."

"He may write as long as he wants. I'd never dream of stopping him."

They both laughed.

"Mason, this is Winnie Graves. Winnie, Mason Remington, otherwise known as the owner of the best soda counter in town."

I nodded. "I know. He's been introduced to me like that before."

Mason did a double-take on me. "You don't look familiar."

"I saw you on my sixth birthday. Sean Spunner brought me for my first fountain cola."

"Spunner?" Mason's eyes lit up. "I remember! He came in with a little brunette all dolled up in ruffles and ribbons. I joked you were his lost love child and he threatened to flatten me when my shift was over. And you, poor thing, got bubbles up your nose with the first sip and sneezed the foam halfway across the counter."

The three of us laughed.

"I went to grammar school with Paterson's uncle and Spunner—before Mr. Finnigan took him in and sent him to private school. They've all got their fine jobs, but I'm still here, slinging sodas since I was your age."

"You have one of the most important jobs in town, Mason," Nathan said. "You give cheer by the glassful."

He chuckled. "During Alabama's Prohibition, that's quite an accomplishment."

"Exactly!" Nathan took my hand. "My girl and I would like two root beer floats, please."

"I promise not to sneeze this time."

"She's a sharp one, Paterson. Hang onto her."

"I plan to." When Mason left to prepare things, Nathan spun on his stool to face me. "I can't believe I don't have the honor of being the first guy to bring you for a soda."

I felt myself glow with his attention. "I've never had a root beer float, so you're the first boy I'll have one with."

"Help me, Winnie," he whispered as he cupped my cheek. "I could drown in your eyes."

"They aren't bright pools of blue water."

"No, nothing common like that." He turned abruptly to his notebook, grabbed his pen, and jotted down several lines.

Nathan shifted between studying me to writing before our floats arrived.

"Thank you," I said when Mason placed mine before me.

"My pleasure, Winnie. I'm glad you finally returned."

"Thanks, Mason." Nathan placed his coins on the counter.

As I was used to the bottles of cola from my father's store, the stronger carbonation of the fountain drink tickled my nose when I took my first sip from the paper straw. But I didn't sneeze. The creaminess of the vanilla blended perfectly with the bite of the root beer.

We chatted and enjoyed our treat over the next quarter of an hour. Even if he was still looking directly at me, his eyes looked beyond my physical form into the distance, a smile or frown curled at the corner of his mouth, and then he'd grab for his notebook.

When we were done, we thanked Mason, and Nathan gathered the books back into the satchel. There was a crowd of shoppers in the pharmacy.

"Could we leave by the back door?" Nathan asked.

Mason looked to the pharmacist, who was busy behind his counter, and nodded.

"Thanks, Mason. I'll see you next time."

"Take care of Spunner's love child," he replied.

Nathan led me down the little hall and through a storage room to a side door. We stepped into an alley and the door clicked shut behind us.

"Why—"

"So we could have a moment of privacy." His arms went around me.

We were almost perfectly matched in height and width. Papa towered over Mama because she was so petite and slim. Even Sean was a head taller than Hattie, though her shape was as broad as his. Did Nathan miss that infusion of masculinity being taller supposedly gave a man? Was I less of a woman in his eyes because I wasn't dainty?

"May I kiss you, Winnie?"

I tilted my head toward him and closed my eyes. His warm lips felt more insistent than they had before. Soon, his tongue was involved and I found myself flinch back at the sensation against my mouth.

"Sorry, Winnie. You taste so good and sweet."

"It's the root beer float."

Nathan laughed.

I had seen kisses between my parents and also the Spunners that looked to be *more*, but I had never thought of it as I attributed it to kissing within marriage, but it seemed natural to explore with him. I accepted his kiss and the flick of his tongue on my lips before being swept away with the surge of passion his tongue against mine created. My arms were about his neck as we explored the other's mouth. Sensuous, odd, and thrilling all at once. Teeth—I had never thought about my teeth unless I had a toothache, but Nathan's tongue tracing them made me think they were truly wondrous. What would it feel like on other parts of my body?

His hands around my waist roamed down my back as he pressed us together while our souls fused. Nathan nuzzled into my neck, hands in a more respectable location as his embrace squeezed me in a hug like no other.

Holding hands, I walked on clouds across town, tumbling back to earth at the site of my mother standing on the front porch with her arms crossed. Nathan opened the gate and escorted me all the way to the porch.

"Good afternoon, Mrs. Graves."

"How dare you say that when my daughter is an hour late coming home?"

"Mama, that's not his fault. I asked to go for a soda after school."

"Without permission?" she snapped.

"You've never needed me for anything directly after school without notifying me beforehand. I didn't think it would be an issue."

"Well, you were wrong." Mama looked to Nathan. "Don't bother coming here in the morning, Nathan Paterson. Winnie's father will drive her to school."

"Yes, ma'am. I'm sorry you've been worried about Winnie this hour. I'll be sure she telephones next time." He retrieved his things from the bag and passed the satchel to me.

Mama's body language shouted there would be no next time, but she stayed silent.

I slung the bag's strap over my shoulders and quickly kissed Nathan's cheek. "Thank you. Everything was wonderful."

He grinned with what I hoped was the shared thought of our minutes in the alley. "Goodbye, Winnie."

I was prepared to watch him all the way to the gate, but my mother took my arm. "Go to your room, Ethelwynne. I want you to stay there until supper."

"Yes, Mama."

I spent the time before supper penning a letter to Nathan and imagining the feel of being in his arms.

Nineteen

Sunday morning, Althea helped me prepare brunch while Sean was at Mass with Brandon. The Mellings were coming over to eat after the cathedral service, with the bonus of allowing our sons time to play together. Pearl was off on Sundays, but Althea typically cooked our Sunday supper. When I asked for her assistance with brunch, claiming she wouldn't need to cook a fresh meal that afternoon, she assured me it was no trouble—and reminded me Sean preferred chicken on Sundays and that it was ready for roasting.

As typical when alone with Althea, I felt an outsider in my own home, though in the new house the feeling was only present in the kitchen. The rest of the house was my domain. I set about juicing oranges while she did all the baking and cooking.

"Mr. and Mrs. Melling have never come before," she stated after sliding the quiche into the oven.

"No, but he's one of Sean's favorite friends."

"Don't I know it." Her lips tightened as she shredded potatoes. "I suppose he's going to show Mr. Melling the painting of his sister while he's here."

I wiped my forearm across my brow to keep from getting the acidic juice near my eyes. "Will he remember it?"

Althea shook her head. "He's never seen it. Before you hung it, I can tell you the only people who laid eyes on that painting could be counted on one hand."

"The painting was a secret?"

"A private Christmas gift from Miss Eliza to Sean Francis. Only the housekeeper from those years and I saw it. Maybe Dr. Woodslow as well."

"Where was it hung?"

She gave me a rare smile. "Over the mantel in his bedroom—same as it is now. He had a collection of her sketches along the wall beside his bed too."

"Similar to the painting?"

"Even bolder."

They must have been full nudes. "What happened to those?"

"When I arrived at his house the afternoon of November 1, 1910, the old housekeeper wouldn't stop complaining about the mess in the master suite. She'd been working hours and was still picking pieces of the glass out of the carpet pilings." Althea shook her head. "I wouldn't have believed it if I hadn't seen it with my own eyes, but Sean Francis had smashed all the frames and looked to have burned the sketches. I didn't see remnants of the painting, but it was missing from the wall as well. I later found it in his closet."

"Did he ever say what happened?"

"Sean Francis told me that night at supper it was time he put Miss Eliza to rest. He needed to let her fade in his mind so he would be ready."

I waited for Althea to say more, but she didn't.

"Ready for what?"

"Ready for you, Miss Hattie. He waited to find you and ain't never looked back. Sean Francis is a devout man, he always has been. He loves God, and he loves his woman. He was seventeen when he lost Winnie to the fever and twenty-five when Eliza Melling was thrown from her horse. He was thirty that Halloween he purged her pictures, then spent two more years clearing his mind in preparation for loving you. Boys like him don't recuperate quickly from heartbreak."

"But why the destruction?"

"He never said, and I didn't ask, but he was changed that day from whatever happened Halloween night."

I set the pitcher of orange juice in the refrigerator and washed my hands.

"Why don't you freshen up. Your guests will be here soon."

"Thank you, Althea. I couldn't have pulled this together without you."

"You're a capable woman, Miss Hattie. Sean Francis is blessed to have you in his life. Don't worry so much about what you can't do and focus on what you can—and it's more than putting a fulfilled smile on that man's face."

I laughed and hung the apron. The doorbell rang as I reached the hall. A deliveryman stood on the veranda with two vases of flowers—one hydrangeas and the other my favorite roses.

"Special delivery, ma'am."

"Thank you." I took the white and pink roses with my name on the card dangling from it, setting them on the coffee table before coming back for the second.

"Have a good day!"

The second envelope said LUCILLE MELLING, so I set the hydrangeas on the dining room table—only realizing then that I hadn't prepared a centerpiece. I rushed back to the parlor to check my card.

Inside the little envelope was an inscription in my husband's own hand:

For my wife and lover,

Thank you for beautifying my life.

The scent of the roses was intoxicating, and I wanted them to fill our bedroom with the aroma of romance. I carried the vase upstairs and cleared a corner of the table beside my reading chair for them as the rumble of Sean's automobile pulled into the yard. I checked my reflection in the full-length mirror. The blue dress was unrumpled, my hair still in the loose chignon. After seeing how becoming the shorter hairstyle was on Ethelwynne, I hoped to get mine cut soon, especially with the summer heat creeping higher.

I checked to make sure the beds were neatly made before descending the stairs. Sean was in the parlor, looking around the space.

"I brought them to our bedroom," I told him as I hugged him. "Thank you for the roses."

"I'm glad you liked them. And Lucy's look lovely on the dining table. Alex mentioned her birthday was next Saturday, so I thought we'd start the week properly for her. I didn't want you getting the wrong idea about me buying another woman flowers."

"Where's Brandon?"

"He's riding from the cathedral with the Mellings."

"What?" I jerked out of Sean's arms.

"It's all right, Hattie. Alex is a safe driver now."

"*Now?*"

"He's been sober for years. He only wrecked automobiles when drunk."

"That's not helping me feel better about the safety of our son." There was no stopping the alarm in my tone.

"Brandon will be fine. Lucy is sitting in the backseat with him and Asher. You know I wouldn't put our son in danger."

I scoffed, then Sean's hands were around me and his infuriating grin lowering to my face. Just before his lips reached mine, an automobile honked.

"That better be them," I said as I stepped out of his reach.

When I got to the veranda, Alexander had the back door of his automobile open. Brandon and towheaded Asher sprang out like little devils, then Alexander helped his wife onto the lawn. Lucy was blonde and nearly as voluptuous as I was with an unrestrained figure. She wore a red lace dress that appeared to be a tea gown from the beginning of the decade. Though dated, it gave her a classic look that dared anyone to challenge her fashion sense.

Sean released Buster into the yard and slung an arm low about my waist.

"Welcome!" He called to them. "I was just talking Hattie out of her worry. Brandon has never ridden with anyone else before. I'm doubly glad you're here safely. I was afraid I'd be banished to the guest room if something happened."

Alexander grinned as he climbed the steps with Lucy on his arm. "All is well, Hattie. No need to punish your husband—unless he likes that."

Sean laughed, gave his friend a one-armed hug, and kissed Lucy's cheek. "I'm glad you're here, Lucy. Allow me to show you inside. Do you realize I've only had one dance with you? Alex simply won't share you at masquerades. All I had was a few minutes on New Year's Eve over a decade ago. If we put on a record after brunch, would you dance with me?"

"If there's time."

Alexander and I stayed out a moment to call for the boys. Like a sheep dog, Buster chased them to the porch.

"Come see my room!" Brandon said to Asher.

"He's a delightful boy, Hattie. You and Sean are blessed."

I stepped through the vestibule with Alexander. "Thank you. Asher seems just as precocious."

The boys were already tramping around upstairs, but Lucy and Sean were in the dining room. She finished reading her card and gazed at Sean with a bright smile.

"Thank you, Sean." She looked to me. "And you, Hattie. Alex, they got me flowers as an early birthday present."

"Sean has always been thoughtful." Alexander looked to me. "And Hattie is a gem."

"Come see the upstairs. We need to check on the boys anyway. The house, Lucy," Sean said as he took her arm, "is a George B. Rogers design like yours."

Alexander took my arm and we followed them up the stairs. "He loves a new audience," I whispered.

He nodded, watching every move of his wife's body as she swayed up the stairs. Sean took the Mellings on to the guest room, and I stopped in Brandon's room. The boys were playing on the rocking horse, Buster on the foot of the bed. I waited in the hall for the tour to come by, and followed them into the master suite.

"Dear God!" Alexander went directly for the fireplace. "Wherever did you find this?"

"Eliza gave it to me that Christmas. I had it hanging in my old bedroom for years. Hattie found it when we moved and thought it would be a fun addition to our boudoir, but didn't know who it was."

Alexander looked back at me with awe. "Hattie, you're a saint."

"It's not a complete nude like her sketches were," Sean said with a smile.

"It's enough." Alexander touched the signature in the corner of the painting. "Eliza Rose, my dear, devious sister. She left the world too soon."

Lucy came to my side. "Eliza's talent was unprecedented, but Sean is much better off with you," she whispered. "No one can fault your good eye for art—or men."

We shared a smile, then she spoke louder. "I love all the bookcases. Every bedroom should be full of books and love."

Sean went on to explain me having use of the den downstairs for my club, and I returned to Brandon's room. The boys had dumped all the blocks out of their bin and were in the process of building castles.

"Now here's a sight we know well—an active boy's room!" Alexander declared.

"Brunch should be ready," I said to Sean. "Allow me to go check while you help the boys wash."

During our meal, Lucy seemed to lose interest from time to time, but Sean played off Alexander's risqué humor like a moth to flame, and Brandon enjoyed every second with Asher.

After eating, Sean and Brandon sang "All Creatures of Our God and King" at the piano. Alexander joined them on the second verse, filling the space with his fine tenor. Not wanting to be left out, Asher stood with the men at the piano and did his best to sing along, but the three-year-old hadn't any natural musical abilities.

After waving our visitors off, Sean carried Brandon in for his nap, Buster following them up the stairs. The dining room was already cleared, so I went into the kitchen where Althea washed dishes.

"Everything was wonderful, Althea. Thank you for helping. Shall I assist with cleanup?"

"Of course not, Miss Hattie." She turned to me and winked. "You go see to Sean Francis."

I found Sean before the mantel in the master suite, gazing at Eliza's beguiling form.

"After spending this time with Alexander, I can finally imagine her antics."

His wide grin beckoned me to join him and his arms enfolded me. "You have no idea."

"Sean, what's wrong with Lucy?"

"What do you mean?"

"She would look happy and engaged, then it's like the light in her mind switches off and she's not there for several seconds or even minutes at a time."

"I think it's a coping mechanism, a way to protect herself when she's overwhelmed."

"But it was just us, not anything taxing."

"Hattie, she hardly leaves her house. Alex has told me she has episodes sometimes. She's emotionally fragile—something that runs in her Easton family. It's sad her life was spared from yellow fever only to be plagued with these troubles." He kissed me. "It's an honor that she came, and I wanted to shower her with pleasantries. That's why I bought the flowers. I saw her fading at the table, so I didn't push for a dance afterward like I wanted."

"She's nearly your type, isn't she?"

"Not anymore." He kissed down my neck, opening my buttons.

"I know you loved Eliza Melling. Why did you destroy her sketches?"

"How—"

"Althea told me you burned them Halloween night six years ago. What made you do it?"

He shook his head.

"Sean, I want to know."

"It's a bedtime story, best told in the dark."

I hurried around the room, closing the heavy drapes against the afternoon sun. Sean laughed and caught me around the waist. Once divested of our clothing, we climbed into bed and snuggled under the sheet, the counterpane kicked to the footboard as the ceiling fan whirled above us.

"I don't know if I was drunk or dreaming or if it really happened, but she came to me that night."

"Was one of your visions of death you've mentioned before?"

"No, it was different. I'd gone to the Halloween Flirts dance, and they'd reused many of the decorations Eliza had painted five years before. I also saw Darla and Henry together for the first time, so I had her artwork and young love on my mind."

I trailed my fingers over his chest, taking in every word he said.

"I'd drunk at the party, then more when I got home to numb my loneliness. When I made it to my bedroom, she stepped out of her painting and teased me. Eliza could tell I hadn't taken a lover since she died—and I hadn't until I met you. She relished in that because she realized the power she had over me. She ribbed me verbally and then showed me all I used to enjoy."

"She was beautiful."

Sean nodded. "And she knew it. She claimed to have met Winifred and was jealous, declaring I chose her because she favored Winnie."

I smiled and shifted closer. "You have a definite type, and I'm happy I fit your preference."

"That's one of the differences between you and her. You graciously acknowledge my taste while she spurned it when she believed it was set without thought to *her*. That night, she taunted my devotion—following me through the house—and told me how she used her wiles in such a way that purged my remaining love for her in seconds." His hands squeezed and caressed my body as a means to comfort himself, and I gloried in his intimate use of me. "The ghost or vision of Eliza, whichever she was, told me she'd cheated on me— with a man of the cloth, no less. And she laughed about it. No shame, no remorse, only pride in her cleverness. And it was true. I asked Alex about it. He didn't know until the end, but Eliza had strung me along the whole time."

"Oh, Sean. How stupid could she be to spurn you?"

"Eliza took advantage of my trust and I raged. I smashed the framed sketches and burned the pictures. I was ready to destroy the painting as well, but she stopped me. She knew I'd regret it, no matter my anger. She was right. These past weeks, it's been a reminder that my youthful follies, no matter their pleasure or pain, have led me to this life with you. Eliza in the painting looks behind her and lusts for what's there." Hot hands on my hips pulled me to him. "You, Hattie Violet Spunner, are my present and future. My perfect match for which I have no need to look back. I walked through Hell to find you and now we have Heaven."

Our lips met with desire, our bodies adding to the fervor. There was no equal to our rhythm, for no two lovers shared what we did in that moment. The humidity of the summer afternoon, the dim privacy of our bed, the forge between two hearts raised fifteen hundred miles apart, and the perfection of our union.

***

I had a full house of the regulars at my Monday club meeting, minus Faith. Jessica informed me of Faith's parents' refusal to allow her to come though she was graduated—all because of Mr. Gentry.

Kate was bold enough to show her face though I was certain she was the cause of Mr. Gentry's interfering. I didn't give her the attention she probably expected, but coolly greeted her.

Ethelwynne had arrived with Marie, saying they'd spent the day together at the Marleys' house. Pleased to see her happy without having been with Nathan, I offered the science room to them whenever they wished during their summer break.

As hurricane season was upon us, Darla thought it best to discuss the tropical storms since Melissa and I had never experienced a major one. Darla's descriptions of the howling winds that ripped roofs off houses and the rising waters that washed acres of sand away from her childhood home on Dauphin Island caused a cold fear to wrap my body in chill bumps despite the afternoon heat. I didn't wish to hear more about destruction and its aftermath, so I sought a way out.

"What of the birds and insects?" I asked. "Does their population suffer?"

"There are less squirrels in our yard after a hurricane," Ethelwynne remarked and the others agreed.

"I wonder if pollination is enhanced or thwarted from these major storms. What do you all think?" I asked, pleased when the conversation was safely away from deadly winds and rain.

Halfway through my spontaneous lecture about pollination, I felt the ladies' attention shift away from me. I knew I was in trouble when Kate eyed someone in the doorway. Sean posed in the entrance—arms across his chest, broad leg stance, and a pompous grin. When our eyes met, he bit his lip.

"Sorry for the interruption, ladies. I need to do a bit of preparation for a case tomorrow, but I had to stop and give my regards. Hearing Hattie speak of pollination is stimulating. I'll have to focus extra hard to get my work done at my desk."

He winked and all the ladies from Grace Anne's tea party laughed. Ethelwynne and Marie blushed.

"You insufferable—"

He was instantaneously before me and kissed my lips. "Punish me later if you must."

I pinched his buttocks before he could get away, causing more laughter from the ladies as he retreated for the stairs.

"How do you do it?" Jessica asked me.

"Do what?"

"Keep such an agreeable relationship with your husband," Mary Margaret replied. "It's no easy feat."

"First off, Sean is one of the most amiable men I've ever met, even when he's posturing like a peacock."

"A man with a form like that is always welcome to posture before me." Kate smirked around her glass of iced-tea.

Grace Anne giggled. "He's a darling, Hattie. I love it when your family joins us for supper. John shouldn't get all the fun when they meet at the men's club."

"The best advice I can give is to be open and honest with your man about *everything*. When you're upset with him, let him know. Don't make him guess what he did wrong. It's doubly the same when he pleases you—whether with a gift, how he plays with the baby, or in the bedroom—tell him immediately. Let there be no question you appreciate his gestures and he'll do them all the more. Men really are simple creatures. Don't complicate things."

Not long after, my guests began to leave. Kate didn't linger, which I was grateful for. After walking to the veranda with the Marley sisters and Ethelwynne, I took my young friend's hand.

"Is all well at home, Winnie?"

She shrugged. "No worse since Mama made a scene before Nathan Thursday afternoon."

"Come here whenever you like—by yourself, with Marie, or even Nathan."

"Thank you, Hattie." She hugged me and followed the others to where they waited for her by the gate.

I waved goodbye in the heavy evening air, and went inside as Althea brought Brandon up the stairs for his bath.

"Check the back porch," she called to me.

I continued through the living hall to the door that led directly to the porch. Sean was on his new rowing machine in nothing but a pair of boxing shorts, back glistening with sweat as his muscles worked under the strain. His leg muscles bulged as he braced himself against the plank at the base. His form was graceful as he flowed back and forth, the gears rolling as the tension cords pulled.

"If you insist on watching me, dearest, will you come around so I might have a view of you at the same time?"

I laughed and took a seat on one of the bottom steps of the exterior stairs within the screened porch. "You mesmerize me."

"You've seen me like this before." He gritted his teeth and grunted through several more pulls before slowing his speed.

"And you're as magnificent as ever."

"As are you, my buxom lady. Come ride with me." He raised his brows. "Straddle my lap and wrap your legs about my waist."

I looked to the open kitchen door where Pearl and her helper worked.

"Naughty woman. You're wearing undies, aren't you?"

"Of course I am."

"Then this will be a test ride. Come see how we'd fit together at this angle."

I shook my head. "Not while the help is here, but I'll look forward to it at another time."

"Pity." His lips went into his favorite pout as he further slowed. "I don't know why I'm bothering to slow my heart rate when all I want to do is chase you up those stairs."

"Is that all you ever think about?" I teased.

"Blame your stimulating talk on pollination." He came to a gliding stop and stood.

I drank in the sight of him dripping with perspiration, muscles twitching from use. My mouth salivated and my center responded with a flood of its own. Gripping the banister, I pulled myself up and hurried to the second floor, Sean close behind me.

He shut the bedroom door and cornered me by the closet. "How do you want me, Hattie?"

I answered his leering smile with one of my own. "However you want to take me, Sean. I know it'll be great."

Our coupling within the closet was beyond anything in recent days. He was already hot, and I was soon as sweaty. The extra layer of walls around us dropped any inhibitions I might have had with Althea in the next room as he took me against the mirror on the closed door. The cool smoothness was tantalizing in contact with our burning skin and the sight deliciously wicked. In the moment I cried with release, I knew what would replace the painting across from our bed and vowed to shop for it first thing in the morning.

Twenty

I spent most of the first days of summer break at Marie's house. Not only did her home have two pianos, but there was also an organ. We often did duets with the pianos—something Mrs. Marley was happy to hear since her other daughters weren't about—but she also instructed me in the basics of playing the organ. I took noon dinner with Marie and her mother three days in a row, then Mama complained and made me stay home until after eating lunch Thursday. I helped with the washing and other cleaning chores that morning and the next.

When I was gathering laundry from the lines at eleven-thirty on Friday, Nathan called to me from the front gate. I pointed him to the driveway on the north side of the property. We met there, and I led him into the old stable.

"Winnie, I've missed you." He kissed my cheek.

I ran my fingers down the sleeve of his suit jacket, smiling. "How's the internship going?"

"Great, so far. I'm working with Uncle Benjamin in the office, but I'll be sent out with a reporter next week. I have tomorrow off and was hoping we could do something together."

"I'd love to, but what? I'll need to ask my parents' permission."

"Another day at Monroe Park would be wonderful or a moving picture show in the afternoon, but I'd be happy sitting on the back stoop with you, Winnie." He caressed my hand he held. "I'll do whatever you're allowed to."

"Could you telephone after supper tonight, around eight? I'll ask my father when he gets home and see what he says."

"Please make sure your mother doesn't answer the telephone."

I laughed. "I'll do my best."

Nathan's forehead went to mine. "I've missed your smile. The clean scent of your hair."

Tilting my face, I met his lips with mine. He tasted me as he had the week before, arms holding me close. I could have stayed like that for hours, but I broke away.

"You need to go before Mama sees you. Give me a minute to get back to the clothesline and then go out the driveway gate."

He kissed me again and held my hand a moment before releasing me. "I'll talk to you tonight, Winnie."

When I carried the basket of dry bath towels inside a minute later, Mama waited like a hawk in the kitchen.

"Is everything okay?"

"Yes, Mama. I'll bring these upstairs."

"Velvet barked and you were gone for longer than usual."

I lifted a shoulder and continued toward the hall. It wasn't a lie because she didn't ask me directly, but I still felt guilty.

Andrew was at the store with Papa for the day, so Mama and I had an awkward luncheon of cold sandwiches and fruit slices. Before I could get away from the kitchen table, she stopped me.

"Winnie, I'm sorry if I've come across as harsh recently, but I'm worried about you."

"I'm good, Mama. For the first time in my life I have places besides home I feel comfortable and a wider circle of friends."

"But these friends, they're mostly above you on the societal ladder. Not to mention all those progressive women. They'll look down on you."

"They don't, Mama. The Spunners never have, and Marie is sweet, even if a maid makes her bed and her mother doesn't cook a thing. There have never been girls my age in our congregation. I was always stuck with the boys and then alienated the past few years. It's wonderful to be talking with Nathan again."

"What could you possibly have to talk about?"

I smiled, thinking of the random conversations on our walks. "We speak of literature. He's a reader like me and writes poetry. He's going to be a reporter, Mama. He worked on the school paper the past two years, and he's interning with his uncle at The Daily Register over the summer. He's smart—almost top of his class—and gentle and sweet."

Rather than joining me in my bliss, my mother's frown deepened.

"He's been a gentleman, Mama," I whispered. "You don't need to worry."

"Sean was sweet and charming too, but he was capable of much mischief." She shook her head. "I'll always worry about you, Winnie. The dangers of men and war are just the beginning of all that can destroy a young woman."

"I understand, Mama, but I need to experience things on my own." Velvet came to my side and rested her chin on my lap. I rubbed her ears before looking back at my mother. "Would you walk with me to the Marleys' house? Meet Marie's mother and see how nice she is. She's raised two other daughters already. Maybe she could put you at ease about my coming-of-age."

She shook her head. "I'd have nothing in common with her."

"They're new money, Mama, not an old Mobile family. There's nothing to be shy about. You're just as well-mannered as her. One of the Marley sisters died from yellow fever the same year you lost your uncle and cousin. I think you'd like Mrs. Marley if you gave her a chance. And seeing their beautiful pianos and organ would be worth the walk, wouldn't it?"

Perhaps she felt the pleading tone in my voice as a cry for peace between us, for she bowed her head and paused. I nudged Velvet off my lap and discreetly pointed her toward Mama. Once her dog was beside her, she reached down to pet the dark fur and offered a little smile. "I'll walk over with you, Winnie. Should I change my dress?"

"Mrs. Marley wears similar blouses and skirts. She isn't pretentious, but leave your apron at home."

My mother wanted to fix her hair so I was instructed to brush mine as well. I pulled back the sides with silver combs. When I met my mother in the downstairs hall, she actually smiled.

"Those look even prettier with your bob than they did with the length." Mama threw her arms about me. Her slight frame and height felt tiny to me for the first time. "Please don't hate me, Ethelwynne. I want what's best for you. I want you safe and happy."

"I know you do, Mama, and I love you, but I need space to grow." I hugged her back.

We left Velvet in the yard and walked three blocks west on Palmetto to Roper Street. On the far side of the quiet intersection, sitting nobly on a slight rise of the lush lawn, was the Marley's two-story abode. The lattice work on the top half of the windows gave it a cottage appearance, but the four square posts across the front supported a large porch roof that was too big to be cozy—though the back porch where Marie and I often sat was small and comfortable.

The maid answered our knock.

"Welcome, Miss Winnie. Ma'am." She curtsied. "Come to the parlor, and I'll let Miss Marie know you're here."

"And Mrs. Marley, please. My mother would like to say hello."

"Of course."

Mama gaped at the wide openings into the parlor and formal dining rooms on either side of the hall that created a large flow across the front of the house. I took her hand and led her to a striped settee in the pink parlor. Pointing to the gleaming grand piano in the corner, I leaned close.

"The tone is exceptional," I whispered. "The other one is in the next room. The organ is in the back hall, but with the acoustics of the stairwell, you can hear it all over the house."

Marie skipped into the room and came to an abrupt halt upon seeing my mother.

"Mrs. Graves, what a surprise!"

"I hope it's not an intrusion, but I thought it was time for me to introduce myself to your mother since Winnie is spending so much time here."

"We're happy to have you, Mrs. Graves. Would you like tea or lemonade?"

"No, thank you."

Round face beaming beneath her halo of silvery blonde hair, Mrs. Marley crossed to my mother, who stood. "Why, you must be Mrs. Graves! My stars, how did a tiny woman like you have such a girl like Winnie?"

"She takes after her father's side of the family. Both my children do."

"Bless your heart. I always say a woman needs claim on at least one child through looks. It isn't fair for us to struggle with them, and then have nothing to show for it years down the road. My Sadie favors me most, but it was Ester who would have been my mirror image, God rest her soul."

"I'm sorry for your loss."

"Nearly twenty years now, but that yellow jack epidemic sometimes feels like it was yesterday. God saw fit to send another angel to me after that loss, so I have Marie. Do sit down."

We all did and Mama continued. "I lost my uncle and closest cousin in 'ninety-seven as well."

"Such a terrible time, those months were. To this day, I cannot stand the sight of yellow fabric." Mrs. Marley clasped her hands together. "But enough of that, I'm glad you're here, Mrs. Graves. Winnie has been a delight this week. I hope you'll allow her to keep coming and join us yourself as well. Luncheon, Wednesday. Would that work?"

"Yes, I believe it would. Thank you."

"I want the girls to keep practicing. They sound lovely together. I think we should host a recital of some kind for them. Invite our friends and allow the girls to show off their skills. What do you think?"

"That would be excellent!" Marie grabbed my hand. "Don't you think so, Winnie?"

"Winnie doesn't perform," Mama said.

"I have at supper parties."

"A few extra family members or friends don't count." My mother straightened in the chair and looked about the grand space. "This would be completely different."

I thought of playing for Nathan—my personal audience of one. "I would like the opportunity."

"And you shall have it, if your mother agrees," Mrs. Marley said with a smile. "A show is something all girls should experience— a night to shine. Her piano tutor would be welcome to attend as well."

"Winnie hasn't had an instructor the last two years, since her teacher retired." Mama looked to me and sighed. "But a small reception would be fine."

Marie squealed. "We could do it by the end of the month, couldn't we?"

"That's just a week," Mrs. Marley said. "We need to give guests some notice, and there's The Fourth of July holiday to consider."

"Mother, please? Especially with the holiday, don't make us wait until after even if the recital is smaller. If it's successful, we could do a larger one next season."

Mrs. Marley retrieved her appointment book from an inlaid secretary desk in the corner. "If you girls can manage to make the invitations tomorrow morning, we could have a messenger deliver them directly for hosting the recital next Saturday, July first. An afternoon recital would be less formal and hopefully not cut into people's supper plans that might already be scheduled. Would that be all right?"

"Yes!" Marie looked to me. "We'll draw up the guest list and draft the invitation now, then work on the invitations all morning."

The excitement fell as I thought of my hopes for a day with Nathan being spurned. Then I realized the chosen date was our typical supper with the Spunners.

"I'll call a courier service and speak to the cook about a menu and hiring on a few more girls to help out next weekend."

Mama looked to Mrs. Marley. "Is there anything I could do?"

"Do advise me, Mrs. Graves. What is your preference between lemonade and punch? Or should we have both?"

"Come on, Winnie. Let's make our guest list." Marie took my hand.

"Don't forget your sisters and grandparents, as well as the Inge and Stuart families."

"Yes, Mother. Is there anyone you wish to especially invite, Mrs. Graves?"

"Winnie will know best."

Marie led me up to her room. There was a lovely cross breeze through the screened windows as the shutters were open on all three exterior walls.

"Isn't this exciting?" She flopped onto her four-poster bed set dramatically in the center of the room beneath a ceiling fan.

"It is, but I was hoping to spend time with Nathan tomorrow. I'm going to talk to my father when he gets home, and Nathan is supposed to telephone after supper to set the details."

"Then invite him here. You can go on with him to wherever after we complete the invitations. Maybe he would even help. You said he's a writer. Is his penmanship good?"

"It is, but—"

"Oh, do. He's so handsome and my mother always laments the lack of boys about. Grace Anne and Sadie both had flocks of boys around in their youth. Mother worries I'm too shy. She even started laying hints that if I want to join a convent, I'd have her blessing."

"You want to be a nun?"

"No, but I know little of the male species beyond my father and brothers-in-law. John is a dear, as you know from Grace Anne's tea, but Sadie's Richard can't be bothered with anything about me. Being around Nathan will be educational."

By the time we returned downstairs with a completed guest list and sample invitation, my mother was gone.

Mrs. Marley looked over the list, smiling. "I'm so glad to see the Spunners included. Marie is enjoying her time at Hattie's club. Who is Nathan Paterson?"

"Winnie's beau. I've told her to invite him to help with the invitations in the morning." Marie giggled.

Mrs. Marley raised her plucked eyebrows. "I didn't know you had a beau, Winnie. I'll be happy to meet him tomorrow. I'll have the cook prepare a luncheon for the three of you."

I smiled and hoped my talk with Papa about my plans for tomorrow would go well.

***

Nathan's telephone call came through at five minutes after eight.

"Good evening, Winnie," he said in response to my hello. "What did your parents say about us getting together tomorrow?"

"Marie's mother is hosting a piano recital for us next Saturday afternoon, so we need to prepare the invitations. Marie wants you to come over to her house with me in the morning and help us write them or at least keep us company while we do. Papa said you're welcome to come here and walk me over."

"I'd be happy to, Winnie. And afterward?"

"I'm sorry, but my parents don't think a moving picture show is appropriate for us to attend, nor do they want us traveling to Monroe Park without a chaperone."

"Then we'll stay nearby. We could sit in Washington Square or your backyard. What time shall I arrive in the morning?"

"Is eight-thirty all right?"

"It can't come soon enough. I'll see you in twelve hours. Goodnight, Winnie."

When I hung the telephone and went for the door, I came face to face with my mother.

"Will you want to host him for dinner tomorrow?" Mama asked.

"Mrs. Marley is providing a luncheon for us, but thank you. If we're not done by then, we will be soon after. The invitations are supposed to be collected for delivery at two o'clock."

"Then I'll expect you home by ten after two."

"Yes, Mama. Goodnight." I hugged her in passing, then went to the parlor to tell my father goodnight.

I prepared for bed but had difficulty falling asleep. At ten, I moved to my hammock on the sleeping porch, but thoughts of Nathan kept me alert for another hour.

The sound of a mockingbird fight woke me in the morning.

I chose a plaid skirt that was full but lightweight and a pale blue blouse that I tucked neatly into the buttoned waistband. Hair brushed, I secured it with my combs as I had the afternoon before.

Downstairs smelled of bacon and pancakes. Papa and Andrew were already at kitchen table, pouring syrup on their hotcakes.

"Do you think Nathan will be here when I get back from the store with Papa?" Andrew asked me when I took my chair. "I want to ask his opinion on my pitch."

"I hope so. I'm sure he'll be happy to play catch for a bit if he is."

My brother smiled and took a forkful of food.

"Nathan is welcome to visit as long as he wishes today," Papa declared.

Mama looked to him from the stove where she turned another skillet full of pancakes.

"If Winnie wishes to invite Nathan to stay for supper," Papa said, "I'll be happy to have him at our table."

"Thank you, Papa. And Mama, I'll give you plenty of notice if he does stay."

She nodded, lips tight. Papa finished eating and went to her at the sink. With an arm around her, he lifted her chin with his other hand and kissed her until she smiled.

"Go on," she whispered. "I'll be fine."

"Drew and I will be back about three. Have a good day, Merri." Papa looked to me. "I know you will, Winnie."

I waited to eat until my mother sat down. She was silent several minutes.

"I'm frying chicken tonight. There will be plenty if Nathan wishes to join us, though your father might not get a late night snack from the ice box if he does."

I laughed. "Papa might rethink his hospitality if his stomach is slighted."

"Boys Nathan's age tend to eat a lot. During those weeks Sean often visited, he would eat one of Althea's meals and then join us here for another one. He was seventeen—the same as Nathan." She gazed at me as though seeing her past. Resting her elbows on the table, she then put her face in her hands. "I was nineteen and should have known better, but no one ever warned me."

"I have an understanding of things, Mama, and Nathan is respectful, as I've told you before."

"But we don't always think logically. Emotions make us all into rash creatures of carnal desires. Thinking it won't happen to you is the worst thing you can do. It lowers your guard because you believe yourself—and the other—to be above it. That's weakness."

"I'll be diligent, Mama."

The doorbell rang while I helped clear the table.

"Do you want to say hello?" I asked.

She shook her head. "I'll see you both when you return from the Marleys."

I hurried through the house, signaled to Velvet to stay, and opened the front door with a smile.

"Hey there, Winnie."

"Good morning." I pulled the door closed behind me, leaving me inches in front of Nathan.

I straightened my shoulders, gaze darting between his blue eyes and lips. His eyes widened as much as his smile as his arm went around my waist. Even with his shirtsleeves rolled to his elbows, the white fabric clung to his neck and shoulders. His lips held the tang of salt, but I didn't mind. The sound of an approaching automobile parted us. Nathan pulled a folded piece of paper from his pant pocket and tucked it into the right front patch pocket of my skirt.

"Don't read it yet," he said with a grin. "Wait until later, when you have a few moments to savor it."

I nodded and took his hand as we went down the front walk. It was the third poem from Nathan and the heat from it practically burned my thigh through the blue and green fabric. Surely there could be no better feeling than reading a poem written for you— knowing you inspired someone to create. My smile grew with each step.

As we crossed Roper Street, I gave him a warning. "Mrs. Marley is liable to pounce, but she's kind."

"I'd face a den of lions to be with you, Winnie." He knocked on the door, and held tight to my hand while we waited.

"Good morning, Miss Winnie. Sir," the maid said. "Come into the parlor."

"Thank you." We passed through the wide front door.

"You came!" Marie squealed and took Nathan's free arm. "Are you here to entertain or help?"

"Both, I hope." His smile was soft as he studied Marie. The thought that he'd end up liking Marie more than me shot through my heart. But just as quickly, it disappeared for Nathan gazed at me with as much tenderness as I could wish. "I'll do whatever is needed to keep beside Winnie all day."

"Y'all are so romantic."

Mrs. Marley breezed into the room in a floral print sundress. "Don't tell me this handsome young man is your beau, Winnie Graves! Welcome, welcome."

Marie took a firm hold on Nathan's right hand and tugged him forward. "Mother, this is Nathan Paterson. He's here to help and entertain us."

"Nathan, I'm so glad to meet you. Do stay and dine with us. I'm having a picnic prepared for the three of you to enjoy after all your work on the invitations."

"I would enjoy that, Mrs. Marley. Thank you for your hospitality."

We spent the next two hours in the small breakfast room, French doors open to the back porch for the breeze. Nathan—though he personally copied three invitations beautifully—was more of a hindrance than a help. Marie chatted with him between each of her invitations, and I couldn't help but look to him often. The way he concentrated as he wrote, purposely keeping his hand lifted off the embossed parchment so he wouldn't smudge the blue ink with the side of his palm, made me yearn to read his latest poem still tucked in my pocket. But it had to wait.

Twenty-one

Directly after lunch Saturday, Sean drove us downtown for the purpose of getting haircuts for both him and Brandon. I had already received a cut earlier in the week and now sported a Castle bob shorter than Ethelwynne's.

Sean and Brandon disappeared into the barber shop, and I into the bookstore.

"Good afternoon, Mrs. Spunner," the shopkeeper called. "I've held back two books that came in this week for you to see before I place them out."

"Thank you, Mr. Lloyd." I lifted my sunhat and used it to fan my face as I approached the front desk. "What manner of science is it this time?"

"Astronomy and chemistry."

"Wonderful!" I happily accepted the books and settled in the chair closest the door.

Opening the astronomy title first, I thought again of my plans of adding a telescope to our home laboratory, but I had yet to broach the topic with Sean. He'd been so generous in furnishing my science room I didn't want to ask for more. Seeing the charts of the night sky caused a rush of gooseflesh up my arms. I settled back and began reading the introduction.

"Mommy!" Brandon threw his arms about my knees what seemed like minutes later.

When I looked up from the book, his adorable flap of hair was significantly shorter, the back neatly trimmed.

"Brandon, you look extra handsome." I set the book aside and pulled him onto my lap, kissing his cheek. He tucked into my shoulder. The rush of love I felt between his form and mine was electric—my mothering instinct pure and strong. "Someone is ready for nap time."

"So am I." Sean bit his lip as my eyes lifted to his, then held out a hand. "Give me the books. I'll purchase them and we can be on our way."

"I'm not sure I want both of them. I haven't even opened the second."

"Brandon and I stood here and watched you for *two minutes* before I set him loose. You were so absorbed in the book you never looked up or even seemed to breathe." He extended his hand. "What has you so captivated?"

"Astronomy. I've always wanted a telescope." I handed him the books, then accepted his help in standing while I held Brandon. Sean kissed me once I was on my feet, and I fingered his smooth face with my free hand. He'd kept his sideburns long, but his hair was trimmed and his beard and mustache gone. His boyish dimples on full display once more. "You're extra handsome as well."

"I'm glad you think so." He winked and then turned for the counter. "We'll take both, Mr. Lloyd."

Sean paid the bill, and we returned to the automobile. Brandon was asleep in my arms within a few blocks.

"The new books will keep you busy for a while."

"Not too busy for you." We shared a smile before his attentions were back on the road.

Sean laid a hand on my thigh as he drove, gently kneading. Once we were parked in the garage, he turned off the motor and took my mouth in a hard kiss.

"Must you always seduce me, Hattie?"

Eyebrows raised, I met his golden stare. "I've done nothing but sit here with our son."

"Some primitive part of you is crying for me—I can sense it. Damn that fertility goddess and her captivating allure." He peppered kisses across my face, slowing as he made his way down my neck. "If you get the doors, I'll carry Brandon to bed."

I led the way with my books, holding the back screen open, then the door to the living hall. Before I could follow Sean upstairs, the doorbell rang. I set my books down and accepted an envelope from a courier with thanks. It was addressed to "Mr. and Mrs. Sean Spunner," so I opened the seal. An invitation for next Saturday afternoon was inside—a piano recital for Ethelwynne and Marie at the Marleys' home. Pleased that my young friends had something exciting to look forward to, I took the invitation upstairs to show Sean.

He was down to his trousers before the new mirror above the mantel in the master suite, studying his shave and cut. The gilt frame hung from a wire off the large hook at an angle, offering a view of the mirror's reflection from the bed directly across from it. Sean had admired the ingenious setup, and both of us had enjoyed it the past several days while Eliza Melling's portrait had been transferred to the guest room.

"You're impeccable, Sean Francis Spunner. I've missed your face beneath the beard."

His grin crinkled the corners of his eyes. "Who was at the door?"

"Delivery." I handed him the invitation, wanting to kiss each dimple but settling for planting my lips on the biggest dent on his right cheek.

I undressed to my foundation garments while he read. He held the paper a full arms' length away to be able to see without glasses. If he wasn't so vain, he'd be wearing spectacles all the time.

"Ethelwynne's first recital! I'll be pleased for the three of us to go see her."

"Sean, the envelope was addressed to the two of us, not the family."

He set the invitation on the mantel and turned to me. "Ethelwynne wouldn't exclude Brandon."

"She's not hosting, the Marleys are."

"But you'll ask her when she comes Monday."

"I don't think would be right to bring him, even if he is allowed."

"He loves music and—"

"And he's extremely vocal about it. We can't expect a boy his age to know how to bridle his passions during something like a recital."

"He does well during Mass with the organ music."

"The cathedral creates awe and reverence. A private residence full of familiar faces will not hush him. I refuse to allow Brandon to be a nuisance at the event."

Sean scowled at me. "You would deny my son this opportunity?"

"No, I'm choosing to delay *our* son's first foray into a society gathering with more than two families in attendance until he has reached an appropriate developmental age to ensure the best possible experience for all those around him."

His frown morphed into a smile and he snatched me around the waist. "You've convinced me, Hattie. That's the power of your scientific mind. I'll arrange Althea to watch Brandon next Saturday. Would you like to make a full outing of it and go to dinner while we're alone?"

"I'd enjoy a bit of private time with you."

Sean's hands moved over my back. "Speaking of privacy, we have that now."

His mouth met mine with a sensual heat. My tongue trailed over his chipped tooth before tasting more as his questing touch stroked my breasts. Desire urged us toward the bed, Sean shedding his pants on the way.

"I had an idea while at the barber shop," he said once we were cuddled on the pillows. "The space is narrower than this room, but the walls are covered in mirrors so you can see the back of your head easily while they're working. How about more mirrors in here?"

I motioned to the one across from us, seeing my arm wave in the reflection. "This isn't enough?"

"It's opened ideas for new possibilities. While I was being shaved, I remembered reading about courtesans and the like who covered their boudoir walls and ceilings with mirrors."

"Ceilings?" I gazed at the expanse above us.

Sean straddled my hips. "Rather than needing to be propped on the pillows to see the mirror across from us, the one on the bottom would have a spectacular view of the one on top."

The rhythm of his grinding against me had me breathless with expectation. I gripped his buttocks through the fabric of his drawers as I arched into him.

"You could watch my flexing muscles as well as feel them—a scientific study of the body in motion during procreation. And I would relish the sight of your splayed hips and poetic curves as I explored your hot depths."

I smiled. "You've nearly convinced me, but I wouldn't want mirrors on the ceiling for everyone to see when we give a house tour."

Lips pursed, he pressed his loins into mine in just the right spot to make me feel the awakening his loving always produced. "I'll think of something."

"I'm sure you will, my debauched genius."

The next morning, I woke before the sun from an impassioned dream. The air was humid and no breeze fluttered the sheer drapes. Sean had stripped down to nothing during the night and his firm thigh was against my backside. His body heat soaked through the thin cotton nightgown as the whirl of the ceiling fan circled above us.

Thinking of nothing but the image of our coupling from my dream, I wiggled out of my clothes. I paused, hand hovering over his nakedness. This was our last day of abstinence, but I didn't want to wait. Darla had called it a safety day—just in case the woman ovulated slightly behind schedule. I knew the risk, but gazing upon my husband's form, I craved him with base desire, proving I was not always able to deny my urges.

He woke to my rhythmic touch, and then I involved my mouth. Sean moaned, hand fisting my hair. When I kissed my way to his neck, there was a playful struggle for dominance to rule the moment. He allowed me to win, assisting in my drive for satisfaction with his practiced ways. Seeing me on the edge, he took control and I watched his broad shoulders in the mirror over the mantel.

"Good morning, Hattie." Sean collapsed beside me. "That was an unexpected way to wake."

"Too much for you, old man?"

"Never!" He was on his knees, looking down on me, in an instant. "I'll take everything you've got and give you more."

"I love to hear that almost as much as I love experiencing it in action." I trailed my hands over his arms, taming the dark hairs. "Worshipping your flesh is heavenly."

He dropped next to me, hugging me to him with arms and legs. "What a way to start the Sabbath."

"You can be my religion, Saint Francis."

"No blasphemy before breakfast, dearest." He kissed me on the lips, and I sought to deepen it but he stilled. "I wasn't supposed to enter you until tomorrow. Hattie, I'm—"

I kissed him to quiet his agitation. "I wanted it, Sean. I needed you, body and soul."

"And if a baby comes from our union?"

"Then the child will be most blessed, along with Brandon." I snuggled closer. "We have too much love not to share."

The tension left his body in a rush and was replaced with glowing warmth. "God knows I love you, Hattie. Everything we share brings me joy."

We lay together until Brandon stirred in the next room. Then, we set about washing and dressing for the day with a quiet calm. Even Brandon was subdued, making me think he could feel the peace between me and Sean. Peace in the fact that whatever happened with our family—within my body—it would be well. I would no longer deny love or delay our passion.

I cooked eggs and toast for breakfast. Sean briefly flipped through the newspaper while we ate and nearly choked.

When his coughing subsided, I looked to him.

"There's an editorial about Mrs. Spunner's science club— covering the scandalous sexual topics discussed along with a side of Darwinism."

"Truly?" I got up to look over his shoulder.

"This has Kate Stuart's name all over it."

"I guess she had to try something else since Mr. Gentry's assault had little effect, yet she still attends."

"What shall you do, Hattie?"

"Nothing whatever. It would only feed her delusions of self-importance."

"You maybe be right, dearest."

I soon kissed Sean and Brandon goodbye when they left for Mass. The astronomy book kept me company on the veranda while they were gone. When they returned, we enjoyed a simple luncheon, piano antics, and nap time. Despite the heat, we all piled on the master bed, me between the two I loved most on this earth.

Late afternoon, we took a leisurely stroll to the Davenports' house. Brandon ran about their backyard with Louisa and Bethany while the adults sat on a double glider swing under the magnolia tree. The oldest Davenport daughter lounged in their screened back porch watching over sleeping Junior while she read.

"Are you writing a response to that anonymous letter in the editorial section about your risqué science club?" Freddy asked me.

"I'm ignoring it," I said.

"There was nothing anonymous about the note. It had Kate Stuart's hand written all over it," Sean said as caressed my knee to the rhythm of the swing. "I warned Hattie about Kate's venom, but she refuses to close her doors to anyone wishing to join the meetings."

"Melissa enjoys them, but I hope it doesn't come back to haunt you," Freddy said.

"Did y'all reply to Bart about his invitation for the island trip?" Sean asked. Bartholomew, with the help of Darla Adams, had planned an excursion to Dauphin Island for Ethelwynne as an early birthday present. Her seventeenth birthday was August third, so she shouldn't suspect anything a month early.

"I spoke to Mr. Graves on the telephone Friday," Melissa said. "Freddy and I will be attending the piano recital on July first, and the whole family will go on the Dauphin Island excursion on the third."

"You aren't bringing Junior to the recital?" Sean questioned.

"We'll be leaving him and Louisa with the Mellings," she replied. "They're just around the corner and it's already the older girls' weekend to be with Lucy."

I captured and squeezed Sean's hand. "I told you it was no place for small children."

"Yes, dearest." He stood on the swing's platform, and looked to his pocket watch. "We should head home in a few minutes so we can bathe Brandon before supper."

"I'll see you tomorrow," I told Melissa. "And Freddy, it will be lovely to see you next weekend."

"Likewise, Hattie." He kissed my cheek. "I look forward to meeting some of these club members you've collected."

***

Monday afternoon, I took Ethelwynne aside while Marie filled her refreshment plate.

"Winnie, is Nathan attending the recital?"

She nodded and smiled, looking more mature than she did even a week ago.

"Warn him about Sean. I'm trying to talk sense into him, but I'm afraid he might say something ridiculous to Nathan in a show of protection. He's already telephoned his uncle to make sure he was in good standing."

"I'm flattered he's gone to that trouble, but Nathan is—"

"A gentleman, I know. But Sean tends to think he knows about *all* young gentlemen, and he isn't impressed with what that means."

I noticed the blush color her cheeks and realized the young couple must have shared some intimacies. With her upbringing, it could have been as innocent as the hand holding and kisses on the cheek I'd witnessed, though it was probably more.

"Sean has no right to question Nathan," she whispered. "My father has known him since he was knee-high."

"I know, Winnie. I'll keep reminding him of his place."

Once everyone assembled, I announced there would be no club meeting next Monday.

"You aren't quitting are you?" Grace Anne asked. "That editorial in the newspaper has me fielding questions as it's known I attend."

"No, I'll never stop the meetings." I sent a brief icy glare at Kate to drive point my home. "The Fourth of July is the following day and many people have family plans. I don't want to intrude on those over a long holiday weekend."

We discussed climate—everything from farming and gardening to the weather's effect on wildlife and human behavior. Melissa shared about her travels abroad in different seasons and how the cultures in different parts of the world were shaped by temperatures.

"In the grand scheme of things, I think we can all safely agree that for a sub-tropical climate like Mobile, society has us wearing too many layers of clothing to be comfortable," Melissa said as she sat with her skirt pulled to her knees, stocking-less legs on display and her shirt still half unbuttoned from when she's nursed Junior. "What do fashion designers in New York, Paris, or London know about humidity like this? Absolutely nothing."

Kate eyed the display of pale skin. "And did you dress like a native when you traveled?"

"When it was appropriate, yes. I've worn sarongs and kimonos, for example, when in an area for a prolonged amount of time or if I was invited to a traditional ceremony where it is respectful to do so. Most of my time in Africa was spent on safaris and expeditions so I wore the traditional garb of adventuring white folks—khaki and white, though I wore a split skirt or trousers rather than a skirt."

Grace Anne gasped and Mary Margaret fluttered her fan faster.

"It saved me considerable distress when I had to climb a tree to escape a charging hippopotamus," Melissa explained.

"I'll be happy to have half the adventures you have," Jessica said with a sigh.

The conversation wound down and the group dispersed earlier than typical because of the stifling heat.

When Sean arrived a few minutes before six, he looked disappointed to see an empty house. Upon hearing the reason, he found an immediate cure.

"I'll purchase a few more oscillating fans. That should keep you ladies comfortable. And at night, we can set them on the tables in our bedroom. A cool breeze on naked flesh is divine in summer." He led me to the parlor and we sat on the sofa together. "Is Brandon already in the bath?"

I nodded. "He was filthy when Horatio and Louisa left."

"What did they do?"

"Mud pies—and Louisa was in a white dress."

"Poor Melissa," he said with an amused smile.

"I offered to allow her to bathe Louisa here, but she took her home to deal with the mess." I rested my head against his shoulder. "I feel guilty for having Althea do most of the labor with Brandon when Melissa has no one."

"She has her husband. Freddy is the most hands-on father I know. He lived alone with his oldest girls for two years before he remarried. Lucy watched the girls during the day, but he did everything else."

"He's a great man, as are you—as long as you don't embarrass Winnie at her recital by threatening Nathan Paterson."

Sean leaned away and frowned.

"Her father is aware of their relationship. He knows Nathan and has set the parameters of their courting. There is no need for you to get aggressive. You'll only embarrass Winnie and possibly yourself."

"Do I humiliate you?"

"Not usually," I said with a sly smile. "But you've come close with your bragging about our bedroom practices."

"*I have?*" He was on his feet, staring down at me. "I merely displayed your passion marks at the gym. Who's the one who bragged about climaxing on my desk at a ladies' tea?"

I burst out laughing and Sean leaned over me, a hand on the back of the sofa.

"You think that's funny?"

"I find it delightful." I smirked and walked my fingers down his shirt from neck to waist. "Seeing you pretend to be upset about me sharing that is almost as enjoyable as the act itself."

Sean flashed his giant grin. "And you, Hattie, are delightfully naughty."

Twenty-two

Eight o'clock Thursday morning, I hung out the wash in hopes of it drying before the typical afternoon rain showers arrived. During the humid months, Mama washed things five days a week so the daily items were fewer. We often had to outsmart the storms and move the laundry to finish drying on the porch—which could take a day or more in the damp air.

My blue cotton dress moved in the breeze about my bare calves, the dewy grass cool beneath my feet, as I pinned one of my cotton slips on the line. Velvet lay under the satsuma trees. When her ears went up, I signaled to the dog to stay quiet and looked to the fence. Nathan waved from between two azalea bushes. I ran over without thinking, Velvet silent at my heels.

"Hey, Winnie." Nathan quickly kissed my cheek when I stopped close to the iron divider.

"Morning, Nathan. How's your internship going?"

"Great! We attended a trial yesterday, and I had to write an article on it, same as the reporter I was shadowing. We turned them into the editorial staff without our names on them, and they chose mine to go to print. Be sure to read my first city newspaper article today."

"That's wonderful! Did they add your name to it?"

"They sure did. And guess what?" He gripped one of the *fleur-de-lis* finials on the fence.

"What?"

"I got write about your friend. The case was one of Sean Spunner's."

"Did he win?"

"You'll have to read to find out."

I laughed and rested my hand on his. "I will, Nathan, and I'm happy for you."

"It's a momentous week for both of us. I want to see you before your recital, Winnie. I can't take any time off during the day today or tomorrow, but I could come over late. Maybe we could meet in the stable for a little while." His voice dropped and he wrapped his fingers through mine. "I miss our conversations. Could you get away at ten o'clock tonight?"

I nodded. "Wait outside the gate until you see me in the yard. Velvet will bark if she hears someone enter the property at night. I'll need to signal to her before I leave the house.

"I'll be near the driveway."

"And I promise to read your article as soon as I finish hanging the wash."

"It's on page three." He slowly removed his hand from mine. "I'll be thinking of you."

I watched him cross Palmetto Street.

By the time I returned to the clothesline, Mama was there. "What was Nathan doing here so early?"

I grabbed her hand. "He stopped to tell me about his article. He's in the newspaper today, page three! He covered one of Sean's trials yesterday. I need to read it when I finish hanging the laundry."

She smiled and touched my cheek. "Go on, I'll finish up here."

"Thank you!"

I dashed inside and found the paper at Papa's place at the kitchen table. In the parlor, I collapsed in the chair nearest the window to use the natural light to read by.

Nathan had written a riveting account of the case—a seafood warehouse worker suing his former employer for lost wages over his broken leg, which happened when a ladder broke beneath him after half a dozen employees complained about the state of it for weeks before the accident. With Nathan's vivid prose, I could imagine Sean pacing before the jury, quoting *The Jungle* by Upton Sinclair as he laid out the plight of not only his client but another worker who had lost his life several months before due to neglected conditions on the property and a dozen more injured that year alone. Sean won the case including eight hundred dollars for his client—of which he would get a handsome percent—and mandatory repairs to be completed on the warehouse property within the month.

"Well?" my mother asked as Velvet followed her into the room.

"It's wonderful! Could I please clip it? I'd like to begin a scrapbook of Nathan's articles."

"Wait until after your father gets home, in case he doesn't finish reading the paper at the store."

"Thank you. It's a thrilling read. Nathan makes Sean sound like a hero." I handed her the paper. "I need to practice my songs if you don't mind."

"Go ahead, Winnie." Mama sat in her chair with the newspaper as I situated myself on the piano bench.

Marie and I were each doing two solos and then a duet for the finale. I'd chosen a Beethoven sonata and also "Precious Savior, Dear Redeemer" from *The Baptist Hymn and Praise Book*, which I would also sing. Our finale was Mozart's "Sonata in D Major for Two Pianos." We had been practicing on our respected pianos from different rooms at the Marley house, but when I arrived today, the pianos were supposed to be set and tuned for the recital so we could practice often the next two days.

I began with Beethoven, then my arrangement of the Mozart piece. Mama stared at the wall, the paper still in her hand, as I played. She looked to be deep in thought, and I imagined she fantasized about Sean charming the jury. When I started on the hymn, she shook herself out of her stupor and watched me play and sing.

"That was wonderful," Mama said when I finished. "Do stand and practice your curtsey."

I did, feeling silly but smiling whole-heartedly.

"What time are you expected at the Marleys?"

"Not until noon. The pianos are being moved and tuned this morning."

"Would you like a new dress, Winnie? There's time to go shopping."

"You bought me a new one a few weeks ago, Mama."

"Yes, but your first recital is important."

"I'd like that. Thank you."

"Would you prefer to go to Gayfer's or back to Mademoiselle Bisset's shop?"

"Mademoiselle Bisset's would be lovely, if we can afford it."

"I may be overly frugal, but we can more than afford another dress for you from there. Let's be on our way as soon as possible."

***

After our trip to the dress shop, we picked up my sheet music from home, and Mama saw me to the Marleys' house. Mrs. Marley invited her to inspect the arrangement. Both grand pianos were in the hall, six feet from the front door. They were opposite each other, the complimentary curves of their bodies nestling together like spooning lovers. Marie sat at the one on to the left with her back to the parlor. Mine was to the right, nearest the dining room.

"Isn't it wonderful? And they sound terrific." Marie pounded out a few chords from her Mozart score. "Now join me, Winnie."

I happily sat on the bench and arranged the pages for our duet.

"From the top?" Marie asked.

I nodded and our mothers settled in the parlor. Marie counted us down and we played with less than a dozen mistakes during the whole duet.

"You both will do splendidly when the time comes," Mrs. Marley said. "For now, we eat. You must join us, Merritt. There is a bounteous luncheon spread that's more than the three of us will be able to eat."

"All right, but I can't stay more than an hour. Winnie's dress is being delivered this afternoon."

Over lunch, our mothers discussed clothing for the recital. Mama described my new dress and as soon as we were done eating, they trouped to Marie's room to compare the two Marie had in mind to get her opinion on which would complement mine. Mrs. Marley wanted me to bring my gown when I came over in the morning so we could do several dress rehearsals.

After Mama left, the afternoon passed quickly with our practice. While Marie worked on her solos, I daydreamed about Nathan. When I did mine, she read *Jane Eyre* on the settee in the parlor. We worked until three o'clock, and then took a tea and cookie break on the back porch. Finally out of earshot from Mrs. Marley, I shared my secret.

"When Nathan stopped by this morning," I whispered, "he told me we wanted to spend time together before the recital."

"When do you get to see him?"

"We're meeting in the stable tonight."

Marie's pale eyes lit with intrigue. "How romantic! I bet he's going to kiss you."

"He kissed my cheek this morning."

"I mean *really* kiss you."

I hadn't told Marie or anyone about the few private kisses I'd shared with Nathan, but I nodded because I wanted to experience them again. "I hope so."

"His article was thrilling. Jessica and Faith were correct about his writing." She had read it as soon as I announced it over our luncheon. "And Mr. Spunner is spectacular. I look forward to seeing him Saturday. Hattie is lucky to have a smart and romantic husband. I think Nathan would be like that too."

We practiced our duet continuously the next hour, followed by our solos.

"I'm done for the day!" Marie declared.

The clock read almost five. "I need to get home, but I'll see you in the morning."

"With your dress and the news about tonight, Winnie."

The air was gray and heavy with summer, the breeze from that morning gone, but I walked as though all was light and beautiful. Coming up the sidewalk on the final block, I noticed the hem of a brown skirt behind the bushes near the driveway gate.

Christina was half hidden, eyes red from tears.

"It's about time." She huffed when I stopped before her. "Your mother said you'd be home at half-past four!"

"I had no idea you were waiting for me. You could have come to Marie's house to fetch me."

She snorted and tossed her ponytail behind her shoulder. "As if I'd grovel to see you in front of that little snot."

"Don't call my friend names." Christina had won me over when she stood up for me three years back, but I'd been blind to her foul attitude toward others because it wasn't directed at me. I could no longer overlook her vile streak. "Why are you here?"

She sucked in a breath and let it out in exasperation. "I thought you'd like to hear that you were right, Ethelwynne Graves. Go ahead and gloat because my life is over."

I had been blind to her dramatics as well, but no more. I rolled my eyes and shifted impatiently.

"He's gone! Luke left town for good and I'll never see him again." Her lips quivered, and then she wailed like a woman in mourning.

Unable to say I was sad to hear the news—because it pleased me to no end—I opened the gate and led her to the stable. She plopped down on a bale of straw and wiped her nose with the hem of her skirt.

"It was your Mr. Spunner, once again." She sniffed.

"What?" Mouth open, I stared down at her.

"Luke has been playing at a couple different clubs to earn money. He heard some fancy gentleman was asking around for him. Mr. Spunner found him at work Wednesday night." Her brown eyes narrowed with anger. "Luke never did anything to anyone but that lawyer cornered him during his break, along with some other man he called Doctor. Mr. Spunner told lies about people in Atlanta looking for Luke and that the local authorities had been alerted to his villainy—whatever that's supposed to mean!"

"I can tell you exactly what it means." I also knew the doctor was John Woodslow, as he and Sean often met at their men's club for supper on Wednesday nights.

Christina ignored my remark. "When I met Luke at our spot, I explained Mr. Spunner was a friend of yours, and his uncle had thought he'd seen him harassing you the other week."

"True on both accounts."

"Nonsense! Luke and I both blame you for him having to leave."

"Why would he need to leave town if he's innocent?"

"And stay here to be bothered by the law?"

"Because he's guilty. And if he loves you, why didn't he take you with him? You're out of school now. Last you told me, he'd spoken of marriage."

"He said he'd send for me when he's settled." She sounded unsure, but I couldn't stop badgering.

"Settled where?"

"I don't know! I went to his boarding house this morning to talk to him, but the man said Luke had left before dawn and owed him two week's rent, and if I knew where he was, I better remind him of the bill he skipped out on. Oh, I'll never see him again!"

Sobs. The tears and frustrations I knew would come to my friend as soon as I laid eyes on Luke poured out of her. I settled beside Christina, arm around her shaking shoulders. She cried for several minutes.

Just as her tears were slowing, Andrew ran into the stable. "Mama's looking for you, Winnie."

"Tell her I'm helping Christina, but I'll be in soon."

"Did she fall? Do you need bandages or anything?"

"No, Drew, but thank you."

He ran out and Christina again wiped at her face with her skirt.

"Would you like something to drink?" I asked.

She shook her head. "I should go so you don't get in trouble for being late."

"There's a piano recital Saturday afternoon at the Marleys' house. Marie and I are performing. It starts at two, if you'd like to come."

"I don't feel like attending parties." She looked at me with half disdain and half jealousy. "You've turned into a prissy society doll."

I stood to get away from her, pushing my glasses up my nose. "I'm still the same person, Christina. You'd know that if you didn't allow Luke to steal your brains and infect you with his lies."

I moved toward the driveway. She followed with a begrudging pace, and I opened the gate wide enough for her to leave, clanging it behind her.

Inside, I quickly washed and then gathered dishes to set the dining room table for supper.

"Is Christina all right?" Mama asked from the stove. Her hair was piled in a bun at the top of her head, sleeves rolled above her elbows as she tried to stay comfortable in the heat.

"No, she realized the man she was in love with didn't love her in return." I took the pile of plates to the dining room.

"Are you reconciled?" Mama asked when I returned for silverware. I never confided in her about Christina's behavior, but she knew I wasn't spending time with her any more.

"I don't think we ever will be."

She asked nothing more.

Papa came home and took me by both shoulders when I came out of the dining room. "Nathan is a clever one, isn't he?"

"Yes, Papa." Pleased one of my parents recognized his talents, I kissed his cheek. "It was a wonderful article."

"It was all the men could talk about," he said as he went to the study and lit a cigarette. "Nothing was said about the front page war news—it was the tidbit from the local court scene that captured everyone's attention. I'm sure Sean is eating up the fame the article gave him."

I perched on the corner chair. "Be sure to tell Nathan at the recital."

He nodded and exhaled a smoke ring. "Did your mother finally take you shopping for a new dress?"

"Finally?"

"I told her as soon as I heard about the recital to take you for something new." He narrowed his eyes and took a deep drag. "She never told you, did she?"

"Not until this morning. We went to Mademoiselle Bisset's."

"Stubborn Merri." Papa sighed, looked toward the kitchen, and then removed his glasses. "She does things in her own time and way, Winnie. I'm sorry you had to wait. It's nothing that needed alterations, is it?"

"No, Mademoiselle says I have a model figure in height and width, that I should always be able to buy off the racks. It's a pretty frock with handkerchief hems and flounces, but not too fussy."

He pinched the bridge of his nose and closed his eyes a moment. "I look forward to seeing it at the recital. Send Drew to me if you happen across him before supper is ready."

"Yes, Papa. I hope you feel better."

"It's just a headache, Winnie, but I'm feeling my forty-two years this summer, that's for sure."

Supper was subdued, except for Andrew's excited prattle about baseball games.

"I'm going to bathe and go to bed," Papa said when Mama presented a lemon ice box pie.

"After dessert?" she asked.

He smiled. "I wouldn't miss a slice of your pie for anything."

Mama dished everyone an equal serving though Andrew kept eyeing the half still in the pie dish. "You may have a second piece after your first is gone, Drew."

Papa stood when he finished. Stopping beside Mama, he leaned down to kiss her. "Still the best lemon pie, Merri. Thank you." He looked to me and Andrew. "Good night, ruffians. Do whatever your mother asks of you this evening. I'll see you two in the morning."

We said our goodnights and then Andrew helped himself to another serving of pie.

"Drew," Mama said as she stood, "I want you to help Winnie clear the table and clean the kitchen. I'm going up for the night as well."

"Does anyone want to use the sleeping porch?" I asked.

"Not tonight, Winnie," Mama replied.

"Maybe," Drew said in between mouthfuls.

I spent the next few minutes trying to think of the best way to dissuade my brother from sleeping on my porch that night. When we were clearing dishes, he solved the issue himself.

"I'm gonna bring Velvet into my room if Mama shut her out of their bedroom. She always looks lonely when that happens. I'd rather her be on my bed than on the porch floor."

When we were done in the kitchen and the house secured, Velvet was sprawled on the hall floor before the closed door. Andrew still hadn't realized that Mama's dog shut out of our parents' room meant they were being intimate.

"I'll bring her into my room while you get ready for bed," I told him.

Velvet came when signaled and happily jumped onto the extra single bed in my room. I sat at my dressing table and brushed my hair until it shone. Staring at my reflection, I tried to see the enchantress within my soft smile and deep eyes Nathan mentioned in his last poem. It looked as though I'd grown prettier in the past month. Did Nathan's attentions make me so or was I only seeing myself through his eyes? Which was the illusion?

"You better not start being one of those primping girls just because you have a beau," Andrew said from the open door.

"Have you ever heard boys say anything about me?"

"Sure, but I threaten to retch all over them if they keep up their chatter."

"That's disgusting, Drew. It's a wonder you have any friends." I went to the door. "What have you heard?"

He rolled his eyes. "That you aren't bad—for a girl. Boys like that you understand baseball and aren't ruffles and bows all the time."

That was hardly the stuff of poems, but before I could question, he continued.

"The older boys always said your glasses kept you from being a true beauty."

That wasn't flattering either, but I elbowed his arm—as close to hugging as we did in recent years. "Thanks for telling me."

He shrugged. "Come on, Velvet."

"Are you going to sleep?"

"I'm gonna read. Jacob loaned me his copy of the newest Tom Swift book."

My dress Nathan admired that morning was a tad limp from the heat of the day. I hung it from a fixture in the bathroom while I showered, hoping it would perk up a bit so I could reuse it for our meeting. It would be easier to explain to my parents if I were caught that I pulled on the day's dress to check something than if I was in a new outfit, and I could easily wear my sleeveless summer nightgown under it.

When I emerged from the bathroom, Andrew was still reading, his door ajar and side table light on. His ceiling fan moved the curtains as much as the breeze outside did. I brought the hanger with my blue dress out to the sleeping porch to continue to air it and forced myself to sit. Rather than reading—for I couldn't concentrate—I fantasied about Nathan but thoughts of poor Christina kept breaking through. She had practically ruined my final week at school and Luke had shaken my faith in men, but the fact that she interrupted my daydreams was another atrocity altogether.

The hour passed with me hyper alert to each person leaving their room to use the bathroom, the creak of the floorboards when they returned, and the click of Andrew's lamp when he finally turned it off at nine-thirty. I folded my dress over my arm, turned off my light, allowed my eyes to adjust to the dark, and shimmied through the partially open door into the hall.

In the faint light, I saw Velvet raise her head on Andrew's bed.

I gave her the hand signals to stay and be quiet.

Barefoot, I crept down the stairs, avoiding the squeaky steps. I buttoned on my dress over my nightgown and snuck out the back door, carefully closing the spring-mounted screen so it wouldn't snap.

I rushed across the lawn, hair bouncing in freedom while I experienced my first act of rebellion—escaping the house without permission to meet a boy at night. I felt completely desirable with the forbidden act and smiled with the thrill of the sensation. I stopped in the open stable.

Dim lantern in hand, Nathan silently climbed over the fence and moved along the shadows of the bushes to meet me in the doorway. Without speaking, he put his arm around my waist and led me next to Papa's automobile. He took off my glasses and set them on the hood of the car beside the lantern, which he turned up slightly.

"So they don't fog over," he whispered as his fingers caressed my cheek.

"Do you like me better without them?"

His face was slightly fuzzy without my spectacles, but I saw his smile. "I like you no matter what, Winnie Graves."

Nathan's lips were on mine a second later, both arms holding me close. I leaned fully against him, not shying from contact as our tongues touched. Running a hand through his wave of blond hair, I followed the curve of his skull. He trailed my hips with both hands, tracing the arch of my backside with his firm touch.

Overwhelmed with the contact, I leaned back. He kissed down my neck.

"Your taste is like the morning dew—pure, sweet, and fresh."

"Will that be in your next poem?"

"Maybe." He took my hands into his, shifting a few inches away. "I love being with you, Winnie."

"And I with you." I led him to the stall where Velvet had kept her puppies. It was swept clean and a blanket was thrown over the partition. "We could use the blanket and sit on the floor."

Nathan shook out the blanket and spread it in the empty stall. We sat cross-legged, facing each other. After a quick kiss, we were holding hands once more.

"Your article was thrilling." My voice was soft. "I could have read dozens more like that."

"Uncle Benjamin said the paper received nearly fifty letters and telephone calls about it. He wants me to turn in at least one article a week the rest of summer."

"I've already clipped today's. I'm going to start a scrapbook of them. It will have to be big if I include everything from the school newspaper next year."

"And what of you? Are you ready for the recital?"

I sighed. "I never knew a duet could be so tricky."

"You'll do well. I look forward to hearing you play."

I leaned toward him too quickly and lost my balance. He caught me, but we fell—him on his side and me on top of him. Laughing, he turned onto his back and looked up. My mouth lowered to his and my legs spread to straddle him. We kissed, his hands roaming my back, until I cuddled along Nathan's left side, resting my head on his shoulder.

His left arm held me tight and his lips brushed my forehead. "These last few weeks have been the best in my life. I love you, Winnie."

I clung to him, fisting his shirt in my hand that was over his heart. I couldn't say the words, I could only feel his warm body beside mine—closer than ever. The rush his declaration gave me collided with the peace I felt in his presence, creating a storm of emotions as my body, heart, and soul tried to make sense of it all.

His hand moved up to my shoulder, which tucked me even closer at the chest. "I know you care for me, but don't feel you have to tell me what I just told you. I'll be with you as long as you'll have me, Winnie. There's no rush."

My hand relaxed, smoothing his shirt I'd wrinkled. I kept it resting over his heart but jerked when something nudged the bottom of my bare foot.

A dark figured towered above us over the half-wall. At the same moment I recognized bare-chested Papa with his shotgun in both arms, Velvet licked my face. Nathan must have seen him too, for we sat up as one.

"Was there no other option for you two to meet? I don't recall forbidding anything, though after this, I might need to."

"Mr. Graves!" Nathan got to his feet and offered a hand, pulling me up. "I'm sorry, it was my idea. We've both had full schedules this week, and I wanted to spend a few quiet minutes talking."

"And it never occurred to enquirer about a post-supper call at the front door in which you could have sat respectfully in the parlor rather than lying on the stable floor?" Papa shifted the shotgun to one hand and rested it against his shoulder.

"No, sir."

"Then you're less intelligent than I gave you credit for." Papa turned to me. "Say goodbye to Nathan, Winnie."

"It was wonderful to spend time with you." I held Nathan's hand and kissed his cheek. "I'll see you at the recital."

"And not before." Papa's voice was gruff for a man wearing only his trousers. "Wait in the yard, Winnie, and don't forget your glasses."

I collected my spectacles from the hood of the automobile and slid them on, looking back at the stall where Nathan shook out the blanket and refolded it.

"You've got a sharp mind in that head of yours," Papa told him as I exited. "I'll have to assume you're addle-brained about my daughter to try something like this. You'll find me a reasonable man, so ask permission to see her next time. But if I ever catch you horizontal with my daughter again, I'll shoot your ass full of birdshot. Do you understand?"

"Yes, Mr. Graves."

I waited in the driveway, worried over Papa's threat. Nathan exited first, giving me a sheepish grin before he went over the fence with his lantern as silently as he'd arrived.

Then Papa was beside me. "I won't tell your mother about this, but I need to know if he did anything improper."

"No, Papa."

"Good. But if he ever does, you kick him in the groin like I told you or do that escape trick you learned from Sean. Now let's hope your mother stays asleep when we go inside."

Twenty-three

The hum of a party spilled from the open windows as Sean led me up the front walk of the Marleys' house at exactly two o'clock. We'd had a lovely noon dinner at an Italian restaurant, and my sleeveless lavender gown was miraculously unspotted from it. The dress swirled about my calves as we climbed the porch steps. It coordinated with Sean's dove gray seersucker suit, and his bowtie was the exact shade as my ensemble, securing the visual to all who saw us that we were united.

Merritt was the first person who laid eyes on us when we walked through the door. She had on her orange gown from Mademoiselle Bisset's shop, but with a lacy cream chemise beneath that modestly covered her chest.

"Hattie and I are pleased to see Ethelwynne's first recital." Sean gave Merritt a rare, reserved smile.

"I thought with seeing each other here this afternoon, it would take the place of our supper tonight. Not to mention the trip on Monday. Is that all right with you?"

"If that's your wish, Merri." He gently lifted her hand and brought his lips to the back of it. "You know I'm always your humble servant."

I merely smiled and lifted the fan that hung from my wrist and fluttered it like a Southern Belle before Sean led me to Mr. and Mrs. Marley.

"Mr. and Mrs. Spunner, how good of you to come. Marie adores those science meetings, no matter that fuss was made about them in the editorial. I'm glad she met Winnie there. She's been great company to Marie."

"Thank you, Mrs. Marley. I've enjoyed having Marie and all your daughters to the club. You have a delightful family."

Sadie approached the group, a dark-haired young man at her side. "Hello, Sean and Hattie. It's good to see you both. Hattie, this is my husband, Richard Beauchamp. Richie, this is the infamous Hattie Spunner." She giggled.

I inclined my head and smiled in greeting.

"Have you heard their news?" Mrs. Marley asked. "Richard and Sadie are to welcome their first child this winter."

"Congratulations, Richard." Sean shook his hand. "Fatherhood is a blessing like no other."

When we moved to the next group within the parlor, I was pleased to get a moment with Darla and her husband, Henry. He worked with Freddy Davenport, and I hadn't caught sight of Melissa.

"Have you seen Melissa and Freddy?" I asked them.

"Junior is under the weather, and Melissa didn't want to leave him. Hopefully he'll be back to rights before Monday's trip," Darla said. "It would be disappointing for them to miss the island."

I nodded. "We're all looking forward to it."

"Hattie, darling!" John Woodslow slung an arm about my waist and kissed my cheek. "You're looking prettier than ever."

"Hands off, Woodslow. She's all mine," Sean said.

"I just want to thank her for what she's done for Gracie." He kissed my cheek once more and then slapped Sean's shoulder. "I hope you know how lucky you are with this catch, Spunner."

"It wasn't luck." Sean straightened. "Hattie is a blessing."

John laughed. "At least you aren't claiming your prowess like Melling would."

As John sauntered away, Nathan wandered into the room, looking over the paintings on the walls rather than the inhabitants.

Sean took my elbow and nodded in the young man's direction. "That's him, isn't it?"

"Yes, but don't—"

He broke from me and strutted to the mantel where Nathan studied the landscape painting above it.

"Allow me to formally introduce myself to the man who painted a flattering portrait of me in court with his eloquent words." Sean bowed and offered Nathan his hand. "Sean Spunner, at your service, Mr. Paterson. I believe you're already acquainted with my wife, Hattie."

Nathan shook Sean's hand. "Yes, I am, but it's wonderful to meet you, Mr. Spunner. I've only attended court one other time, but I don't see how a finer performance could have been displayed on behalf of the innocent."

Sean gave a smug smile, arrogance on full display, and I pitied Nathan for what would spew from my husband next. "You have a firm grasp on words for one so young, Mr. Paterson. Did you know my quotes were from *The Jungle,* or did you have to ask someone?"

"I recognized them at once," he stammered and blushed under Sean's direct gaze, "though the senior reporter I was with had no idea what it was other than it wasn't Shakespeare."

"Is that so?" Sean raised his brow and struck once more. "Winnie is well-read too. I've been loaning her books from my collection since she was a little girl."

"Then I must thank you, Mr. Spunner. Literary talks with Winnie are some of my favorite times with her."

"I've known Ethelwynne since she was born and am very protective of her."

"I'm glad Winnie has people looking out for her, but Mr. Graves has already threatened me this week—not that it was needed." Nathan fidgeted with his tie.

"And what, pray tell, did the old man say?"

"He promised to shoot my ass full of birdshot if I do anything with Winnie," Nathan stated, his blush deepening.

Sean's full laugh rang out, turning heads. As though recognizing the sound, Ethelwynne came around the corner as quickly as decorum would allow. Looking lovely in a beige dress, tiered to best accent her figure, and trimmed in a golden color much like Sean's eyes. She looked like a wood sprite, earthy and calm.

"Hattie!" She hugged me and then looked to the men. "And Sean, I'm glad you met Nathan."

Sean hugged her and kissed her cheek. "Yes, you lovely creature. His intelligence is a great match for yours."

Ethelwynne smiled and took hold of Nathan's hand. "I'm happy you approve."

"Come with me, Sean," I said. "We need to find Grace Anne and say hello before the recital begins."

"Excuse us," he said as he tucked my arm around his. Leaning close, he whispered. "He out-witted me for a moment."

"You deserved it."

"Sean and Hattie!" Grace Anne, pretty in pink, leaned in to kiss each of us.

"We saw John a few minutes ago, and he praised Hattie to no end," Sean said with a wink.

"Dear Hattie—all the husbands of the science club women owe her much. You're extra gorgeous today. However do you accomplish it?"

Sean leaned closer. "An afterglow from lovemaking."

"Even after your wallflower years, that old cad is still in you. Don't deny it. Come get a good seat." Grace Anne led me to the area beside the stairs, Sean following. "You'll see Winnie well from here. The recital begins in five minutes."

"Thank you, Grace Anne."

Sean gallantly saw me to the armchair and stood behind it, helping me sit. I ignored my first thought that he believed me incapable of placing my rear on a seat directly behind me and reminded myself it was his chivalrous nature—how he was raised. Then he leaned over and whispered in my ear.

"I have the best view from here—straight down your cleavage." He kissed below my ear. "Will you be my supper date tonight?"

I smiled up at him. "I'd love to."

"I shall return before it begins." He squeezed my shoulder and went for the back of the house.

Bartholomew stopped by a moment later. "Merri just told me you weren't coming over for supper."

"Sean and I are going to have supper out instead. Althea is already watching Brandon today."

"I'm glad you're both here for this. It means a lot to Winnie." He joined his wife in the dining room—just out of sight from my chair.

Sean returned, leaving a caressing touch on my neck as he took his place behind me.

Mrs. Marley stood before the front door and rang a silver bell until the house quieted. "Thank you all for coming as my husband and I, along with Mr. and Mrs. Graves, present our daughters for your entertainment this fine afternoon. The recital will begin in a moment, if you would like to get comfortable."

The hum of chatter returned as people shifted closer to the pianos. I opened the fan on my wrist and waved it beneath my face to give a bit of a breeze in the stagnant hall. The view was great but at the expense of air flow.

Marie, dressed in a mauve gown, took the piano by the parlor. A smattering of applause sounded and she dipped her head in acknowledgement. Her piece began bold and fast.

"Tchaikovsky," Sean whispered.

The next few minutes were a filled with racing chords and Marie's dramatic facial expressions to match the tune. Afterward, the house filled with applause.

Marie returned to her bench as Ethelwynne approached the opposite piano. Her tune was softer than Marie's but equally complex.

Sean squeezed my shoulder. "A Beethoven sonata."

Ethelwynne did splendidly and glowed when she curtsied. She smiled toward where her parents were and to us, but her eyes lingered longest on Nathan.

"She's all grown up now," Sean lamented before Marie started on a ragtime tune that Sean said was Scott Joplin.

Several people tapped their feet, and Sadie and her husband started dancing which, based on Marie's shallow smile, created a bit of family drama between the sisters.

In direct contrast to the dance tune, Ethelwynne started on a hymn as soon as the clapping stopped. Not only did she play, she sang "Precious Savior, Dear Redeemer." Her sweet melody shrouded the house in a reverent hush. Even if the Catholic majority of the gathering was unfamiliar with the hymn, many were moved to tears as Ethelwynne sang. I used my fan to dry the moisture pricking at the corners of my eyes, and Nathan never looked away from the angelic figure at the piano.

Ethelwynne curtsied to a standing ovation at the completion of all three verses.

The finale was surprisingly a duet. Sean gave an audible gasp when the girls played in tandem. He was so mesmerized he didn't tell me the name of the composer. It was glorious to witness something I'd never seen before. The idea to have Marie and Ethelwynne discuss how the different tones and melodies worked together at a forthcoming club meeting crossed my mind but didn't stay. I could dwell on nothing but the miracle happening across two keyboards.

"What was it?" I asked over the ringing sound of clapping and whistling for another standing ovation.

"Mozart's 'Sonata in D Major for Two Pianos'," Sean practically shouted for me to hear him.

As the girls curtsied, their fathers each brought them a bunch of roses—Ethelwynne's pink and Marie's white, which complimented their dresses. During the rush of congratulations, the dining room table was laid with a fresh assortment of appetizers and drinks. Sean brought us around to pay our compliments to Marie and Ethelwynne, and then he filled a plate for us to share and poured two glasses of wine. Alabama was supposedly a dry state, but most Mobilians refused to give up their alcohol. Even Sean had a stash of several dozen bottles at home.

Halfway through our refreshments, Sean excused himself. I finished off the fruit salad and sipped at my white wine. Merritt strolled by and sneered at my glass but beyond her, I saw Bartholomew sling back a shot of something.

The post-recital chatter calmed and conversations returned to the typical remarks about weather, the help, and children home for the summer. I stared out the window, listening to it all but hearing nothing as my thoughts were on Sean's odd disappearance. He was usually attentive. Each minute without him felt like a betrayal.

"Are you all right, Hattie?" Marie asked. "Should I get John?"

I rapidly blinked to clear the fog that had drifted into my mind. "I'm well, thank you. And you did a terrific job. I was only wondering what was keeping Sean."

"I saw him on the telephone."

"I hope Brandon is all right," I replied.

"He looked happy, not upset," Marie said before continuing to the next group of guests.

Wine finished, I set my used plate and glass on the maid's tray when she came by and murmured my thanks. Hoping to find Sean, I wove through the crowded front rooms. At the refreshments, I helped myself to another glass of wine and walked aimlessly through the rooms.

Ethelwynne and Nathan were cozy together on the back parlor settee. The other guests were too involved in their own conversations to notice the blossom of young love in their midst as Nathan took her hand into his, fingers caressing.

"There you are!" Sean kissed me. "Are you ready to leave?"

I nodded and he brought me across the room to Ethelwynne.

"We enjoyed the recital, Winnie," he said. "Would you and Marie be willing to play for Brandon the next time you come over? He'd love to hear you, even if it couldn't be the duet."

"Of course." She smiled. "Though if Hattie can bring him here one day next week, we could do the duet."

"That would be terrific." Sean shook Nathan's hand. "Behave yourself, Mr. Paterson."

Before more could be said, I turned my husband around and nudged him toward the door.

"I love it when you're forceful."

After saying farewell to Mr. and Mrs. Marley, Sean whistled our way to the automobile and handed me inside.

"What is going on with you this afternoon?" I asked as soon as he sat behind the wheel.

His grin was huge, his amber eyes shining. "I'm pleased to have a day with my lovely wife."

I scooted across the leather seat until our sides touched. Fingers trailing the column of my neck, his mouth lowered to mine. Deep passion ruled the kiss.

"Look, Darla. The Spunners are going at it like a couple of reckless co-eds." Henry Adams knocked on the hood of the automobile.

Sean took his time ending our connection and then laughed. "Don't be jealous, Adams."

"Of you, old man? I've got my own wife, thank you very much." He laid a quick kiss on Darla. "We'll see you at Mass and first thing Monday morning."

Rather than turning homeward, Sean drove toward the city. Figuring we were on a pleasure ride, I enjoyed the architecture and people watching as we traveled all the way to the courthouse before turning north onto Royal Street. He parked in front of the Battle House and a footman opened the door for me.

Sean passed his automobile key and a dollar to the valet and offered his arm to me. Thinking he was bringing me to the Trellis Room to eat, I spoke. "I'm not hungry for supper."

"Good, because that's not what I have in mind."

A concierge met us in the lobby. "Mr. and Mrs. Spunner, we are happy to host you today."

"Thank you." Sean inclined his head. "Is everything ready for us?"

"Yes, Mr. Spunner." He snapped his fingers and a bellhop was immediately beside him. "Michael saw to everything. He will bring you to your room."

Room? In all our visits to the hotel for suppers and parties, we had never stayed in a room.

We rode the elevator to the fifth floor then followed the bellhop down a twisting corridor. Once opened, Sean looked inside the corner room, turned back to fist several dollars into the bellhop's hand, and accepted the key from him.

"That's all for now, Michael. Thank you."

The young man smiled as he hurried away and Sean caught my hand.

"Welcome to our next adventure, Hattie. It's all inspired by you, my lover, my wife."

On the table in the wallpapered room were two striped boxes from Mademoiselle Bisset's shop, a simple toiletry bag, a box of chocolates, two crystal flutes, and a bottle of decades old French wine from our house—given to us on our wedding day by Uncle Patrick. Sean always told me he was saving it for a special occasion, and I had expected it to be for an anniversary.

"How—"

"Don't worry about logistics, Hattie. Enjoy it."

He motioned further into the room, and I stared in puzzlement at the wooden backsides of tall furniture barricading the bed area. Moving closer, I recognized the backs of full-length dressing mirrors. They surround the double bed on all sides. The coverlet and top sheet had been folded down to the end, leaving an expanse of white sheets from pillows to footboard. The headboard had even been moved away from the wall to place three mirrors side-by-side behind it. A slim gap on either side of the bed to allow entrance into the space was all the opening the love nest held.

"Sean, I don't know what to say." I looked from the mirrored space to my husband.

"I've been obsessed with the thought since we spoke of mirrors the other week. And yes, there's a carpenter by the name of Paul Rollins working on a custom bed for us, but I wanted something to experience now. I remembered you lamented our travels have been long overdue. Today offered us the perfect time to take advantage of a clear social calendar and a caregiver for Brandon. Tonight is ours, Hattie, from this moment until checkout tomorrow.

Room service will bring whatever we wish, but we can go out for supper or dancing if you'd like."

"I don't wish to share you with anyone." I hugged him. "I don't ask to be spoiled, but it's amazing to experience."

"Let's see what Mademoiselle sent for you. I requested a boudoir ensemble and an evening gown, both with all the trimmings."

I went for the smaller box on top. Lifting the lid and removing the tissue paper, I gasped at the beauty of the finery.

"She never disappoints," Sean murmured as he lifted the skimpy blue gown by the thin straps, beneath which were a matching robe and mules. The lacework covered the bust area, trimming the empire waist line with a scalloped band. Blue silk fell from below the bust in a simple A-line that looked like it would end mid-thigh on me. He bit his lip before grinning. "Not too long to get in the way and loose enough to billow around us. Perfection!"

"I'd like to try it on."

"Just the gown—and don't ruin it with undies."

I retreated behind the dressing screen, tucked my shoes into the corner, and hung my lavender ensemble over the top of the partition as I undressed. The décolletage of the dressing gown was extremely low, allowing me to set my breasts so they were in a flirty position for Sean to enjoy. When I stepped back into the room, he was down to his underdrawers, his suit draped over an armchair. His eyes widened at the sight of me.

"Finish disrobing and bring me to our exploration chamber," I commanded him.

"With pleasure, dearest."

Tantalizing. The intimacy of seeing all of ourselves from different angles created a rush of forbidden pleasure as though we were voyeurs within our own marriage.

"You're so beautiful, Hattie. Being surrounded by you, I don't know where to look."

I captured his face with my hands. "Always return here if you're unsure. I love sharing a connection with you."

"Your eyes are extra blue with that gown and the white backdrop. It's like heaven in here." His hands were in my hair, fingers caressing my scalp as he pulled me closer.

His touch soon flowed south, grasping at my curves in such a way that caused me to undulate against him as our kiss deepened. The movement of our bodies was hypnotizing, the experience electric as I watched us shift between control and surrender during the next hour.

Gazing at his profile as I caught my breath, I couldn't help smiling. "You've taught me three things this afternoon, Sean Francis Spunner."

He propped onto his elbow and looked over at me. "What are those?"

"I'm more of a wanton than I thought, my tits are as amazing as you've always claimed, and you've got the tightest buttocks imaginable."

"Just wait until our bed is finished and you can view my backside from a canopy mirror."

Twenty-four

Monday morning, the sound of someone coming into my room roused me in the pre-dawn darkness.

"Winnie," Papa said, "you need to get dressed."

Immediately alert, I raised my head. "Is something wrong?"

"On the contrary—all is well. Wear something comfortable you don't mind getting dirty. And bring a good sun hat. We'll be traveling."

"Are we going to Grand Bay for the holiday? Do I need to pack for a few days?"

"No more questions, Winnie. Do as you're told and prepare for a day trip."

"Yes, Papa."

He turned into the light of the hall on his way to the stairs, and I saw the brown trousers and a plain button down shirt he typically wore to work around the house.

Before I made it to the bathroom, Andrew hurried out of his room fully dressed in knickers and a play shirt.

"Mornin' Winnie." He ran down the stairs, following the scent of bacon and pancakes that wafted from the kitchen.

I washed my face and dressed in a beige checkered dress that buttoned down the front and tied it with a navy sash.

Glasses on for the day, I looked over Nathan's second clipping from The Daily Register I had tucked in the corner of my mirror as I brushed my hair. I reread what appeared on The Social Side page the day before.

*Mr. and Mrs. Philip Marley and Mr. and Mrs.
Bartholomew Graves were pleased to welcome over
forty souls into the Marley house on the afternoon of
July 1. The two families presented their daughters,
Marie Marley and Ethelwynne Graves, in a rousing
piano recital that covered the classics as well as a hymn
and a popular tune from recent years. Miss Marley
was pretty in pink and Miss Graves elegant in an
earthy palette. The grand finale that stunned the lucky
audience was Mozart's "Sonata in D Major for Two
Pianos." With their talent and beauty, these young
ladies will go far.*

Smiling, I carried my wide brimmed straw hat downstairs and found my whole family at the kitchen table. Even my mother was sitting down to eat.

"Good morning," I said. "It smells wonderful, Mama."

Papa looked at the clock on the wall. "We've got about twenty minutes before we need to head out. It's already been blessed."

Andrew reached for more bacon, but Mama bopped his hand. "No second helpings until Winnie dishes up."

We ate in silence but the others kept exchanging furtive smiles.

"Could I help with the dishes, Mama?" I asked when I finished eating.

"I'm just rinsing them, but thank you."

Rinsing? My mother never left anything half done, but she rinsed the syrup from my plate and stacked it on top the others. Then she took Velvet's leash off the hook by the back door and fastened it onto the dog's collar.

"Velvet is coming?"

She nodded and signaled the dog to stay. She removed the apron and smoothed her white blouse and gray skirt. "I need to collect my hat and then I'll be ready."

I grabbed my hat too and joined Andrew in the yard. We waited for Papa to back the automobile out of the stable, then Mama motioned Velvet to jump in the front, sitting between her and Papa as I got into the back. Andrew held the gate open and joined me once the car was on the street.

Expecting to head west, I was surprised when Papa turned toward downtown. None of us were dressed for the city. Remembering his admonition not to question, I stayed silent though Andrew looked increasingly excited.

Papa parked the automobile near the river. Darla Adams stood by a pier with her husband and son.

Mama and Andrew headed toward the Adamses with Velvet and two picnic baskets, but Papa stopped me.

"We're here for your adventure, Winnie. I've secured a boat, and a few friends are coming along for a day on Dauphin Island. Happy early birthday."

"Thank you, Papa!" I hugged him.

"I hope you enjoy your day."

Papa started toward Darla, Henry, and little Horatio, who were joined by a hatted man from the boat who was almost the size of Papa.

"Thank you for your help with this, Darla," I said. "Thanks to everyone!"

Darla motioned to the man with his shirtsleeves rolled above his elbows. "Mr. Graves and Winnie, this is Captain Douglas Campbell. He'll be bringing us to and from the island on *Fare Marie II*, a sturdy sixty foot steamer."

He lifted his cap, displaying short brown hair, and shook hands with my father and nodded at me. "And I'll be nearby while you're on the island as well," he said with a slight Scottish brogue. "My wife, Maggie, and Darla are good friends, and we figured a few more children around wouldn't hurt anything. My oldest is a wee bit younger than your son."

"That's fine," Papa said. "All are welcome."

"Come aboard and meet my first mate, Emmett. His father owns the fleet. I'm sure you'll see more of the Walker family on the island."

We went down the pier, crossed the gangplank, and then I stood upon a ship for the first time. I took my father's arm for a second to steady my body from the gentle sway.

"Emmett!" The captain called to a young man about my age who lifted his cap off his shaggy, dark blond hair. "Emmett, this is Mr. Graves and his daughter, Winnie. Be sure to help them out with whatever they need while they're with us."

"I will, Captain." Emmett's grin turned on me as my father moved on to join Mama on a bench. "You must be the birthday girl."

"It's not for another month, but yes."

"In a few years, I'll be captain of my own boat." He looked down at my bare calves between my boots and dress hem and my wide stance for balance. "How are your sea legs?"

"I have no idea." I laughed. "This is my first time on anything larger than a rowboat."

"Good thing I'm here. I'll stay close, Winnie." He touched my arm as though to steady me, eyes bright.

"Emmett!" Darla called from the pier. "Her beau is coming, so give her some space."

He looked at me with disappointment. "You have a fellow?"

I smiled as I nodded, pleased with the news that Nathan was coming along.

"Figures, a girl like you. Still, it's my job to help. Holler if you need me."

"Thank you, Emmett."

Mama scowled until Papa kissed her cheek. "You've got yourself a pretty daughter, Merri. Boys are bound to give her attention, even when she isn't seeking it."

A minute later, the Spunners' automobile parked next to Papa's. Marie jumped out of the back, followed by Brandon and Nathan.

I returned to the pier.

Marie ran to me. "Isn't this the most exciting thing ever?"

"Yes." I hugged her, then Brandon, who had followed close behind.

"We're riding the boat with you, Winnie!" He lunged for the gangplank but Nathan caught him by the arm.

"Easy there."

Sean collected his son and set him on his shoulders, giving Brandon control of his Brownie Box camera. "And how are you feeling, Winnie, after being written up about in the society page?"

I laughed. "I'm well and surprised. I had no idea this was happening today. Thank you all for coming."

Hattie arrived with a picnic basket and blanket.

"Is that everyone, Darla?" the captain asked.

She looked back toward the parking area. "The Davenports."

Hattie shook her head. "Melissa telephoned. Junior started running a fever last night. They had to cancel."

"That's too bad," Captain Campbell said.

Darla sighed. "Then I guess we're all here."

"Come aboard, everyone, and get comfortable," the captain said. "If you don't do well with the movement of the boat, stay with Henry at the bow. He's guaranteed to be a shade greener than you."

Darla laughed. "Poor Henry, but he does love the island— once he gets there. I'm glad we have a relatively calm day for the trip."

Nathan held my hand as we crossed the gangplank. Emmett was already eyeing Marie as we gathered around the captain.

"There's much to see on the way south," Captain Campbell said. "Darla and Emmett can point out anything as well as or better than me since they were raised on the island. I've only been here a decade. Emmett, prepare to disembark."

Henry Adams was at the very front of the boat, his son at his side. Sean set Brandon on his feet and they joined them.

"Where do you wish to sit, Winnie?" Nathan asked.

"The shore side, I think. I'd like to see the lay of the land."

Nathan looked over my shoulder at Marie. "Are you joining us?"

She nodded, but watched everything Emmett did as he released the boat from the dock. We settled on a bench bolted to the floor on the opposite side from my parents and observed the beginning of the journey as we backed into the river and turned to face South.

Acting as hostess, Darla made her way between the passengers with an easy gait. Hattie had taken a spot near my parents, and Andrew was welcomed into the wheelhouse by the captain.

"Is everyone feeling okay?" Darla asked us once we were out on the open bay.

"Yes, though I don't think I'm ready to walk around yet," I replied.

Nathan squeezed my hand he held. "I'm good as well."

"I'm feeling a little off," Marie admitted.

Emmett was there in a flash. "Allow me to see you to the railing."

I watched Marie cling to his strong arm as he slowly walked her to the side. Darla went to Hattie next, leaving Nathan and I a bit of privacy.

I pressed my shoulder to his. "It's thrilling, isn't it?"

"There's no other place I'd rather be than by your side on this adventure." He pressed his lips to my cheek. "I hope you have a magical day, Winnie. I know I will."

We watched the shoreline breeze past and the seagulls fly above, my head on Nathan's shoulder as I soaked it all in.

Several minutes later, Brandon and Horatio ran from their fathers at the bow. Darla intercepted them with a reminder not to run on a boat and took each of their hands. I couldn't help watching Sean as he went for Brandon. He looked out of his element though he tried to hide it with a smile at Hattie.

"You're doing well," Hattie called to him, and I knew she thought the same thing I did.

"He can command a courtroom but looks helpless right now," Nathan whispered.

"I don't think I could do any better."

"I didn't mean to sound snobbish, but it's nice to see a man like that has his weaknesses. There's hope for all us mere mortals when the mighty show the chinks in their armor."

We spent the remainder of the voyage pacing the deck and looking over the railing from different vantage points. After losing my hat twice, I took Nathans's advice of using my waist sash to tie the hat on my head. I felt like a country girl with a bonnet, but it kept my hands free. Marie joined us when Emmett wasn't showing her around. Her hat was secured with a hat pin—something I no longer had enough hair to use. For several minutes, we kept Henry company at the bow while Darla chased Horatio around. Mama stayed on the bench, but Papa moved about, talking to the captain and everyone else.

Approaching the east end of the island, I marveled at the smallness of the settlement beyond the sandbars. Trees were plentiful on this side, but the sand stretch far into the west like a white ribbon amid the blue water under the glaring sun.

I turned to the local I knew best. "It's gorgeous, Darla! Why did you leave?"

"My parents and brothers died when I was eighteen, and my uncle in Mobile sent for me. I've been in the city ever since, though I visit the Campbells and Walkers as often as possible."

Everyone gathered at the railings for the final half mile. Hattie held Brandon on her hip and Horatio stood on a coil of rope to see over the side with Sean beside him because Darla was with her husband. With a slight bump and a swaying jerk when the moors were set, the boat was officially at port. Captain Campbell shut down the engines and finished his procedures.

Without the breeze traveling created, the morning sun heated me beyond comfortable levels. Darla suggested bringing our supplies to the Campbells' house and then exploring the shell mounds, saving our picnic for the beach midday.

"It's your choice, Winnie," Papa told me. "What would you like to do?"

All eyes turned to me, but I wasn't self-conscious in that group of friendly faces. "Darla's suggestion sound fine."

"Aye, that's the best thing," the captain said. "Emmett, let your family know where to find us. Any are welcome to join the fun."

"Yes, sir." He tipped his cap and ran off the dock.

We moved as a group, following Darla's lead. The Spunners stayed in the front with the Adamses, and Andrew stuck with Captain Campbell, asking a hundred questions about everything from ship to shore. Papa and Mama were last in line with Velvet.

At the Campbells' tidy home, we left our supplies and accepted fresh iced-tea from Mrs. Campbell for a brief respite before exploring. As we left the little house, Emmett arrived with a freckled redheaded boy who fell in with the Campbells' oldest son. They welcomed Andrew into their fold and took off in the lead. Darla and Henry had charge of Horatio and Brandon, as well as the captain's youngest son.

Through the oaks, pines, palmettos, and tangles of vines we tromped. Nathan kept by my side, often jotting notes in his pocket-sized journal. At the top of one of the highest peaks of the shell mound ridge formed by the accumulation of discarded shells by the native tribes that for centuries used the island for seasonal harvests, he sat cross-legged and wrote in earnest for ten minutes. I used the time to thank my parents, once again. Papa hugged me and Mama looked content, Velvet at her side.

Sean stopped before her, grinning in his youthful way. "Merri, thank you for inviting us."

"It was Bart's idea." Her mouth set in a deep line.

"Enough!" Sean passed Hattie his camera and snatched Mama around the waist, throwing her over his shoulder. "I swear if you don't smile at me, Merritt Hall Graves, I'll toss you in the gulf!"

Velvet barked and jumped at him, ready to play.

"Sean, put me down!"

"Take the leash, Bart," he commanded.

As soon as Papa did, Sean ran down the trail, Mama shrieking as she hung over his back. He ran up the next rise of earth and down the far side. Papa and Hattie exchanged weary glances and followed.

"What's going on with Mr. Spunner? Is the heat getting to his head?" Nathan asked.

I laughed. "That's how he is with my mother. Old family friends, remember?"

He nodded, slipping his notebook into his pocket. Seeing all the attention was directed the way Sean had run, Nathan's arms went around me, and he left a soft kiss on my lips.

"Were you taking down descriptions or working on a poem?"

"Both." He smiled and took my hand.

By the time we caught up with the group, Papa had Mama in his arms. I looked to Hattie with the unspoken question in my eyes.

She immediately smiled. "All is well."

"How long will it last?" I couldn't help asking.

Hattie laughed. "I think for good. At least I hope so."

Sean trailed his hand around his wife as he joined us. "It will be. Supper the first Saturday in August will be at our house in celebration of Ethelwynne's seventeenth birthday."

***

Two hours later, I waded in the Gulf of Mexico with Marie while the boys swam and the younger children splashed, overseen by the men. Sean was waist deep, stripped down to his trousers and helping Brandon float. Emmett and Nathan had Kade Campbell and Abraham Walker on their shoulders, keeping balance in the surf as the younger boys tried to knock each other off the other guy's shoulders.

"Emmett sure is tan and muscular, isn't he?" Marie remarked.

"A laboring man, my mother calls them."

"Mr. Spunner is no laboring man and his shoulders are just as broad, his arms as thick," Marie countered.

"But he's as pale as Nathan." I watched Nathan's lean form as he held strong beneath the assault of the rambunctious boys. "Is it wicked of me to want to touch Nathan—feel his body?"

"I hope not." Marie giggled. "I want to touch and kiss Emmett. Maybe even lick the saltwater from his skin."

"Marie!"

"Sadie told me tongues are important when showing affection." She looked sideways at me. "Have you used your tongue when kissing Nathan?"

I nodded, guilt creeping over my face in the form of heat though it was invisible under the bright sun.

"Then don't play pious, Winnie Graves."

Not wishing to continue the inappropriate conversation, I went for the picnic area. Crossing the glaring expanse of white sand, my body welcomed the cooling relief the pine trees offered when I stepped into the forest line. Mama, Hattie, Darla, Mrs. Campbell, and Mrs. Walker lounged on blankets spread between the rough trunks of the Southern pines.

"Is Marie all right by herself?" Mama asked.

"Oh, she's fine." I plopped onto the corner of one of the blankets and untied my hat. "She can't keep her eyes off Emmett."

Mrs. Walker laughed. "Do I need to send for my girls and Maggie's daughter to keep her occupied?"

"At the stage she's in, it wouldn't do any good," Hattie remarked. "Lust conquers all when it comes to attention, but girls of all ages need their fantasies."

"And some of us are lucky enough to marry ours," Mrs. Campbell said with a smile, causing the women to laugh—even Mama.

I retrieved a glass jar of lemonade and unscrewed the lid to drink from it. "Are we allowed to eat or do we need to wait for everyone?"

"Help yourself from any basket, Winnie," Mama said. "There's plenty to last all afternoon."

By the time my plate was filled with fruit, chicken, and bread, Nathan joined me on the edge of the picnic. His wet pants, still rolled to his knees, clung to his legs and his naked torso glistened.

I touched his shoulder, watching the spot turn from red to white and back again when I lifted my hand. "You're sunburnt."

His smile gleamed amid his ruddy face. "It was worth it. The freckles will be too."

"Dry your hands on my skirt and get some food."

Captivated by his form, I watched Nathan check the baskets and select a bit of everything he saw. As he ate, he jotted phrases into his notebook as I looked over his bare shoulder.

warm blanket of water

turquoise swell

beauty amid the white sands

waves caressing as her touch

He caught me when he looked up and snapped the book closed, tucking it back into his shirt pocket on the blanket beside us. "Those are incomplete thoughts, Winnie. Nothing worth reading."

Nathan finished eating, then helped me stand. "Is it all right if Winnie and I go for a walk down the beach to look for shells?"

Mama looked to the others finally emerging from the water to eat. "Don't go too far."

"Rinse out your lemonade glass and put your collection in there," Mrs. Campbell said. "I won't miss a few canning jars."

"Thank you." I retied my hat.

Mama looked relieved when Nathan pulled on his shirt, but frowned when he didn't button it. I clutched the jar to my chest with one hand, the other linked with Nathan's. Papa and Sean both gave him a slant-eyed stare as we passed them, but Emmett winked and Marie giggled.

We walked straight into the azure water, ankle-deep. I rinsed the jar and lid in the salt water to remove all traces of the lemonade.

"I want to fill it with shells and rocks and any other interesting tidbits we find to help me remember this day."

Nathan's eyes were like blue fire amid his sun-fried face. "May I kiss you each time you place an item inside?"

"Let's start with a bit of the sand." I slipped the lid and ring into my pocket and the lifted the hem of my dress to dry the inside of the jar. "Would you get a small handful for me?"

He went several strides into the dry, loose sand. Returning with a palm full, he positioned his fist over the jar and released a trickling stream of white grains into the glass. He paused as the last of the sand spilled out, and then gifted a kiss on my knuckles holding the jar. I wished to throw my arms about him and kiss his lips, but settled on smiling upon him because I knew we were watched.

We strolled down the shoreline for several minutes, collecting a few shells followed by kisses upon my hands. Secure with our distance from the group, he kissed my cheek when I added a small piece of driftwood, then my ear for a piece of a sand dollar. We continued on, combing the beach as we enjoyed the intimacy of stolen kisses, sand-dusted skin, and bare legs.

When we next paused, I noticed the shoreline had curved inland and the slight rise of a dune momentarily blocked our view from the picnic spot.

"Nathan," I whispered as my free hand touched his exposed chest over his heart. My fingers trailed down. I smiled over his caught breath and wide eyes, leaning closer. "I love you."

His mouth was on mine, an arm about my waist and the other around my shoulders as we kissed. My hand not holding the jar was pressed between us. I maneuvered it free and round his back, feeling more of his hot skin beneath his shirt as his kiss deepened. My fingers came to a rest at the back of his waistband, and he shivered a moment before breaking the connection.

"Winnie, we need to stop or your father and Mr. Spunner will be fighting over which one gets to kill me. Captain Walker looks a bit rough and might offer to help hide my body."

I laughed, but took a step away. "I think that was worth half a dozen new items in my collection. Help me look."

We were raking through the compact sand of the outgoing tide when Sean, Hattie, and Brandon came around the corner.

I looked to Sean's shirtless form. "Did you draw lots with Papa? Were you the winner or loser to come after us?"

Hattie laughed. "I told you she wouldn't appreciate it."

"Brandon wanted to collect shells too," Sean said, eyes cutting toward Nathan.

"I've got a jar, Winnie! And shells!" Brandon held up his prize.

"Good for you, Brandon. I think I'm nearly done, though I was hoping for a full sand dollar."

"Did you ever see a live one—how they move with their little spines?" Hattie asked.

"No, I haven't."

"Neither have I," Nathan added.

She grinned, looking between us. "It's fascinating."

"Shall I find one, dearest?"

"Only hunt for a few minutes." Hattie watched Sean run into the surf and then partially disappear as he grappled with the shifting sands, seeking a treasure to please his wife.

Brandon tugged on my dress. "Winnie, will you help me with shells?"

"Sure, Brandon." I looked to Hattie. "Is it all right if we walk him a little further?"

"Of course."

Brandon ran beside Nathan a couple dozen yards down the shoreline. I stopped to collect what they missed, arriving at their destination with several new items.

"How many did you find?" Nathan asked.

I held up four fingers, expecting him to kiss my hand. Instead, his hands cupped my face and he left a gentle kiss on each cheek and then my forehead. He paused, smiled at me in his dazzling way, and then brought our mouths together with a force of passion we never enjoyed with an audience.

"I want to kiss Winnie too!" Brandon jumped circles around us.

Laughing, Nathan looked down at the boy. "You little imp."

I knelt beside him and he smooched my cheek, leaving a damp, sandy film where his lips were.

"My jar is full," Brandon declared.

When we were almost back to Hattie, Sean sprang out of the water, waving his arm above his head. "I got one!"

Hattie waited in the ankle-deep water like a child on Christmas, hands clasped and eyes shining as Sean joined her. She reverently accepted the gift as though from a knight returning from battle with his spoils of war.

"Brandon, Winnie, and Nathan, come see the hairy spines moving in coordination!"

I'd never seen her look so excited, or Sean's attention on Hattie brighter than it was in that moment. When I gazed upon the disc the color of wet sand, I was disappointed. As I listened to Hattie discuss the symmetry, show the mouth, and briefly set it down on the sand so we could watch it move, I began to see the odd beauty of the creature. Nathan held it a few minutes and then pulled out his notebook as Hattie gently dipped it back in the water before passing it to me.

It felt like a thousand spider legs crossing my palm. "Someone take it, quick!" I squealed.

Hattie came to my rescue and bent down to Brandon with the sand dollar.

"I never would have taken you for being squeamish," Sean said with an amused grin as I washed my hands in the water lapping around my ankles.

"It felt unnatural, like nothing of this earth."

"You should feel an octopus," Sean teased.

"No, thank you."

I went for the dry sand and settled above the reach of the tide, watching the Spunners share their love of knowledge with their son while Nathan recorded the happenings in his notes. My admiration for Hattie was still there, but I knew I wasn't like her. That was fine because I was growing into my own shape and discovering love with an amazing young man—all on my own timeline.

Twenty-five

Tuesday afternoon, I soaked in a tepid bath in an attempt to wash the sweat from my body. Sean insisted on taking Brandon downtown for the Fourth of July parade that morning, which went against my better judgement after our twelve-hour island adventure the day before. But the pull of Brandon's reaction to marching bands was stronger than my exhaustion. I tolerated the searing heat and humidity to see Brandon shouting colors as the parade passed in front of Sean's office. Around us, the men spoke of President Wilson and rumors of The United States entering the European war. I had focused on my family—my husband safely beyond the age of enlistment and our precocious son—rather than the unease of the topics of the crowd under the graying skies.

I toweled off, buttoned on a cotton housedress, and quickly brushed through my short hair. On the back porch, Sean and Brandon were in their underdrawers upon the hammock, an oscillating fan moving the air back and forth across them from the side and the ceiling fan above helping with a breeze.

Brandon was passed out atop Sean's glistening chest—both of their arms spread wide as though seeking to cool themselves. Their skin was probably melted together. If only it were winter and they were on a bed I could climb upon with them. Buster lifted his head from the bare floor when I went to move away. I scratched behind his ear before gazing out the balcony view between the screened latticework. The neighborhood was quiet in the heat despite the holiday. I stretched flat on my back on the daybed a few feet away from the hammock, one pillow beneath my head and no blankets. It was stifling, but I managed to drift off to the sound of the whirling fans.

I woke to the sensation of cool air blowing across my legs. Shifting, I bent my knee, causing my dress to fall to my thigh as I stretched my arms overhead.

"You're the sexiest woman I've ever seen."

Smiling, I opened my eyes and found Sean gazing down at me in the same state of undress he'd napped in. He held the tabletop fan that was previously on the floor, pointing it at me.

"And you, holding that electric breeze, are the most appreciated man ever."

He pulled a chair over and set the fan on it so the circulation would more easily reach me on the bed. "I didn't wake when you joined us."

"You were both sleeping like angels."

"Then it's time for some devilishness." He leapt upon the bed beside me, leering down as his hand caressed my exposed thigh.

"It's too hot. And where's Brandon?"

"On the veranda with Althea. He's helping snap the green beans for supper, and she promised to entertain him until she needs to cook." Sean's hand didn't stop exploring as he spoke. The moment he realized there was nothing under my dress, he bit his lip.

"I suppose I could take another bath before supper because sweat is known to be therapeutic."

"Then we'll sweat and bathe together, Hattie. And pray for cool rain."

"Lots of rain, Saint Francis. It will take a deluge to cool Mobile."

"It shall be done." Sean stood, crossed himself, and slipped out of his remaining clothes. He was upon me once again, trailing kisses as he opened my buttons.

We had never had sex on the sleeping porch before. Sean laved attentions on me, my frenzy increasing each minute until I burst with a cry I realized I should have stopped as Brandon shouted "purple," and Althea gave an answering laugh.

"Now let's set off some real fireworks," Sean said.

We were playful in everything, from banter to touching. Afterward, I opted for a shower rather than a bath because I didn't want to lose track of time, but Sean managed to keep it interesting.

While he was toweling off in front of one of the fans situated on a bedroom side table, I kissed his neck. "I love you."

"And I love you, dearest." His countenance glowed with love.

I returned to buttoning on a fresh gown, pretending to look in the mirror at my own reflection, but I was looking behind me at Sean pulling on a pair of navy trousers. He skipped an undershirt and went right to buttoning on a white shirt.

"I'm going to check on Brandon. I'll bring him to the piano if he's done with the beans. Come with me, Hattie. He loves to sing for you and there's no sight I enjoy better than your form no matter where I am."

An hour later, Brandon and Sean were still going strong with music when the telephone rang. I was surprised to find Ethelwynne on the line.

"I hope I'm not bothering you," she said.

"Not at all, Winnie. We're taking it easy this afternoon, though we did go to the parade this morning."

"So did Nathan, Drew, and I. It was great. I hear the piano. That's why I've called. You wanted me and Marie to play our recital pieces for Brandon, but I was wondering if I could come in the morning to do mine rather than waiting until next Monday."

"You're always welcome, with our without music."

"Is eight or eight-thirty good?"

"Either is fine."

"Thank you. I'll see you then, Hattie."

I woke in the pre-dawn darkness. Sean and I were spooned together on the daybed on the sleeping porch and Brandon and Buster were in the hammock. A breeze blew in the screen and Sean fidgeted. Turning to his increased agitation, I tried to shush him with gentle strokes across exposed skin.

"Sean, it's okay. You're dreaming." I took a firm hold of his shoulders and shook. "Sean, wake up. You're having a nightmare. Sean—"

His hands latched onto my forearms and squeezed.

Fearful of bruising from his deadly grip, I leaned my head against his and spoke louder. "Sean, wake up, please!"

He didn't stop until I pressed my lips to his. Eyes blinked open, a look of horror on his face. Staring at me as though unsure where he was, I spoke calmly to reassure him.

"Sean, you've been dreaming. We're home and you're awake, but you need to release me. You're hurting my arms."

Fear melted from his face as his grip relaxed, anguish taking its place. His lips trembled just as Brandon's did before tears erupted.

"It's all right. I know you didn't mean to hurt me. It was a nightmare, but we're fine now." I held him to my chest, his tears wetting my nightgown.

The sky lightened but the wind increased, bringing with it a few stray raindrops. Several minutes later, the tears slowed though he still trembled. I kissed his cheeks and rubbed his back, hoping to bring him peace.

"I love you, Sean. Whatever the dream was, we're together— right here, right now."

He pressed his salty lips to mine and then used the pillowcase to wipe his face. "It was a vision."

Sean had alluded to having had visions before someone close to him died, but he was vague about them. I thought he must think me too science-minded to believe in otherworldly messages.

I brushed the wave of brown hair off his forehead, noticing how his hairline was slowly receding. "You can trust me," I whispered. "I'm your wife, your partner, your lover."

He exhaled a shaky breath.

"You can tell me, Sean. I think you've told me everything about yourself except this one aspect. I won't discredit your experiences."

"I have visions, Hattie. Megan calls it my second sight."

"Your cousin knows?"

"About the first two." He stared at me in the gray dawn. "Merri and Uncle Patrick knew of the third, nineteen years past. It's been ten years and seven months since the last vision, but only the person whom it was about knew of that one."

Placing the names—spoken and unspoken—and dates into a timeline, I gasped as I caught his fear. "Sean, was it—"

"Not family, but heartache for dear friends. Oh, God, how will the Davenports bear it?"

"Freddy?" I took Sean's hand into my own.

"Little Junior. He won't survive what's plagued him since the day of the recital."

"Can't we warn them?"

He shook his head, fresh tears dripping down his nose. "The visions come days or weeks before the death, but there's nothing to be done to stop the events. I tried. God knows I tried with Eliza. I saw her thrown from her horse, and she avoided riding at my insistence for two weeks, but it wasn't enough."

"And Winifred, from the fever?"

He nodded. "And my parents in the train accident. All tragic, all pain-filled, except Granny. She died in her sleep of old age."

I couldn't refute or explain his experiences. They weren't rational, but there was no denying his belief in them—or the fact that it had happened four times, with the looming possibility of a fifth.

I cuddled closer amid the wind now steadily blowing through the porch. "What can we do?"

"Be there for Melissa, and I'll do what I can for Freddy. I've known him most of my life and witnessed him go through other heartbreaks. If he does what he's done in the past, I'll be going to the gym with more regularity, to hold the punching bag, row with him on the machines, or possibly even spar with him in the ring if I think I can be of service."

We lay in silence, the northern gusts growing strong enough to cause raindrops to cling to the screen in a shimmering sheet.

"This isn't a typical storm," Sean whispered.

"You prayed for rain yesterday, Saint Francis. What have you unleashed?"

"You'll find out tonight, dearest." His wide smile was back, eyebrows raised, for a brief moment of humor. "Allow me to get to the office and check with my contacts. I want you to stay home—all of you—and wait for my telephone call."

"Winnie is supposed to come."

"Hopefully she doesn't, but if she shows up and things aren't better, keep her here."

Brandon woke the same time Sean was ready to leave and reached to be lifted out of the hammock. He carried our son downstairs on his back, set him on the landing four steps up so they would be about eye-level.

"You're in charge of the house today, Brandon. The weather is going from bad to worse, so be sure Mommy and Miss Althea stay inside."

"And Winnie!"

"And Winnie, if she makes it over."

"And Buster!"

"Buster has permission to go outside to do his business."

"Yes, sir!" He thumped his bare chest and then giggled. "I'm Daddy!"

"Not you aren't, you rascal." Sean scooped him into his arms and blew raspberries on Brandon's belly.

Once Sean set Brandon down, he looked to me as his joy fell.

I embraced him. "I'll keep him safe."

"I know you will. And I'll be careful as well. Stay near the telephone."

We kissed and parted.

Althea was on the back porch. "Shall I make breakfast or see to Brandon Patrick?"

"Breakfast, please. Thank you, Althea."

"Miss Thea, I'm Daddy today!"

She smiled. "You sure look like him, running around with no pants on."

"I'm strong!" Brandon posed like one of the boxers at the gym, showcasing his spindly limbs.

After exchanging smiles with Althea, Buster was set outside, and I saw Brandon back up the stairs. He dressed, and then I told him to play in his room while I got ready. I skipped shapewear and chose a simple green dress with a crossover style bust that helped camouflage things. I checked that all the windows were secure on that level before helping Brandon gather a few toys from his room to bring to the parlor.

"Buster hasn't left the stoop," Althea called to me on the porch through the open kitchen door.

"I'll try the front yard. Come on, Buster."

He shook off the rain that had blown onto his fur before tromping through the house. I opened the front door.

"Don't go outside, Mommy!"

"Buster is scared, so I need to walk him onto the veranda. I'll stay under the roof. Come with me to make sure I'm safe."

Brandon took my hand. The dog sniffed the air nervously. There was an atmosphere of unease that caused my skin to prickle and my mind to buzz with dangerous possibilities. The change of weather in less than twenty-four hours was unbelievable. Were destructive tornados and deadly tides headed our way? Like Sean's visions, I couldn't refute the stinging raindrops that pelted my feet with the next gust or my dress billowing around my bare legs like a hot air balloon. Buster ran into the yard, making quick work of his business.

The telephone rang as we came back inside.

"Hello?"

"Hattie," Sean said, "there's talk of it being a hurricane. Has Althea come over yet?"

"Yes, she's fixing breakfast."

"Tell her to grab whatever she might need from her apartment because I don't want her out there until this thing passes. Have you heard from Ethelwynne?"

"No."

"I'll telephone Merri and see if she's left yet. And Bart at the store." He took a breath. "I already called Freddy. I telephoned him first, hoping to catch him before he left the house—and I did. The last thing Melissa needs is to be worried about him while she's home with the children."

"Is Junior—"

"He's not doing well. They tried to get a doctor to house yesterday but didn't have any luck catching one on the holiday."

"What about John?"

"He's a surgeon, dearest. He hasn't made a house call in years. I'm going to finish up a few things at the office, but I'll be home by ten. Try not to worry. Althea knows what to do to prepare for the hurricane. We've been through it before."

But I hadn't. I had only read about the power of tropical cyclones and heard the horror stories at my science meetings.

"I love you, Hattie, but I need to make more telephone calls to safeguard our family and friends. Don't worry—I'll see you soon."

Don't worry when there was a hurricane coming and my husband was miles away and Ethelwynne was on her way over? I shouldn't be mad at Sean even though he didn't telephone me first, but it was much easier to be angry than scared. I tried to push those feelings back and stay focused on what I could do.

"Breakfast is ready!" Althea called from the kitchen.

Brandon and I met Althea in the breakfast room.

I dropped my voice as Brandon climbed into his chair. "Sean telephoned. It might be a hurricane. He said for you to get what you need from your apartment because he doesn't want you crossing the yard until this is over. And he wants you to make preparations when you're done getting your things."

"I'll pack while you're eating."

The grits with Gruyère cheese, pepper, and sautéed shrimp were wonderful, but I wasn't hungry. I had to force myself to eat because I knew I'd need the energy. Brandon, as typical, ate hardily for his little body.

When Althea returned, Brandon frowned at the rain spots on her dress and put his hands on his hips while he sat in his highchair like it was a throne. "You went outside Miss Thea?"

"Your father sent word for me to get a few things from my apartment, so yes, to obey him, I did."

"Oh." He went back to drinking his milk.

"You're doing a fine job keeping us on track, Brandon Patrick."

The doorbell rang.

"Stay and eat, Miss Hattie. I'll get it."

"It might be Winnie." I looked to lace curtains covering the windows and shivered at the grayness beyond the intricate needlework.

"Hattie?" Ethelwynne called as she hurried through the formal dining room to the breakfast room doorway. "Miss Althea says it's a hurricane."

"Yes, Sean was supposed to telephone your parents. You're welcome to stay here, but call home and find out."

"Nathan is here too. He met me on Government and we rode the streetcar around to have a few minutes together."

"After you're done, have him telephone to find out what he needs to do. We won't send him off in this weather if he doesn't need to get to work."

"And then come in here for some food. There's plenty." Althea looked to me and nodded at my bowl. "And you keep eating. Miss Winnie knows her way around."

Althea brought in two more place settings.

Ethelwynne returned, looking slightly relieved. "Mama said Papa would pick me up on his way home. He's supposed to close the store before eleven."

"Good, you can visit for a little while. Would you like some shrimp and grits?"

"It smells wonderful. Thank you."

"I'm cancelled for work today," Nathan said before taking the chair beside Ethelwynne's. "I told my mother I wasn't coming home until I was sure Winnie was safe with her family."

"Papa could drop you off when he gets me."

Nathan nodded and took a spoonful of grits. "I've never had grits like this."

"It's the Gruyère cheese—Sean's favorite."

"He has fine taste."

Several minutes later, I was on the parlor sofa—Buster at my feet—overseeing Ethelwynne and Brandon singing at the piano while Althea and Nathan closed the storm shutters upstairs. I tried not to listen to the wind over the piano chords, but it was difficult to ignore the largest of the howling gusts that caused me to flinch.

Three songs later, my concentration waned, and I nearly missed clapping for them. Ethelwynne started on one of her recital pieces, and Brandon watched every move her fingers made. Nerves frayed with fear of the unknown, I turned to my childhood training and Sean's devout beliefs for help. I did the sign of the cross and gave a silent prayer for my husband's safe return.

During the next song, the door to the hall from the back porch snapped open and shut, making me jump.

"Is there a reason why Nathan Paterson is hanging out one of our bedroom windows?"

"Sean!" I ran and threw my arms around him. "I prayed you'd come home safely."

He took my arms and held me away from him so he could look me over. "Are you truly my Hattie?"

I made a grab to pinch his backside. "Don't be an ass!"

"You're Hattie all right." He grinned and raised his eyebrows. "It takes a hurricane to make a believer out of you."

I fell against his solid chest, hugging him to me. "I don't like this, Sean."

He kissed my forehead and squeezed me in return. "It will be over before you know it, dearest."

"Daddy, Winnie's playing the piano for me."

Sean released me to lift Brandon for a hug and kiss. "And it sounds wonderful, but I need to go see what's going on upstairs. I'll be back soon."

Brandon immediately returned to the piano. I started following Sean up the stairs, but he stopped on the landing.

"Stay with them," he whispered as he cupped my face and left a kiss on my lips. "It looks like Nathan has most of the shutters closed, but I want to check on things."

I paced the hall and looked to Althea when she came down a minute later.

"The shutters are secure and they're putting the porch furniture into the back room, Miss Hattie. I'm going to bake cookies."

When they descended the stairs, Sean and Nathan went immediately out the front door. One by one, they shuttered the windows around the veranda and carried the porch furniture to the carriage house. Then, Nathan climbed the ladder while Sean held it so they could secure the remaining downstairs windows.

The transformation to a tomb was complete. We were sealed alive in what was supposed to be a home of love and light.

Twenty-six

Seeing Hattie's fright in the darkness, I switched on a side table light on my way to her in the hall. "I'm glad Nathan is here to help."

"Yes." She managed to smile. "He's been terrific."

"Winnie, will you play more colors?"

Hoping to keep Brandon occupied so he wouldn't notice his mother's unrest, I returned to the piano where he was trying to copy my Beethoven sonata.

Marveling over how much he could pluck out with one finger, I looked to his grinning face. "How did you get so smart?"

"Mommy and Daddy made me."

I laughed. "They sure did. You're a blessed boy, Brandon."

"Hattie!" Sean hollered from the back porch.

Eyes wide, she disappeared out the back. A moment later, she hurried up the stairs, soon returning to pace the hall, her mouth in a tight line.

I tried to work with Brandon on the fingering for the Beethoven piece, but his hands were too small. I switched to teaching him "Precious Savior, Dear Redeemer," which was easily adapted to be played with one finger without losing the tune. Using the blank music sheets Sean had purchased, I created a simplified version of the score, which Brandon happily worked on. Singing along to his playing, he finished the first verse surprisingly well.

Sean joined us with hearty applause, his hair damp but fresh clothing dry. "Winnie, I'd like to hire you as Brandon's piano tutor, two hour-long lessons a week. How about it?"

"I don't mind helping him. I'm happy to come at no expense."

"Nonsense. You, Ethelwynne Graves, have a talent, and you can't go through life giving it away. Capitalize on it when you can." He motioned to the simplified version of the hymn I'd written. "That's a skill. Not every pianist can figure out how to adapt a score like that. It's just what Brandon needs at this time. After the storm, I'll speak to your parents about hiring you and set your schedule for tutoring when it's convenient for you and Hattie. Does that sound reasonable?"

I nodded, looking beyond him to Nathan, who'd just come down. He wore one of Sean's white shirts—too big on his shoulders—and pants supported by a pair of suspenders.

Sean laughed. "I may not be the biggest at the gym, but seeing Nathan in my clothes helps me feel powerful."

"You've got two decades on me, and I'm still growing." Nathan gave his good-natured smile.

"I think he's great the way he is," I said.

"The favor of a lady is important. I guess you're safe, Nathan." Sean strode to the piano. "Now allow me a front row seat for this new piece. Hattie, come join me."

As the wind and rain beat upon the Spunners' house, Sean watched Brandon at the piano, arms around Hattie as she perched stiffly on his lap in the armchair beside the instrument. Smiling at Nathan, I took his hand and led him into the darkened club room. Nathan kissed my lips and tucked me against his shoulder.

Then it struck me with a flood of memories and everything felt wrong.

The items from Sean's wardrobe clothed Nathan in the man's scent—the one I'd known since childhood. The smell of Sean as I sat on his shoulders while we saw to the glass bottles in the grove, beside him at the supper table, and on his knee at the piano. At one point in my life, I would have relished being held within that aroma of French cologne, but no more. I wanted Nathan's scent of soap and young man, which had lately been seasoned with newspaper ink.

I nosed into his hair and kissed his ear. "I love you. I'm glad we're together right now because it means less time to worry about you when we're separated."

We sat together on the settee, hands clasped and shoulders close. A few minutes later, Sean stood in the doorway, arms crossed and a look of incredulousness on his face. I met his annoyance with complete serenity.

"I'm going to get some grits. When I come back from the kitchen, I expect you two to be at the table with me while I eat or in the parlor with Hattie and Brandon."

"Yes, sir," Nathan said before Sean walked away.

Smiling, I kissed Nathan on the cheek and went for the parlor. Nathan paused in the hallway, grabbed his notebook from his satchel on the bench, and went for the dining room. I wanted to hear what he and Sean would talk about, but knew Hattie needed me more. She was pale, fists tight, and stared unseeingly as Brandon sung his heart out. When his song was over, I went to his side.

"Your daddy is eating his breakfast, if you want to join him."

Brandon was across the house in a flash, Buster following. I sat beside Hattie on the sofa.

"Hurricanes are scary, but this house is solid, Hattie. Sean, Brandon, and even Althea are here. Y'all will be safe."

"I'm a wobbly yearling," she whispered. "You and Nathan are so composed, but I feel like my world is shattering with every howl of the wind."

"It's natural to feel that way during your first storm. We're overdue for a hurricane. It's been a decade since the last big one. I was a crying mess during the '06 hurricane, and the fear stayed through every thunderstorm afterward for months."

"But you were a girl," she said with exasperation. "I should be able to handle a weather situation I understand on a scientific level without breaking down."

"We all have our limits, Hattie, and Nature is a reasonable thing to fear."

But her eyes showcased the pain that she believed she shouldn't be so fragile.

The boys were coming through the hall with Sean when the telephone rang. He veered to the side to answer it.

"Yes, she's here and safe as can be," Sean said as I came closer. "Is Bart getting dotty in his old age?" He paused.

"A likely excuse." Sean laughed, then listened. "Should I bring her home?"

I shook my head and pointed to the floor and then toward the parlor, where Hattie was once again pacing.

"Well, the fact is, Hattie has never been through a hurricane and she's nervous. Ethelwynne is helping her stay calm." A pause. "Sure, she's right here."

Sean waved me closer. "It's your mother. She gave the shop boy the message for your father to pick you up on his way home, but he forgot to pass it on."

"Hello, Mama."

"Are you comfortable with the Spunners?"

"Yes, but I'm worried about Hattie. She's frightened, and I'm afraid Brandon will become upset if he catches her mood."

"Isn't Althea there?"

"She's busy in the kitchen."

"I'd hate to send Sean out in this mess if Hattie is that poorly."

"She'd not survive, Mama."

"I should send your father for you. Drew is helping him shutter the windows right now, but afterward—"

"It will only get worse. Why don't I stay here? Things should be clear by tomorrow."

"We'll lose the telephone lines and the streets might be impassable for days."

"But you know I'll be safe here. There aren't any large trees nearby, and the house is built like a fortress."

"Then you'll be safer than us. Give the telephone back to Sean."

Sean went back to my mother's call. "She'll be a huge help, Merri. I'll send word as soon as possible on our end. Yes, call back whenever, though I doubt the lines will last the evening." He smiled. "You're a darling. We love you all too. God speed."

"I'm staying?" I asked as soon as he hung the receiver on the box.

"Yes, though it will be no vacation, as you well know." He looked to the other room. "Nathan, a word with you, please."

Sean waved me away, but I listened from the parlor.

"It appears your opportunity for a ride is lost. Bart is already home and securing his house. Winnie will be staying with us for a day or more, depending on the aftermath. Ordinarily, I'd offer you a ride, but I won't leave Hattie alone or force her out in this mess. I don't wish to send you out on foot, so the best I can do is offer you shelter here, unless your family can collect you."

"Thank you, Mr. Spunner. I'll telephone home and see what would be best."

"You're a good man, Nathan. I appreciate all your help this morning, but please call me Sean." He went directly for Hattie, put a loving arm around her, and led her to the sofa. She curled up beside him, head on his shoulder, and Brandon took the opposite side.

"Winnie is staying with us, Hattie. That will be an extra set of helping hands around here." He kissed her forehead. "For now, we'll all keep on as we are as long as possible, having dinner together and playing this afternoon. When the winds get stronger as the eye gets closer, we'll gather in the hall. I'll bring in furniture and make it comfortable for everyone. If it worsens terribly or it sounds like a tornado is coming, we'll all pile in the silver room, but I don't expect that to happen."

"You don't?"

"No, dearest. But we will lose electricity and telephone service. With a gas range and plenty of food, we'll be fine. Althea already filled buckets and pitchers in case the water service is affected. Trust me to keep you safe. You and Brandon, plus Althea and Winnie."

Nathan returned from his telephone call and linked fingers with me in the parlor doorway. "My father is supposed to pick me up within the hour." He slowly led us back into the hall, then into the club room where he kissed me. "I wish I was staying with you. I'll check in as soon as things clear. For now, I need to pack my bag and gather my wet laundry from upstairs."

"Leave the clothes. It will be an excuse to return."

"I love your mind, Winnie Graves." He spun us around until I was in the far corner. His hands trailed my back as we kissed. Heightened passions wouldn't cure the emptiness when we parted, but they were wonderful in the moment.

"Winnie!" Brandon hollered, causing Nathan and I to break apart.

We stepped into the hall, him going for his satchel and I for Brandon.

"Winnie, please sing with me." Brandon reached for me from his spot on the sofa beside his parents.

I picked him up and settled in a side chair, Brandon on my lap and Buster at our feet. "What do you wish to sing?"

"Piano!"

"We can sing without the piano. Have you looked inside the piano and seen the little hammers striking the strings?"

"Daddy showed me."

"Well, our voices are instruments too. Feel my strings vibrating. They're called vocal chords." I rested his hand on my throat and sang the first verse of "Precious Savior, Dear Redeemer".

"Winnie," Sean said, "that was genius. I've never thought to explain singing like that. You'll be worth every dollar when you begin tutoring.

Brandon's face grew rosy with excitement. "Winnie sings pink and orange and yellow!"

"Like a sunset?" Sean asked from the sofa.

"Yes, Winnie sings the prettiest!"

Smiling, Sean looked to Nathan. "Are you ready to leave?"

He stepped back. "Yes, sir. Unless you wish your clothes back."

"Bring them another day."

Sean stepped into the vestibule when Mr. Paterson arrived. The force of the storm moved all the drapes when the door opened and closed. Althea arrived in the hall to pass a cheesecloth-wrapped bundle of cookies to Nathan, who slipped it into his satchel before coming into the parlor to say goodbye.

"I love you," I whispered when he leaned over to kiss my cheek.

"It's a good thing he's going home," Hattie remarked after Nathan left. "I wouldn't want to be responsible for chaperoning you two tonight."

Sean locked the door to keep the wind from blowing it open.

Brandon tugged on his father's pant leg. "Piano, Daddy!"

Sean and I took turns at the piano with Brandon, though we often sang when not accompanying the tune. I took a break when Nathan telephoned to say he'd made it home, but then I was back to the music.

For the midday dinner, we dined at the formal table. The storm often shook the chandelier, causing Hattie's hands to tremble.

After eating, Sean took Brandon to the sofa for his nap while Hattie and I went through her fossil collection. Sharing her love of science kept her mind from focusing on the increasing storm.

After Brandon woke, I brought him to the work table in the club room with a box of crayons and several papers while Sean cuddled with Hattie on the parlor sofa.

"Draw what your favorite songs look like," I instructed Brandon.

He worked for a quarter of an hour with the same concentration he gave music, which was eerie in one so young. There weren't any distinguishable characters on the pages, but the colors were vivid and some patterns emerged from the chaos.

Sean came up behind me, hands on my shoulders as he leaned over the workspace. "What do we have here?"

"I drew songs for Winnie." Brandon held up his last creation, a purple and pink swirl that mixed with blues. "This is my Mommy song."

"Then you must show her right away." When Brandon hurried out of the room with his picture, Sean squeezed my shoulders. "Did you instruct him to draw the songs?"

"Yes."

"Why?"

Sean stayed behind me so I couldn't read his face. "He's always shouting about colors when he hears music, so I thought he would enjoy drawing the songs."

"Bless you for understanding him so well. You're the friend and mentor he needs." Sean kissed the top of my head. "The power has flickered twice in the past half hour. I think it's time we move into the center of the house and have candles at the ready. This room doesn't have the veranda around it for protection like the parlor does."

Gathering the other pages from the table, Sean motioned me out in front of him and closed the folding doors.

***

Brandon and Ethelwynne were in the middle of singing "Love Is Mine" when the power flashed off and stayed out. There was still enough ambient gray light coming through the cracks of the shuttered windows that we weren't in complete darkness, but I gave a shriek as the sound of the wind switched direction to batter the south side of the house rather than the north.

"Stay where you are, Hattie," Sean spoke in an even tone as he patted my hand and stood. "I'm going to Althea to make sure she has candles and matches, and then try to get Buster to go out before it's dark. I'll be back."

Brandon beside Ethelwynne on the piano bench held her hand. "I protect you."

But no one was beside me for comfort. My heart hammered to the steady rhythm of the driving rain.

A few agonizing minutes later, Sean came through the house looking like he'd jumped in a lake. He was in nothing but clinging underdrawers and every bit of hair on his body was black from the rain.

"Your candles will be a few more minutes in coming. Buster wouldn't go out unless I did. I left my clothes on the porch so I wouldn't leave too big of a mess."

"It appears you left your brain out there as well." My sarcasm was as thick as his thigh muscles. "Winnie is here, in case you forgot."

He waved a hand in dismissal as he went for the stairs. "She has a father and brother. Not to mention a beau—though I pray she hasn't seen Nathan like this."

"I don't believe I would have survived the experience if I had," Ethelwynne said with candor.

Sean laughed as he climbed the stairs. "You've always been a darling, but you're becoming even better company as you age. Witty women are the best companions, especially during a hurricane."

We had supper by candlelight held aloft in one of the silver candelabras. Afterward, I sent Ethelwynne to wash and ready for bed though she refused one of my nightgowns.

Althea insisted on sleeping in the kitchen, so there was one less body in the living hall. Sean had brought Brandon's mattress down, and it was against the stair wall where the bench usually was. The bench had been relocated to the club room, and the sofa now blocked that doorway. The dining room and parlor doors were also closed, creating a snug cocoon, though the transoms over them remained open to help with airflow. A side table beside where I rigidly sat on the sofa held a burning candle to light the space.

Brandon was already curled in one corner of the bed, Buster at his feet, when Ethelwynne returned from the bathroom.

"If you want, I'll keep Brandon on the sofa with us or put Buster in the kitchen with Althea," I told her.

"No, he's fine—they both are. I'm used to little boys and dogs."

She stretched out on the edge of the mattress and pulled the separate blanket over herself.

Brandon's little hand patted her back. "Goodnight, Winnie. I love you."

She turned to him and kissed his cheek. "I thought you were already asleep. Goodnight, Brandon."

"The storm's music is black and silver," he whispered.

Sean descended the stairs. The candle made his bare torso golden, his eyes fiery. He blew out the candle and settled beside me on the sofa, whispering words that were softer than the howling winds.

The house shuddered with the force of the hurricane, causing the windows and doors to rattle louder than my clattering teeth. I clung to Sean tighter with each cry of the storm, thinking the next blast would flatten our home. Our family. My fingers flexed into the hot skin of his back like talons from a vulture clinging to a chunk of carrion. He was my livelihood—a promised morsel to keep me alive.

"I'm not going anywhere, dearest," he whispered in my ear.

I nodded, my head rubbing against his chest, but I couldn't speak. Every muscle in my body had a mind of its own and they all screamed, violently quivering amid the onslaught of nature battering our castle walls.

"I'll hold you all night, dearest. You needn't fear." His warm lips kissed across my cheek to my ear. "I'll protect you, Hattie. Always."

I cleaved all the more, my body locking around Sean's pillar of strength. What seemed like hours later, I managed to fall into exhausted asleep against his chest, but woke in the dark.

The wind was a low moan, but I could still hear the patter of raindrops on the windows. I whimpered, and Sean hugged me tighter as his kiss found my forehead.

"The worst is over, Hattie," he whispered. "We survived the hurricane. Take a deep breath and relax."

I was near hyperventilating. Sean stroked my back as though calming a baby.

Across the shadowed cavern, Ethelwynne rose from the mattress. She knelt at our side, put her arms around me, and added her voice to Sean's loving words.

"We're safe, Hattie. I'm glad to have been here with you and your family. There's nothing to fear in this wonderful house of love."

Twenty-seven

I paced the veranda on the second Monday in September. According to the social calendar, it was officially Autumn, though Mobile liked to hang onto summer weather for another month.

Brandon ran the yard with Buster. He had grown an inch or more in the last eight weeks, about the same as the child within me. Only Sean, Althea, and Darla—my midwife—knew of our growing family, but I was itching to share the news. I thought today would be a good time to do so, if there were any guests for the science club.

The hurricane in July halted all meetings as the inhabitants of the city dealt with the aftermath. August was spotty with the Marley sisters and Kate Stuart across the bay on the Eastern Shore for the worst of the summer heat, and Mary Margaret Easton didn't attend without Kate or Grace Anne. Kate had never apologized for sending Mr. Gentry to try to break up my club or the editorial in the newspaper, but I would never bar her entrance. Faith was now employed as a secretary and working on her teacher's certificate. Out of respect for her parents, she let me know she would never return. Jessica only managed one meeting in August before moving. She was now settled at Mount Saint Agnes College in Baltimore. I had received a glowing letter from her a few days before.

Each Monday afternoon, Darla brought Horatio to play with Brandon, but Melissa hadn't visited since Junior died from pneumonia after the hurricane. I stopped by the Davenports' house at least weekly, usually sitting on the front porch with Melissa for an hour while Louisa and Brandon played. We never said much as we sipped iced-tea, but Melissa seemed to enjoy the company. Sean spent an hour or more at the gym nearly every day after work with Freddy. They didn't talk either, but Freddy rowed, lifted, punched, and boxed until he could barely walk to the showers.

But Ethelwynne Graves was there without fail each Monday, as well as two other times during the week for music tutoring. Brandon excelled under Ethelwynne's guidance, for she instinctively knew how to channel his excitement. Today would be her first time coming directly from school, and I expected Nathan to accompany her.

A woman stopped at the front gate. Not recognizing the lady in a wide-brimmed hat with stooped posture, I descended the steps and crossed the walkway.

"Hello, Mrs. Spunner."

As I drew closer, I clearly saw her face though I hadn't spoken to her since the beginning of summer. "Christina, what a surprise. Are you returning to the club?"

"No, but I knew I'd find you out here at this time. I can't stay long, but I wanted to thank you. I was mad at Winnie and your husband for months, but I know they had my well-being at heart. Luke never loved me, I know that now."

"Shall I pass word to Winnie?"

"No." Her prominent, dark eyes went wider with fright. "She doesn't need to hear from me anymore. But I wanted to thank you for what you're doing with this club. I learned a lot, but I was too far gone with Luke when I heard about things."

I narrowed my eyes, not sure if I understood the unspoken words. Then Christina's hand went to her stomach.

"Ooh, Christina. Do you need help?"

She shook her head. "My parents registered me with a home up north. One of those places for girls like me. They'll board me and see to my medical needs until I deliver. Then the home finds a family to adopt the baby. I'll be able to stay on a few more weeks to recover before coming home—if I decide to come back. I might enjoy a fresh start somewhere else because I know my parents will never look at me the same again."

"It wasn't your fault, Christina. Luke was a chronic seducer, preying on young girls."

"I knew enough to know better. Please don't tell Winnie about me, but be sure she stays innocent. Send Mr. Spunner after that pretty boy Nathan Paterson if needed."

"We're watching over her."

"I wish I had someone like you when I was her age. Goodbye, Mrs. Spunner. And thank you."

"Stay brave, Christina."

When she was two houses up Houston Street, Ethelwynne and Nathan came from the main road.

"How was school?" I asked, opening the gate.

"Terrific," Ethelwynne said. "Nathan got me on the staff of the school paper, one of only six students from the girls' school."

"Your writing got you on staff. You were voted in unanimously."

I followed them up the walk. "It's great to see you both. Are you stopping in for a few minutes, Nathan?"

"Yes, thank you. I'd forgotten what a walk this was. I've grown soft riding streetcars over the summer."

Althea came onto the veranda with the tray for the children, greeting Ethelwynne and Nathan as they went for the front door. By the time they helped themselves to refreshments, Darla arrived, followed soon thereafter by Grace Anne and Marie who said Sadie was at home resting, feeling the heat extra in her condition.

"Don't hurry away, Nathan," Marie said. "I haven't seen you in weeks."

"I know when to leave a gathering like this. Invite me to another recital if you wish for more time with me."

"Mother was just saying yesterday that we should plan a Christmas concert. Would you agree to it, Winnie?"

"I'd like that. I'll see Nathan out now."

"Just tell him goodbye here. We all know you're going to kiss."

Ethelwynne followed Nathan from the room, returning a minute later with reddened lips.

Marie sighed. "You're so lucky, Winnie. I think he's even handsomer now than he was three months ago."

"Boys change a lot around this age," Grace Anne said. "They go from boys to men right before your eyes. Don't discredit the lackluster ones. They often peak later and last longer than the early bloomers."

"Females typically reach maturity before males," Darla said.

As a discussion on growth ensued, I coolly welcomed Kate and Mary Margaret. After everyone was settled, I waited for a pause.

"I have news to share. If all goes well, Sean and I will be welcoming a baby into our family when the azaleas bloom next spring."

"It's about time," Kate said with a smirk. "I wondered if your unorthodox means of copulating were detrimental to reproduction."

Mary Margaret gave a grim smile. "Have as many as you can, as quickly as you can. Pregnancy only gets worse as you age and you had a late start."

"Hattie will do well," Darla said.

As pregnancy chatter continued, I couldn't help but think of Christina, destined to go through her journey with strangers. Hopefully, she would find friends and a surrogate family in her temporary home.

"And what of Melissa?" Grace Anne asked. "I haven't seen her since the hurricane."

"I visit her regularly," I said, "but she isn't ready for social events. The pain is too raw."

Darla nodded. "I go for short visits as well. She'll return when she feels up to it."

"And Frederick, the poor man," Kate said. "I passed him on the sidewalk last week and couldn't get over how hard his face was set. I haven't seen him like that since Alexander stole his wife."

We chatted about our lives since the hurricane. Having experienced a major event with the rest of the community, I finally felt like I belonged.

Ethelwynne stopped beside me. "I'm happy for you and Sean."

"Thank you, Winnie. Will you tell your mother when you get home? I wanted to say something at supper the other day, but I felt I needed to wait a bit more before sharing."

"I will, Hattie. Can I get you something while I'm up?"

"Another sandwich and cookie, if you don't mind."

"Careful," Kate said when Winnie and Marie went to the dining room, "don't think you can eat too much extra and not receive the unflattering effects."

I raised my brow in challenge to the gossip queen. "My husband is man enough to handle all my curves, in any position."

That got the ladies laughing and the conversation returned to tamer subjects the remainder of the gathering.

After saying goodbye to everyone, Althea took Brandon up for his bath while Pearl and her Monday helper cleared the dining room in preparation for supper. I took a few minutes to rest with my feet up on the sofa.

Sean found me there and studied me from my bobbed hair to bare toes, smiling.

"Once again, you're luminescent in your motherhood. My seed is a perfect match for you."

I smiled as he swaggered closer and accepted his kiss. "I told the ladies today."

"Then I'm sure half the town already knows that you're filled with my—"

I yanked his arm until he was within kissing distance. "Keep your lips occupied on more important matters than being a braggart."

The telephone rang and Sean grinned. "And the congratulations begin!"

"Says who?" I followed him to the hall.

"Hello? Yes, John, you heard correct."

Laughter—over something inappropriate, I had no doubt. "You're the doctor. You figure it out. Yes, I'll tell her and you tell Gracie she wins the quickest mouth in town award for today. Why don't you try putting *that* to work for you, Woodslow?" More laughter before the receiver was replaced.

"John sends his congratulations to my spirited wife—the one who announced to her club that I'm man enough to handle everything you have, in any position. That sounds like a challenge that needs proving."

"You know it's true, and our new bed gives ample means of witnessing it." I smiled at the memory of the times Sean and I spent within the mirrored panels. They were closed around the sides of our bed like a roll top desk while we coupled. During the day, the four inch panels hid on their tracks behind curtains at each of the four corner posts beneath the mirrored canopy.

The telephone rang again and I beat him to it. "Hello?"

"Winnie told me the news. Congratulations, Hattie."

"Thank you, Merritt."

"Is Sean home?"

"Yes." I stepped to the side, passing the earpiece to Sean so he could take the call, but he put an arm around me to keep me with him.

"Good evening, Merri."

"I know you've always wanted a passel of children and this is giving you a great start. Bart is thrilled as well. We'll be sure to have an extra special supper in October to celebrate. Allow me to host."

"Of course, and we appreciate your joy over our news, Merri. Goodnight."

Sean hung the earpiece on the cradle and turned to me. "This is a great day."

"It will only get better, year after year, Sean Francis Spunner."

"Especially with your dear face and that mischievous twinkle in your eyes."

"Always, my fine specimen of a man, but I'll keep you humble."

"Impossible, Hattie. I know a good thing when I see it and with you by my side, I can't be anything but perfect."

THE END

Author's Note

I'd like to start off with the beautiful cover art this trilogy is graced with. Mobile Bay area artist Amanda Herman (@amandawithmagic on Instagram) enthusiastically accepted my commission for home portraits featuring three real-life historic homes my fictional characters live in. This cover features 19 Columns, historically known as the Bessie Fearn-Syson House, on the corner of Old Government and Houston Streets. This George B. Rogers designed masterpiece has been lovingly restored by Bryant J. Olson. You can learn more about the house's past and present on "19 Columns Restoration" group on Facebook.

Once again, much love and thanks to my inner circle—my family and my Dial-A-Nerd/critique buddies. Candice Marley Conner, Joyce Scarbrough, Lee Ann Ward, and MeLeesa Swann are still the best and my family is awesome in their unconditional love.

Members of Dalby's Darklings were there for me, offering name ideas and more support than I could ask for. Beta reader—and Darkling member—Jennifer Lamont dove in, once again, into uncharted territory. Thank you for loving my people as much as I do. And special thanks to Sean Connell for his massive undertaking with edits. It's been a great journey to the heart of the story.

Read Next

Look for *Severed Legacies*, the final novel in the Malevolent Trilogy, to find out how World War I affects the Spunner and Graves households.

If you want to know more about Sean Spunner and Eliza Melling, be sure to check out *Mosaic of Seduction* (Possession Chronicles #1.5 novella) and the short story "The Portrait of Eliza Melling", found in the *Halloween Pieces* anthology by Mobile Writers Guild.

Sean and Hattie's first meeting—and altercation with Mr. Gentry—can be found in the short story "Natural Selection in Life and Love," first published in the *Homeroom Heroes* anthology by Bienvenue Press.

Check Carrie Dalby's website for book information, sales links, and more.

https://carriedalby.com

About the Author

While experiencing the typical adventures of growing up, Carrie Dalby called several places in California home, but she's lived on the Alabama Gulf Coast since 1996. Serving two terms as president of Mobile Writers' Guild and five years as the Mobile area Local Liaison for the Society of Children's Book Writers and Illustrators are two of the writing-related volunteer positions she's held. When Carrie isn't reading, writing, browsing bookstores/libraries, or homeschooling her children, she can often be found knitting or attending concerts.

Carrie writes for both teens and adults. *Fortitude* is listed as a Best Historical Book for Kids by Grateful American Foundation. The Possession Chronicles, a Southern Gothic family saga series, is her largest body of work for adults. She has also published several short stories that can be found in different anthologies.

For more information, visit Carrie Dalby's website:

carriedalby.com

CPSIA information can be obtained
at www.ICGtesting.com
Printed in the USA
BVHW050830080223
658123BV00003B/194

9 781957 892054